A TIME TO DIE

A TIME TO DIE

THE OUT OF TIME SERIES — BOOK ONE

NADINE BRANDES

ENCLAVE

PUBLISHING

Published by Enclave Publishing
5025 N. Central Ave., #635
Phoenix, AZ 85012
www.enclavepublishing.com

ISBN (paper): 978-1-62184-029-9

A Time to Die

Published in the United States by Enclave Publishing, an imprint of
Third Day Books, LLC, Phoenix, Arizona.

This is a work of fiction. Names, characters, places, and incidents are
products of the author's imagination or are used fictitiously. Any similar-
ity to actual people, organizations, and/or events is purely coincidental.

Cover design: Kirk DouPonce, DogEared Design
www.dogeareddesign.com

Printed in the United States of America

*This book is dedicated to the personal and loving
Master of my life, the bringer of shalom, Yahweh.*

*In memory of James Frank Harrison, IV.
From your death, I questioned life,
and God answered me with this book.
I look forward to meeting you.*

1

000.364.07.05.16

There was once a time when only God knew the day you'd die.

At least that's what they tell me. I wasn't alive then—back when life bore adventure and death held surprise. I guess God decided to share the coveted knowledge. Either that, or we stole it from Him. Personally, I think He just gave the world what it thought it wanted: control.

My thin rectangular Clock sits on the carved shelf across the room, clicking its red digital numbers—red like blood. Today marks the first day of my last year alive.

000.364.07.05.16

Three hundred sixty-four days, seven hours, five minutes, and sixteen—no, *fifteen*—seconds to live. I've always thought it cruel they include the seconds. But people want absolutes. They demand fine lines in a fuzzy world.

My toes curl like pill bugs when they touch the cold wood floor. I creep to the open window, flick a shivering spider off the sill into the October breeze, and close the shutters. Wind still howls through.

I pull on a pair of wool socks—a frequent Christmas gift of which I never grow weary—and ignore the mirror. It's the same face every morning: tangled hair, bleary chocolate eyes, and a waspish glare that doesn't leave until after coffee.

I push through the bedroom door into the kitchen and just miss a collision with my mother. She sweeps past bearing a mixing bowl of steaming cinnamon oatmeal. Pity her morning greeting isn't as warm as the breakfast she slams on the table. "Twenty minutes, Parvin."

"It's *my* time I waste sleeping, not yours."

The rectangular kitchen glows under the heat of the cooking fire on the opposite wall. A metal wash tin and a red water pump sit to my left, beneath our only glass window. Cold morning light reflects off the soapsuds. The rough kitchen table crowds most of the walking space unless all four chairs are pushed in tight. I plop into the closest seat.

"It's already six-thirty." She blows a stray hair away from her face. "You've wasted seventeen years, let's not spoil your last one."

Ah, mother-daughter love.

She slides a wooden mug filled with coffee across the table with one hand, and reaches for the creamer with the other. My morning pick-me-up splashes over the rim. I shrug. More room for cream.

Once I've transformed my coffee into a liquid dessert, I spoon oatmeal into a dish and calculate my schedule: Five minutes to eat, five minutes to change, ten minutes to walk there. If I stick to my planned detour, I'll be late for Assessment. I don't care. The hearing is more important.

My coffee turns to vinegar. I force a swallow against my shaking nerves. I won't be nervous today. I have to be strong.

A life depends on it.

"Get out of those thin shorts." Mother barks the command as she stokes the cooking fire, then places the blackened kettle over it once more. "And stop sleeping with the window open. No wonder you're cold at night—you've got legs like twigs. I don't know why you make such impractical clothing."

"They're practical in summer." *And more comfortable to sleep in than the wool underclothes you insist on wearing.*

"It's October."

I take a bite of oatmeal. My sewing fetish is my version of rebellion and independence. At least I'm in control in *some* manner, although sewing never helped my popularity.

After three more mouthfuls of oatmeal, I practically inhale my coffee before going to change into a grey wool shirt and black vest—self-tailored to fit my short torso. I pull on my double-layered cotton trousers and boots lined with speckled rabbit fur. The blend of dark colors makes me feel serious and firm—exactly what I need for the hearing.

Mother brushes my hair into a burgundy-umber fluff. I scowl and braid it down one side before jamming on an ivory cap.

She tucks my Clock into my vest pocket. "Forty minutes."

No way I'll be home in forty minutes. "Eighty." I'll probably be longer.

I stride up the uneven stone sidewalk of Straight Street. Mother never bids farewell anymore, not now that the real Good-bye is so near.

Weak rays of dawn peek over rows of identical wood-and-thatch houses. Flickering morning candlelight shines through every shutter. In the few homes with glass windows, homemade gadgets or goods line the sills—socks, herb teas, paper notebooks, candles, wax tablets, hair ribbons. Tiny price cards sit beside them.

Sill trading.

I scan the sills for an old newspaper, rubbing my fingers over the last coin in my pocket. Crumpled black-and-white paper catches my eye. I stop and scan the headline:

10th Anniversary of Worldwide Currency 'Specie'
Celebrated with Increased Dividends

My eyes flit to the date to confirm my sinking hopes: *October 06, 2148*

Three days ago. I've already read it. Besides, the price card tells me it costs two specie, and I have only one to spend.

With a sigh, I look between the houses to the horizon still shrouded in shadow. Barely, just barely, the Wall is visible through morning fog. The stone spine looks as menacing as ever, stretching a thousand feet high along the west border of my state, Missouri. It's hard to imagine it encircles the Earth's longitude, but that's what they say.

I break my stare and quicken my pace. Red maple leaves fly through the air like autumn snowflakes. I hug myself and cross the narrow, muddy street, nodding to the milkman on the corner as he organizes his various bottles between the wood slats of his pushcart. He waves a gloved hand, which returns to his side as if out of habit, rubbing a square bulge in his trouser pocket.

I've seen his Clock—four more years and a thimble-full of days until his zeroes line up. Longer than I have even though I'm younger, but I don't begrudge him. We're all a population of walking second-hands, ticking toward the end.

A wooden arrow painted white points toward the center of town—Father's handiwork from his carpentry shop. My fingers brush across the smooth top of the sign. The black letters glisten, painted to withstand the upcoming winter: *Unity Village Square.*

Unity Village. The insinuation in the name is far from the disposition of its people. Seventeen years haven't been long enough for me to change this. Instead, I've conformed to the cold separateness we cling to. The concept of unity is now a nostalgic whim from the past—like gentlemen doffing fedoras, free ice cream on a hot afternoon, barefooted children hoop-rolling. Selfless consideration is rare, except from the Mentors. And they only fake it.

Mentor. The word turns my stomach and my shoulders tense.

Assessment Day.

A few yards from the village square, my trudging slows like a dying wind-up toy. I stop and allow the mud to creep its fingernails into my boot leather. Straight ahead, a weathered wooden platform rests dead center inside a square of empty market booths. Leafless dogwood trees surround the square as if trying to fill the silent space.

Harman, the master gardener, stands rigid between his stocked vegetable stand and the Enforcer car parked beside him. It shines like a black stinkbug, its warning to the meager crowd of onlookers as palpable as any stench. A painted gold backward *E* shimmers against the black paint as the sun peeks over a thatched roof.

Atop the platform stands a middle-aged stranger. Grey facial hair quivers as he chews on his upper lip. Two Enforcers flank him, statue-like, with black coats brushing the dirty platform floor. A backward black *E* marks the left side of each of their faces.

I avoid their eyes and grip the Clock in my pocket. *God, let today be the day.*

"Martin Foster is reported of being an unregistered Radical," the Enforcer on the right says. "Is there anyone to vouch for his Clock?"

The square remains silent. A handful of people mingle, as if trying to ignore the question.

"Can anyone vouch he has a Clock?" The Enforcer widens his stance and clasps his fist behind his back.

Mister Foster's chewing stops. He stares at his feet.

Look up, I think to him, as if he'll catch my projection of courage. *Be brave.* I've never seen his Clock, but I went to school with his son. Mister Foster has a life. He has purpose. He has a family.

"I vouch for his life," I squeak.

The Enforcer glares at me. "That is not applicable to the question at hand, nor will it affect our decision."

"But his life matters. Not his Clock."

The other spectators avoid my eyes. Will they ever speak out? Can't my village come together to save a single life?

Mr. Foster's gaze lifts, finding mine. This moment will burn in my dreams tonight, like with every other Radical I've unsuccessfully vouched for these past three months. Not that it's done any good. If only I'd started doing this sooner. Years ago.

His eyes hold glassy hope—not that his life will be saved, but that his life has made a difference and someone has noticed.

I have. But I'm helpless.

"If no one can vouch for Martin Foster's Numbers"—the Enforcer shifts into mechanical monotone—"then he is sentenced to the Wall."

"No!" I step forward. "That's not the law. Register him as a Radical."

The Enforcers lead Mr. Foster back to the car in three swift steps.

"He can choose relocation!" My courage withers. I can't swallow. My eyes never leave Mr. Foster's, even when a thick film of tears blurs the scene.

The door shuts and the car rolls away through the mud with a high-pitched electric whine.

I sink to my knees, immune to the wet chill the mud sends through my pants. Today wasn't the day. Another innocent will die, sacrificed to the mystery of the Wall. *God, why do You allow this?*

My Clock is cool against my sweating palm. I didn't even realize I had pulled it from my pocket. I can't look at it. I want to smash it, but if I do, I'll be the one on the platform.

My sorrow returns to its cage of resignation. I stand and leave the square, tense against the probing stares of others. When I reach the border of Unity Village, I stop.

The slick county building towers like a bland government pillar, resembling a giant Time Clock tilted up on one side. Even the windows have red rims like the Numbers. A long electronic post board covers the outside wall facing the village, still blinking: *Hearings: Martin Foster—Oct. 09.*

I hate Clocks. Each one is a constant reminder that my life is not, and has never been, in my hands. The possessive, all-controlling nature in me rears its irate head, but it can rear all it likes—

The Numbers are never wrong.

I move toward the county building, and my fingers stray again to the lump in my pocket. *364. 364. That's plenty of time.* Deep breath, chin high, and a perfected look of defiance. I ascend the steps and enter through the heavy doors.

The lobby has a marble floor with a trickling water fountain and stiff yellow lighting—one of the few Unity buildings with plumbing and electricity. My steps echo. A rat-nosed receptionist sits behind a desk across the room. She doesn't look up, but I don't care.

Instead, my eyes wander to the grinning man with dark hair standing beside the woman's post. My persona slips and I break into a run. *"Reid!"*

His arms envelop me and I breathe in his scent of forest and travel. "My little Brielle."

I laugh at the name to keep from crying. I haven't heard my brother's voice in almost a year. *Brielle* is my middle name—a name only Reid calls me because, he says, *"It sounds so soft."*

"I didn't think you'd come back so soon," I mumble into his coat.

"We're in this together, sis. You're not alone."

I sniff and survey his face. "You got freckles."

"Too much sun tends to do that." He tilts his head. "You got thinner."

Most girls seek this form of compliment, but when Mother calls me Twig Legs and Reid says I'm thinner in the same day, I'm irked. "So what?" I step away. Why must he point out my smallness the very moment we're reunited?

He frowns a little, but he'll say nothing more. I read his face as well as my own since they're nearly identical. We're triplets, well, what's left of them. Our older brother, William, died at birth.

"Parvin Brielle Blackwater?" Rat Nose asks in a nasal, smoker's voice. I flinch. Reid gives my arm a comforting squeeze.

I turn to her. "Yes?"

"You're here for your Last-Year Assessment?"

"Mm-hmm." I haven't allowed myself to consider how I want my life to end. It seems too morbid. Truth is, I've been too scared to think about it. Now . . .

I have to.

She peers at me through oval glasses. "Your Mentor, Mr. Trevor Rain, will see you." Then she turns to Reid. "And now that *she's* here"—she jerks her head in my direction—"will you please join Ms. Monica Lamb? She's on a tight schedule."

"Aren't we all?" Reid murmurs.

I giggle. It feels foreign. I lean close to him and lower my voice. "Thanks for waiting for me." I eye the snappy receptionist.

"Why were you late?"

Mr. Foster's face flits across my mind's eye. I sigh. "Oh, you know me—slept in too long." Someday I'll tell Reid about my recent attempts to vouch for Radicals. Someday . . . when I save someone.

We step into the elevator. As the door closes, I place one hand on a wall and the other on Reid's arm. I never get used to moving upward in this metal box. I should have taken the stairs.

Mirrors cover three walls and I stare at Reid. He's grown taller, more rugged, and now he sports a five o'clock shadow. It's strange seeing something so adult as facial hair on him.

I pull the wood box from my pocket. "Do you want the Numbers?" Each second taps against my fingertips with a dull *click*.

"Ah, who cares about protocol? You keep it. Trevor's stricter about checking Numbers. I'll pretend I forgot mine. Monica loves to add another tally to her list of why men are immature and irresponsible. If today's the day our Mentors discover we've illegally shared a Clock, so be it. We've made it seventeen years."

We told the Mentors we have two Clocks with the same Numbers. It's a common occurrence between close friends or siblings, which often means they'll die from the same cause: a boating accident, natural disaster, or something of the sort. But our single Clock was an unfortunate mishap.

The elevator doors slide open. I try to clear my throat but seem to have forgotten how. To compensate, I take a deep breath and lift my chin.

"There's the confident mask I hate so much." But Reid adopts his own carefree façade and struts down the hall to Monica Lamb's door.

"I'll see you at home." I walk the opposite direction.

I push open the maple-paneled door into Trevor's long, blank office. He sits on one side of a mahogany desk, perusing my thin file, perhaps to appear as if he remembers me. An empty plush red chair rests on the other side of his desk, facing him.

My soft boots *tap-tap* over the slick marble floor. Trevor looks up. His hair is black, dusted with grey. A strand falls into his face and catches in his rectangular glasses for a moment. He pulls a comb from his suit pocket and smooths the strands back. His smile doesn't reach his eyes. It hardly makes crinkles in his face.

"Ah, Parvin." His voice is annoyingly soothing, as if he knows I don't want to be here.

I resist responding with, *"Ah, Trevor."* Instead, I give a curt nod.

He gestures to the plush chair in front of him. Like there's anyplace else to sit. "How are you feeling?"

Should I be honest? I settle for neutral. "I'm okay." I lower myself into the seat.

"Did you bring your Numbers?"

I place my Clock upright on his desk. He squints at it, then at the open manila folder. "You turn eighteen in April?"

"Yes."

"Your brother too?"

"Yes."

"And both of your Clocks have the same Good-bye, next October?"

I gulp. "Yeah."

The word sticks at the back of my throat, and something pinches in my chest. Every lie I tell is a mental tattoo that glows in the dark when I try to shut it out, to pretend I didn't say it. But this lie I *must* tell—to protect Reid's and my dwindling lives. Right now, Reid's probably lying, too. Does he feel the same guilt I do, or am I merely weak?

My eyes stray to the thin wooden box. The Numbers face away from me. If we could get a second Clock, then we wouldn't have to hide the fact we're stuck with just the one—and that we don't know whose it is. But no one controls the Numbers, not even the government. And Clocks are merged to a person at conception.

I dread this Last Year because one of us will zero out and the other will become a Radical with no Clock. We don't know which one will die.

I hope it's me.

Trevor closes my file with one hand and slaps it on the desk. His eyes—so professional, so full of feigned interest—meet mine. "Let's start with your Good-bye. It might help you relax."

Well, of course. Because discussing how I want to die will leave me floating on air. Thanks, Trevor. He stares at me for several seconds. Is he waiting on me? I look around. "What? I just . . . jump in?"

"Do you know how you want your Good-bye to be?"

"Painless, of course."

He plasters on the phony smile. "Of course. We can only hope."

Why are we discussing this? It's all a pretense. I mean, like the government can actually affect our Good-byes. No one knows what my Good-bye will look like—except God, I guess. I could get struck by lightning, trampled by a horse, or hit in the head with a stone that puts me in a coma.

Or, God willing, I could fall asleep and never wake up.

I vote for that one.

Maybe Trevor just wants to know how confident I am about dying—about the end of my life. I straighten in the chair. "I don't need to talk about it."

He glances down. "Let's move on to your past dreams."

Past dreams. The life-long goals I decided for myself at age thirteen—as if I had a clue what I wanted. What did I tell him the last time we met?

"You wanted to travel."

My heart sinks as pictures of foreign terrain and lands of discovery flash across my mind. Places I'll never see. "I haven't had the chance." Or should I say, the courage?

He opens a desk drawer and pulls out a large, thin electrobook. I sneak a peek at the electronic cursive designed to appear handwritten. A date marks every top corner that slides across the screen. He stops on the year *2148* and runs a finger down a long list.

"We have . . . a three-month opening in Egypt starting in December." He scrolls over a page that says 2149. "A . . . two-week opening in England next January, four weeks in Italy, a week in Canada if you want something short, or eight months in Brazil." He peers over his glasses.

I shake my head. "Staged settlements with good food and fake natives? There's no authenticity in that."

"You don't want to travel anymore?" He props his elbow on the armrest. "If you want something more local, we can send you any of the thirty-one states. All you have to do is pick one."

"No." Traveling, even inside the USE, no longer appeals. It sounds . . . daunting. Reid's done it, and his stories are enough to make me feel like I've seen the entire country. I don't want to copy him. I want to do my own thing. Problem is . . .

I don't know what that *thing* is.

Trevor pulls my file toward him again, opens it, and crosses something out. "Have you been kissed yet?"

I turn cold and sit a little straighter. *"Excuse* me?"

He raises his eyebrows. "One of your dreams listed is to have a boyfriend—or as you put it, a *soul mate*—and be kissed."

I resist the urge to snatch my file from him and read it myself. "I was thirteen. A one-track mind." Heat sweeps up my cheeks. "But no, neither happened." How could it, when I've lived in tiny Unity Village my whole life? All eligible prospects moved away the moment they had the opportunity.

A new window surfaces on Trevor's electrobook. This one has several blank screens and scribbled lists.

"I have a few gentlemen in Unity Village desiring a relationship." He scans the page. "Robbie Contrast is nineteen, would like an intimate relationship, and says Good-bye in two hundred and twenty-three days."

Is he kidding? He *has* to be kidding.

"Or Dusten Grunt." Trevor drones on. "Eighteen, with the desire for a girlfriend. His Good-bye is in twenty-two months. There's also Finn Foster, who is in his Last Year and seeks marriage. If you start now, you could have a child three months before your Good-bye. Would you like photos?"

"N-*No!* I don't want any of them!"

Trevor is speaking as if I don't know these men, but each one is burned into my memory. I still recall Dusten Grunt's conceited face four years ago as he whispered through the school window of the girl's bathroom, *Empty Numbers! Empty Numbers! Parvin's just got empty Numbers!*

And Finn Foster . . . his father was sentenced to death today.

Trevor puts the list away. "I suppose I could send in a request for a male actor or model willing to give you a couple months."

My legs propel me out of the chair. "That's *not* what I want." I look around the room, searching for the right words and willing my temper to settle. Releasing a deep breath, I sink back down. "I've changed."

"Changed?" He takes off his reading glasses.

My fingers stray to the silver cross ring on my pinky—a gift from Reid. I twist it round and round, rubbing the tiny rubies lining the band. "Well, I . . ."

Trevor's gaze shifts to my hands, and the corner of his mouth turns down. "You believe in that old-fashioned spiritual stuff?"

I place my hands in my lap. Why am I embarrassed? "Yes, I do." My voice comes out quiet. Angry.

Trevor lets out an "Ah" and replaces his glasses. "Be careful. Unity Village is unusually tolerant, but other places are not. Your parents should remain cautious too. I hope they're not teaching it to you. You can't get away with religion in any of the High Cities." He swipes over a page and squints at the screen. "But because this is your Last Year, I might be able to find a good religion-boy for you in a neighboring town."

I bite the inside of my cheek, willing myself not to scream. "I don't want a fake relationship." Does he not understand the meaning of a soul mate?

Unfazed, he flips to a fresh slide. "Let's move on. What are your *new* desires?"

The dreaded question. I've spent the past two weeks trying to analyze that exact thing. It felt like forcing out a Christmas list of things I didn't even want. Only one real desire stands out, and it sounds so shallow a croak escapes my lips when I share it.

Trevor stares. "Pardon?"

I close my eyes for a moment and take a deep breath. "I want a year-long free subscription to the local and national newspapers."

The room falls silent. I open my eyes. Trevor is tapping out information on his electrobook. I raise my eyebrows and release a small shrug. It must be protocol to abstain from saying my desires are lame. Who wants a year's subscription to a newspaper to fulfill their last days?

I do. I'm tired of scrounging for coins and snitching newspapers off the street to satisfy my interest in the outside world. I'm ready to open the door to a paper on my threshold every morning, like rich people in the Upper and High Cities.

Trevor looks up. "What else?"

I shake my head.

"Nothing else?"

I don't want to tell him, but I have to. I must be honest with my Mentor. As unpleasant as he may be, Trevor is trying to help—or so the government says.

What *do* I want? My plaguing question has no answers except ones that don't match Mentor criteria. I want to fix the broken law system in Unity Village. I want to unify the people so Radicals don't have to die. I want my short life to *mean* something.

"I want . . . to be remembered." I suck in a small gasp. Of all the dreams I could have mentioned, this is the one that creeps past my lips?

Trevor's forehead scrunches. "That's a tough one."

"Excuse me?"

He rubs a finger over his lips. "Well, we could set up a heroic act, or send you to a broadcast center to get your face known. I could even make some flyers with your name and we can put them on post-boards—*The Girl Who Wants To Be Remembered*." He claps his hands. "Yes, I believe that could work."

"I don't want you to make me remembered." I exhale. "I just . . . want to be remembered." My eyes stray to the round analog clock on the wall. Fifteen precious minutes of my Last Year have been wasted discussing dreams I don't want.

"How would you do that, Parvin?"

The second hand ticks in slow motion. The clock is round, like the Earth. The hour hand points to the seven and the minute hand is poised on the one, forming an angled longitudinal line up the clock's face.

"What happens to people on the other side of the Wall?" A shiver runs through me. Did I really ask that? Out loud?

Trevor coughs and his calm mask slips for a moment. "Parvin, no one goes through the Wall unless they're an unregistered Radical or a convict."

"But what if, hypothetically, I *wanted* to cross the Wall—as my Last-Year's desire?" I say this with passion even though the idea entered my head twelve seconds ago. "I'd just die on that side instead of here." Like Mr. Foster.

A small sigh escapes Trevor. "After the terrorist tragedy and those meteorites, our ancestors chose the East side of the Wall—the government side. You should send up religious prayers of thanks. If not for them, you might have been an Independent trying to survive in an uncontrolled, primitive environment. Who knows if anyone even survived on the West side? We send Radicals there for a reason—and it's not for adventure." Trevor shakes his head. "I'm sorry. It can't be done."

I put back on the bored, confident face. "I understand, Mr. Rain." My question was, after all, hypothetical.

He leans back. "Can you think of any other Last-Year dreams?"

None that he could comprehend. I can't tell him I want more time to relive what I've already wasted, that I want to be someone else, or that I want to know for sure whose Clock is in my pocket. He can't understand because he's a Mentor. Mentors are required to outlive their clients, and Trevor has over fifty years left to his Numbers.

I remain quiet for a long time, but then . . .

A new plan forms. I won't have to lie. "I want to be a biographer."

His knuckles crack. "You can't be a biographer. You have only a year—you don't have time to write about someone else's entire life. The government wouldn't pay or publish you."

He's right, but this new idea is motivation enough for me to overlook the odds. I'll tell the world about the illegal sentencing of Radicals going on in Unity Village. I'll even show that it's possible to live without a Clock. Reid and I have been doing it our whole lives. I am strong. I *will* be remembered. This is my ticket.

"You misunderstand. I want to be my own biographer."

His mouth sags, and who can blame him? No biographer has ever told his or her own story. But I can do this. I know I can. Besides . . .

What better way to be remembered than to do something no one else has ever done before?

2

000.364.06.05.09

"Mother, I need your journal." I ease the door closed.

Her hand freezes over the water pump. Perhaps I should have said *Hello* first. She straightens, flexes her fingers, and delivers a powerful push to the red lever. "In the safe."

Water gushes into the wash tin, swirling among wood dishware. I roll my eyes and toss my hat onto the entrance table. "Combination?" But I doubt she'll reveal the numbers she's kept secret the past seventeen-and-a-half years.

"26-17-27."

Now *I* freeze, balancing on one foot and tugging my boot off the other. Reid opens the front door and knocks me in the backside with the metal latch. I sprawl forward and crack my chin against the plank floor.

An immature guffaw bursts from his mouth and Mother shrieks, "Reid!" in a decibel not intended for human ears. I ought to have included, *Reid is back* in the *Hello* I never offered.

I raise myself to all fours. A splash of blood ripples on the wood floor. I touch my chin. It burns. The red liquid on my fingers reminds me of the red Numbers on my Clock.

Reid hoists me to my feet, and Mother slaps a damp rag to my chin as she rushes into his embrace. I too might bypass a bleeding daughter for a hug from Reid.

The rag on my face smells old, like spoiled chicken. I toss it into the sink. "You gave me the combination . . . why?"

Mother wipes at her eyes, though I see no tears. She gulps. Reid releases her and she brushes past me to the cupboard. "I knew anything could happen today and I readied myself for it. It's your Last Year—you get whatever you want."

In the seriousness of her statement, I still cannot repress a stinging grin. "Anything?"

Mother pulls a crisp white cloth from the shelf. "Don't push your luck."

Blood or not, Last Year or not, the three of us laugh. Reid is home, and that means laughter. Mother squeezes my fingers as she hands me the fresh rag. Reid and I sit at the table. He takes the cloth and wipes it across my chin.

"How did Assessment go?" Mother asks, pushing the kettle over the constant fire. She sets a carved wooden mug in front of each of us—products of Father's occupation. "I'm assuming this is why you returned early, Reid?"

He wraps his hands around the mug even though it's empty. "I can't face our Last Year without Parvin." He avoids my gaze, probably because he knows I'll see the truth in his eyes.

I'd be a mess without *him,* not the other way around. I was born as the needy triplet. Maybe it's because I'm a girl, or I'm four minutes younger than he, or I'm skinny and twiggish, but I need Reid. He doesn't seem to need me. He *loves* me, but he's always been self-sufficient.

Mother studies him. "So how *did* Assessment go, Reid?"

He shrugs. "Told Monica I wanted to be sporadic in my Last Year. No plans."

"Sporadic? You? That sounds more like Parvin. Monica believed you?" Mother spoons tiny mounds of sugar into our cups.

"She doesn't know I'm an obnoxious, plan-every-detail kind of guy, Mother. She's a Mentor. She shook her head and gave a 'That's-just-like-a-boy' face."

A drop of blood splashes the back of my hand. I pick up the cloth from beside Reid and press it to my chin.

"I asked for my Last-Year funds."

At his quiet words, Mother knocks over her mug of sugar, and my cloth slips from my hand onto my lap. "What?"

He pulls a camel-colored drawstring pouch from his pocket and tips it upside down. Thick coins tumble out. A silver one rolls along a crack in the table and drops to the floor with a *clink!* Mother scoops it up in a flash and sets it back on the table.

"That's the first six months." Reid organizes the coins into piles. "At the next Assessment, I'll get more."

"She's robbing you," Mother says in an undertone.

"I know, but not as much as if I let her plan my last days." He smirks. "Besides, she deserves a little tip for putting up with me."

I snort. "Monica's a man-hating snake."

Mother shakes her head. "What are you going to do with all this specie? Travel?"

I can't take my gaze off the coins. Though Mother's right and Monica Lamb *is* hoarding half of Reid's rightful Last-Year funds, there's more specie on this table than I've ever seen in one pile in my life. Wistful dreams of glass windows, wood roofing, and endless rolls of wool socks drift across my mind. Why didn't *I* ask for my Last-Year funds? Now that I think about it, what is Trevor going to do with my specie? I asked him for only a newspaper subscription. Will he keep the rest?

"I have some ideas." Reid's response interrupts the growing rage at my Mentor. "I want to keep half of it with me and leave the other half here for whichever one of us survives the Clock."

"What do you mean?" I ask.

"Once one of us zeroes out, the one who survives will be an unregistered Radical, whether we like it or not." He separates the pile into two even halves. "The government hunts unregistered Radicals, and it'll be near impossible to get a job. This specie can help us live until we figure out what to do—maybe get to another city that will register us."

Mother nods. I gape with my mouth open. I haven't spared a single thought about life after zeroes, mostly because I'm positive it's my Clock and therefore will *have* no life after zeroes.

Mother looks at me. "So how did *your* Assessment go, Parvin?"

Reid plucks the drying rag from my lap and holds it out to me with a smirk. "Yeah, you sprinted home."

The kettle steams and I pull at my collar. "Shouldn't we wait for Father?" I've never been good at stalling. What will they think if I tell them my plan?

Father walks through the door, a howl of wind announcing his presence and making his blond beard quiver. Mother takes his coat and hangs it on the only peg that's not loose. They exchange a quick kiss. He enters the kitchen and eyes my bloody cloth before planting a whiskery kiss on my forehead. He and Reid then go through an awkward father-son reunion—shaking hands and grunting what I assume must be words of manly affection and delight.

Father places a handful of wooden serving spoons on the table. "Some extras I made today."

Mother scoops them up with one hand. "Thank you."

"What's all this specie?" The warmth of Father's deep, mustache-muffled voice pours comfort into my nervous soul. The anxiety of sharing my biographer plan lessens. After all, this is my family. They deserve maskless authenticity. We'll go through Last Year together, like every other family. I can't leave them out.

"The results of Reid's Assessment." Mother lifts the kettle from the hook with a thick mitt.

"Oh?" Father grabs a mug from the cupboard and pulls up a chair. "Tell me."

Reid shoots me a wink. "Actually, Parvin was going to share *her* Last-Year plans with us. She seems to have a lot running through her head."

I glare. Once Mother pours the tea and sits down, I take a deep breath. Reid squeezes my hand under the table and reassurance dissolves my tension.

"I'm going to be my own biographer," I blurt, not meeting their eyes.

Mother opens her mouth, but says nothing, Father stares into his watery tea—probably assessing the flaws, and Reid cocks his head to one side.

"I want to start from the beginning." I'm determined not to quail beneath judgment. "From my birth. And I want to write it *all*."

As she usually does when she disapproves of something, Mother finds her voice. "But Parvin, you don't exactly have an interesting story to tell. You've led a very . . . calm life."

That's a nice way to say I've wasted my life. Reading, sewing, daydreaming, why did it take me so long to realize those things weren't worth the time I sacrificed for them? I've only recently woken up from my apathy.

"I have interesting *secrets* to tell." My eyes meet Reid's.

He blinks. *"Our* secret? You want everyone to know we've illegally shared a Clock for seventeen years?"

My skin grows hot. "That's one of the secrets. I want people to know life is possible without having an absolute Clock. And . . . I want to reveal the injustice behind the Unity Village system. Radicals shouldn't be killed—they're not causing harm."

Reid shakes his head. "Radicals *smash* their Clocks. They openly defy the government."

"Not all Radicals." Has Reid even been to a hearing? Mister Foster didn't appear rebellious. None of the Radicals I've seen looked defiant—they just wanted to survive.

I force my voice to remain controlled. "Most people are Radicals on accident, like us. Mother didn't know she was having triplets. She didn't know she'd need a third Clock when she got pregnant. Now look at us—one of us will be a Radical this time next year. It's the government's fault Clocks are matchable only at conception. They shouldn't punish *us* for their limited inventions."

Reid blows on his tea. "But Radicals are relocated or chucked over the Wall to die. If you reveal our secret, they'll consider *both* of us Radicals. You know what Unity Village is like—the Enforcers won't register us, they won't give us an option. Radicals go straight to the Wall."

"That's why I need to do this!" Why can't he see? "For the sake of all the other Radicals dying without a choice. As long as you and I find a way to *register* ourselves as Radicals, maybe in a different village, we'd be safe." I've protested at every city square hearing for the past three months, and the Enforcers never even checked my Clock. I hold up my hand with the cross ring. "You've told me God will protect us."

Mother casts a quick glance out the window. "Speak softer."

"Parvin and I are almost eighteen, Mother. You don't have to be afraid of breaking the law."

"If someone hears and thinks we've been teaching you—"

"They won't hear." Reid sounds weary. "No one in Unity Village cares if you teach us about God before we're adults."

"Do you even believe He'll protect us?" I hiss to Reid, trying to get us back on track. "Telling our secret will get my biography noticed and published."

"Not through the government." Mother sniffs. "They'll burn the copies and sentence you anyway, especially if you start spouting about their injustice."

My voice comes out in a whisper. "I would go through a publishing company *not* owned by the government."

Father scoots his chair closer to the table. It grates against the floor with a loud squeak. "I've never heard of one. Besides, if the government knows one of you doesn't have a Clock, neither of you will receive medical services, even if you're registered. You won't be given jobs and your Mentor won't give you any dividends. You would *both* be sent across the Wall before the Clock times out."

The government cannot control our minutes or hours, but they do run our lives by them. "It's a risk we'll have to take," I say. "Besides, in a year one of us will be gone. The government will know then, whether we like it or not."

"Not necessarily." Reid slides his stacked coins to the side. "You've never written anything before, Parvin. Why spend your Last Year doing this?"

"I've read plenty of books," I snap. "I can manage. Besides how can you deny me my Last-Year desire? It could save lives. And those school jerks will see that I *do* have worth!"

His eyes soften. "Not everyone who bullied you then is still a bully now. And even if they are, do you think they'll have remorse when they read about your pain? You'd be telling them they won."

"No." I push my fist against the smooth table wood. "They didn't win. I'd be teaching them a lesson—life is worth more than Numbers. You don't have to agree with me. In fact, you should be thankful writing a biography is all I want. I *considered* asking to cross the Wall."

I expected shouts of surprise like, "No!" "You can't!" or "Parvin!", but my family's corpse-like silence unnerves me more than any uproar would have. I should've bitten my tongue.

"You want to die *there?*" Mother croaks. "*If* people survived over there, they descended from rioters, maniacs, and government rebels."

My hands tighten around my mug; the heat sears my palms. "It's not that I want to die there, I just entertained the idea of doing something . . . different. I need action in my life. Like a final act of—"

"Insanity?" Reid's face holds no smile.

My gaze narrows. "I was going to say bravery."

"You hate the Wall," he says. "You can't even watch the sunset because you'd have to look at the Wall to see it, even though the Wall is miles away. You never went on the school fieldtrip."

"You can't get through." Father speaks in a low, firm voice, redirecting the growing argument. "Only Radicals are sent through, and then only as a death sentence. No voluntary passage is allowed."

My breath quickens. "It was a moment's thought!"

"Where did it come from?" Reid frowns. "You would be *alone* for our Good-bye."

I sip my tea. It burns, but not as much as my family's criticism. "Maybe I'm curious. Everyone's curious. Even if I *did* want to go—which I don't—you couldn't tell me not to, Reid, when *you've* spent your entire life traveling and fulfilling all your dreams."

Mother pours more hot water into her mug. "No one knows what's happened to the other side."

"That's not true. A wall can't quench human thirst. People have tried to cross on purpose and the government never even cared. The leaders of the United States of the East—the members of the Council—must have some knowledge of the mysteries of the West, that's why convicts and Radicals are sacrificed. The Council must *know* it's a deathtrap or wasteland."

"Can we return to the first desire?" Father turns to me. "You want to be your own biographer."

I tear my eyes away from Reid. "I want to write my story, even if it's bland. I want to start from the beginning—from our birth, which is why I need Mother's journal. My story about illegally sharing a Clock might catch the eye of a publisher. Then, inside the biography, I'll share the injustice that takes place in Unity Village."

Is any of this making sense to them? My words aren't matching my clarity of thought. "I have to do this for the sake of all those murdered Radicals that no one knows about. People will see that there is injustice in the Low Cities like Unity. Maybe they'll even see that it's possible to live without solid knowledge of our Numbers. Reid and I have been fine without that knowledge. We're not a threat to society."

Something stirs inside me—a desperate, unplaced passion. "I need to take some sort of action and this makes sense to me. I can't accept that these measly seventeen years are all God planned for me . . ." My voice trails off and I put my face in my hands. Blood trickles down my neck from my chin wound.

"You're being impulsive," Mother says. "Just like all your other ideas."

"What other ideas? I've never even left Unity Village. I've never had a job! You think I'm impulsive, but look where I am—*nowhere*, with nothing to my name!"

Mother frowns at me. "Your life isn't as bad as you think. You don't need to write a biography or go through the Wall to get some sort of recognition. How long have you wanted this, exactly?"

I leap to my feet and my chair topples backward. "What does it matter? I've wasted my life!" It stands out to me clearer than any other thought. "I'm empty Numbers, Mother. Numbers that will be missed only by my three family members, if I'm lucky!"

Reid's mouth opens, and his eyes widen with a tinge of hurt. I throw my scalding mug across the kitchen. It smashes through the window above the sink. Hot tea sprays across Mother's drying dishes.

Ashamed, I rush to my room and slam the door. The jolt causes my stack of library books and old newspapers to topple off my desk. I refuse to permit myself a dramatic sob into my pillow. Instead, I stride across the room, open the brown shutters, and battle against the wind to climb out.

The near-frozen dirt in the wasted garden sends a zing of greeting into my bare feet, but the defiance in me doesn't care. I close the shutters behind me and sit against the side of the house. Wind pulls strands of hair from my braid and blows the wet blood along my chin line. A leaf sticks to my neck.

The chill is calming, entering my lungs like a cold hug. A long stick-bug clings to the wall of the house next to mine, its spindly legs quivering in the wind. What does the life of a stick-bug look like? Short? Misunderstood? Has a bird ever plucked one from the ground to build a nest and enjoyed an unexpected meal instead?

"Little Brielle . . ." Reid peeks his head around the corner of the house, blocking the morning sun. He must have come from the front door.

I rest my forehead on my knees. *Why did Assessment have to be so complicated?*

He sits beside me. "I like your biographer plan. I'm jealous you thought of it first."

"Then you should do it," I grumble. After all, he's the one who does everything. Reid finishes his education. Reid travels. Reid goes on adventures. Reid gets a job. Reid makes friends. Life has been a permanent competition, and he's won every time. The only thing Reid can't do is sew, which is why I spent seventeen years of my life creating ridiculous articles of clothing—clothing I hoped would show me who I am, but it didn't. I have more personas in my closet than Numbers to my name.

"I'll go with you through the Wall if you really want to go."

My first impulse is to shout "No!" but I hold it in, surprised at his changed attitude. I don't want to go through. He's right—it terrifies me. It's tall, black, and cold, and hundreds of Radicals have died there.

Even more than this though, I don't want Reid to go. The Wall is something he's never done. It's the one idea to which I beat him. If anyone's going to claim this idea, it's me. I must have claim to *something* original, even if it's an idea I'm not using.

"I'm not going through the Wall. I never was."

"Why not?" He removes the leaf from my neck and twirls it. Blood cakes one side like broken veins.

"I changed my mind. It was an impulse." I cringe with the last word. "I want to say Good-bye over here, with you." At least with this confession, he won't leave me and cross the Wall on his own.

Reid says nothing.

My nose is cold. I wrap my arms around my knees and release an elephant-like huff. "I didn't mean to break the window."

"I'll buy a new one with my Last-Year funds."

I shake my head. "I'll pay for it." Glass windows are rare in Low Cities like Unity. We only had the one—a 20th anniversary gift from Father to Mother. Reid and I used to fight over who got to wash it.

"You're not empty Numbers," Reid says in a low voice, not looking at me. "You've never been empty Numbers, despite what kids at school used to say. God doesn't make empty Numbers."

My retort forms in a deep breath but sticks in my throat like a ball of wet dough. I look at Reid—his eyes scan my face.

"You know that, don't you?" he asks.

My ball of dough melts and comes out as a dry sob. *Empty Numbers! Empty Numbers! Parvin's just got empty Numbers!*

They never said it to Reid, even though they thought we had the same Numbers. Everyone knew he would use his well.

He stands. "I'll help you with your biography. I'll convince Mother to let you do it. I don't mind if our secret is revealed. They're our Numbers, after all."

I look up. He seems taller against the sun. "I don't think I should write it anymore. It sounds like it might be too dangerous . . . for everyone."

"Don't be so indecisive. Have confidence in your choices." He holds out a hand. "Sometimes impulsive thoughts are the best ones."

Why couldn't I have been born with his confidence? Someday—at least one of the remaining 364—I *will* be like Reid, but for now I take his hand and allow him to pull me to my feet.

"Okay." I sniff and rub a sleeve along my nose. "Maybe I can get it published right before our Good-byes. No risk of being evicted because of it."

"If that's what you want. Mother will give in easier."

I wipe my forearm across my chin. "Do you think she'll stay upset with me?"

We walk around to the entrance where precious shattered glass decorates the brick sidewalk. "Oh, she's already set up punishment."

My stomach drops and I peek through the broken window. "Punishment?"

Reid grins and opens the door before whispering in my ear, "Stitches."

3

The four stitches on my chin look like man-stubble.

Mother chose the thread, Father sterilized the fishing hook, and Reid assured me it wouldn't hurt much.

He lied.

Though anesthesia is preferred, I avoided the medical center in Nether Town. Their admittance procedures grow more finicky by the day, and I don't want to raise unnecessary questions with my dwindling Numbers.

My Clock blinks 363 days now, and I carve the number on the top edge of my wax tablet with my stylus. When Mother sewed me up, Reid explained his reasoning behind approving my biography. She relented. My discouragement morphed into determination, which I will channel into this biography. My restlessness must be tamed.

The scratches form white numbers in the black wax. I haven't used my wax tablet for anything but sewing plans and book lists since leaving school. Now it will hold my story.

I glance at the sewing plans now and realize my problem at once—my tablet isn't big enough for a biography. It has a middle flap with wax on both sides and a wax coating on the two cover flaps—four pages of wax.

I'll need paper.

I set down the stylus, pointing the needle-side away from me. I thought I was brilliant when I replaced the dull tip of my stylus with a sewing needle last year. It makes a smoother line in the wax and allows me more room to write, but that will be nothing like writing on paper. I won't have to think about wax pieces or the heat of the day or the pressure of the stylus.

"Paper," I whisper to the empty room. The idea of keeping words somewhere permanent sounds surreal. I would be able to draw a design without having to memorize it or erase two days later.

Mother won't like the idea of spending precious specie on paper after I just broke our window. Maybe I can sell some clothing at the market square. But I can't wait for the paper. I must start my biography now on my four good pages of wax.

I stare at the black wax and my eyes glaze over. How does a biographer begin a book? God started with *In the beginning*. Fairy tales begin with *Once upon a time*. Neither sounds right. I'm not God and I'll never be a fairy.

I scratch:

I was born.

It looks so boring—an accurate depiction of my life. I press the scraped wax into the top right corner of the tablet and stare at the three words. A tiny fist in my heart squeezes out a drop of sorrow. *Why did You let me be born, God, if You knew I'd just waste my Numbers?*

I was born. Who cares?

New plan.

Mother, Father, and Reid are out on a reminiscent walk. Unlike me, they find pleasure in tromping through mud and licking chapped lips against the wind. I do it out of necessity.

I grab my overdue library books, wrap a scarf around my threaded facial hair, and then stomp out of the house toward Unity's one-year-old library. Twenty-six minutes later, I return home with a pile of last year's hottest biographies—still in paper form due to Unity's low-class status. It's ironic to me that paper books are considered "low status" when my family still can't afford paper. I'm tempted to tear out the blank pages from the backs of the biographies to use for myself.

As I lift the latch to the front door, my foot rolls over something round. I fall against the doorframe and the biographies topple into the October mud. I glare at them. Gunk seeps into their pages.

"Great," I mutter, scooping them up one by one.

On the doorstep lie two newspapers. Trevor followed through. One is Unity's own *Weekly Unit*. The other is a fresh feast for my news-hungry eyes. A fancy electrosheet—weatherproof and programmed to curl into a single roll. The title, *The Daily Hemisphere*, lines the front and the warped pictures pop with color. A line on the top border is marked with an asterisk:

Self-updating electrosheet

Perfect. Don't lose it.

I stumble inside, drop the mud-soaked books onto my desk, and snatch the news from the doorstep. I open *The Daily Hemisphere* first, never having held an electrosheet before, let alone one carrying national news. It's lightweight but stiff, and unfurls when I slide my closed fingers down the length of it. Once opened, it's half the size of a paper newspaper. The first heading reads, *President Garraty Approves Increase in Assigned Enforcers.*

The article states every village, town, and city must have three Enforcers per population thousand. A picture beside the article shows three men, same height, standing shoulder to shoulder with pointy backward black *E*s tattooed on their left temples.

Fifteen more Enforcers are coming to Unity? The six we already have cause enough harm. I shudder and set down the electrosheet. New Enforcers won't know my village or the people. They'll Clock-check everyone and more people will go through the Wall, even though the rest of the nation registers Radicals and gives them a choice—relocation or the Wall. At least, that's what the newspapers say the rest of the nation does. I wouldn't know.

Stupid Low-City status. The Enforcers here don't register Radicals because they're lazy. I guess it takes too much paperwork, specie, and tracking devices. It must be easier to murder someone.

I scan the rest of the electrosheet. The words scroll up when my gaze reaches the bottom of the screen. I spend the next several minutes directing the pages with my eyes. It's so strange I set it down, wary and slightly dizzy, but excited. I've never owned something so advanced. "No wonder paper isn't the norm anymore."

I leave my new stash of reading material and make a cup of coffee. News will wait. It's time to read about those who died. Maybe I'll get some ideas for how to write about my own life.

The first biography opens with a long description about flowing wheat fields. Boring. Book two starts with a joke. Rejected. Book three coaxes me into its pages like a handsome salesman. I resurface after four intriguing chapters about Gloria Pak—a mathematician.

I flip to the cover. Only a gifted biographer could make the life of an arithmetic-savvy reclusive woman from a spit of a town sound interesting. My eyes find the author's name: *Skelley Chase.*

My new hero.

I scan the spines of my dwindling stack. The flowing script of *Chase* covers all books except the two in the reject pile. How have I never heard of this author before? I should have branched away from the fiction section more often. This man must have never-ending Numbers to follow the lives of so many people. Four biographies last year? He's a miracle-worker. Nothing but a miracle will fix my bland life and get this thing published.

For the second time today, I leave the house on an inspired mission. My heart pounds in time with my purposeful footsteps. Impulse. It's my oxygen.

The excitement in my chest transforms into abrupt nervousness when I reach the county building. My last meeting with Trevor feels like weeks ago, not yesterday morning. Do I want to see him again?

No. But I *need* to see him again.

I don't allow myself to hesitate. This is my Last Year—I must not waste it with cowardice. The pulse in my clenched fingers sends a panic signal up my arm. I enter. When I reach the desk, Rat Nose looks up from her *Sacred Seconds* magazine electrosheet with obvious reluctance.

"Can I help you?" she wheezes.

My eyes stray to the magazine picture. I glimpse a clean-shaven, thirty-something gentleman with a handsome smirk and a green fedora.

Rat Nose flips the sheet over. "He's good looking, too old for you, and wouldn't waste the seconds of a receptionist."

I squirm. "Um, I'm here to see Trevor."

Rat Nose jerks a thumb toward the elevator and returns to her electrosheet. I skirt around the desk and avoid my own gaze in the elevator mirror. The third-floor light dings and the doors open. I lift my chin like a tightrope walker.

Confidence.

Trevor's door stands cracked open. I enter with an abrupt knock. Trevor glances up with bulging cheeks. His office reeks of fish. My attempt at a deep breath claws its way down my throat and I swallow a cough. I make a point not to look at the lunch plate before him.

"Uh hi, Trevor. Do you have a moment?"

He nods and swallows, sweeping a hand toward the same chair as yesterday.

I choose to stand. I won't stay long. "Can I add something to my Last-Year list?"

He nods again, either still swallowing or choosing not to speak. One hand pushes his plate away and the other reaches into a drawer on his side of the desk. My folder makes its appearance. "What's on your mind?" His voice comes out in the usual collected manner, but raspy. Must be the fish.

"I want to meet with a biographer for writing advice."

His fingers tap dance on the screen surface and he picks up a thin pointer pen. "Name?"

"Skelley Chase."

The pen stops mid stroke. Trevor takes off his glasses and looks at me. He inclines his head.

I scratch my nose. "What?"

Trevor's eyes jerk to a spot over my shoulder and swift footsteps precede a loud, nasal voice behind me. "Hiya, Trevor I need a new list."

I jump and turn around. A young man Reid's height with a receding chin, small mouth, and dusty-blond hair swept to one side, strides past me without a care. He places his hands on Trevor's desk. Trevor closes my file with his finger saving the spot. The stranger taps his forefinger on my file. I bristle.

"I've already met the chicks you listed and it's no good. They're not interested. I need to extend the list. Broaden my search." He stands straight and flings his arms wide, inches away from my face. "I need to have an open mind and a willingness to sacrifice meaningless criteria. I'm no longer afraid of dating someone unattractive."

It takes me twenty seconds to assess the young man who interrupts, ignores, and nearly backhands me with his hairy knuckles. My conclusion? Instant dislike.

"This is not your file, Dusten," Trevor says.

Dusten? Dusten Grunt. The childhood "Empty Numbers" chanter. None of his cute-kid looks survived into his teen years. I internally cheer. Sometimes mean people deserve to turn out ugly.

Trevor pulls my file to his chest. I'm pleased to see this measure of confidentiality. "You need to speak with your own Mentor."

"Monica's given up on me. She says I need to find a new wish." Dusten lowers his arms. "Seriously, Trevor—three girls say their Goodbye in the next two years. That's not much to choose from."

Trevor points toward me with my file. Dusten turns and flinches when our eyes meet. I raise an eyebrow and fold my arms.

"She's got a beard."

My hand jerks to my chin and heat sweeps from forehead to stitches.

Trevor's mouth twitches. "I think it's temporary." He releases a little cough. "Besides, I pointed at her because we are in a meeting. She's not one of your options. You will have to wait until we are finished."

"This is important." What a whiner. "I haven't got much time."

He doesn't remember me. I couldn't be more thrilled, though I *would* like to give him a hard kick in the shins. So, he has empty Numbers too.

Hypocrite. Even so, I pity Dusten's determination to pursue a relationship with dwindling Numbers. No girl will have him with such little life left to his Clock. Even if he hadn't remained a bully.

He's still in a better position than you, my conscience nags. I ignore it.

Trevor places his glasses back on his face. "You will have to wait."

I'm liking Trevor a little more.

Dusten plops himself into the red chair on this side of the desk. I roll my eyes and give Trevor a shrug. As long as nasally Dusten is silent, I can tolerate his presence.

"Parvin, you can't meet Skelley Chase."

My momentary approval disappears. "Why not?"

Dusten swings around in the chair and looks at me with his head cocked. "Parvin?"

"Shut *up!*" I forgot that detail—my memorable name.

Trevor reopens my file. "Mr. Chase is famous and busy."

"He's busy with biographies. I'm *writing* a biography. Wouldn't he be interested?"

Trevor runs his tongue over his teeth. "Probably not. Biographying isn't his only job."

Dusten still watches me, but his eyes narrow. I force myself to stare at Trevor. "Yesterday, you said you could get me a famous actor. Why can't you get a biographer?"

"Different circumstances."

"Please, Trevor." My voice sounds desperate and I grit my teeth. "I want to talk to him about how he writes. I need some pointers."

He closes my file. "I can't."

"What sort of Mentor are you?" I fight the urge to pound his desk. "I can't cross the Wall. I can't be a biographer. I can't even *meet* a biographer." I tick off each statement with my fingers and then throw my hands in the air. "Oh, but I can travel to foreign countries and find a boy to kiss me."

Dusten's eyes widen like a raccoon's. I want to slap away his stare. Instead, I place my hands on Trevor's desk and lean forward. "I want my Last-Year funds." He opens his mouth, but I slam my fist on his fish-ridden desk. "Now."

A strand of his combed hair falls out of place. His glasses reflect his wide eyes. Hesitant, with cautious movements, he opens a lower drawer in his desk with a tiny key. Inside sit four camel-colored pouches like the one Reid brought home yesterday, each with a name hanging from the drawstring. "You get half now. You may request the rest at your six-month Assessment."

"Fine."

He pours coins into an empty pouch while I watch every move. It looks like half. I wish he'd try and cheat me so I could vent my anger with a few more shouts. The moment he ties the pouch, I snatch it from his hand, turn on my heel, and stride from the office. I jab the elevator button so hard I jam my finger. With a growl, I take the stairs instead, shaking my hand.

As the stairwell door closes, I hear an amused whisper behind me. "*Empty Numbers.*"

I run the rest of the way down and burst into the entry lobby. The receptionist looks up, but I stalk past her desk. "I can still write my biography on my own." I push open the double doors like a bandit exiting a saloon. "I still have sources."

On my way home, I splurge on a stack of paper from a street shop. I don't have time to wait. I have to write this biography *now*. Though I'd planned to keep Mother's journal for later inspiration, a quote from her private thoughts may be the juicy intro I need for my story.

I turn the corner to Straight Street and trip over a bale of hay bound by twine.

"Watch it!" a voice shouts and I catch myself with my right hand on the rough side of the first house.

My temper is in no mood for this. I push my body back to a standing position. "The middle of the *street*?" I gesture to the bale and search for the culprit. "There's no better place for you to put this?" I meet my target's eyes, and my temper fizzles into an embarrassed squeak.

What's a handsome man doing on Straight Street? Okay, he's not pure handsome, but he's no Dusten Grunt. And he's a *man*. On *my* street.

He's not from Unity Village; I would have noticed him before. Maybe he's a registered Radical, relocated here.

Soul mate material?

He tilts his head to one side, a gently disapproving frown on his shadowed face. His nose is a little crooked and his short hair is dark— or is it the shadow from the house? His skin is pale, but in an attractive way. He's older than I am—just a couple years—and holds no traces of immature boy.

"Good eve. Sorry about that, I'm trying to get the new thatch up before dark."

I glance back at what I now realize is a bale of thick roof thatch. "Are you moving here?"

"No." His frown turns into a soft grin. "Enforcers live at the county building."

All thoughts of handsomeness pop like a punctured balloon. "You're an Enforcer?"

He steps out of the house shadows and I make out the pointy backward *E* on his left temple. A few strands of his hair, which I now see is dark blond, rest over the tattoo. He doesn't seem so likable anymore.

I lose my words and inch around him. "Um . . . okay. Nice to meet you."

"Tally ho."

Tally ho? What does that mean? Enforcer lingo?

I turn and walk five houses down to my own house, mentally kicking myself. Nice to meet you? We didn't even meet. Did I have to be so nervous? If he thinks I'm nervous he'll think I have sketchy Numbers. He'll Clock-check me. I'll be sent across the Wall early. I'll never finish my biography.

I shut the door behind me, catch my reflection in the entrance mirror, and groan. I'd forgotten about my stitches. Just what I wanted to do: make an unforgettable impression on an Enforcer who now knows where I live. My throat grows tight, but I push myself to stay focused.

Somehow I remember the combination to Mother's safe from amidst yesterday's bleeding, arguments, and scalding tea. Good thing, too because I doubt she would give it to me again.

The fire crackles in the grate, attempting to warm the kitchen despite the broken window. The warmth soothes my irritation. Sometimes Mother complains about the small size of our house, but I've always liked it. The cooking fire and wood stove heat all three rooms. With the kitchen in the center and a bedroom off each side, the heat filters everywhere except the outhouse.

I knock on Mother and Father's door before entering. It's empty. Their bed sits opposite the dresser, nicely made with two wool blankets. I shove back the coats in their cramped closet and kneel beside the black safe. The combination takes two tries, but once unlocked, the door opens without a sound. A stack of yellowed papers tumbles into my lap along with four blank Clocks—the only free gifts from our government.

I set aside the two blank Clocks belonging to Mother in case she has more children. I blame the government for Reid's and my predicament. It gives women two Clocks in case of twins. It doesn't account for triplets. And yet, Reid and I will get blamed and punished if caught with our single Clock.

The other two blank Clocks linger in my fingers. Mine . . . for my potential children. They'll be destroyed once I say Good-bye, childless. I don't mind, though I squirm at the memory of the thick needle piercing the soft inner skin by each hip. I was alone when the medic arrived at our house on my ninth birthday. Mother and Reid were out gathering ingredients for a birthday cake. Two small ovachips were inserted into my body, programmed to detect a conception and initiate the Clock.

My gut clenches, knowing something electronic with a mind of its own is swimming around in my body. That's enough incentive for me not to get pregnant.

I put them down, then shove aside birth certificates, immunization records, and an old wooden Clock stuck on *000.000.00.00.00.*

William's, the oldest of we three triplets. It figures that one of the two Clocks turned out to be his. Ironic. He never needed it, yet here it is. Expired.

No sense fuming about things I can never change. Reid and I will know soon enough whom our Clock belongs to. Behind William's Clock is the real treasure—a floppy leather journal with finger-worn corners. The cover is black, like secrets.

I thrust the other items back inside, swing the door shut, spin the dial, and retreat to my room. After slipping on a fresh pair of socks, I curl on my bed and flip to April 2, 2131—my birthday. Mother's handwriting is barbaric and doesn't follow the lines, but the challenge of deciphering makes this feel more like an adventure and less like an invasion.

04.02.2131
I want to see my son before he dies. The contractions have begun and midwife Bridget is late. I'm afraid he'll die before he's born.

This is all she writes? Happy birthday to me. The entire page is filled with one to three-sentence entries per date. I turn back a page and find the same format. Why so cryptic? After a few thumb-flips, I realize every entry is like this. Mother's short, to-the-point conversation habits seem to have leaked into her writing.

I return to my birthday entry and read it again. The woman gives birth to three children—one dead, one expected, and one a surprise— yet she writes only three sentences in her journal? Why even keep a journal? Beneath the words is a small black handprint. Mother scribbled the name *William* beneath it. My forefinger traces the handprint of its own accord.

No mention of me. I can't start a biography with *this*. I lick my fingers and turn the page. Two more handprints cover the surface—one in blue and the other in faded pink. Mine is miniscule—smaller than both Reid's and William's.

I hold my hand, palm up, against the page beside the corresponding pink one. The seventeen years between my hand sizes zip through my mind like a fly fisher's cast. Not much stands out: playing with Reid, backing out of dares, being bullied at school, quitting school after eight years, snitching newspapers, sewing random clothing I never sell or share, and waiting . . . waiting for the end. Waiting to see if this year is the end.

My eyes stray to the next entry on the bottom of the page and I find the opening line for my biography.

04.03.2131
  I have a daughter. I'm cursed.

4

000.362.18.40.56

Mother and I are not best friends. We don't have girl talk or squeal about my future wedding. We don't paint our nails together. We seldom hug. But we *are* friends...in our own way. We have coffee in the morning, and occasionally she does my hair. Sometimes we go sill shopping and, when I was little, I held her hand.

I imagined her first thoughts about me as positive—Parvin, the surprise baby, the life replacing death. Not as a *curse*.

My eyes smart. What did I expect? I close the journal and, with it, my heart. I won't assume and I won't ask. I may be her curse, but I won't risk what relationship we *do* have in my Last Year. Not yet, anyway.

The front door opens with a burst of jabbering. Reid's voice holds its usual upbeat dance. It's refreshing having him home, even if he insists on sleeping in the room above Father's shop instead of our house—always so independent.

My fingers brush over my stitches and I slide off my bed, leaving the blanket crooked.

Reid enters my room like a rhino. The door rebounds off the wall. He stops it with his foot and throws his arms wide. "Ribbons! Long ones, short ones, ones for every mood." He does a little dance to the singsong rhythm. "Thin ones, thick ones, and ones to tie your shoes!"

I giggle. "You can't rhyme."

He wiggles his fingers in front of my face. Ribbons are tied to each one—silk, velvet, lace, smooth, curly, and shiny. Though I never wear ribbons—I'm not even sure *how* to wear ribbons—I can't stop the sigh. "They're beautiful."

"Like my sister." He slides them off, one by one.

"They'll get lost in all my crazy hair." I wrap one around my pinky finger.

"Then tie them to your beard."

Mother interrupts Reid's laugh with a holler. "Supper!"

I make a face, not very hungry, but we enter the kitchen and take our seats anyway. Crumpled street vendor wrappings sit beside four steaming plates of food on each edge of the table.

Baked fish.

I warn my gag reflex to behave. Mother takes the ribbons from Reid and steps up behind me. She loosens my braid and brushes my hair with her fingers. Something in me wants to pull away, but the hidden soft side—that Brielle persona—keeps me still. In fact, it urges me to enjoy the moment.

"Aren't you going to eat?" I ask her.

"In a minute." She pulls back strands from my face.

Reid bows his head.

I close my eyes, trying not to disrupt Mother's fingers.

"Our Father in heaven," he says. "Hallowed be Your name . . ."

My mind drifts from his formal prayer. He and I don't pray the same. Maybe it's because I don't often pray. Does this prayer touch his heart? I've heard it so often I can't seem to focus on the meaning. It seems so . . . impersonal sometimes.

". . . but deliver us from evil. Amen."

I open my eyes.

Mother says, "Now, tell us about your day, Parvin."

Father and Reid dig into the crappie with vigor, releasing its fumes like stirred cow manure. Reid throws me a wink. I feign throwing my fork at him.

It takes a minute to register Mother's request and even longer to recall the day's events. *Library, Skelley Chase, Trevor, Dusten, Enforcer, journal.* I don't want to tell them much. They look so content. But they're family—*my* family. I can't leave them out, so I insert lightheartedness into my descriptions.

I brush off disappointments. I leave out the journal. Mother French braids ribbons into my hair while I speak. My throat feels thick from her touch. I want to believe she loves me. I want this show of affection to be real. But I can't help wondering if she's thinking of me as her curse. I want my assurance back.

"Did you see the Enforcer on the corner of Straight Street?" I pick at my crappie.

"Enforcer?" Reid looks up, a frown creasing his brow.

Father sets down his fork. "A new family is moving into the empty house—an evicted family. I'd guess he's their escort."

Now it's my turn to frown. "I didn't know Enforcers escorted evicted families. I thought they just kicked them out of their home city—downgraded and relocated them."

"Enforcers from Upper or High Cities provide escorts as a security measure," Reid says. "The law in those cities is a lot more structured and humane. They have to register the Radicals and monitor the number of re-located Radicals in each city."

"This is why many Low Cities deteriorate," Father says. "If there are too many registered Radicals, the job market and population get adulterated. Low Cities turn into Dead Cities because the government gives less specie and the Mentors move away. That's one reason I think Unity Village is hesitant to register all the illegal Radicals."

I look between Father and Reid—how do they know this? No one seems concerned about the Enforcer on our street. Isn't Reid nervous? After all, I have our Numbers with me. If that young Enforcer on the corner had stopped Reid and asked for his Numbers, Reid could have been sentenced to cross the Wall then and there.

"Parvin, I have some news." Reid's grip tightens around his fork. Mother binds my hair, pats my shoulder, then she and Father retreat to their room with their meals.

"Bad news?" I croak as their door closes. They'll be listening.

"Depends on your perspective."

I bite my tongue. "I won't panic." Sometimes saying it makes me believe I can restrain myself. He runs a hand through his hair. I do the same until my fingers catch in the ribbons.

"Should I beat around the bush—?"

"Just say it, Reid." My anxiety swells and my mind skims possibilities: He wants to cross the Wall. The government knows about our Numbers. He knows about my outburst with Trevor. An Enforcer caught him without his Clock—

"I'm leaving."

I let out a sound somewhere between a gasp and a squawk. "L-Leaving?" I focus all my strength on restraining the over-reactive emotions welling in my eyes. He won't look at me. I can't bring myself to ask why, when, or for how long.

"I only came home for a couple days. I'll return for the six-month Assessment."

All willpower drains from me and I rest my face in my hands. First Mother and now Reid. Am I important to them at all?

Deep breaths. A few tears drop. "I-Is it because of my plan?" I choke. "B-because I want to be a biographer? Is it because I upset you yesterday?" Silence. I look up. His face is in his hands, too. "I'm sorry, Reid."

He shakes his head and then meets my eyes. I see the anguish in his gaze before his brave smile makes an entrance. "No, Parvin. It's not because of your plan. It's because Florida is *my* plan. I can leave now knowing you have something to pour the rest of your time into—your biography."

"What's *in* Florida? You haven't even told me about it. Why do you love it so much?"

He releases a long breath and cracks his thumb knuckle. "I'll write to you about it, okay?"

Resignation takes its hold—something I've mastered. I'll watch Reid leave on an adventure again, envying him, but not daring to follow. I restrain myself from begging, *But you said you came to go through Last Year with me. You said you wouldn't let me face it alone.* A sigh escapes my tense lips. "When do you leave?"

"Tomorrow. The train departs at dusk."

I dip my head. "Thanks for telling me."

"Parvin . . ."

I hold up a hand and stand. "I'm fine, Reid. Just let me swallow it tonight."

"Your ribbons look nice."

"Thanks."

I enter my room and shut the door softly, like a whisper. If I could unbutton my soul and hang it up, its downtrodden state might dry off by morning. Instead, I lie on my bed and let it float in my swirling emotions.

Reid was right—I have something to pour the rest of my life into, but I do it because of his absence and my stirring restlessness. With no writing experience, no brother, and nothing else to do, I commit every second to my biography. It's difficult rebelling against my former habit of wasting time. When the pull to quit is too strong, I walk through the town square clutching my Clock as a reminder of the urgency.

Sometimes I read my Bible because Reid would want me to, but the words gloss together. The information won't seep into my heart, no matter what I read. The verses, the books, the stories . . . all seem so boring. What am I missing?

The dipping pen Father carved drips blotches of Mother's ink onto the page as I scribble sentence after sentence. The ink is made from blueberries and smells like summer—a hopeful scent in these winter days. Mother places the extra ink on the windowsill for trade.

Weeks pass and I delve into the works of Skelley Chase—fascinated by his ability to turn the most boring story into a midnight-candle read. My weathered wood desk grows stained from ink. The local newspapers lean in uneven piles. The electrosheet brings drama from Upper Cities and depressing changes in Low City regulations.

Hearing after hearing swallow up my weak protests, leaving me with more ghost eyes of doomed Radicals. I pour every experience, every attempt at saving them, into my biography. Someone will read this. Someone will change this.

I cry through the recollection of my limited school years, but take care that no tears smudge my pages. After much internal squirming, I change the names of the bullies. I can't bring myself to give them the honor of having their names published.

The hardest part of writing my own story is filling in the blanks. I have a lot of blanks: staying at home and doing nothing but dream, read, sit outside and make pictures in the snow, stare at the sky and envy Reid's confidence, sew, sew, sew. These aren't things people want to read about.

I resign myself to a short biography.

When I'm in need of inspiration, I flip through Mother's journal to find some mention of Reid or myself. My name appears several times in her short cryptic sentences, but no entries hold emotion. Just raw facts.

01.12.2140—"I wish the government would give us a better dividend so I could buy Parvin some boots."

06.01.2141—"Oliver gave me a glass window yesterday. It's so clean. Parvin and Reid made faces in it all day long."

09.10.2142—"Reid saved Parvin from the bullies at school today. I'm so proud of him."

I manage to write two pages from these last two sentences after Mother's entry jogs a long-forgotten memory. Reid always saved me— from bullies, from depression, from loneliness . . . all the way up until our Last Year.

Now he has deserted me.

Every time I finish with Mother's journal, I place it back in the safe when she's not looking. For all I know, she doesn't even realize I'm reading it.

The six-month mark approaches and Mother turns more snappish, yet somehow softer, in her interactions with me. Maybe it's because she'll miss me. Perhaps she already misses me. I don't often leave my room and our visiting has dwindled to the necessity of mealtime. My birthday passes without card, cake, or Reid. Apparently Mother and Father don't think eighteen is an important age since it marks the year I'll die.

Mother does leave me a Bible verse scribbled on a scrap of paper. Something about God completing what He started in me. I toss it among the stacks of Unity newspapers. Now that I'm eighteen it seems she's not afraid of being arrested for sharing a Bible verse.

Half of my Last Year is gone, and I've spent it holed in these four walls, filling the air with the aroma of blueberry ink. Even with the scratched-out rough draft of my life sitting on my desk, I am unfulfilled—and plagued by that fact. But it seems to plague Mother more.

"I don't know what you expect from my Last Year, Mother," I say the afternoon of my six-month Assessment. "If you were my Mentor, what would you have me do?"

She throws a dishrag into the sink and pumps the water handle with unnecessary fervor. "I don't understand why you want your biography published. Why do you want people to know you disobeyed the government or you quit school or you sew all the time?" Water gushes from the pump and she shoves the stopper into the sink bottom.

"It's not just about me. It's about the Radicals who are sentenced on that platform in the square every month." I wrap a thin orange scarf around my neck and bypass the basket of gloves. The weather has lightened and spring awaits the sun's call, but brooding clouds hold the war flag at the moment. "This can heal people, Mother."

"No one's broken."

"Everyone's broken," I breathe. "Our village has lost its unity."

"You don't make sense."

"At least I'm *doing* something." The words feel like a lie. My soul pounds its fists on my sternum from the inside, screaming, *It's not enough!* But I don't know what *is* enough. I must keep searching. I must keep moving.

It's no fair growing restless when, six months from now, I'll be in "eternal rest," according to Reid and the Bible. I'm not even tired yet.

"The government won't publish your story." Mother pulls her hands from the icy dishwater and rubs them together.

"They have to. I'll make it a Last-Year wish. I'm bringing the manuscript to Trevor Rain right now." I can't allow myself to think I'm spending my Last Year in vain. One hundred and eighty-one days remain to my life and it's still as bland as watered-down coffee.

She gives no reply. I hoist the satchel containing my biography onto my shoulder, blow her a kiss she doesn't see, and tromp into the afternoon rays. It's already two hours past noon, but today's a lazy day. Mrs. Newton stands on the corner, washing her street window.

Mother and I figured the Newtons have a lot of specie from their previous city because every window in their new house has glass in it—pure single sheets of glass. Our new kitchen window is made of twelve square panes connected to crisscrossed wood framing. Aside from the windows, their two young girls wear different clothing almost every day.

"Good noon, Parvin." Mrs. Newton waves her rag at me—the friendliest soul on Straight Street.

"Good afternoon."

An Enforcer steps out of Mrs. Newton's front door—the young one who thatched their roof. I jolt to a stop and my hand flies to my Clock in my pocket.

He sees me and smiles, crinkling the black backward E on his temple. "Good noon, Miss."

"G-Good . . . uh . . ." I take tiny steps, inching to the other side of the street.

"This is Parvin Blackwater."

I want to scream at Mrs. Newton to be silent.

"Pleasure to meet you, Miss Blackwater," he says. "Off to the market?"

I shake my head. "M-my six-month A-Assessment."

His smile fades. "Oh, I'm sorry. Well, enjoy the spring warmth on your walk to the county building."

"Thank you." I turn onto Center Road toward the square and try not to flee. Deafening thumps pound my eardrums as my blood pulses. Why is he with the Newtons? They're not *friends* with an Enforcer are they? And why did he want to know where I was going?

I glance over my shoulder. He's not following. Does he suspect anything?

It doesn't matter. I have our Clock. He can't do anything to me. My heart rate slows and I try to push my thoughts to positive things.

Reid comes home today. What would he say to my second encounter with this Enforcer? Maybe nothing. Maybe he would shrug it off. Maybe our reunion will be like last Assessment Day, joking in the entrance of the county building and riding the elevator together. But when I arrive, the entrance is empty of all except Rat Nose. She's wearing new glasses.

I approach her desk. She looks up and her eyes narrow. "Parvin Brielle Blackwater?"

I flinch at the name Brielle. "Is my brother here?" She squints at an electronic screen set into the face of her desk. I lean over the marble counter and stare at the screen. "Is that new?"

A miniature calendar blinks from under her coffee cup. "The government gave us a few benefits. It's about time they updated our system.

These documenters make my job easier." She moves the cup and taps the screen. Today's square grows large. "Your brother has not arrived yet."

"He'll probably be a little late." I shake off the disappointment. When does his train arrive? Home has been bogged with depression since he left. I want him back and I don't ever want him to leave again.

"Mr. Rain will see you now," she rasps, pursing her lips.

I trudge into the elevator and stare at the reflection. Nothing new—I'm a bit heavier than last time from all the sitting I've done. Reid will like that.

I knock on Trevor's door. He lets out a muffled, "Come in."

When I enter, someone's in my chair. Trevor beckons me forward. The broad-shouldered, shorthaired stranger turns and releases an unnatural smile. He has a prominent jaw with a brown goatee and holds an asparagus-colored fedora in his lap. I've seen him somewhere before—he's attractive, mid-thirties, with a tanned complexion.

"Mr. Sacred Seconds?" I place his face to the memory of Rat Nose's old magazine.

"Ah, you read magazines?" His voice is low with a little warble and sounds almost bored.

"No, but I saw you on the cover once."

He raises an eyebrow before turning back to Trevor. I rub the toe of my boot on the floor. My Clock is in one hand and my satchel dangles from the other.

"Parvin." Trevor smiles—a real smile, making me step back in surprise. I eye him, but he goes on. "I'd like you to meet Mr. Skelley Chase."

5

000.181.23.20.16

Shock. People react to it in different ways. Some scream, some drop things, some babble. Me? My brain enters an instant sludge of numbness and idiocy. My tongue muscles recover sooner than my mental ones and I spew foolishness. "You have a goatee."

Trevor gives an embarrassed laugh—the type that comes from a parent when his or her child does something unusually stupid.

The shock lessens, but leaves behind the debris of silent questions. Why is he so young? Why is he here? Why isn't he a wiry, pointy-nosed, bookworm with glasses?

I attempt to remedy my declaration of immaturity. "Excuse me, Mr. Chase." I step forward with my hand extended. "Parvin Blackwater. My surprise in seeing you rendered me thinkless."

At first I think he may ignore my hand and salutation altogether, but perhaps he likes my creation of the word *thinkless*—being a fellow writer and all—because, after a moment, he shakes my hand with his thumb and first two fingers.

Not too friendly, but he's my miracle worker and it will take more than an aloof handshake to wipe away my admiration.

"I believe you wished to meet with him." Trevor must have abandoned his embarrassment because now he's beaming. His humanlike happiness unnerves me.

"Yes, I did—*do*."

Skelley Chase tosses his fedora onto his head and stands from the chair. "Shall we have a day of it? I have only a day."

I look to Trevor. He rests his hand on top of my closed file. "We'll meet next week, Parvin. We don't have to hit the exact six-month mark."

Skelley Chase leads the way out of the room, carrying a brown leather briefcase. The elevator ride passes in formal silence.

When we stride across the cold entrance, the receptionist squeaks and jumps to her feet, clutching a marker and a wrinkled paper version of *Sacred Seconds* to her chest. Skelley Chase walks on. Rat Nose opens and closes her mouth several times. We leave the county building before any sound emerges from her lips.

"Should I bother driving?"

Only now do I notice the sleek, forest-green car plugged into the county building's electric port. It glimmers in the sun like a dropped coin.

The color reminds me of his hat.

"There's nowhere to park." I glance around. "And the streets are too small."

Not to mention all the booths and vendors in the way. I can't remember the last car in Unity Village that wasn't a black Enforcer beetle. The train is Unity's transportation, and the people are better off spending their limited specie on provisions or real windows than on roads or charging ports.

I frown. "I thought personal automobiles were banned in the Low Cities." This recent piece of national news popped up on *The Daily Hemisphere* just yesterday. I suspect the USE doesn't want to develop Low Cities any further than it has to. Now only government cars are allowed.

"This is my first visit to a Low City." He adjusts his fedora.

He didn't answer my question. He must already know about the ban. Perhaps biographers are exempt, or maybe he wants to make it clear he's higher class.

"I come from a High City."

I assumed no less. Upper and High Cities are filled with media-food: politicians, actors, actresses, athletes, musicians, etc—those who have Numbers long enough to affect the world.

"Have you ever visited one?"

"No." I respond in a clipped voice. I haven't even *seen* an Upper City. I've read about how they compare to the average city before the Wall—technology, Internet, automobiles, plumbing, copy-paste apartments, stores filled with mass-produced food—but a person must apply to live there. Anyone can live in a Low City.

Unity Village may be impersonal and a bit run-down, but I'm proud to live here. The people are stiff and determined to work hard. We survive without too much government assistance.

"Lead on." Skelley Chase waves his hand at me.

Something in my chest tightens. "Where do you want to go?" My voice comes out timid, and queasiness plays against my stomach like a drummer. Where can I take him? What will we talk about? What did he mean earlier by, "Make a day of it"? I force myself to swallow the illness and inhale some fresh confidence.

"Does your village sell coffee?" His sarcasm is masked just enough to appear casual.

Coffee. My mind takes a mental sprint through the limited map of Unity. A street vendor sells coffee grounds on Sunday mornings. I doubt Unity Village has anything Skelley Chase might call classy.

My mind skids to a stop on the steps of a glass-windowed, red-awning café I've never entered. It was built a year ago. It's the top of style for us. It will have to do. "Yes." I'm relieved to hear more confidence in my voice. Or is it defiance?

I lead the way, avoiding the muddier streets for the sake of Skelley Chase's polished shoes, but he doesn't seem to mind the mud. By the time we reach *Faveurs*, splatters and muck cover the rim of his ironed slacks.

Four two-seater round tables with burgundy tablecloths and a tiny vase of fresh magnolias on each surface flank the propped door. Pink magnolia trees always bloom first in Unity Village before the dogwoods.

Skelley Chase takes a seat on the right at the table furthest from the door. I sink into my own cushioned wicker chair. Wreaths and garlands of woven magnolias twirl around the awning's framework, trickling down to tickle the top of the door.

This is my first time here. I've never had the coin or desire to visit before. Mother's black sludge from the morning fire tastes good enough to me. I think the café owner built *Faveurs* in an attempt to provide the people of Unity Village with a sense of dignity, but our dignity comes from something far more valuable than a luxury coffee shop.

A waitress, who could pass as a model, floats out the door in a white spring dress with blue trim and matching high-heels. Heels? She can't be from Unity Village.

She places a folded cloth napkin before each of us with a manicured hand. Goosebumps dot her tiny pale arms. "*Bonjour.* What may I get you?" she asks in a soft French accent.

Certainly not from Unity Village, but I'm grateful for the high-class feel of the café. Skelley Chase might lose his sarcasm.

"Double cappuccino, extra dry, breve, please," he drones.

Frenchie nods as if she hears this every day. I've never heard, read, or spoken these words in my life. Is he ordering food or a drink? Skelley Chase watches me. I jump and Frenchie blinks long, fake eyelashes.

"Um, nothing, thank you." My pockets are empty and I don't speak coffee except for two words: *hot* and *sweet.*

"Nonsense." Skelley Chase plops his fedora on the table beside his napkin, frowns, and surveys me. Despite my skill at a calm façade, I know my face betrays surprise. He squints, taps his finger a moment, and turns back to the waitress. "She'll have a single vanilla mocha, extra hot, no foam, and a little whip." He considers me for a quick second then adds, "Better make hers breve, too."

Frenchie retreats with the order. I pray she can write me up a tab and trust I'll return later to pay for whatever monstrosity he ordered.

"Let's get to business." Skelley Chase eyes me. "Why am I here?"

I push my tab worries aside to make room for the wave of new worries that flow in. Deep, calming breath. I am in control. "I need your advice."

He folds his hands.

I fidget with the napkin before continuing. "I'm six months into my Last Year. I wrote my own biography and I want your opinion."

He holds up a finger. "Writing your own biography makes that an *auto*biography. Why do you want my opinion?"

"Because you're the best. I've read several of your biographies. My biog—*auto*biography needs to be good enough to get published. Maybe you could even connect me with a publisher?"

He sighs. "You want to die famous and well-known."

The way he says it makes me feel ashamed. "Remembered," I supply. "I want to be remembered."

"Doesn't everyone?"

Frenchie arrives with a tiny cup topped with milk foam and a dusting of cinnamon for Skelley Chase. She places what looks like a birthday dessert in front of me. "Eez there anything else you need?"

"A plate of lemon rinds, please."

Skelley Chase's request is so absurd, I snort. He picks up a tiny cinnamon cookie that arrived with his drink and raises a single eyebrow. "Manuscript?"

I stop laughing and pull the wad of tied papers from my satchel. He looks at the stack with half-closed eyes. My confidence dwindles. Did I expect a cry of delight?

He removes the brown twine and reads the first page while sipping his coffee. Is he impressed it's written on paper?

Page two. Silence. Page nine is where I reveal the secret about Reid's and my Clock. How will he react? Am I making a mistake by sharing that long-protected information?

By page three, I pick up my own sugar-topped drink and take a sip. The whipped cream goes up my nose. I snatch my napkin from the table and wipe my face. He's still reading. The swallow I manage to obtain from beneath the cream mountain is thick and sweet, like a liquid candy bar—just how I like it.

"This will never get published." Skelley Chase sets aside page four.

I drop my cup back onto the table. "Why not?"

"It's bland."

My calm dissolves. "You've read four pages!" Are my thoughts and words so worthless?

"Four pages too much. Your only good line is the one your Mother wrote in her journal. Other than that, it's you writing about your own life for yourself. You're not writing for a reader, which is why I'm bored with it already. I'm not you." He pushes it toward me.

"It's supposed to show people who I am, so they can know me."

He sniffs. "Why should anyone care about knowing you?"

My heart ices over. Why? Because I'm someone with depth. I matter, despite my Low City status. "I-I n-need your help to make this better. Please keep reading. It won't get published without you."

"That will take more than a day."

I slump in my chair. My great plan now seems ridiculous. Any passion floats away in the chilled breeze. I don't have the time to rewrite the autobiography. Mother was right—I'm being reckless. Six months wasted. Six months to go until all opportunity for meaning is gone.

I make a last-ditch effort, my voice deadened. "Can't you at least read the whole thing? Maybe you could stay an extra day." I cringe at the selfishness in my request. Skelley Chase is famous. Who am I? Why should he stay? My attitude is distancing me further from his respect.

He takes the twine and binds it around my papers again. "That depends on Mr. Rain. I'm not cheap."

I straighten. "He's *paying* you to be here?" My Last-Year funds are financing this torture?

"Time is money."

"Please, for the sake of my Last Year, just read through it." I'm begging, but without Skelley Chase's miracle I can do nothing but give up. I've given up my entire life so far. It can't end the same way.

He wipes a coffee drip off the side of his white cup with his thumb. "My train leaves at seven tomorrow morning. I'll be here for my morning coffee at six-thirty. You may gather your manuscript then. I'll try and write in a few pointers, but don't count on them for publication."

He stands as Frenchie arrives with a plate of lemon peels. He pulls a plastic bag from his briefcase and dumps them inside. He then hands her a specie—more than enough for both our coffees. "That covers tomorrow morning as well." Without another word to me, he leaves *Faveurs* the way we came.

"Thank you," I mutter, though he's already turning the corner onto the main street.

I sip the rest of my drink to thaw my heart. When I leave, I pluck a flower from one of the wreaths and twirl it between my thumb and forefinger. Skelley Chase doesn't think I matter. He's branded me because of my city status.

"Stupid Low City." I squeeze the flower stem until it crunches and wets my fingers. "Just because where I live is considered obsolete doesn't mean I have to match it."

I walk past Father's carpentry shop. His spring display consists of sugar bowls and dessert plates with carved flowers around the edges, sitting dainty behind a small lattice window. A thin coating of dust blurs the detail. My hands itch to wipe the dishes clean, as I did so often when I helped out here.

The door is closed and the *Enter* sign flipped around. Reid must be home. I place the flower in the door latch and quicken my pace. How could I have forgotten Reid? He missed his own six-month Assessment. His Mentor, Monica Lamb, probably enjoyed the free half hour.

Programmed anticipation urges me to run home, but I resist. I'm lacking the excitement I used to have when Reid came home. This time, I'm not sure what to expect. Last time, he left me and, though he'd promised, he never wrote. I thought we'd have a year to bid farewell to the Earth and each other, and we now have only six months. Or do we? What if he's home again just for a few days?

I round the corner to Straight Street and run into a human brick wall. I stumble backward with a gasp and the man catches my forearm before I fall. "Excuse me," I say, still recovering from the collision.

"Clock?" The one word comes out in a deep rumble. I look up into the serious face of a black man with a pointy *E* tattooed backward on his left temple.

My hands fly to my spring jacket, but the square lump isn't there. "Um . . ." My arms begin to shake. "I just had it."

His grip tightens and my free hand fumbles in my satchel. Down at the bottom, my fingers close around the cold wooden box and my knees weaken. I pull the Numbers out and hold them in front of his face, not looking into his eyes.

"These are your Numbers?"

"Yes." I'm panting now and pull against his grip. "I've lived here my whole life."

"You don't have much longer."

"I know."

He releases me, and I sprint to my house. I look back up the street before entering. The Enforcer approaches the Newton's door. He raises his fist. I slip into my house before I can hear his knock. The front door creaks when I close it and the safety of home washes over me.

I fall back against the wall, holding my Numbers over my heart. I've never been Clock-checked before. The new Enforcers have been here a month. They must be getting bored if they're wandering by my street. I can't blame them. There's not much to do since few people leave or move to Unity.

I spare a thought for the Newtons. They've been here six months. They were *escorted* here for relocation. How does that work if they're registered Radicals? Will this Enforcer allow them to stay or do they have to move again?

The kitchen is empty and the fire laps up its last coals. The chairs sit crooked along the table. I hang my scarf on a loose peg in the entrance beside Mother's sage-green shawl and then snag a log from the home-made wood box.

Mother bursts from her bedroom. I jerk, and the log slips from my fingers, leaving behind a thick splinter in my skin. "*Mother!*" I suck breath through my teeth and clutch my wounded hand, squeezing away the pain.

Her hair has fallen from its loose brown knot and her hand jumps to her throat when she sees me. "Parvin." My name comes out in a gush of air.

"What?" I bark. My hand throbs and I increase the pressure.

Her gaze darts around the kitchen and lands on the log on the floor. "We're leaving."

"Leaving where?" I hold my hand away from myself and pick at the tip of the sliver.

She strides forward, slaps away my attempts, and yanks the splinter free, leaving behind tiny specks of wood and a burst of blood.

"Ouch!" I throw her a glare. She drops my hand and snatches her shawl from the entry. She looks confused and . . . frazzled. Mother is never frazzled. "Mother, what's wrong?"

Her eyes lock with mine, wide and fierce. "Reid's train derailed."

6

Mother's fingers squeeze around my wrist like cold handcuffs, but not as tight as the fear shackling my heart. We stumble through the streets of Unity Village until we reach the dirt path leading to Nether Town—it follows the train tracks like a wavy shadow. The crisp air sears my gasping lungs like red-hot nails.

"Mother," I wheeze. "What happened?"

"Father read a notice on the village postboard this afternoon," she grinds out. "The train crashed this morning—all survivors are in Nether Hospital."

My numbness turns into a welling of tears. "Is Reid one of the survivors?"

"We don't know." She continues to drag me.

I can't think. One word repeats like a broken record in my mind. *Reid. Reid. Reid. Reid.* I wrench from Mother's grasp and stop, gulping for air. My need for oxygen has nothing to do with exhaustion.

"Parvin, hurry!" Her voice cuts into my emotions. She says my name with no comfort, only accusation and panic.

I cover my eyes with my fists and scream, "Why didn't I *feel* anything, Mother? He's my triplet!" Shouldn't I have sensed a stab of fear? Apprehension? Alarm in the moment of tragedy?

"You haven't felt much of anything lately." The harshness in her voice pales in comparison to the slap of her words. She tightens her knitted shawl around her shoulders and continues to walk, leaving me behind.

How can she say I haven't felt much? I've been pouring every emotion and suffocating memory onto paper. Does she think I don't love Reid? *He's* the one who deserted *me*. Maybe she blames me for the accident. Reid wouldn't have tried to come home if not for me.

The train derailment wouldn't be an issue if Reid had his own Clock. We'd know how long he has to live and we'd worry only about his physical or mental status, praying he hadn't broken anything permanent. But I'm sure it's my Clock—it must be—which means he could be dead.

I don't care now that he left me six months ago or that I envy his confidence or that I didn't sense his danger. I want him with me for these last six months. If he dies, then I'm really alone. I can't face the end without him.

I run with endless, desperate energy. I pass Mother and my distress blinds me to the stitch in my side, the ache in my legs, and the burning in my lungs. My heart pounds like a miner's hammer—pulling me forward with each beat. When I see the first shingled housetop of Nether Town, I slow.

I veer through the houses and stores until I reach the red brick hospital. People wander around outside. Someone is sobbing. My panic ebbs away into determination and forced strength. I must be prepared for anything, but can anyone prepare for tragedy?

I shove through the heavy glass door and enter a packed waiting room. Seats with worn ivory cushions line the walls and equally worn pale people fill each one. Three Enforcers in boots and cross-backed, bullet-lined, military suspenders mill among the distraught. One of them watches as I stride to the high front desk. A nurse with curly brown hair glances up from a pile of paper-thin electronic documents—electrosheets. She closes her tired eyes for a moment and rubs her temple.

"Reid Antony Blackwater, please," I say in a firm, business-like tone. She slides two electrosheets toward me. One says, *DECEASED* in sharp, black letters and the other says, *WOUNDED*. There's no list for uninjured survivors.

The electronic page scrolls upward as I scan the wounded list. I stop at section B. The scrolling stills.

. . . *Benson, Bjork, Blade, Brown* . . .

No Blackwater.

Beside each name tiny digital blood-red Numbers click. Some of the names have minutes left. *Blade* clicks to *000.000.00.00.00.* and the name disappears from the screen. My fingers shake as I pick up the

Deceased list. I scroll down too fast and almost pass the Bs. Up an inch. *Blade* is now there, but still no *Blackwater*.

"He's not on either of these." Relief douses me.

Mother arrives behind me, gasping for air.

"He's not on a list," I say. "Are you sure he was on the train?"

Mother grows pale. "Of course. Has everyone been recovered from the accident?" Her knuckles whiten, clutched on the counter.

My mind reels. "What if he's still trapped in the train, *dying?*"

The nurse holds up a hand. "Everyone has been recovered, madam. The *Lower Missouri Transit* is a carbon-fiber train with high crash energy absorption. There is no need to panic. You are family, I assume?"

Mother and I nod in mute silence.

"Then you must know his Numbers." She rolls her eyes. "I'm surprised at the alarm this caused. It's as if half the families never prepared a farewell party for their deceased. How can this be a *shock?*"

Then it hits me like the train that never made it to our village. "Reid didn't have his Numbers!"

The nurse's eyes widen so much her eyelashes touch her arched penciled eyebrows. She snatches back the lists. "It is protocol to carry your Numbers at all times." Her gaze flits to the Enforcers and back to me.

My gut tenses and I lower my voice. "I have his here, in my satchel." I scramble in my bag, shoving aside crinkled pieces of paper and ribbons. For the first time, the Numbers are warm in my hand—a lifeline instead of a death sentence.

The nurse frowns at the Clock. "Where are *your* Numbers?"

My tongue sticks to the roof of my mouth and I'm sure my panic-stricken face gives me away, but Mother lies like a professional. "We didn't bring ours. We rushed from the house and ran here from Unity Village. We knew Reid needed his Numbers as soon as possible so he could receive medical care if injured."

"It's *protocol.*" The nurse squeezes her lips together and turns my Clock over in her hands. She lets out a skeptical "hmm" and mutters something sounding like "careless."

I hold my breath.

"He may be in the Radical Ward. You'll have to identify him before he receives services. Keep in mind his Numbers have only six months left. He's not eligible to receive a Medibot, which means any medical assistance will be on a more natural level. Depending on his injuries, he may not be entitled to care at all."

She leaves the desk and my blood mutates into liquid lead. *What if he's not there?*

We pass through a thick metal door after the nurse opens it with a detailed hand-scan. Rows of rooms line a hallway. Some doors are propped open to show families at the bedsides of half-coherent loved ones. Some are shut with mysteries of sorrow or joy behind them.

Three hallways and two elevator rides later, we step onto a floor with a different feel: light grey walls with no doors, no windows, and no warmth. I shiver. Beds form four rows in the open floor, some with hangings, some with restraining belts, and some empty.

"This is the Radical Ward," the nurse explains in a cool, detached voice, as if emotional response to this revolting display of care is prohibited. "The injured who have chosen to live without their Numbers are placed here until the board decides what to do with them. Often times we send them home to heal before eviction or they remain here until their Good-bye. For economical reasons, they receive no medical care."

A groan splits the air, followed by a hoarse sob.

"You put Reid in here?" I choke. Mother walks from bed to bed, but I scan with my eyes. In the back left corner a scruffy man sits beside an occupied bed. "Father?" My voice rebounds off the walls and metal bed frames.

Father looks up and the shine of hope surges into his face. My legs propel me down the main aisle. My gaze locks on the unconscious form in the bed. I stumble and collapse on the hard straw mattress. My fingers fumble through the sheets until they find Reid's hand. It's stiff and covered in blood, but I clutch it to my chest.

His mouth is open and blood cakes his lips, face, and hair. A tooth is missing. Someone had the decency to fold a thick cloth over what must be a head gash. Trembling, I touch a purple bruise on his left cheekbone with my fingertips.

"I couldn't do anything," Father croaks. "I couldn't do anything about his Clock."

"I-Is he alive?" I rasp.

Mother sits with Father, more pale than I've ever seen her, but the nurse steps to the bedside with our Clock. "Of course he's alive. If these are his Numbers, it seems he has a solid six months left."

No one responds. What if he's seconds away from death? I clutch his hand tighter. It's cold. I stare at the thin sheet, willing it to rise and fall to indicate breathing. The nurse pries Reid's hand from mine.

I glare at her. "What are you doing?"

She pulls from an apron pocket what looks like an electronic rubber pacifier with a needle on the end. Pressing a tiny button on the bottom, she pricks Reid's thumb. His body twitches and I jump.

He's alive.

"I'm sending this blood to the lab to enter him into the computer." She holds the needle upward. "I'll need to take his Clock as well."

"You pricked him for blood?" I spring to my feet. High emotions, fear, and disgust at this ward don't make a good mix. "He's *drenched* in blood. You couldn't take some of that?"

"Fresh blood is preferred."

"You've allowed *fresh* blood to drain out of him for the past *twelve hours*."

She purses her lips and places the pacifier in a steel container before tucking it in a pouch on her uniform. "I understand you are battling many emotions. According to his Numbers, he'll survive until autumn."

"But in what state? Weak? Sickly?" Hot tears match the heat of my temper. "What if he never wakes up and stays in a coma for the next six months?"

"I'm sorry for your distress," she says in a soothing voice. "Sometimes it is difficult to accept the form of Good-bye a loved one will take. I will fetch the doctor and have Mr. Blackwater moved to a higher ward. He will provide you with an assessment of Reid's status."

She leaves and I slump back onto Reid's bed. Mother and Father do not speak. Several minutes later, two men place Reid on a gurney and wheel him into the elevator. Though I'm relieved, I can't help but wonder . . .

How many of the unconscious or injured Radicals in this ward will die painful, untreated deaths? Do their families have to adjust to the panic that comes with an injury, knowing their loved ones receive nothing but a straw mattress to soak up the free-flowing blood?

The elevator doors slide shut, blocking the Radical Ward from the sight and minds of the hospital workers—but not from me.

I will never forget.

For twelve hours, Reid was a Radical.

000.181.17.20.11

The hospital devotes twenty precious minutes to transforming Reid into a warm, colorless, octopus. Tubes and wires cling to his body like electronic intravenous birthday streamers. Mother, Father, and I observe in an ignorant stupor. When my voice resurfaces, I demand details. "What's that beeping?"

"His heart rate." The new, male nurse's voice is smooth and calming, like the coffee color of his black skin. His smile elicits relief and trust. "The hospital bed contains sensors to detect his pulse."

"Thank you for speaking to the doctor," Mother says in a quiet voice. "We didn't know what to do when he first denied services."

The nurse shrugs. "We have extra beds and a recent monetary increase from the government. He didn't have a right to deny services yet. Not with six months to Reid's Clock."

"What's that tube?" I point.

"It provides fluids and nutrients." He unwraps what looks like a pea-sized nugget of cookie dough and pushes it into Reid's right ear canal. Before I can ask, he says, "This dissolves over the course of several hours and reports temperature changes to this screen." He taps a black panel in the foot of the bed. "Everything is conveyed electronically." With that, he exits the hospital room.

I feign understanding, though the acronyms and changing numbers on the panel mean nothing to me.

Numbers.

The question hangs in the air—what if Reid dies today? Tomorrow? What if this train wreck is his end? "I don't want to say Good-bye like this."

"How *do* you want to say Good-bye?" Mother asks. Her eyes turn hard. Father sits beside her, silent.

Is she angry with me? Does she think this is my fault?

I scrape my brain like a rake on a leaf-strewn lawn, trying to process her question and figure out my answer. A mental picture enters my mind—Reid and me sitting together against the outer wall of our house, chatting lightly on October seventh at one twenty-five in the afternoon, and one of us fading away in death. It would be quick, maybe even comfortable. We wouldn't try to control our Good-bye like some do—jumping off a cliff for a last thrill or hiding in the house hoping it doesn't happen. We'd be brave.

"It's always been a competition between you two," Mother says. "You can't stand watching him travel or make friends or learn a trade. You've hated every birthday because you had to share it."

I'm not sure why she's bringing this up right now, but my blood boils. "That's because every birthday I was invisible. Reid had ten friends over and I had *none*. You just squeezed my name on the cake to make me feel included."

"What will make you feel victorious, Parvin, outliving him?"

I stop and press a hand over my heart, trying to hold in the shock. "That's not what this is about. It's not about winning."

"It's not?"

Father puts a hand on Mother's shoulder and she turns away. I pace to the beep of Reid's monitor. Mother holds Reid's hand as if she hasn't just shattered my brittle composure. Father stares into space, and I allow my thoughts to join the circus—trapezing, tumbling, and jumping at will.

Is my autobiography about winning? Am I obsessed with doing something Reid hasn't? What caused me to sit and write every day for the past six months? What pushed me through Mother's doubting remarks and discouragement? Determination? Rebellion? Passion?

Restlessness.

The growing urge makes me wring my hands and tap my foot every time I sit down—an urge toward movement, action. It has little to do with Reid—he's a small factor in my purpose. While we are both alive, it's only to await the answer to our pulsing question, *Who will die? Who will die? Who will die in six months?* The one left behind is evidence of successful life without a Clock. People need to know it's possible. Radicals—registered or not—don't need to be killed.

Despair links its fingers with mine. All my life I've wondered what my purpose is. Today, I realize with a twist in my gut, that all my wondering and waiting hindered me from *seeking* a purpose. I could have done so much more if I'd braved intentionality sooner.

I swallow my pride and sit beside Mother. After a still moment, I rest my head on her shoulder, pushing aside her hurtful words. I need her.

She takes my hand and rubs her thumb over my clenched knuckles. We stare at Reid. Father stands by us and, even in the torment, we are united—united through blood, worry, and love. What would Unity Village be like if everyone felt this way for a single day?

Everything would be different.

Everything.

In my head, I mail a spiritual 'thank you' card to God for this minute. He understands why I'm thankful, even if I don't. A certain peace rests upon me, knowing I've invited Him into our unified clump. My fingers stray to the silver cross ring on my pinky.

Wake. I mentally whisper to Reid's sleeping form. *Please, Reid, wake. We need you. I need you.*

000.181.07.55.40

Reid's eyes find mine first. It may be luck-of-the-draw due to my close proximity, but I like to think it is intentional. I lean forward, silent. His eyes are blank, like the sheets of paper I stared at when scrawling my autobiography. My heartbeat quickens and pulses in my ears. He blinks in quick succession. After several breathless seconds, a wave of awareness, recognition, and life seeps into his brown irises. His gaze breaks from mine and sweeps the room before scanning my face.

He parts his lips and licks them before mouthing, *"Parvin."*

He must have meant to say it out loud because he frowns and gives a little cough. Mother jerks awake and shakes Father out of his snore.

"My Brielle," Reid rasps.

I release my breath. "Hey," I say in a voice like a five-year-old. It seems appropriate at the moment.

He smiles and the window of relief opens. Mother manages to stay calm and presses the button on the black screen for the nurse. Father slumps in his chair. The black nurse returns to perform assessments and ask Reid questions. My body turns shaky and I excuse myself into the hallway.

The floor slides up to meet me, and I prop myself against a wall. Reid is okay. His speech is hoarse, he's weak, and he still resembles a medical squid, but so far his memory is intact. He knows who I am.

"Parvin." Mother emerges from the hospital room.

I have an abrupt desire to spout all my thoughts and fears to her, not in anger, but in overflowing desperation. "Why did God allow us to have the Clocks?"

Mother doesn't seem surprised by my question. Perhaps she's expected the serious questions to come now that my potential Goodbye is closer. She peeks up and down the hall before replying in a low voice. "You need to ask *Him* that."

"He doesn't talk."

She sits beside me. "No? Then why do you wear that ring? Why do you say you believe God's real?"

I twist my ring and bite back the generic, "I don't know." I can't evade this question. I need to know the answer myself. Why *do* I wear the ring? Why did I tell Trevor Rain I'd changed if I'm not willing to own up to it? *Have* I changed? Reid told me a year ago how important God is—how I haven't ever truly put Him first. He was right, but he still never told me how to *do* that . . . or why I would want to. God's not welcome in our village, why would I isolate myself further from my peers?

"Reid says God wants what's best for us, but these Clocks *aren't* what's best. If they *were*, wouldn't I have a better life? What's the use in knowing how long I've got if it doesn't make me accomplish anything?"

"The Clock isn't what pushes you to action." Mother's voice grows gentle, which means her next words will be hard to receive. "Action is a step *you* must take. Whether you know your Numbers or not, look what you've done with the time on that Clock. You still took it for granted."

A lump rises in my throat, pushing tears to my eyes. Mother strokes my arm. It doesn't help.

I push myself to my feet. "Well, six months isn't enough time for anything. I guess I missed my chance."

As I return to Reid's room, my thoughts stray back to God. *Didn't You want my life to have meaning? Why did You even make me? You never did anything with my life.*

It feels good accusing Him for the state I'm in, but something inside nags at me. Did I ever really surrender my life to Him?

The nurse inserts something into one of Reid's tubes and presses a purple button on the side of the bed. A light scans from the top of

Reid's pillow to the tucked-in corners around his feet. The bed releases a mechanical groan, bending upward several inches, elevating his feet, and arching beneath his knees.

"The bed adjusts according to the patient's stiffness," the nurse explains. "This helps keep the joints loose and contributes to better circulation, which fights against blood clots."

Father stands and surveys the electronic screen, then bends toward the purple button. He'll push it once the nurse leaves.

God . . . I take a deep breath. *Reid says never hesitate to ask the impossible.* The nurse looks into Reid's mouth with a light and tongue depressor. *If I really give You my life, could You do something with it in these next six months? Could You take it somewhere fulfilling?*

The word *impossible* drifts inside my consciousness, but I shrug it off. At least I asked. I sever the communication with God. He has my request. The next step is up to Him.

"How's the biography coming, Parvin?" Reid's voice sounds stronger. The nurse clicks off the mini flashlight and leaves the room.

I scuff my shoe back and forth on the polished hospital floor. "First of all, it's an *auto*biography." Reid's grin reveals the hole in his mouth from his missing tooth. "And it's not very long, but it's finished."

Part of me wants him to read it. The other part wants to burn it. *"This will never get published . . . It's bland."*

"I'm proud of you."

I avoid his gaze. Will he still be proud when I tell him Skelley Chase's conclusion?

Mother takes Father's hand. "We are going to see what food they have available for visitors." This translates into, *"It's your problem. Think of Reid and deal with this biography thing like an adult."*

It's inevitable that I'll deal with it incorrectly, no matter how adult it seems to me.

"I brought you home a gift." Reid looks around the tasteless hospital room. "Did they gather my belongings from the train?"

I grasp the escape topic. "All belongings are locked in a storeroom. What did you get me?"

"You'll see. It's in celebration of writing your biography."

*"Auto*biography." My playfulness dies away as Mother and Father disappear through the doorway.

"What have you planned so far? Have you given it to a biographer or Bio-publisher yet? Are you going to get it published right away or wait until our Good-bye?"

"I met with a professional biographer." I place myself back on my bedside perch. "I was hoping he could polish it for me."

"Did he read it?"

"I gave it to him yesterday. He said he'd read as much as he could overnight." The clock in the top right corner of Reid's electronic bed screen says *6am*. Like always, time has disappeared and I can't account for the missing hours.

"When do you meet with him again?"

His excitement cuts at my heart and I remember, with tightening guilt, my frustration and anger toward him the last six months. "His train leaves town today at seven. That's in an hour."

Reid's smile wilts. "You're not going to meet with him?"

His dismay hurts even more than his excitement. "The man won't publish it, Reid. He says it's bland—"

"No! Don't stay here for me, go get your manuscript! Tell him your plan—our secret, even." He grasps my hand, taking me by surprise. "You've got to follow through. Remember the passion you had when you first told us about your idea?"

I yank my hand from his bandaged one. "Remember the passion you *didn't* have? Why are you so earnest now?"

He slumps back against the pillows, pale and sweaty. Beeping on his screen increases and he touches his wrapped forehead with trembling fingers.

"Reid, I'm sorry!" I place a palm on his face. He closes his eyes and breathes in deep, shuddering breaths. "Shh." I stroke his cheek, willing his body to calm and regain its energy. "What do you need? Water? The nurse?"

"I'm just . . . proud of you," he rasps, drawing my attention back to his face. "I know how . . . badly you want to . . . finish something." He opens his eyes and places a shaking hand over my own. "I want to help you with this, Parvin." His gaze turns distant.

Finish something. That's what Reid thinks. He doesn't realize I'm restless to *start* something. The autobiography didn't do it. It's like standing at a hearing again, watching another Radical led to the Enforcer car, sentenced to the Wall. I can't save them. I may not save a

A TIME TO DIE

single one before my Good-bye. If I keep pushing forward, can I reach a place of wholeness? Success? Victory?

I let out a defeated groan and lay my head on the blanket. I can't tell Reid about my doubts and how I'm starting to fear the end. He's determined to believe I'll proceed on to greatness in a matter of months. He's proud.

The beeping slows and Reid's breathing deepens. He's sinking back to sleep. He needs it.

As I still my own nerves, the restless dragon scratches against my lungs, urging me forward. It builds like a halted breath, growing, pushing. The dragon needs air—it needs *action*. I must appease it, whether Mother approves or not. I stand and scribble a note on the bedside electropad for her and Father.

Gone back to Unity to finish my autobiography.

But that's not all I'm going for. The autobiography is not enough to tame my agitation. I don't know what is, but I plan to find out.

7

A flash of lightning punctuates my entrance into *Faveurs*. My hair sticks to my rain-soaked face and I close the door against the dripping sunrise. The French waitress squeaks and slams a delicate hand over her heart.

"What time is it?" I gasp, but there's no need. My eyes find the clock behind the counter. *7:04am.* I'm late. Skelley Chase's train left four minutes ago.

The interior of the café is furnished with tables identical to the ones outside yesterday. A polished wood floor rests beneath my feet, already covered in a small puddle. Wide lattice windows line the entry and back walls, coated in dark rain. A counter rests before me against the right wall weighed down with coffee machines and jars of syrup. Frenchie stares at me with eyes wider than a newborn baby's.

I place my hands on my knees, sucking in deep breaths after running the entire way here from the hospital in a downpour. Running has never been my forte.

I'm too late—the story of my life. I straighten, holding a fist against my sternum. "Is there a note for me?"

Frenchie shakes her head, no.

"A package? Anything?"

She shakes her head again.

Figures. Now I don't even have my manuscript. "Fine. I'll have whatever I had yesterday." Since I'm here and shivering, I might as well indulge in something hot and soothing. Then I remember my pouch of coins is at home. "Never mind. I have no specie."

"I do." The low, bored warble flips my heart like a spatula.

I turn and see the asparagus-colored fedora before I register the brown goatee and trimmed scruff. Skelley Chase nods to the waitress, who gives a coy smile and retrieves a tall, clear glass.

"You're here." I can't believe it.

His eyes scan me from head to toe and back again. I must look desperate, drenched without a coin in my pocket. I struggle to pick up my dignity from the gutter.

"You have a skill for noting the obvious. There's been a train delay."

My heart lurches. "Yeah, it derailed."

"So I heard." He smells like lemons. Did he eat the lemon peels he gathered yesterday?

"My brother was on it."

Skelley Chase shrugs. "Supposedly he still has six months."

How dare he shrug off my brother's injury? I take a breath to spew an angry response, but something in his insensitive comment halts my fury. "You've read my manuscript?"

He places a hand on my shoulder and steers me to a table by the corner window. My manuscript lies on the crisp tablecloth. "I'm going to make you famous." He says this in a stoic, professional manner.

I choke on air. "Famous?"

He pats my back and pulls out my chair. I plop into it while my thoughts scream on a mental merry-go-round. Does this mean I'll be published? Reid will be so proud, and I'll have something to my name. Mother can never say I wasted my life. Unregistered Radicals won't be sacrificed anymore.

A deep breath precedes my forced calm. "Explain." I adopt his same businesslike tone while my hope sails through the ceiling.

He lays a manicured hand on the curling first page of my manuscript. "Most of your manuscript is worthless, but I'll spruce it up. I'll have it published within a month if I can pull it off."

My jaw drops and I don't bother to maintain my calm façade. "Why? Why did you change your mind?"

"Because your story has a lot of promise if you work it right."

"Work it right?"

He steeples fingers together and leans his chin on them. "You should go through the Wall."

The bold statement hits my heart like a frozen sledgehammer. "The *Wall?*"

He closes his eyes for a moment. When he opens them again, he speaks slowly. "You and your brother have one Clock. You don't know who will die in six months. You say you want to live out adventure, well this makes an excellent story—you go through the Wall and then return before your Clock runs out. You'll tell your story, and I'll make you famous. Your voice will be so loud, the government will *have* to do something about the injustice you mentioned happens in this village."

"The government would capture and sentence me to some sort of punishment if I did any of that."

"They wouldn't dare. Not if you're famous. Besides, I'll vouch for you against any punishment."

"You can do that?" "

"I can do anything." He winks. "I'm going to edit and publish your novel in the next month to build up a following over the remainder of your time. Along with your book, I'll have press releases and follow-up stories on postboards."

Overwhelmed. That's the word that comes to mind when he leans back and surveys my reaction. This project is too much. Press releases? Building a following? Fame? I'll be remembered.

The Wall.

"I can't." But my heart pounds with thrill.

Skelley Chase swirls his cinnamon cookie in the cappuccino foam. "You're the one who wants to find your purpose."

There are too many holes. If I allow him to publish my story in a month, where will that put Reid? If he's still in the hospital, the government would terminate his medical services once they knew the Clock might not be his. He'd be back in the Radical Ward. And then there's the other issue . . .

"I can't go through the Wall."

"It's your last six months. I've seen a lot of people die disappointed and unfulfilled. If there's ever a time to be spontaneous, it is now."

Mother would slap him upside the head for recommending spontaneity to me. She's tried to squash impulse out of me my whole life so I'd be like Reid—calm, collected, and planned out. Now that I have an opportunity to be as impulsive as I like, will I refuse to take it?

"No one's ever done it before," he continues.

"Done what?" My voice still hasn't returned to a normal pitch. "Died in an abandoned wasteland with the bones of convicts and Radicals? Someone does that every other week here in Unity." My mind conjures images of the long stretch of grey stone on the west horizon, mere miles away from Unity Village. Cold. Unwelcoming. "There's nothing over there. Just death. No one comes back to our side. No one survives."

"You could return," Skelley Chase pushes. "Plan a date of return and I'll make sure the door is open for you." Before I can respond, he holds up a hand. "Sleep on it."

"Sleep won't tell me anything except that I'm one day closer to my death." Frenchie places my drink before me with careful hands. I'd almost forgotten about it. "Thank you."

She opens her mouth, but her eyes jerk to the door and her already pale skin turns sickly white. I place a hand on her arm. "Are you okay?" I twist in my chair to see what stole her blood. The black Enforcer who Clock-checked me last evening stands in the entry, scanning the coffee shop with narrowed eyes. The backward *E* stands out against his wet skin. My hand falls from Frenchie's arm.

My Clock is with Reid.

As if sensing our instant terror, the Enforcer walks up to our table. Frenchie is still pasty white, but she manages a polite whisper, "*Bonjour.* What can I get you?"

"Your Clock," he rumbles.

Her lower lip quivers and she tries to inch around him, but he grabs her arm like he did mine the day before—it left bruises. I'm surprised it doesn't snap her tiny bones in two.

"Clock."

"Eet's in zee back!" But even I can tell her panic runs deeper than simple fear of the Enforcer's mannerism. She doesn't have a Clock.

She's a Radical.

"Let's go get it," the Enforcer says, but she tries to squirm from his grasp.

"Madame!" she shrieks toward the coffee counter.

A heavyset woman with frizzy hair emerges from the back room. She places her fists on her aproned hips. "Let my employee get back to work."

He turns to her. "Clock?"

"Is that the only word you know?" She pulls her own Clock from her apron and thrusts a solid thirty-two years, seven months, and four days in his face.

"Where's hers?" He gives Frenchie a little shake. She whimpers.

"It got burned inside your black heart," Madame snaps, pulling on Frenchie's other arm. "We got her estimated Numbers written down from her memory, though. Fourteen years solid."

He stands his ground. "She's breaking the law without a Clock. It's the Wall for her unless someone vouches at her hearing."

Madame leans right up in his face, but he doesn't react. "Her cottage burned down a year ago and her Clock with it! And if you want to bring up breaking the law, then you better throw *yourself* across the Wall. Radicals get *two* options—relocation is one of them. Go register this girl! I'm sick of watching innocents thrown into that abandoned, feral, no-man's-land just because our village happens to be within train distance."

My desire to even *think* about the Wall again sinks into an inner abyss. No matter Skelley Chase's offer, no matter my dreams of success, I will never cross it.

The Enforcer turns toward the door and drags the screaming, frantic French waitress behind him. I leap to my feet, but my tongue sticks to the roof of my mouth. What can I do?

Madame throws a cappuccino cup at his head and it shatters against the doorpost. He doesn't stop. The downpour is swept inside when the Enforcer opens the door and Frenchie's wail is lost to the wind. *Faveur's* entrance bell tinkles as the latch shuts behind them. No one in the shop seems to breathe except Skelley Chase.

He takes a loud sip of his cappuccino, then rises to his feet. "I'll be back in an hour." He picks up a black umbrella from the corner, slips on his wool overcoat, walks to the door, and tips his fedora at Madame. "I'll bring back your French waitress." With that, he enters the gale and disappears.

The café remains silent. I stand, shaking, by our table. Madame walks to the counter with balled fists—the movement awakens my muscles. I want to follow Skelley Chase and see how he plans to convince an Enforcer with a hollow heart to release Frenchie; instead, my desire to avoid these growing encounters with Enforcers wins me over. I sit down.

Can he save the waitress? I've never seen anyone stand up to the Enforcers and win. What sort of man is this?

My manuscript rests on the table. Already, my precious blueberry words are marked with his own scratchy black pen. I don't read them—they might make me change my mind about this whole autobiography thing.

A half hour later, the entry bell tinkles and Skelley Chase walks back in, leading Frenchie to the counter. They're both sopping wet, but his coat rests over her shoulders. Her cheeks are flushed and she beams at him.

"Go warm up," he says.

The café is dead silent. Madame stares at Skelley Chase with her mouth half open. He walks up the stairs to the rooms above the café and returns to my table moments later in dry clothes.

"How did you save her?"

"I told you, I can do anything." He leans back in his chair and surveys me. "You haven't changed your mind?"

I tangle my fingers beneath the table. Will he be angry? Disappointed? This hero—this famous man—is offering me help and I want to meet his approval, but I must stand on my decision. "Nope. No Wall."

"Well then, let's just rewrite this thing."

I raise my eyebrows. "You're still going to publish it?"

"Yes."

"In a month?"

"Yes."

I scratch at a spot on the tablecloth. "I'd prefer you not to publish it until my Good-bye in six months. With Reid in the hospital, I want to make sure he still gets medical benefits. I can't put him in danger."

Skelley Chase glances back at my scribbles. "Okay, I'll try."

My thumb rolls my cross ring around my pinky. I'm not sure what else to say. Thank you? Maybe. But am I grateful? We're continuing my autobiography, but it didn't bring fulfillment the first time around. My restless dragon is still pacing inside. Is this the thing I want to pour my last months into? Will I feel fulfilled afterward?

I look at Skelley Chase. "So why do you need me here?"

"Your manuscript is now mine. Together, we will meet here to edit and rewrite it."

"You're staying here?"

"Yes. I've taken on a new biography—yours. And"—he toasts his cup to me—"the train is derailed."

I frown. "But . . . you have a car. You could leave whenever you want."

"I don't like to put on so much unnecessary mileage. I'd rather transport it on the train. The train delay gives a wonderful excuse to my publishers, editors, and other . . . people demanding my return."

I dislike his abruptness, but I can't help appreciating the effort he's putting into my *bland* novel.

"Now to make this biography work, you need to be open with me."

I bristle. I'm not open with anyone, except maybe Reid. How open is open?

Skelley Chase must notice my hesitance because he raises an eyebrow. "*Completely* open, Parvin."

It's the first time he's said my name. It comes out like an order—something an impersonal father might say to his daughter after giving her a lashing. I fold my arms. "I'll be as open as I want."

He slides a thin, electronic gadget across the table. "Let's get started then."

It looks like a cross between a camera and a book with a tiny coin-sized button on the side.

"What's that?"

"My sentra."

I lean closer. "What's a sentra?"

He stares at me for a moment. A sigh precedes his dull-voiced explanation. "It records a snapshot of your emotions. The button on the side takes the emotigraph. You'll be pressing that button often. Readers thrive off emotigraphs; they draw them into the plight of the character—you, in this instance. The more your readers connect, the more they remember you."

"Woah." Things like this exist? I understand cameras taking pictures of scenes and people, but pictures of emotions? I want one. "There aren't any emotigraphs in the biographies you write, though."

"Not in the paper copies. All Upper and High Cities use X-books."

I bite my lip, not wanting to continue my naivety, but craving answers. "I've seen mention of X-books in *The Daily Hemisphere*. What are they?"

Skelley Chase sets aside his empty cappuccino cup and blinks once. "Really, Parvin? Your hobby is reading the news. I would have thought you'd understand a little more of the higher life."

I clench my fists. "Well, I'm sorry I wasn't born with your Numbers, Mr. High-City. *I* would have thought that, with your profession, you'd learn a bit more tact within other cultures."

We sit in silence for a moment. How dare he blame me for not knowing about High-City life? It's not my fault the school refused to teach me further because of my low Numbers. How can he still see me as lowlife trash after he's read my story?

Skelley Chase's bored warble interrupts my seething. "An X-book is an experience-book. They've been replacing E-books for the past seven years since the release and success of emotigraphs. Your biography will be an X-book, which means that every time you feel a twinge of emotion—good *or* bad—I want you to press this button."

He points to the tiny dot on the side of the sentra. I press the button with my forefinger. A sharp prick makes me jump. "Ouch."

"You'll get used to it."

I glare at him. "Have fun feeling *that* emotigraph."

"Your spunk is humorous. Now let's edit."

I force myself to exhale my pride and peer at the first page of my hard work. "You scratched out my Bible verse."

He waves a hand. "Boring and dangerous—an interesting mixture. You have a level of unmatchable ignorance. Do you read the news at all?"

I falter. "Well, I've been spending most of my time writing." When *was* the last time I read through *The Daily Hemisphere*?

"This religion stuff you include in here would get you—and your parents—arrested in a High City. It could even get you arrested *here*. Then again, you're not exactly the law-abiding type. No one cares about the verse, pushing your faith is illegal, and it makes you look bad to your readers."

I sit back in my chair. "So you want me to erase my beliefs?"

"No, I want you to keep them to yourself so this plan works. You haven't hit me with your beliefs yet, so don't do it to your readers just because they're picking up your book."

I stare at the harsh line through the verse. My cheeks warm. Why did I even put it in? Did I include it because I wear my cross ring? Is it out of obligation?

"Did your parents raise you with these beliefs?"

I still the spring of fear that enters my chest. "No. They know they're not allowed to raise me in a religion before I'm eighteen. Reid influenced my faith. "

He remains silent. I can't meet his eyes. I've kept my faith to myself my whole life. Why is it so tempting to continue doing it? Am I that weak?

"Okay," I say. "We can take out the verses, but not the parts that talk about when I started believing in God. He is part of my story, it needs to stay in." I look up.

Skelley Chase adjusts his nanobook. "Fair enough."

We turn into a sort of team over the next several days—pouring over my ever-changing biography with pens and thoughts. My new diet consists of mochas and whipped cream. He asks about childhood memories, desires—both the abandoned and fulfilled—and beliefs. Every word I decide to grant him is recorded on his personal nanobook. My finger soon grows immune to the prick of the sentra.

When I give reserved answers, he presses for detail, forcing me to be honest. I find myself opening up more than I expected. It's refreshing to share—or should I say vent—my feelings about my empty life. He nods—a practiced listening gesture, but it makes me feel important. It makes me feel *heard*.

Somehow, spouting out every thought, regret, and memory puts my life back in perspective for me. My heart starts to hurt and cry a little inside me with each day of writing. Eighteen dead years. Why didn't I see them dying? Why didn't I feel my time wilting? I spent so much of my life lounging in regrets and sipping bitterness that I abandoned any thought of creating *happy* memories; instead, I wasted. Just wasted.

A letter from Mother and Father arrives five days later, written on one of the hospital napkins. Reid is healing well, but still requires a lot of day-to-day care. They are coming home on the new train, leaving him at the hospital for a few days. I look forward to seeing them once Skelley Chase and I finish. The house has been cold and lonely, the wind louder through the shutters, and I can't say I've cooked much.

Mrs. Newton and one of her blond daughters visited three nights after my return. She stood on the doorstep holding a cloth-covered dish with potholders. An Enforcer stood beside her. Two others flanked the door to her house, standing like tattooed sculptures in the rain.

"I saw you home alone and made a meal for you. Is your family okay?"

Steam issued from the dish carrying the scent of baked potatoes with cheese and bacon. "Reid is in the Nether Town hospital. He was injured by the train derailment."

Her brows creased and I sensed that, if she hadn't been holding my gift of dinner, she would have hugged me. "I'm sorry."

I wanted to ask her about the Enforcers standing guard at her door, but couldn't bring myself to say anything while the black-coated tattooed official stood right behind her. Were the Newtons in trouble?

Mrs. Newton handed me the dish and her daughter held up a small basket also covered in a flowery cloth. "Bread!"

I took the basket and she grinned, half toothless. "Thank you," I whispered as they returned to their house.

This morning, on my way to *Faveurs*, the Enforcers were gone. I knocked on the Newton's door, but no one answered. The village postboard never announced a hearing. I have to hope they were relocated, but guilt has since wrapped its chilled arms around me. I should have asked the Enforcers why they were there, but my Clock is at the Nether Hospital. I couldn't risk being caught. Not now. Not when I'm so close to grafting purpose into my life.

"This is the final draft," Skelley Chase says. I peer at the organized nanobook. He taps it with its pointer pen.

The skimming words fill my story with meaning. Something in me swells—not the restless dragon, but something else. Pride? Joy? Why do I feel the urge to cry? I swallow hard. "Thank you, Mr. Chase."

He tucks the nanobook into his briefcase. "Don't thank me yet. We're not done."

"We're not?"

He stands, flicks Frenchie a coin, and strides out of the coffee shop. He must expect me to follow. Of course, I do. His polished shoes click on the cobbled sidewalk and we cross the main street, heading east toward the edge of town. Magnolia trees are in full bloom, arching over the bright yellow forsythias.

Now that we're finished with the biography, Skelley Chase will leave. The thought makes me a little sad. Though his get-it-done manner dominated our every meeting, he's a man of action—a person who makes his Numbers look good and used. If only I could be as efficient.

He walks up the steps of the county building and, out of habit, my breath quickens. I'd almost forgotten about Trevor Rain. How much has Skelley Chase cost over these several days? Will I need to return some of my Last-Year funds? It's worth it.

Rat Nose squeaks from behind her desk and Skelley Chase throws her a wink.

Flirt. That wink just made her day—probably her whole year.

We don't take the stairs but he leads me down a long hallway across from the reception desk on the right side of the wide entry.

"Where are we going?" I've never ventured to this portion of the county building.

"Here." He holds a glass door open for me to the left.

Inside is a thick wooden desk next to a small corridor. A man sits behind the desk, tapping something onto the surface screen. He looks up and my nerves send a shock up my spine. A spiked, backward black *E* covers his left temple.

"This is Parvin Blackwater," Skelley Chase says from behind me. "She's a Radical."

000.175.19.01.00

My blood turns to frozen tar. Over the course of a second, I register what feels like a thousand thoughts: I'm in danger. They know my name. I don't have my Numbers.

He betrayed me.

The Enforcer stands from his desk, knocking the edge with his knee. His chair scrapes backward.

I bolt.

My shoulder clips Skelley Chase as I slam through the swinging glass door with both hands, fleeing the sounds of frantic shuffles behind me. My legs feel like weighted baggage and my arms shake almost as fast as my unnerved heartbeats. I sprint across the entry, eyes fixed upon the exit.

Oh God, oh, God, oh, God . . . The desperate plea sounds over and over. I dare a look over my shoulder just as the Enforcer tackles me. I scream.

We fall to the ground and the back of my head cracks against the marble. My body tumbles to a limp stop, pinned under his weight. Pain overtakes all sensation. I shut my eyes, but flashes of light and thick blackness invade my vision. I groan. My head rolls to the side. The cold marble soothes my flushed cheek as every zing of panic ebbs into a thick pool of surrender.

God . . .

The Enforcer moves to the side, holding my arms with one hand. My wrist bones press against each other, grinding, bruising. My head throbs. I moan. "Stop."

I need to hold my head. It pulses, begging for relief. The grip relents and I pull my arms close to my body. He must know I can't flee now. I curl into a ball and slide my shaking fingers up my cheeks, through my hair, and around my head.

"Only a Radical would run like that," the Enforcer says. "Thank you, Mr. Chase."

"Is everything okay?" I know this voice—Rat Nose. Her rasp comes as an odd comfort and her next words sound confused. "She can't be a Radical. She's been meeting with Mentor Trevor Rain for her Last Year."

"She's a Radical. Unregistered, at that."

Skelly Chase's voice erases my agony. I open my eyes. "Traitor . . ." I intended to scream at him, but my voice is weak, pinched by too many negative emotions.

Rat Nose looks between us with a frown.

Blood pounds inside my head so I close my eyes again, taking a deep breath. The Enforcer hauls me to my feet, but my legs are still weak.

"Stand up," he grunts, but I bounce on useless puppet legs until he throws me over his shoulder. Humiliated, I squirm, despite the continued ache in my head, and he sets me back on my feet. I cooperate this time, swaying a little, but determined not to crumple.

"Take me to my parents." They must be back by now. Mother will know what to do. I close my eyes against ripples of nausea.

"You're going to the containment center until we set up a hearing."

"A hearing?" I'm dizzy. Is this really happening? "I've lived in Unity my entire life. I was *born* here. An Enforcer checked my Clock just last week!" But I know better than to think he'll listen. I watched that other Enforcer drag Frenchie away.

I look at Skelley Chase. I may have never finished schooling and I may have wasted my life, but I inherited my Mother's cunning and it's not hard to see his plan. "You're using me for a good story." Chilled fury rises inside.

He just stares down at me with a creased brow and his lips pursed to one side. He pulls the sentra from his pocket and holds it in front of my face. "Press this."

I let out a sharp, "Ha!"

He grabs my bruised wrist and presses the button with my palm. I yank my hand away. "Yes." He smiles now and returns the sentra to his pocket. "I'm getting a good story."

He turns and walks away. Rat Nose trots behind him with a nervous glance over her shoulder. The Enforcer yanks me toward the exit.

How did this happen?

I don't register the trudge to the containment center until the Enforcer shoves me into a cell made up of bars and a single wooden bench. "What happens now?" I lean against the bars. My heart pounds my chest. "Can I see my parents?"

"You get a hearing tomorrow morning. You'll see them then . . . if they come." The Enforcer walks into a different room and out of sight.

"They don't even know I'm here!" I cry after him. "You have to tell them!"

He doesn't respond. A shiver races down my spine and I twitch as goose bumps follow like a swift shadow. Why didn't I suspect Skelley Chase—a famous biographer knowing all my secrets and wanting to help? How stupid could I be?

I lower myself onto the bench. I should have seen it coming. I was too desperate—desperate to trust, desperate to share my story, desperate to tame my restless dragon. I trusted the wrong person.

Or was my mistake in trusting You, God?

Hasn't He seen my fears of the Wall? My desperation to help Radicals? Why would He do this to me? Is it because I took the Bible verses out of my biography?

"Why would You do this?" He and I seldom talk unless I'm angry. I tried to be nice to Him on the hospital floor last week, when I asked Him to do something with my dwindling time. But I think when He decided to form Parvin Brielle Blackwater He wrote my story on a pitch-black canvas with a stark ending.

I'm in a cell and will be given a hearing tomorrow—*me*, with nothing to my name. Yet now I'm a criminal. Will my village turn up to save me?

The bench is rough against my clothing. I sit on the floor, curled against the one wall not made of bars. I've never joined in the world's ability to throw the topic of death around in flippant afternoon chatter. I can't treat death lightly because Reid and I have never *known* when we'll die. Without knowing, I can't prepare myself—not for my own death or for his. Is this how people lived before Numbers? Uncertain? Fearful?

I pull my knees close and rest my forehead on them. My stomach growls, I swallow some tears to feed it. As my thoughts swirl themselves into a hopeless stupor, I think of nothing. It's calming. I've heard men can do it—think about nothing—and women aren't supposed to be able to, but I must have stolen a few of Reid's triplet genes.

I drift in and out of consciousness, aware of the growing hardness of the floor and agony in my head. It's pulsing again. Someone once said falling asleep can be dangerous with a head injury. Right now, I don't mind the idea of danger. My thoughts go blank. I'm running back from Nether Town. It's raining. I trip and land in mud, startling myself awake, only to drift back into a dream of Mother arriving at my cell.

She's here. She can fix it. She's Mother.

The rays of dawn arrive with a clatter on the bars of my door. I look around and my heart slips. Mother's not here. No one is, except an Enforcer with a stern face. He opens my door and pulls me to my feet. I'm still groggy and the saliva in my mouth feels thick. It's hard to swallow.

His face spins a bit before I'm able to focus. Are all Enforcers cold and stoic? Are they trained that way? Don't they have hearts?

He leads me out of the containment center and into a black beetle car small enough to fit three people and squeeze through the narrow streets of Unity Village. I pass the painted gold backward E on the exterior. We climb inside and it moves with a high-pitched electric whine toward the village square.

Is this what other Radicals experienced? Did they feel alone and ashamed? Wonder who would show up at their hearing? Now more than ever, I'm thankful I vouched at hearings, even if I never succeeded. At least the Radicals had someone on their side.

Mud squelches beneath the wheels. "This is my first time in a car," I say to my Enforcer. Someone might as well know.

We arrive at the square at 5:20 a.m.—the hour most people in Unity rise to make the most of their Numbers. I'm led to the weathered, wooden platform in the center, surrounded by bare dogwood trees, due to bloom any day. Will I even see them?

We walk up the warped steps next to the empty vegetable stand. Master Gardener Harman isn't here yet. I wish he were, to attest I grew up in Unity, but my parents will testify.

On top of the platform, flanked by two Enforcers, I wipe the sweat off my hands before looking up. The twelve people at the base of my guilty podium are all I have to show for my empty life. More than half are probably here out of curiosity. They want to see if I'll cry or plead, scream or faint, freeze or run.

I square my shoulders and look out at them. I'll explain what happened. I'll remind them who I am. I'll show them I'm worth saving.

I scan the faces. My chin quivers of its own accord and I bite my lip. Mother's not here. I would have spotted her in a moment. Is she ashamed of me? Father's here, though. He stands in the center of the tiny crowd. The Newtons aren't present, but I meet the eyes of the young Enforcer who helped repair their roof thatch. His mouth forms a grim line and his eyes slant downward. A tiny crease brings his eyebrows together. I don't remember him looking so sad before.

"Parvin Brielle Blackwater is reported of being an unregistered Radical," the black Enforcer beside me says in a detached voice. Can't he at least act like I'm human instead of talking like I'm an old potato? I want to smash his Clock and see how he talks then. "Is there anyone to vouch for her Clock?"

I don't even get a moment to defend myself. No Radicals ever do. Words push against my throat, but I must let others speak first.

The black Enforcer stares ahead without a twitch. The Enforcer on my left gives my arm a tiny squeeze. Father stares past me with a set jaw.

I imagine him running at the platform and thrashing the Enforcers for my freedom, but he stands stiff and silent. Isn't he going to save me? The stillness of raw morning drifts around us.

"She was born and raised in Unity Village," Father finally says.

And I'm your daughter. This means far more to me than being raised in Unity.

"I went to school with her." It's Dusten Grunt, speaking from the back of the crowd. People turn to look at him and he shrugs. "I'm just sayin' she's been here as long as me."

How could I have allowed my loathing to have sunk so deep for Dusten? He's standing up for me when all I've ever wanted to do is kick him.

"Has anyone seen her *Numbers*?" The Enforcer returns to the original question. No matter how well people know me, it all comes down to the Clock. My palms sweat even though the morning air numbs the tip of my nose.

Both Father and Dusten say, "I have."

My skin tingles and, instead of relief at their support, I grow nervous. My heart beats faster.

"They were empty Numbers," Dusten says and I renew my desire to kick him. "She's only got a few months left."

"I've seen her Clock, too."

I jerk my head around at this voice. Trevor Rain stands to the side of the platform, hands in his pockets. I've never seen him stand before. He has a tiny potbelly and unusually short legs for his height. "I'm her Mentor."

Bless his heart for coming out of his office. He wants to be a good Mentor after all. The Enforcers attend to him because his voice and words hold weight. Why don't they talk to the Mentors before holding an unbalanced hearing like they do? Government is government, I suppose. That doesn't mean it's efficient.

"I vouch for her Clock," Trevor says.

I can't stop the growing panic. Even if he can vouch for my Clock, then I'll need to *produce* my Clock, but it's in Nether Town with Reid.

More people trickle into the square and I glare at them. Stop staring! I want off the platform. I want to be safe in Father's arms or asking Mother why she's not here.

A voice from beneath a green fedora startles my already frantic heartbeat. "She's been sharing a Clock with her brother."

I zone in on Skelley Chase, who appears from the shadow of the glasswork shop. He looks bored even though he just revealed my life-protected secret to the people of my village, the Enforcers, and my Mentor.

Trevor Rain's eyes transform into question marks and he looks between Skelley Chase and me. I've never considered myself a violent person, but thoughts of murder enter my mind.

What if I take Skelley Chase down before they send me across the Wall? But I can't change his Numbers. I couldn't murder Skelley Chase even if I made him swallow dynamite.

"She's been *sharing* Numbers?" someone asks. "How?"

"They're twins with one Clock." Skelley Chase shrugs. "Passing it back and forth."

I can see Trevor piecing together this news with my odd answers and the meetings without my Clock.

"Isn't Reid in the hospital?" someone asks. "They wouldn't let him in unless he had a Clock, right?"

My mouth goes dry. If people don't know whose Clock it is, the Enforcers will terminate services. Reid will go back into the Radical Ward. My mind screeches like the train whistle. *God, do something!*

"But whose is it originally?" the same person asks. "Is it hers or Reid's?"

Mine! Mine! Mine! But I can't forget the memory of Reid's pale body on the straw mattress, blood dripping down his skin. He needs these months.

Skelley Chase looks at me for several silent seconds. He's giving me a choice. I clench and unclench my fists. My body shivers like when I stepped into the Radical Ward. He turns to the Enforcers and takes a breath.

"It's Reid's!" I lurch from the Enforcers' grasp.

The freedom behind my force startles me and I stumble off the platform. I land on my hands and knees in the mud. "It's Reid's Clock!" I look at the surprised faces above.

Father pushes through the stunned crowd. The Enforcers jump from the platform after me, but I launch myself into Father's open arms. I want to be held before I die now that I've sealed my fate.

He holds me tight to his chest and I inhale the scent of sawdust and fresh soap from his clothes. I add my own dose of tears and a choked sob, "It's Reid's." Father strokes my hair.

The Enforcers yank me out of his embrace and back onto the platform. "You stole your brother's Clock?" The black Enforcer grips my arm tighter than before.

I gulp once and nod, daring Skelley Chase to refute my next words. "I'm a Radical."

Father shrinks to the back of the murmuring crowd, covering his face with his hands. My heart breaks for him.

"How *dare* you!" a woman shrieks. "You've been offsetting our system? Our village resources are diluted by unregistered Radicals."

"We don't make our goods to support rebellion." The milkman chimes in. "At least other Radicals were *accidental.*"

"My boy could have gone to school earlier if you hadn't taken his opening," a pudgy lady squawks. I've bought fabric from her store once a month the past four years.

I bite back a sob as my own people assume I've taken advantage of them my entire life. They don't remember me. I hid in my own life too long to imprint their memories.

I used to think Unity Village was my safe haven. I was so wrong. My village comes together when it's against something—and right now they're against *me*.

With a hard swallow, I stand with my chin up like a brick wall because I'm finally standing for something: Reid. My family. Radicals.

I am strong. I am confident.

At last, my restless dragon is tamed.

9

000.175.06.55.12

My first impulse when Skelley Chase steps into the containment center is to reach through the bars and grab a fistful of his hair, not letting go until they cut off either his head or my hand. I'd prefer the former. My internal violence is held at bay long enough for him to get a few words out.

"I plan to help you, Parvin."

If I could work up a decent spit, I'd soil his shoes. "How?"

"You won't go through the Wall today."

I hate this man. I do, but a tiny part inside me cries with relief at his words, even though I know they're laced with ulterior motives. "Why not?"

"I want you to be ready."

I stare at his grey-black eyes. He doesn't break eye contact. We had a partnership. He broke it. I thought I knew him until the moment he turned me in, yet I feel like he's still on my side somehow. I want to trust him, but I don't understand his actions.

"If not today, then when?"

"Tomorrow morning."

A chill clenches my stomach. I still have to go. My hands grip the bars and I break our gaze. Sweat lines my palms and I squeeze my fingers tighter around the metal. "Why do I get extra time?"

Mother steps into my line of vision from the entrance. "To prepare you."

I straighten with a jerk and my hands fall to my sides. My voice is unstable and defeated when I speak. "Where were you?"

She was the one person I wanted at my hearing and she's the one person who didn't come to save me. Doesn't she care about her daughter?

"I was doing other things." Her eyes flick to Skelley Chase and back to me.

My gaze narrows. "*What* other things?"

Before she can answer, Skelley Chase steps in. "The Enforcers are granting you a day to gather your belongings and bid Farewell. Be grateful I got you that much."

"A Farewell party? That's like postponing a hanging for a convict's birthday." Not that I consider myself a convict. Thanks, Skelley Chase. Throw me to the wolves, but bring the cake candles.

I sigh. It may not make sense, but I'll take it. The more time between me and that Wall, the better.

Enforcers unlock my cell and lead me out. When we pass through the entrance lobby, my attention drifts to the young Enforcer from my hearing—the one who helped the Newtons with their thatch.

He's leaning over the receiving desk, speaking heatedly with the Lead Enforcer. "I escorted them here, Sachem. They were *assigned* to Unity Village for their relocation! They were registered and safe under the Law."

The Lead Enforcer doesn't blink. "The Law does not support Radicals, Hawke."

So that's his name. Hawke. The only part about him representing a hawk is the fierceness in his eyes.

"They weren't all Radicals! I registered them myself. They were in the monitor system. Unity Village had enough spaces for this Radical family." Hawke puts his head in his hands and releases a muffled groan.

"What's done is done," the Lead Enforcer says. "They decided to stay together. They had the option to let Mr. Newton cross the Wall alone."

My throat constricts. *The Newtons?*

Hawke looks up, his jaw and fists so tight the veins stand out like raised scars. "You have no compassion." He glances at my entourage. Swifter than an owl snatching a gopher, he grabs my arm and yanks me out of my escort. "And this girl, Miss Blackwater! It's not her fault she has no Numbers. She needs to be registered in the Radical system. Let me imbed the tracking chip. I'll even escort her to a different eviction site—a job *you're* supposed to do."

The Lead Enforcer's gaze flashes to Skelley Chase for a sliver of a second, then back to Hawke. "She's going across the Wall."

Hawke's grip on my arm is tight—too tight to escape, not that I want to. He seems on my side. My fingers throb from lack of blood. The other

Enforcers stand beside me, but Mother and Skelley Chase wait by the door.

Shaking takes hold of my body and worsens as the silent seconds pass. I don't know what to do. My voice holds as much weight as a tea-leaf right now. I have no power to fight for my fate.

Hawke looks down into my eyes. I can't comprehend the full emotion in his wrinkled brow and grinding jaw, but his eyes hold deeper sorrow than I've ever witnessed in my short life. In this moment, I realize how very different sorrow is from pity.

"I'm sorry," he whispers and his grip loosens.

My four Enforcers retrieve me and pull me toward the door. His hand slides down my arm, like he's reluctant to break the contact. But when fingertips meet fingertips, he lets the air separate us. I can't stop myself from watching his face until I'm outside.

Keep fighting for me, I urge, but even Hawke has given up on my fate.

As we walk, I keep my head down and choke on the impulse to run. My heart sinks into a crevice of despair so deep it will never resurface. The Newtons were sent across the Wall to die—my *neighbors*.

I close my eyes against the imagined aroma of cheesy potatoes and bread. Even with an Enforcer's protection, they died. I will be following them in less than twenty-four hours. My family didn't fight for me. My lone ally was a young man who represents the enemy.

Everyone we pass stares at me as if they know what I've done—as if they blame me as the villagers at my hearing did. My face warms, though I can't consider myself guilty. What else could I have done?

We reach the front door and the Enforcers take their places—two at the front and two at the back by the outhouse, like they did to the Newtons. I guess they're staying. Well, they're not invited to my Farewell party.

Once inside, I grasp for the comfort feeling of home, but it's not here. Tension floats in the air. Father rises from the table, looking over the three of us before opening his arms for an embrace. I enter it, biting my lip. I want a hug from Mother more than anything, but she takes her place at the sink like it's a regular morning and she's late making the coffee. Skelley Chase seats himself at our table without an invitation.

I step out of Father's arms. "Get out."

"*Parvin,*" Mother chides. Father sits across the table.

"*He* did this, Mother!" I point straight at Skelley Chase's bored face. "He's the one tearing our family apart, stealing my secrets. He wants me *dead!*"

"Hush." She swipes at me with a wooden spoon. "Our walls are thin. The Enforcers are outside."

This shuts me up, even though the shouting feels good, but Mother is tolerating and defending Skelley Chase. *Why?*

"What's your plan?" I sit beside Father.

Skelley Chase leans on his elbows and pulls in every ounce of my focus with his intensity. "We prepare you as best we can for the Wall. You'll cross with exactly five months and three weeks until your Clock runs out. I will open the Wall the last week before your Good-bye. You *must* be at the Wall in the time I get for you. During your time in the West, I shall spread your name and bravery to the public in the East. I will meet you back on this side, and we'll finish your story."

The plan sounds flawless except for one thing. "I don't want to go."

"Tough."

"What makes you think I'll survive? It's our country's *death sentence.*"

Skelley Chase shrugs. "Cross your fingers and hope it's a utopia over there. If you die, I'll still use your biography. It carries so much promise. Either way, you get your wish."

Mother says *hate* is a strong word, but I'm certain the fullness of its strength courses through my blood as I stare him down. There are so many floating question marks. What's on the other side of the Wall? Utopia or not, I've never been mentally or physically sharp enough for self-survival.

"You'll have to be honest in your writing on the other side," Skelley Chase continues. "Write every feeling, fear, doubt, surprise, lesson, and observation. Start today."

"Writing?" I suck in an emotional shudder. Don't cry. Don't cry. Don't cry.

He pulls a leather-bound square no bigger than the palm of my hand from his briefcase. He unfolds it twice to form a larger square and hands it to me. I take it from him with hesitant hands. It's stiff and weighty.

"A journal?" I sneer. Nothing is written on the cover, but instead of paper inside there's a smooth blank screen. No cracks or hinges reveal its folding capabilities.

"It's much more than a journal. It's a nanobook. Every ounce of your last-year funds went into that and some of my own donations."

My fingernails bite my palms. "You had no right to take my last-year funds!"

"You're a Radical! You *have* no funds. You have no right to a Mentor, but Trevor Rain is one of the few gracious people left in this nation and allowed me to use your funds for this item." He gestures to the nanobook. "You'll have plenty of time to fiddle with it and discover the ins and outs. It's your link with me—with the East side of the Wall. It will transmit any information you desire back to me."

My brain numbs. "Transmit? Like computers? Like Internet?"

He rolls his eyes. "Yes."

"How do you know the West has Internet?"

"You have a lot to learn about today's technology, Parvin. I purchased P.I., a portable Internet source, embedded inside. You could take it to the moon and it would still transmit."

Now I don't mind that he spent my Last-Year funds. "Do people do that?"

"That and more. I want daily updates. I want to know about every single living organism you encounter in the West, *especially* if you come across any people. Understand? And I want it back when you return, so don't lose it."

He still doesn't understand I won't return. I won't *survive*. An odd aroma wafts from the cover. "It smells like lemon." It smells like him.

"I always make it a point to associate an event with a particular smell. Helps me remember more details in the future."

I'll be sure to rub it in dirt the moment I cross the Wall.

If there *is* dirt.

He holds out another item—a long thin box. The hinges pop the lid open under the slightest pressure from my fingertips. Inside sits a blue watch. A digital date blinks on the face behind the rotating hands. "Why are you giving me all this?"

"This is an early Farewell gift."

I don't allow myself to say thank you. He's gift-wrapping my death sentence. "Why do I have to stay in the West for the rest of my time? Why can't you open the Wall for me again after a couple weeks?"

Skelley Chase stands and snaps his briefcase shut. "Because your life is in my hands and you don't have a choice. Be thankful I'm even securing you a return."

"Stop telling me to be thankful for your betrayal."

"You're the one who wanted a meaningful life." He shrugs. "Did you really think you could find meaning in a couple weeks? You'll be lucky if five months is enough."

He tips his fedora to Mother and Father. They give no physical or verbal response and I swell a little. He turns and leaves our house. The kitchen is contaminated with the residue of his presence.

All three of us sigh at once. Mother puts the kettle on the wood stove instead of making a fire, and plops a cloth pouch of coffee grounds into the water. "Your father is going to fetch Reid from the Nether Hospital tonight."

"No." I shake my head. "Reid shouldn't come. He shouldn't even *know*." If he knows what I've done, he'll do anything to stop the Enforcers. He'll tell about our Clock or try and convince me to escape. He'll doom himself to an identical fate or kill himself trying.

"He has a right to know," Father grunts. "This involves him, too. He'll be questioned anyway—they may even be doing it now." He stands. "I'm going to get him."

I open my mouth, but he squeezes my shoulder and strides from the kitchen into the morning rays. Mother doesn't even wait for coffee before she announces, "I'm going to organize your Farewell party." So saying, she leaves the house, too.

Are they afraid to be with me? I don't blame them, I've transformed into some sort of purpose-crazed monster in my Last Year. I don't make sense. Even when my life was purposeless I still felt logical. Now? I can't understand myself. My desires and determination change daily.

I'm frightened, despite my outward desire to know Skelley Chase's plan and to stand up for Reid. My Clock has just been reduced to a single day, *that* much I know. I can't survive twenty-four hours across that Wall.

I've heard too many rumors—there's a paradise on the other side, it's a wasteland of dirt and rocks, the Independents have a lifestyle free from corrupt power or greed, the Independents caught a widespread disease that turned them deranged and feral.

Tomorrow, I'll find out the truth.

Right before I die.

10

000.174.16.25.59

Reid lifts Mother's expensive toast glass. "To my little Brielle." He sports multiple bandages and a sling with one of my ribbons tied to it—the reddish-brown lace one. Apparently it reminded him of my hair.

"You didn't have hide all day, Parvin." Mother lifts her glass. "Some people stopped to visit. Even that young Enforcer, Hawke, came for a moment."

"He just came to inspect her nanobook." Reid hands his glass to Father. "The Enforcers are suspicious."

I take Mother's glass for my sip. "It's done with."

Our foursome toast feels like freedom and captivity all at the same time. I ingest the bubbly-something with trembling lips. We will never be together in this house again.

The fire pops. Chills sweep up my body and down again with the liquid I swallow, like soap on a washboard. The Numbers tick on the mantel. I wish they weren't displayed.

000.174.16.21.13

One hundred and seventy-four days, sixteen hours, and twenty-one minutes. I'll spend tomorrow with an Enforcer on the train. No one else is allowed to accompany me to the Wall. I'll cross and then die.

Alone.

Gifts from my family rest on the table—I don't know why we give presents at Farewell parties. Those with Good-byes can never enjoy or use them.

Reid gave me his own handmade canvas shoulder-pack with wool padding sewn into the straps. Father gave me a knife the length of my forearm and a wooden sheath. It will be useful if I survive long enough to encounter monsters or cannibals.

Mother's gift is an elegant mixture of practical and lovely—black leggings and a skirt with a fur hem and triple layered with brown, green, and grey wool. It's knee-length with a high waist and pockets around the wide band.

The colors are for camouflage and the skirt can be untied to spread like a blanket. She made it last night after a visit from Skelley Chase, while I was in the containment center.

My hands clench my glass as I'm seized by an instant of sorrow and longing. "I want to live to make you all proud."

What I don't say is how I also wish to die and leave Mother happy with her faultless son . . . how I want to avoid the terrors and trials of the mysterious West, to apologize to God for a wasted life . . . how I hope He still allows me a glimpse of polished gold streets.

Mother hastily wipes away a tear. Her sorrow comforts me. Am I being too hard on everyone? She lifts her chin and relapses into poised indifference.

Reid squeezes my hand. "It's okay to be afraid."

I shudder and sniff. They're all trying to make this a positive evening, but don't they realize how frightening a Good-bye is? I expected Reid to understand after the train accident, but he doesn't show any understanding. In fact, he isn't showing much emotion except fake pleasantness.

When he first stepped through the door, he gave me a long hug as best he could against the pain, but he never said, "Let's switch." Or "Take the Clock and run." He just spoke two words:

"I'm sorry."

I wanted to see him upset about the situation. I wanted to see him sad I might die early, but he took it with a brave smile. I had all my arguments ready.

No, Reid. It's my choice.

You can't go instead. I'm doing this for you.

You have a better life to live. Keep the Clock.

They all sounded so heroic, but I didn't get to use a single one. He doesn't seem to mind that I'm being shoved through the Wall against my will.

I am alone.

During the gift giving, he grew giddy like he does every Christmas. In his excitement, he almost always blurts out the contents before the opener even unwraps it. But tonight I wanted to see him solemn.

Once I'm gone, maybe he'll grieve.

I scan my family. My throat closes. "Thank you."

Mother doesn't meet my eyes and I allow a resigned abandonment to blanket my heart. Everyone has faces on. I want them to be real—to cry and be fearful with me. Beyond all this is a strange desire for them to pray with me—*for* me. But their false fronts make me feel more flawed and alone than ever.

"Off to bed." Father tosses another log into the fire. "The train leaves at six. I'll wake you at five."

There's no need for him to remind me. I won't sleep in tomorrow. I'll be lucky to sleep at all. I was always told the Farewell party is joyous and calm, but that's from people who've had their entire lifetime to accept their Numbers. What would it be like to feel calm at this moment? I can't even remember calm, not since before Reid's accident.

All I feel now is emptiness.

000.174.08.30.11

My senses sharpen the moment I wake up. I hear the rush of each raindrop before it crashes against the wood of the shutters. I smell the new fire in the kitchen holding a warm good-bye in its ashes. I breathe in the weight of my life—the memories, the dreams, the mistakes, the regrets. Even now, my life feels thin and light.

I sit up and swing my feet over the edge of the bed. The sound of my socks brushing the floor kisses my ears and I welcome the goose bumps on my shoulders. I am more alive today than ever before because one phrase repeats in my mind.

Never again. Never again. Never again. Never again will I feel, see, touch, smell, or hear these things. I run my hand over the smooth desk Father carved. The wood is slick and warm with love and invitation.

I dress in my new skirt, leggings, boots, and my favorite sturdy, long-sleeved shirt beneath my vest. I don't know what to pack—how does one prepare for death?

The first thing to go in after a scan of my room is my Bible, like I'm taking God with me. I toss in a half-used box of matches, some wool socks, underwear, my self-updating *Daily Hemisphere*, an extra shirt, and—for sentimental reasons—my pocket-sized sewing kit. Last, is Skelley Chase's electronic journal and watch—not that I'll use them much.

I squeeze the watch in my fist, half wishing I could crush it. I think back to the hope I held in my heart that he would even *read* my autobiography on Assessment Day. Now he's writing it, both on electric paper and across my life—taking charge.

Dressed and packed, I enter the kitchen. Mother sits at the table with a mug between her hands and heavy eyes. She looks up and breathes, "Parvin."

My name sounds like a lily spoken into a breeze—soft, treasured. I'm young, new, and hopeful, like I'm ready to start life, not end it.

She rises from the table and greets me with a tight hug. For the first time she's not bustling around with everyone's to-do lists running through her mind. "I love you," she whispers.

I've never heard her say these words with such meaning. She speaks them while we hug so I can't see her face. She never liked showing emotion.

"I love you." And I mean it. Why did we ever argue when life was this short? I didn't have time to argue with her. I should have loved her better. I pull away and blurt the one question I must have answered before I die: "Why did you write in your journal that I was your curse?"

With a sniff, she seems to overcome her weakened state and turns to the wood stove where a pot sits heating. "I didn't say you were my curse."

"'I have a daughter. I'm cursed.' Why did you write that?"

Her shoulders rise and fall with a breath. "The midwife told me I was cursed. I wrote her words."

I plop at the table and glance at the clock—5:00 a.m. We have time for this discussion. "What did her words mean to you? Why were they so important?"

Mother stirs the contents of the pot and I inhale cinnamon oatmeal with a hint of honey. "I never wanted to forget," she mutters. "I never wanted to forget to appreciate you."

My mind reels backward. "But . . . I thought you *regretted* having me."

The slam of the cast-iron lid onto the pot startles me, and she turns with eyes as hot as the fire. "You are my *blessing*, Parvin. You were the hope that saved me from despair that night. Don't *ever* think I regretted you."

"But . . ." I bite my lip. *You always seemed to love Reid more.* "Why say you're cursed?"

"I'm cursed because I have to lose three children instead of two."

Things start to make sense. Mother's harshness this past year stemmed from her fear of losing another child. She felt cursed knowing she'd probably watch us all die before her Clock even showed a single permanent zero.

Father bursts from his room and strides to my door before spotting me at the table.

"Good morning," I say.

He smiles, but a second later his chin quivers and his face crumples into tearful wrinkles. He strides right back into his own room. I pound my fist once against the table followed by my head. I groan.

"Don't give yourself brain damage," Mother says from the stove. "It's a hard morning. Just bear through it."

"That's easy coming from your heart of steel," I mutter from my arms. "You can bear through anything with a deep breath and soap suds. I don't have as much practice."

She hands me a spoon. "Today's a perfect day to practice."

I mope and stab the table with my spoon. "Today is *not* a perfect day." But the playful grumblings between us lighten my heart. The day may not be perfect, but it suddenly feels normal.

She nudges my chin with the knuckle of her forefinger and places a tiny bowl of chocolate puff cereal in front of me. I gasp. "Did you make this? Where did you get wheat?" I inhale the chocolate puffs like they're my last meal. I guess they kind of are.

"I found a cereal bag at the Newtons," she says in a somber voice. "Mrs. Newton would have . . . wanted us to use their food."

My cereal sticks to my throat. I knew something was wrong when I first saw the Enforcers outside their door. Why didn't I do anything?

Reid enters the house. The chill from his entrance lingers in the doorway. He sits at a kitchen chair, taking slow breaths against his cracked ribs. He scans my face with hollow eyes, then stares at the wood.

Looks like I'm going to have to be the strong one. Today, my feelings and emotions don't matter. They'll be snuffed out all too soon. I might as well suck it up and leave this world with backbone.

Once Father collects his tears, he emerges from his room with a coat, a coiled rope, and a walking stick. "Time to go."

"Almost." Mother hands me several bundles wrapped in clean rags and tied with thick cords. "Banana bread and some of my butter spreads. The other rags hold herbs for sickness, tea leaves, and a paste for rashes and burns."

She holds up the largest bundle. "Dried corn kernels, beans, noodles, beef, and a cupful of salt. The salt and corn will preserve the meat. Noodles will fill your stomach." She pulls out a leather water pouch with a wooden stopper and places it beneath the sink pump.

"You don't even know if I'll live," I say, numb. "We don't know what's on the other side of the Wall."

Mother loads her medley of supplies into my bag and includes the coffee pot. I don't bother asking how she got noodles—maybe the Newtons had those, too.

Her eyes fill with tears, Father coughs, and I feel very grown-up. I kiss Mother on the cheek, place the canteen in my pack, and pat Reid on the shoulder because he doesn't move to get up. I pull my most sturdy coat off the loose wall peg and relish the weight and comfort it brings.

"Parvin."

I turn at Reid's voice, but don't get a chance to see his face before he's out of his chair and I'm enveloped in the warmth of his coat, breathing in his forest-travel scent. Will my dead body take on that smell as I lie in the unknown behind the Wall?

When he lets go, I look up and wish I hadn't. His face is scrunched and tears blur his irises. I've seen this face once before, when he found me in the mud with a broken leg after I'd fled from the school bullies. Yet here I am, about to die, and those bullies all have greater Numbers than I do.

He holds out a brown book stuffed to the fullest with papers and items taped inside. "It's my journal."

I frown and sniff at the same time, fighting the pout of my lower lip. "How did you get all this paper? I didn't even know you kept a journal."

"There's a lot you may find you don't know about me," he says with forced cheer.

I'm realizing that.

"And *this*"—he pulls out a thin, familiar, electronic gadget—"is a sentra. It takes emotigraphs." He points to a button on the top. "You don't even have to aim, but if you want a photograph to come out along with the emotigraph, you hold down the button when you aim."

"I've used one before." But I avoid saying Skelley Chase's name.

Reid holds it up to the morning light coming through the window and clicks the button. "When the emotigraph comes out of here"—he points to a slit on one side of the sentra as a thin electrosheet emerges— "it will have a tiny button for you to push to feel the emotion you recorded. This was the gift I brought back for you."

"I've never seen it spit out a sheet like that before."

Reid pulls the emotigraph from the slot and shoves it in his journal before I can press the flat grey button on the corner. "It's an older generation sentra. I got it in an Upper City."

"You've been to an Upper City?" I place the strange object in my pack. "When?"

He taps my pack. "Journal, little Brielle. Read the journal."

My throat makes a funny sound, like a kitten's cry. *God, why are You making this harder?* I won't live long enough to discover the Reid I thought I knew. "Reid, no one will remember me."

Reid makes no move to comfort me, but Mother quotes from behind us, "'He who began a good work in you will bring it to completion . . .'"

"But God hasn't started anything in me." My shoulders sag. "There's nothing to complete."

"Ah, little Brielle." Reid flicks a stray eyelash from my cheek. "I love you, sis." This is all he says. Somehow, it's all I need.

Mother snatches a hairbrush from her room and brushes my hair until it's fluffier than an autumn dandelion. For once, I don't fight, though I do pocket a few hair ties for later. Father opens the door. It's not raining anymore. We step outside, leaving Mother behind, still holding the hairbrush. Reid stands behind her, solemn and bleak.

Two Enforcers step from their posts to intersect us. Everything in my throat and eyes tightens, squeezing out tears hotter than winter tea. My quivering lips prevent any final words as Father and I walk down Straight Street for the last time.

Mother speaks in a whisper more precious to my heart than embroidered gold. "Good-bye."

11

000.174.05.48.04

The shoulder of my coat still holds the stain of Father's tears. His sobbing cracked my already fragile heart and I don't think I'll ever recover. I kissed him on the cheek—a small token that will never repay what I owe for his endless love and care.

I now face Wall Opening Three out of the four circling the globe. This one is placed in the top west corner of my own state of Missouri—one of the remaining thirty-one states. The wide Missouri River lies behind me, flowing with a hushed whisper. I want to jump off the arched bridge we just crossed—jump into the river's brownish-red waters and let it carry me back toward Unity Village.

My Enforcer holds each of my arms at the wrist with a grip like human handcuffs. My heartbeat has long since abandoned the word *steady* and pumps blood like a frantic firehose trying to douse the crackle in my nerves.

Some people on the train blew me kisses and squeezed my arm as I exited—clearly not residents of Unity. Some people fear death, but everyone fears the Wall. The unknown. The passengers had a special grace I needed. This is the only stop in a stretch of two hundred miles North and it feels abandoned—like my future.

Father demanded I bring a thin coil of rope. A loop slips off my shoulder as I walk, so I readjust. The black Enforcer and I follow a marked path toward the towering stone structure. I've seen the top edge of the Wall all my life. The sun sets behind it every night, leaving a menacing orange-red glow. I now stand at its base for the first time.

It's colossal—stretching to each side like an endless guard with a chilled grey heart. How could anyone build this and call it an improvement to society? God certainly didn't. I can't imagine Him speaking the Wall into existence and saying, "It is good."

Tiny early-morning snowdots dance through the air, windless, but swirling of their own accord—unusual for April, but appropriate for the chill in my soul. None seem to land, but they brush my face as though in cool reassurance.

The guardhouse leans to one side, rickety and breezy. It loses my gaze to the frosty Opening beside it. Even when the guard and Skelley Chase emerge from the guardhouse I can't stop staring at the carved arch enveloping a smooth, steel door. There's no handle. I imagine the tunnel stretching for miles through cold rock, infested with bugs and animals anxious to escape the abandoned West.

"You're late," the guard barks. "It's already seven-thirty!"

I can't breathe. I can't look away. I'm already trapped in that Wall, clawing against the door, trying to come back to this side. My fingers ache, my ears fill with distraction, my eyes sting. I sway.

My Enforcer gives me a rough shake. I gasp and my clenched hands relax. A tear slides down my cheek.

"Don't panic yet." The guard is in his mid-forties, with a cropped haircut, stained brown uniform, and squinty eyes. "It's even freakier inside."

I want to flee—the most I've wanted to do since leaving Unity Village. The entire ride on the train passed in blurry shadow. I don't even remember blinking.

Skelley Chase strides forward. "Ready?"

I don't move, but the Enforcer shoves me forward. Skelley Chase lowers his voice as we walk to the Wall. "I'll have one week in October for you to return, so don't miss it. Keep a sharp eye on the dates. And watch for news or updates from me."

Panic swells again. Skelley Chase holds out his sentra. "Take this. Use it on the other side and send them to me through your nanobook."

"I have one," I whisper.

He raises an eyebrow. "You do?"

"Reid gave it to me."

Skelley Chase shrugs. "Then press this."

I do and don't even register the prick. "Is this emotion going in the autobiography?"

"It's just a biography now. And yes, this is the final emotigraph. Readers will have to follow the rest of your story through updates to their

X-books. And trust me, they'll follow. People love to *feel* what you're feeling."

I doubt any reader wants to feel the terror coating my spine. *God, are You with me?* I shudder at the idea of meeting Him face to face. What will He say? Not, "Well done, good and faithful servant." This little phrase is inscribed on the inner Bible flaps of the few steadfast souls. I'll probably get, "You did okay, wasteful and fickle Parvin."

I squeeze my fingers together and release a long breath. My terror settles into a petrified calm, filling my body like it's an empty lemonade pitcher. I allow the silence to dominate.

"Two minutes, girly." The guard's compassion must have died with his first Wall victim.

I can't do this. I breathe deep and think what I wish I could scream: *I don't want to die. I don't want to leave this shadow of a footprint behind for my life.*

The guard holds a blank wooden Clock next to a large square hole in the Wall. He sets it inside, places a heavy metal lid over the hole, and pushes a stone button with his thumb. A strong suction sound precedes a loud *clunk!* The Clock is gone when he takes away the lid.

Skelley Chase stands beside the guard with a slick camera floating at eye height. A round, black disc sits on the grass beneath it. I can't tell if it's stone or metal. A red light blinks on the levitating camera. I don't ask. I don't care. I can't bring myself to say anything.

This is Skelley Chase's doing.

He tips his fedora. I look away and take my first willing step toward the Wall.

"Why do you have on all that traveling stuff, eh?" The guard gestures to my shoulder pack, rope, and garb. "Think you're gonna survive or something?"

"It makes me feel more at home." It's the truth—I'm carrying a bit of each family member with me. Maybe it's false comfort.

The guard shrugs. "Whatever makes the Good-bye less painful, I guess." He scratches the stubble on his chin, takes a deep breath, and spews his next words with the speed of an auctioneer. "May you find peace in the afterlife in which you choose to believe and may all hopes and dreams come to fulfillment in your heart and soul as you lie down to rest. I wish you luck, joy, and all spiritual wellness in the course of whatever form death may take in these last minutes. Good-bye." He takes a breath. "That's a message from the government of the United States of the East."

He holds up a wristwatch shaped like a mini-Clock. "The East Door—this one—will open for fifteen seconds. The West Door's already opened, but it'll close after ten minutes. It's a long tunnel. Better walk fast so you don't get trapped inside. Ain't no getting back."

I look at Skelley Chase, but he gives a slight shake of his head. I guess he has his ways. He can do anything, right? Not that I'll live to see it.

I stare at the cold door with scrape marks where it's opened before. The door glides sideways into the Wall, revealing a black tunnel with no lanterns and no sound except my breathing rebounding off the shadow. I step backward.

"Fifteen seconds, girly."

Does the guard really have to count down?

The black tunnel is endless, cold, and hollow. I'm looking into the darkness of hell.

"I can't—" I choke, taking another step back. "I can't go in there." I meet the pressure of the Enforcer's body behind me.

"Ten . . . nine . . . eight . . ." The guard holds his watch up to his face.

I want to die in the light. I can't see ahead. What if it's an endless tunnel with no exit to the West? The guard's voice rings out behind me like an echoing pendulum, "Three . . . two . . . *One!*" With a shout, the Enforcer shoves me over the rutted threshold.

I twist around, reach out my hand, and release a strangled cry. *"Wait!"*

The steel door slides shut, slicing away my last beam of familiar light. I barely maintain my footing. The last bit of light fades from my pupils, taking with it the outline of my outstretched hand. My heart pounds so hard it's bound to leave bruises.

I turn back around, gasping. Everything ahead is new—pitch black and unexplored. I swallow hard and a lump of ice hits my stomach. Packed dirt scrapes under my boots as I force my feet to carry me forward. Hands outstretched like Christ on the cross, my fingers run along the crude parallel rock walls. A pink glow appears ahead—symbolic of old sayings portraying death as the light at the end of the tunnel. With foot over leaden foot, I walk to my death—deep breath, chin high, and a perfected look of defiance.

Sound does not exist. Breath does not exist. I start to wonder if I even exist. My mind shuts out memories with the closing of the East Door. Reid, Skelley Chase, Unity Village, Mother, Father . . . they all fade like dying electric light bulbs. My former acute awareness to the senses dulls into a numbness that not even fear can penetrate. Encompassed in light at the end of all the darkness, death looks less daunting.

I lose the sense of time, but process the fact that the bright arch is growing, growing. I reach out a hand toward the West this time and see my fingers splayed in front of me. Now I run. I sprint toward the light.

Sounds explode from my movement—pebbles skirting across the worn path, my panting grating the walls, the bouncing of my rope as loops slide off my shoulder and trail behind me like a dead snake. The loudest sound is the scrape of boots on dirt as I skid to a halt on the threshold of the West.

A similar steel door waits inside the Wall to cut me off from the half of the world I've come to know. I squint into the light of the West and see what no one in the East has seen.

Across the threshold, two feet from the tips of my toes, is air.

Just . . .

Air.

Red dirt crumbles away into an abyss. Misty clouds with a shadowy cover form a base blanket, as if I'm standing on the tip of a mountain peak. The sun hasn't made it to this side yet. I stabilize myself against the inner Wall and lean out, glancing to my left and right. The Wall stretches on, like the East side, but the ground extends a foot or less for a hundred feet each direction at the Wall's base before curving out into a more supportive plateau.

Stretching straight ahead is a lake of sky. There's no ground—apparently demolished by an earthquake or some other natural disaster caused by the meteor that smashed the West so long ago. The only way out is down—and the guard said this door would close after ten minutes. That could be any moment.

Now I know how I'll die. I've always wanted to fly.

For one silent, peaceful moment, I inhale and survey the scene before me. I'm on the other side of the Wall—a mystery none but the dead have seen. The Newtons, Mr. Foster, and all the other Radicals are waiting for me.

The sun sends light rays above, breaking over the Wall edge, brushing the clouds, and twinkling in each wispy snowdot. A bird flies in the distance, but no people or cities are present—none of the government-free Independents. I suppose we did end up needing the government to survive.

The air smells cold and a rush of wind along the Wall blows my free hair across my face. I don't care if it tangles, these are my last minutes. I don't need to fear if I'll survive. The answer lies before me in cloud form: Death.

I spread my arms high, embracing the chill, and scoot my boots to the edge of the cliff. My toes raise me up in a short second of final balance. A smile graces my lips. I lean forward at the same moment the door zips shut. The last feelings I register are the lurch of my stomach as I entrust my bodyweight to gravity, the rush of air around my tense face, and a fierce thrill over my searing heart.

12

Something crawls around my neck and up my left arm—a blazing serpent, licking blisters on my skin. Stretching. Igniting. Hammers on my head. Hammers. I can't breathe. The serpent tightens, turning red-hot then black. My Numbers scream.

My eyes snap open. Awareness follows an instant later. The world is twisted, upside-down and confused.

No, *I* am confused. I shake my throbbing head. The hammers don't stop. The burning around my arm and neck isn't a snake, it's my rope, twisted three times around my suspended arm like a candy cane stripe, holding all my weight.

My blurry eyes struggle to focus on the stretches and crinkles in my exposed skin, straining against the rough fibers. The end of the rope is caught around my shoulder pack, coat, and hair. I'm lucky I wasn't hung.

A groan reaches my ears. It comes from my own choked voice. *Choked.* The rope rubs like a dull saw on my neck. My senses awaken and with it my survival instinct. Things seem clear now. The scraggy rock face scratches my shoulder blades, my feet dangle like wind chimes below me. Blood trickles down the creases of my left cheek. My right arm clutches a handful of my coat and vest over my heart.

My heart.

I'm alive.

Why?

The pain in my arm takes precedence over the questions in my head. I grab the rope and pull up, loosening the tension. With my free hand, I spin myself to face the cliff and unloop the cord from my neck and head. The slack releases the rope from my shoulder pack and I rotate, unraveling my body. Now my feeble strength holds me up.

Several yards above, the taut rope stretches over the edge of the cliff. Is it caught in the closed door? All desire to free fall and plummet to my death disappears.

If I climb down, the rope will have to remain here against the cliff, abandoned. I could climb up, though—shimmy to my left until the ledge fans out to solid ground. I should at least climb back up to the closed door and leave a note for the next Radical, not that they have much choice against a plunge.

My feet scrabble for a hold, but the rock face slants away from my body. Using both hands, I pull against the rope. My elbows bend a fraction of an inch. Muscles tremble. I kick against the stone, but drop back against the cliff. Limp. Weak. Flimsy.

Already, my arms fight for strength. I need to make a decision. Soon. Climbing up isn't going to work—not with my pathetic muscles. Reid was right. I'm too skinny, too frail.

Below me, ragged rock and crumbling red dirt plunge into the misty clouds. There must be a bottom. I can always find a trail to hike back to the top. Maybe the Newtons are down there. They might have climbed.

The blood flows back into my throbbing arm. Needles sweep through my skin. I lower myself a few inches. Hand-over-hand, I descend the rope. My body is so heavy. I mustn't fall now.

My arms quiver. Once I start, I go faster—faster than my body's ready to handle. The grain in the rope fibers burns my hands. My own weight pulls against me. A few minutes later, my feet kick the air and scrape rock pebbles into the abyss. I've reached the end of the rope.

I hang for a moment, tempted to drop and hope there's a canyon bottom somewhere within two hundred feet of the mist. I take a deep breath and peruse the rock in front of my face. The cracks are defined and thick. I could fit several fingers in them. Rock bumps and crevices stretch below me. Somewhat promising.

The transfer from rope to rock is precarious. My boots are clumsy and I scuffle for a foothold, but my fingers clamp the rock with muscles I didn't know they possessed. I hold my breath, feeling fifty pounds heavier without the rope as a lifeline. If my fingers don't hold me, every bit of my body will plunge to the canyon bottom.

I try to peer at my feet, but my forehead hits the rock. "Okay, rock wall. Cooperate now. I've never done this before."

Climbing down proves much trickier than I expected. My fingernails scrape against rutted stone and gather dirt and grime. Some split and snap backward. I wince. My head is heavy and dislikes balancing on my aching neck. The blood from my forehead snakes down my neck into the collar of my shirt.

I straddle a small rock spine and hug it with my knees and elbows, locating cracks and bumps with the eyes in my fingers. My thumb snags a spider web. A large crevice to my right runs deep into the cliffside shadows.

My downward movement slows as I enter the cloud. The silence turns eerie now that the light is more hidden. A tiny ledge provides a few minutes of rest. My forearms tense, shaking. I continue. Mist thickens. I grip the rock in a moment of panic. What if there isn't an end to this descent? What if this canyon was caused by an earthquake and split the Earth so deep that it's an endless abyss? How long do I descend?

I peer back up. Mist. Below me, mist. Dare I keep going?

God, I'm afraid. My arms shake. I close my eyes and inch downward. The rock is cold against my fingers.

Mere minutes later, the cliff base meets piles of giant boulders like they're old friends. My foot tests for stability, then I rest my full weight on a boulder—and collapse against the rocks. Sweat soaks my vest beneath my pack and my sticky hair clings to exposed skin. My shoulders whimper beneath my pack and I adjust it before crawling to the next boulder.

I squeeze down in a crack between two boulders and meet hard dirt with tiptoes. The bottom. Bluish-grey mist blurs the shadows of scraggly trees fifty or sixty yards ahead and silence rests on the air.

I survived.

I step from the rocks into the openness of the canyon floor and slip on a stray chunk of rock. I flop to the ground with a yelp. My tailbone meets an unrelenting stick. I yank it out from under me and throw it. It clacks against something else. With a squint through the mist, I recognize its form.

A long, white bone.

Human.

Ahead, my foot rests on a small human skull staring sideways into my eyes. I gasp and kick it away. I scramble to my feet and scan the canyon floor with hitched breathing.

Skeletons surround me like a lifeless welcoming committee. Their pieces stretch across the visible space to the sparse forest ahead. Spiders in eye-sockets, web-strung nets between ribs, scraps of torn clothing, pale elbows and knees bent upward and backward, scattered fingers clawing the earth—Halloween spread on the ground like a human carpet.

This would have been my grave. This is what I would be, had my rope not stopped me—empty Numbers lying with other empty Numbers.

I scream.

My fists squeeze over my eyes and I stumble backward, back to the cliff, to the boulders. Pounding. Pounding. My heart won't stop. It won't slow. My legs shake beneath me. The bones rattle.

I open my eyes. The ground *is* shaking. The bones clack like a morbid symphony. Mist starts to rise, sunbeams peek over the cliff ledge and sift through the cloud. The treetops across the open graveyard move in drunken sways. Earthquake?

The shaking continues, growing stronger. Bones clacking. Clacking. Growls. Snarls. Yapping. Howls.

I retreat in slow motion, too terrified to look away from the forest and run. Where can I run? Where can I climb? What's coming?

My pack hits the boulder and I stop, holding in any sound or air that might break loose. My nerves trample my skin like a stampede of hysteria. I fight it until my eyes land on what plows through the trees to meet me with wide open jaws, bristled grey hair, and manic eyes.

Wolves.

Enough wolves to tear me in more directions than I ever want to travel. They slow to a menacing advance, paw over paw, lips twitching for blood. Behind them, three bears—two black and one grizzly—sit on matted haunches. Hesitating in the trees, a line of coyotes waiting for the wolves to move aside. Leaning backward over the boulder, me. Paralyzed. But the dinner guests know as well as the meal that there's no way out.

I imagine the beasts charging—it will take a second. There are so many, I'm bound to die quickly. But a quick death is as far as my optimism goes.

Run? Freeze? Yell? My impulse is to flee, but I can't bear to turn my back on death. Why didn't I let go of the rope and die from impact when I had the chance? I survived for *this*?

The wolves stare at me, unblinking and unmoving apart from their ragged breath. I stare back, stiff and weak-hearted. Time stretches, swallowed by tense silence. Seconds remain before one of us moves. What can I do? What do wolves fear?

I don't know. I've never known. I've never even gone camping let alone encountered wolves in a canyon. Reid would know. He would survive.

No. Reid's not here. It's just me and I'm not Reid. I never have been. I never will be. I no longer *want* to be. I've survived a dive off a canyon and a climb of torture. Wolves, bears, and coyotes still trump the two, but I feel uncharacteristically determined to die with a fight.

I inch my left hand toward the ground, slower than a cat stalking a mole. My raw fingertips brush over a smooth, cold bone. It's long and thick. A femur.

Just what I want.

In the moment my hand grasps my weapon, the leading grey wolf blinks and breaks from the pack like a stone from a slingshot. I screech and swing the femur. It catches Grey under the chin and he releases an angry yelp. He skids among the bones, regains his footing, and leaps once more. I duck, turn, and scramble up one of the boulders, banging my knee against the stone.

I flip onto my back and flail my heels, catching Grey in the mouth. I scream again and pull my boot from the wolf's jaws. The femur is no longer in my hand. The roars, snarls, and yaps double in ferocity. Every ounce of fur and drool charges.

The coyotes head toward my surrounding boulders and the wolves follow Grey straight for me. The bears are slow on the uptake, but their roars shake me from the inside out like ravenous kettledrums. I'm on my feet in a flash then scramble up the boulders and leap from the highest one toward the cliff. I thank God with every particle of gushed oxygen that I land on a tiny cliff ledge on the canyon wall.

I reel backward for a moment, but my right hand clings to a crack. My pinky keeps me from falling, curled like a bolt inside the crevice. A peek over my shoulder reveals Grey crouching, settling his shoulders for a spring.

"Stop!" My shout is in vain.

He sails through the air with a mighty launch. I squeeze my eyes shut and cower against the lumpy cliff. One hundred pounds of fur and muscle smash my face into the rock. Grey's jaws clamp around my left arm and claws rake down my leg as he scrambles for balance.

I ball my right hand into a fist inside the crack. Every muscle tenses in obedience to my frantic brain. Why can't I stop screaming? Grey's teeth rip from my arm and something sharp swipes across my back. I fall from the ledge, but my fist anchors me to the rough stone. My eyes spring open. Grey's mass hits the ground with a deadly thump. I release the air of relief.

God, please let him be dead.

The other wolves, coyotes, and advancing bears seem less daunting . . . until Grey regains his footing. He looks up with a snarl and circles back toward the boulder.

God, please . . .

It's all I manage. The scratches on my legs burn like branding irons. Blood drips over my hand in the crevice. God must be listening extra hard today because, five yards above and to my right, is an overhang with a defined lip. I ascend.

My legs and left arm quiver against seeping, sticky warmth, yet I climb. My limbs find mysterious strength to pull me up—defying my previous weakness. Handholds appear like sprinkled miracles and the overhang seems nothing more than a minor challenge. When I crawl onto the ledge, the miracles don't stop—it's not a ledge, it's a tiny God-thumbprint pressed into the rock face.

I scoot under its angled roof and dare to dangle my legs over the edge. My dinner party paces below among fragments of clothing and skeletons, waiting for me to jump. I'd rather starve in this haven, picked to the bone by spiders, than face the beasts again. Some of the material beneath their paws looks familiar, as if a little Newton girl wore it once.

I look away and curl against the cavern wall, entwining my blood-slicked fingers around my ankles to hug my knees to my chest. By this point, my tears, heart, and lungs remember how to function. Shaking sets in like a spring drizzle and grows until I'm drenched in panic and freezing sweat. My eyes squeeze against the burning pillaging my body. Tears slink down my face, but they taste of relief.

"Mother?" I crave her firm hands of care. I hurt. I *hurt*. I've never hurt like this. *"Mother!"*

My heart beats rhythm against my knees—solid and invincible while at the same time chilled and feverish. This awareness of life lifts my head from my knees. I stare through a watery film to the opposite wall of grey stone. Wild tangled hair sticks to my cheeks, my neck, my wounds, my blood.

I wanted this. I wanted life. I wanted a second chance, and God is giving it to me. Granted, my second chance twirls among a pinwheel of rabid, starved animals inside a crater, but it's a second chance nonetheless. God wouldn't allow me to survive a death-plunge only to be devoured, would He?

The thin cross ring spins easily under the pressure of my forefinger, slathered as it is with blood. God is all I have now. Mother's not here. Reid's not here. The name *Parvin* is a clean slate without the chalk marks of passivity. Today, my name marks a new beginning wrought with blood, loneliness, and fear.

My pack slides from my shoulders and I rummage through with my right hand, wiping tears with my left, smearing blood and sticky hair across my face. I want to pull out the nanobook Skelley Chase gave me and beg for rescue, but there's too much blood on my hands to experiment with it. Besides, my betrayer wouldn't help me and I don't want the reading world to know I wanted to give up so early.

My hair clings to wounds. When I pull it away, the strands slide against my raw skin like paper cuts. I rummage for a ribbon to tie it back, but my fingers find Father's smooth dagger first. I slide off the wooden sheath, wrap my hair in my free hand, and run the dagger in a sawing motion through the sticky strands. The slicing sound is pleasant, rhythmic.

I feel no remorse for cutting my hair, though I regret using my bloody hand to hold it, now having to pick each loose strand from the thick red coating of life. What's left is still long enough for a small braid. I find a ribbon and, as I tie my hair back, a sense of assurance secures itself among the ribbon.

Now the wounds. I close my eyes and assess. I encounter pain first on my face, then my neck. Blood and grime covers too much of my skin for me to locate gashes or deep cuts—my raw, torn fingers have little feeling in them anyway. Instead of feeling around, I pinpoint the strongest pain: my left arm, my back, and my legs—all bearing gashes from Grey's teeth and claws. A shudder pulses down my body and I glance over the cave ledge.

The beasts are gone.

I scan the tree line. No shadows. No haunting eyes. My wariness increases, but I cannot allow myself to dwell in paranoia. The pain in my back is sharp and thrums with furious beat, harder and harder. With a grunt, I remove my coat and curve my right arm back, brushing shaking fingers over my vest. There are no holes in the thick material, but it is soaked and sticky. I peel it away from my skin and a zing shoots through my nerves. Three defined gashes pour my life onto the stone.

I know little of healing or care for the body. How much blood loss is too much? Though I'm not a healer, I'm not ignorant. I need bandages, water, a fishhook, and a fire. I've seen Mother do stitches plenty of times.

Bandages I can make, and I have my leather water pouch, but no wood for a fire. My mind rests on the needle in my pocket-sized sewing kit. I didn't think I'd need to use it on myself.

I shudder. I can't reach the wounds on my back, but my thighs and calves bear similar lacerations that could heal with some fishing twine. Too bad I'm stuck with regular sewing thread.

A sigh escapes into the breeze. I could have prepared so much better, but I was distracted by my death. I didn't weigh other possibilities. I didn't count on miracles.

I didn't count on surviving.

I give my head a small shake, and the rope burn on my neck screams. I ignore it as best I can.

Get to work.

Father's knife becomes my hero, slicing away the grey layer of my skirt and cutting long, even bandages. I dampen one rag enough to wipe blood away from my calves and off my back. Snowdots sprinkle the air again, dancing with more energy than before. The chill slows the bleeding.

For now, I use bandages—the needlework will have to wait until courage catches up with me. I tie cloth strips as tight as my weak arms and stiff fingers allow. The wool scratches against my wounds like sandpaper.

My leggings are torn in several places, but still hold together. I refrain from cutting them. Instead, I pull their shreds over the bandages to help hold them in place. My left shirtsleeve is almost rent in two from Grey's teeth, so I rip it off and wrap my arm.

My back is the most difficult as I struggle to cover the entire wound. For good measure, I smear a little of Mother's burn paste on the bandage to keep the gashes from stiffening too much—at least, that's what I hope it does. I also lather it on the uncovered rope-burn portions of my left arm and around my neck. It's slimy and uncomfortable, but it will encourage healing.

When the last knot is tied, my body succumbs to dizziness and fatigue. I knew it would come, but I admire my own stamina—I never knew I *had* any.

I spread out the two remaining layers of my skirt and curl beneath them. The sun no longer shines in the snow-dusted canyon. Wind picks up and my bruised knee throbs against the bending. I attempt to rest on my side, but the pain rolls me over to a different position. Grunting, gasping, and tender turning bring me to my stomach—still an uncomfortable state, but the least painful so far.

My head rests against my shoulder pack. The bump from falling against the cliff-face throbs, but what can I do? I throw the worries aside and spare a moment to register this is my first time ever sleeping outside, even though it's daytime.

I'm camping. I'm alive. I can do this. Yet I still start to cry. I hurt, far deeper than physical wounds. How could Skelley Chase do this to me? How could my family allow it?

God? Are You even here?

I Am.

Imagined? Felt? Heard? It doesn't matter. His response soothes my sorrow. As my mind's-eye slow-dances with the sandman, I dare to believe for a moment that I might survive.

13

000.173.20.05.50

I never absorbed the definition of *agony* until now. The word somer-saults through my mind on repeat, bouncing off the awareness of pain in my back, over my leg, across my face, on my arm, in my hands . . .

It won't stop.

I don't know how long I slept or if I just wafted in and out of con-sciousness. The light is nearly gone. Its glow fades like melting sugar.

Agony.

Dratted word. Sitting in this chilled cave, waiting for myself to heal, almost takes more energy than action might.

I sit up, the action accompanied by a fiery scream from my back wounds. I rummage through my pack for a syringe of distraction. My numb fingers close around the leather-bound electric journal from Skelley Chase. It still smells like lemons.

The blood on my hands is dried and doesn't smear the cover. When I unfold and open it, my arm spasms. I grimace. The blank screen looks cold and aloof. My brain is sluggish, but I must write. Everything must be written. I wanted survival and adventure. I just never expected to get them.

Though my hand shakes, I tap the screen. Nothing happens. I run my fingers along the smooth sides of the square. They slide across a long slit in one side and meet an indentation on the top. I press my finger into it and the screen lightens to an aqua blue with a small chime sound. Two sea-green bubbles float on the screen. A single black scripted word sits inside each. One says, *Contact*, the other says, *Journal*. I touch *Journal*.

A blank page opens with several tiny screen-buttons lining the top. The first has a swirly *Ss* inside of it and another has the words *"Talk/Type."* Others have single letters or symbols I don't understand.

"No instruction manual?" Before I finish speaking, words flow onto the page like an invisible calligrapher is writing them.

No instruction manual?

I gape at the screen. Could it be this simple? "My name is Parvin Brielle Blackwater."

My name is Parvin Bree-yell Blackwater

So it has some spelling issues, but writing just got a whole lot easier. I scan the other bubbles. Inside are the letters *S, P, E,* and *N.* I tap the *P,* and nothing on the screen changes. I tap the *E* and a little rectangle bubble pops up in the middle of the screen that asks, *Erase?*

"Yes." Nothing changes. I repeat myself, louder. "Yes."

The bubble floats, unchanging. I tap it with my finger. It pops, but nothing erases. I press the *N* and a new blank page shows up. Easy enough.

Deep breath. Where do I start? I snag the blue watch from my pack and squint at the date. "April sixteenth, twenty-one forty-nine."

No words show up on the screen. I release a frustrated grunt and tap the "talk/type" button harder than necessary. "April sixteenth, twenty-one forty-nine." The graceful script flows across the top.

I sigh. "Finally."

Finally.

"What? No! Useless thing."

What? No! Useless thing.

And I thought this would be easy. My head reminds me of the pulsing agony. I tap a few extra buttons, accidentally change fonts, try commands like, *New paragraph* and *Erase,* and at last manage a small entry with enough details to jog my memory in the future . . .

Assuming, of course, I have one.

4.16.2149

A cliff on West Wall. I fell, climbed down. Graveyard. Stampede of wolves, coyotes, and bears. Fought. God saved me. In cave bleeding. Snowing.

I press the bubble *Ss* to save my work. A miniature Clock counts down from 5 seconds to 0 before a screen message says, "Saved and Sent to Skelley Chase."

Skelley Chase—invading every part of my life. He must have programmed this before giving it to me. I wouldn't have sent my entry to him yet. I might as well get used to it, but I didn't want to share my first survival moment with him.

I reread my short entry and breathe in thick pride. I may be bleeding and freezing, but the past several hours of unexpected life have held more action, tears, thoughts, and excitement than all my time on the East Side. Even the sticky sorrow coating every minute now is refreshing.

Reid. Has he ever felt real sorrow? What did he feel when I left home? Did he experience panic or passion for life? Does he miss me? Does he embrace any hope of seeing me again?

My optimism vanishes with the closing snap of the journal. "How do I get out of here?" My voice startles me and I glance toward the darkening forest. Nothing emerges. "What do I do?" I whisper it this time.

My agony disappears with the blaze of a mental candle. Seconds later, I hold in my lap Reid's sentra and journal. I start at the end of his journal and flip backward until I reach the most recent entry.

04.15.2149, Time: 23:45

Parvin is afraid. She's afraid of dying and she's afraid of me dying. God, give her perseverance and peace. Help her pursue Your shalom.

This is dated last night. He was right—I was afraid. I still am. At the bottom of the page, in tiny print, is an asterisk.

Shalom—wholeness and completeness in God. The way things were intended to be.

This is much deeper than my understanding of the strange word. I thought it meant *peace* in a different language.

04.08.2149 Time: 05:00

It's strange heading back to Unity . . . alone. Sometimes I question if this was the right thing to do. But Parvin needs me. I can't abandon her. Besides, she needs to know.

Reid wrote this the day of the train crash—a week after our eighteenth birthday. He felt alone? What did I need to know? Even though my pain and dizziness increases by the minute, I read the entry again. Did he regret coming home from Florida? Did he regret coming to be with me? This thought hurts my heart more than any wolf bite could. Why did I think his journal would hold answers?

I close the pages and examine the sentra. It's older than Skelley Chase's. I press the small button on the edge. A tiny grating sound comes from the sentra. A slot in its side expels a thin electrosheet the size of a playing card. The sheet shows a picture of my boot with another button on the top right corner. I suppose I should have aimed the lens. I reach up and press the button on the emotigraph with my thumb. It pokes me, but I feel nothing else. I click it again. Nothing. Is it broken?

My eyelids grate like sandpaper when I blink and pressure pulls my head toward the cave floor. I set aside the sentra and release a ragged breath. I try to relax. Not much time passes before my mind swims itself back into painful sleep.

I bob in and out of slumber like an anchorless buoy, sipping water when I'm conscious enough. At one point, snow rests upon me like a cloud blanket, kissing my skin with shivers and goose bumps. I can't die this way.

God, where are You?

000.172.04.35.01

Three days before my thirteen-year-old Assessment, I woke with heavy eyelids, endless sweat, and the sensation of anvils spread across my body, pressing out my breath with each ticking minute. The thought of talking had soared out the window with the little energy I'd abandoned.

This morning, I feel the same, only there is no Mother to smooth my hair back and wash the sickness off my skin with cloths warmed from the fire.

I vomit over the cave edge and possess enough gumption to glare in the direction of the hiding wolves. That's all they get from me.

I roll onto my back with a groan and wipe my mouth with the bandage on my arm. Every spike and bump in the rock digs bruises into my aching muscles. The invisible weight presses on my forehead, but I push myself to a sitting position. My mental-smoke clears and, with several blinks, I survey the sunlit clearing below me. The skeletons look less threatening and the forest twinkles in welcome. I want to walk in it. The idea of flickering leaves and bird chirps floats in my head. I want to be there—sick or not.

God, take me into the forest.

I close my eyes to breathe in the mental picture. When I open them, I'm lying down again and the lighting has changed. I must have fallen back asleep. The cave is frigid, but the snow has stopped. I roll my heavy head to the side and groan. My cheek connects with the bitter stone.

Sitting up, blackness wafts over my vision for a moment. It relents and I see the trees. They still sparkle under the sun. My fear of the animals lessens, either from incoherence or boredom.

I check the bandages and swallow bile. The amount of dried blood covering me looks like new mottled skin. I dab water on some of the cuts and take a long drink. Parched. The loss of blood carried my hydration onto the stone. Abandoning restraint, I gulp down three more swallows. The last sip is more like a slurp. I try again. No luck. My water's gone, but I don't have energy to worry.

Tiny rocks fall from the top of the cliff and clatter among the bones. I pause in tying my last knot and peer upward. A shadow grows through the thin cloud wisps and a falling body pulls a gasp from my throat. Before the man plummets into the hard earth, he releases a screech, and I squeeze my eyes shut.

Another victim of the Wall.

A familiar pounding breaks the morning silence. Pounding that prefaced my own encounter with death cloaked in fur. Growls and yaps join the noise of the stampede. I bury my face in my pack.

"Oh God, oh God, oh God." I pray for relief from the sounds of animal mayhem. Alarm closes around me like a cocoon. Wind increases, carrying unnerving howls to my ears and stray snowflakes to my cheeks.

At least this man's death was quick. My death will be anything but. I have slow options—freeze, starve, die from infection, or feed the wolves. I've never been good at making decisions.

As the throaty grunts and animal sounds quiet, I dare a peek at the animals, all the while trying to suppress the wave of guilt that hits me remembering the Newtons. They were in trouble with the Enforcers, but what could I have done? Did they die like this?

The Wall victim is nothing but a pile of clothes. Familiar clothes. Thick and brown, a little stained. It's the Wall Keeper who sent me through a few days ago! Was it a few days? I've lost count already. Two? Three? How long have I tossed in delirious sleep?

The beasts retreat, satiated. So this is how they live—a feast is handed to them practically every day.

I place a shaking hand over my mouth and look away. How did the packs know more meat had arrived? Did they hear the impact? They couldn't smell him that fast.

His scream echoes in my mind, like a dinner bell. I look back at the animals. Slimy bones and clumps of clothing are all that remain now. The coyotes sniff around, making certain not to miss a bite.

A bird takes flight from a nearby tree, yet not a single ear twitches or nose lifts. A rabbit hops from a clump of trees to the right. It halts, staring at a wolf. The wolf sees it, but turns away. The rabbit flees back into the underbrush.

My sluggish brain turns its cogs through sleepy tar and I remember Reid telling me about dog training and other animal instruction—repetition and association. Repeat instruction and associate the desired action with a reward, sound, or command. Could these animals be so conditioned to receiving free meals they won't chase down their own food?

I shake my head and chide my stupidity. They chased *me* didn't they? They're not immune to the thrill of the hunt. But they're responsive to a scream—a scream means food. My thoughts speed up like a child at the end of a footrace. Didn't I scream when I realized I stood in a graveyard of Radical bones? My own terror brought the animals out for food. If they're full right now, couldn't I, if I keep silent, make my way down the cliff and into the forest?

Calm down. I take a mental step backward. I can't let my thoughts carry me into death, but my options are limited—stay in my cave and die or put forth an effort for survival . . . and probably die. I slurp from my water pouch before remembering nothing is left. Grey still paces for my blood. He glances up at me every few steps.

What am I doing sitting here? I thought I'd die off that cliff, but God's given me a clear message: I LET YOU LIVE.

I have my second chance and I'm spending it bleeding to death in a cave. It's time for action.

The thought goes against every physical plea in my body, but God knows my Numbers. I can't waste them again. If I'm going to believe He's got a plan, then that belief needs to start now.

In Nether Hospital, what seems like months ago, I thought I asked the impossible of Him. I asked Him to take my life somewhere fulfilling and to *do* something with it in the next six months. Now, here I am in a land no one's explored with a chance to travel and return home. I asked God for six months. He's giving them to me. The Clock *must* be mine. I'm invincible until October. Which means . . .

I meet Grey's eyes.

"You can't touch me."

14

4.18.2149 – 13:04

Going to walk through a pack of wolves. Need water. Thirsty. Sleeping and bleeding a lot. I'm invincible.

I don't say the Clock is mine. I don't trust Skelley Chase's word anymore and I doubt he'll wait to publish my biography until the Clock zeroes out. When he publishes it, the world will know our secret and Reid might lose medical care. He may even be put to trial like me. The less attention I bring to our Clock, the better.

Shoving the journal into my pack, I take one large bite of Mother's banana bread. It crawls down my throat with a thin coating of saliva.

Buckling the pack around my shoulders makes me lightheaded, but I wait with my legs dangling over the edge until my vision straightens out. The animals haven't noticed my movement yet.

I slide over the rock edge on my stomach. The bending of my spine cracks open my dried back wounds. I gasp, but hold in any sound.

The cave waves good-bye, painted with blood. My clothes are soaked and crusty. I grasp the stone for holds with shaking arms and chilled fingers. Everything is weak, except my motivation. My mind is foggy from pain and illness, my body is tired from hunger and cold, and my muscles have never been of much use. I have to move fast or I'll fall.

I let out a small pant as I shift down, trying to bend my rope-burned neck to look at my feet. My elbows and knees release tiny pops. Most of my weight rests on my toes as I work my way to the ground because my fingers and muscles seem incapable of squeezing the rock like I tell them. They've been sleeping too long. Bleeding too long.

I'm fifteen feet from the ground when the rock beneath the tip of my boot crumbles. The jerk of my body weight rips my limp hands from their holds. I slide along the cliff face and connect with the ground, hard. A small cry escapes when my legs buckle and I land on my side, banging my head against a nearby boulder. A black flash blinds me for a moment, but all I can think is, *Don't scream, don't scream, don't scream.*

Heat spreads through my body from raw agony. I whimper, praying my sounds are muffled behind the boulder. My pack is sideways and the straps pull against my throbbing wounds. I lie on the ground for a few minutes until my breathing regulates and I'm sure the wolves aren't running to eat me. My hands and the right side of my face are grated and tender.

I push myself to my knees and lean back on my heels. I place Reid's sentra in my left skirt pocket then take Father's knife from the pack, leaving the sheath inside. The blade still holds smears from when I wiped off my blood.

My world stops spinning and slowly, tenderly, I pull myself to my feet with a grimace. I'm still alive—with almost six months promised to me. These wounds will heal. I won't die of infection or pain.

God got me out of the cave. I couldn't do this alone. I've never been strong enough to descend a cliff with a fever and wounded body. My perseverance must be coming from Him.

With a deep breath, I creep between the boulder and the cliff. A small peek through a crack reveals the animals mulling around the clearing. Some coyotes sniff at old bones. A few wolves lie on the ground with their heads on their paws—Grey is one of them. Where are the bears?

My motivation is smeared somewhere on the rock and I start to shake. I can't do this. What if they're still hungry? What if I was wrong?

Over-thinking—never something I've done before. But my impulse is a little broken today.

I close my eyes and take a deep breath through my nose. My energy seeps into the frozen dirt the longer I stand by the boulder. I straighten my pack and it scrapes my wounds. *I have to start somewhere, right, God?*

My eyes open and dart to a lump on the ground between the boulder and cliff. My rope. I look up. This is near where the Wall Keeper fell. My rope must have been caught in the closed door until it opened again for the next victim.

I stuff it in my pack, tangled and unorganized. I'll coil it later. Right now, I'm just thankful to have it back.

The lazy animals settle in the afternoon sun.

Don't think. Not the wisest motivational thought, but enough to make me move. I squeeze between the boulder crack before I can back down and walk toward the beasts—not tiptoeing because that makes me nervous. Not thinking because I know I'll panic. Just regular heel-to-toe steps, slowed to a near crawl.

They continue about their business. I'm a few feet away from the first coyote. He balances on three legs and licks his paw. I stare straight ahead, but monitor his movements through the corner of my eye. He watches me pass.

My pace increases, but I will myself not to run. Every muscle tightens with each coyote and wolf head that looks up. I meet none of their eyes. Grey is ahead. He's staring at me. I barely breathe, clenching my tongue between my teeth to keep from muttering like a maniac. Before I even reach him, Grey lifts the corner of a lip and releases a wet snarl.

God, God, God . . .

My fist clutches my little knife and I keep walking. Faster. Faster. Movement behind me tickles my ears—licking sounds. I imagine the pack preparing to charge. After all, I still *smell* like dinner. I smell like human. Why didn't I think of that? I'm covered in blood.

I break my statuesque gait and peek over my shoulder. A line of coyotes and wolves lick my dripping blood off the ground. I suck in a breath through my teeth. The smell of dirty, matted hair reaches my nose. Gag.

I return my gaze forward and reach my left hand into my pocket. I inch the sentra out enough so the lens aims toward the wolves. The small movement captures Grey's attention even more. I press the button and push it back into my pocket as it makes the grinding sound to expel the picture.

Grey raises himself to all fours, but he takes his time. A tiny wheeze interrupts his snarls and his front leg buckles. Could he be wounded from his plummet from the rock face?

Serves him right for shredding me like a round of cheese.

Six months, right God?

My fear dissipates. There's no logical reason for it to leave—I'm still surrounded by carnivores craving human flesh—but the fear is gone. Completely. My muscles relax, my stride turns normal, and I look Grey in his cold reflective eyes.

"I've been promised six months."

He snarls.

Chin up. Deep breath. I stride toward the forest. Grey doesn't move, doesn't blink. I enter the line of trees, kicking aside a skull on my way. Grey's growls die with the light once I'm among the forestry. The other animals remain on the tree line, bored and wandering. My heartbeat quickens, like my apprehensive nerves are working again. A headache pounds. I press my palm against the scrape on my scalp.

Keep walking.

Breathing grows difficult. I slow my pace and suck in air, pushing the licking sounds out of my mind and surveying my newest scenery. The forest had looked thin from my thumbprint cave, but now that I'm in it, the thickness increases a few yards in.

I duck beneath spiky pine branches and weave through oaks. My hair snags old spider webs and their strands snap like miniature harp strings. I brush a hand over my head to rid it of any spiders, but regret the movement as my bandage slides over the cuts on my head.

Though I hurry through the forest as best I can, pain reminds me of my needs. I need to care for the wounds. I need water. I need heat. I need to eat. My stomach gnaws on my small bite of banana bread like cow cud. It'll have to do for now because I mustn't stop until I'm well into the thicket—well away from this cliff trap.

My legs feel clumsy after not using them for so long. I trip on branches more often than I step over them. Pushing aside curled parched ferns with my shins takes as much effort as bending the stiff tree tufts in my path.

I won't last long.

My muscles already shake when I brush forest dust off my bandages. My determination to walk to safety competes with my need to rest.

A river. That's all I need. I'll stop at the river, but I don't hear the rush of a single water droplet. There must be one near. Where do the wolves drink? They can't live off blood.

I stop trekking as if to allow my stupidity to slide off my shoulders. I can't go to the river. If it's the lone source of water, that's where the wolves will go. I need to get *away* from them.

"But I need water." The forest gobbles up my voice and I resume my painful walk. I wiggle my fingers against the knife in my hand, reminding myself it's there.

Water. I can't stop thinking about it and, now that my mind is fixated, the word turns into a chant. *Water. Water. Water.* I swallow, but my saliva disintegrates into the dry folds of my throat. The forest air smells like dust, which aggravates my thirst.

Water. Water. Water.

I stumble and catch myself on a tree. The bark is lined with sap. I pull my hand away and rub the goop on my skirt.

The light doesn't change as I walk. Is time even passing? I stick and unstick my fingers with every few steps. The movement is like a clock ticking away the mindless time. My eyelids droop and I stop trying to lift my feet over the dead branches claimed by winter. Something crawls along the back of my neck. I swat it and grimace.

God, where am I even going? Where can I go? I don't know what's ahead or what's above. I don't have a purpose other than leaving the wolves behind. *Where do You want me to go?*

He urged me to go in the forest and He knows I need to find the river. I have to keep walking until He gets me to it. "Can we find the river *today*?" I ask with the little breath I have to spare. "I don't think I can wait until tomorrow."

The light is fading. Or are the trees thickening? I blink upward. Dust falls in my eyes. As I rub them with my fists, I stumble. My momentum propels me forward, but I can't see and collide with a tree. I spin, disoriented. My hands and knees meet the underbrush. Sticks poke through my already torn leggings and the impact jolts my shoulders. I lower myself to the forest floor. It's so good to be down.

Rest. Calm. Silent.

Wolves.

I lift my head with a groan. The foul beasts won't let my mind relax until I'm safe away from them. I squint ahead and my breathing pauses. A glint. A flicker. Sunlight blinds my eyes for a millisecond.

I'm on my feet, running with the last bit of energy in my limbs. A branch slaps my face, but I break through without slowing. I stagger onto a stretch of mud in a clearing. Mere yards ahead, a lake laps a ragged shore in welcome. The sun glints off its surface like a polished pocket watch and the canyon wall stretches high in the distance. To the left, the forest inclines up rolling hills. Out of the canyon, maybe?

I fumble for my water pouch, hands shaking, and walk toward shore. My breath quickens and my throat grows even drier, yearning for liquid. I glance around. No wolves, but the mud sports hundreds of paw prints. Are they from wolves or coyotes? Either way, something occupies this stretch of lake on a regular basis.

I should get water and leave, but the thought of walking any further weighs my heart like an anchor. Tears spring up like daisies. I don't allow them to fall . . . yet. I don't have time for a breakdown.

The lake stretches away like a glorious carpet, flanked by thick forest trees until it curves out of sight. I kneel down, resisting the urge to leap in. The water is smoky with dirt. I hold the pouch poised over the surface. Water to my left looks a little cleaner so I scoot over a few steps and dunk the pouch, averting my eyes from floating gunk. If the animals can drink it and survive, so can I.

The first gulp is cool and desperate, like heaven in liquid form. I gasp and take another sip. The heaven feeling fades when something slimy slides down my throat. I gag and lower the water pouch. I cough twice before spitting pathetically in the lake. The desperation of my thirst isn't enough to stop me from imagining frog eggs hatching in my stomach.

Mother used to boil our water before she and Father installed a kitchen pump. Boiling kills all things dangerous—including frog eggs. I thank God for her logic in packing her coffee pot for me. *She* thought of the danger of drinking frog eggs.

I lean back on my heels. The pressure on my legs moves me to a sitting position. My bandages are so dirty they almost blend with my clothes. They smell rancid. I need to wash. Just the idea saps my energy. The lake is already blurry to my vision. I need to rest. I need to find a place *to* rest. I need to clean. I need to eat. I need a fire.

Which comes first?

A shiver sends me hunting for wood. Forget the wolves—I'm building a fire here. I'm not heading back into the woods where they can lurk behind trees. They're afraid of fire, right? Or is that from storybooks?

"I guess I'll test it." I'm growing more comfortable with the sound of my voice echoing off the blank atmosphere.

Dead branches line the edge of the lake. Even though it snowed recently, the tiny flakes never made it through the treetops and the branches are dry. Winter wind must have been fierce because my supply of fallen wood is endless. I gather as much as I can through the pain of bending and stretching. Every time I want to rest I force myself to pick up one more stick. I need enough to last through the night and, if there's anything I know how to do—other than sewing—it's how to build and maintain a fire.

The fire takes mere seconds to set ablaze. A couple blank pages from Reid's journal spur the kindling. I'd like to think it would have started without the help of paper, but I'm more concerned about my low supply of matches than my pride. I have fewer than thirty.

The blaze grows. I build a second fire a few yards away. With plenty of wood to keep both going strong through the night, I feel more protected sleeping between them.

The mud is cold when I sit down—half frozen and half wet. I shiver and my wounds twinge. I stare at my injuries. They're swollen and smell like something dead and decayed. They must be infected. What do I do against infection? The longer I stare at them, the faster my heart races. If the Clock isn't mine, I could die in my sleep. Tonight. All because of these wounds.

I can't sleep yet. I mustn't, despite my body's exhausted pleading. My small pouch of threads and needles tumbles out of my bag as I try to find it. I grip it tight.

It's time to sew.

15

If I could sterilize my brain like I'm sterilizing my needle, I'd burn the wolves right out of it. My sewing needle rests on the shiny surface of the knife held as close to the fire as I can get it. It is bent like a crude fishhook, the product of my careful pounding with a rock. It still might snap in half.

I hold my hand still so the needle doesn't slip. The heat licks my skin. My adrenaline still pumps and I take advantage of my courage while it lingers.

My injuries sting from scrubbing them with the lake water. Reddish streaks line my arms and legs, radiating from the wound. I washed the bandages and my wounds one last time with boiled water from the kettle, then hung the bandages on sticks shoved in the mud between the fires. They're almost dry. Perfect timing.

I start stitching on my leg. The skin is swollen and separated. I clamp my lips shut. The doubled black thread hanging from my needle might as well be a noose. I can't do this.

With a deep breath, I poise the needle tip by my skin. Five stitches. Five stitches and it will be over. The gash needs twice that amount, but I need a less daunting goal.

My thumb and forefinger tense, squeezing the needle. I press the point into my skin with a squeal. My skin moves from the pressure, but I feel nothing. I frown at the cut and push again. The needle goes through my skin, leaving the black thread hanging like a tail out the other side. I tap my leg with my forefinger. Nothing.

Health-wise, this can't be good. Stitches-wise, it's exactly what I need.

Once I get past the sickening fact I'm sewing my own skin, I tie up nine painless stitches. My arm is not so lucky. Every point and tug against the lacerations draws a choked, "Ouch," from my lips. I leave the other cuts to fend for themselves—bandages will have to do once they're dry.

My arm throbs and my leg is cold and bleeding, but I stitched myself up like a regular doctor. Reid would never believe me. Mother would say it's about time.

Pride. It flows over me. I even pull out the sentra, aim it at my stitched leg, and press the button. I giggle at the prick in my thumb compared to the needle I shoved through my skin.

I place the expelled emotigraph between the pages of Reid's journal for safekeeping and take out my first one from when I sat in the cave. The emotigraph is thin, but stiff. I resist the urge to snap it in half. It's durable—an electronic device of the twenty-second century. The indented grey button on the top right corner beckons me. I succumb.

The prick is followed by a wave of uncontrolled sadness and fear—fear of death, despair at the loss of Reid's companionship. He hadn't wanted to come home to see me on our six-month Assessment. Didn't he care about me?

Moments after I think this, the negative emotions vanish and my state of pride and victory return. I almost can't remember the despair. I turn over the thin emotigraph.

"Wow."

It works. I just took a swallow of emotions opposite to my mood. They didn't feel like mine. Emotigraphs—pictures of emotions. The name makes more sense now. The concept, however, remains foreign. How does a tiny button collect and record that? Are emotions something that run in my *blood*? I spent a week giving Skelley Chase my emotions, but never experienced this side of the emotigraph. This is what my readers will feel.

A headache flicks my temple with a torturous rhythm. Darkness is thick beyond my fires. I can't bear to look at it, to provide my imagination with ammunition for nightmares.

I adjust my pack as a pillow. The bandages are dry, but I allow my cuts to gather air until morning. Before going to sleep, I eat a full slice of Mother's banana bread and add thick branches to my fires.

The night is restless and cold. I don't move much due to the pain from my injuries. Twice, I wake to nothing but glowing coals before piling on more wood in a frenzy. Fitful hours later, light arrives over the treetops with welcomed warmth. My fires crackle high, the sun beats on my skin, and yet I shiver.

A fever.

I rummage in my bag, pull out the banana bread, and slather a slice with Mother's caramel apple butter. My first bite brings memories of last Christmas, when Mother served it with milk toast for breakfast. The thick butter sauce glides across my tongue. The fragrance of December and spices hits my nose.

I chew the soft bread longer than necessary, savoring every texture, every flavor. After this, it's dried meat from the rag holding Mother's funny mixture of food. If only I could thank her. Instead, I'd scoffed at her attempts to help me survive. I was too obsessed with my own death.

The dried meat takes more effort to chew than I'm willing to give. My jaw grows tired and my headache increases as I try, so I resign to suck on it. My sick, empty body welcomes the salt. I take another nap while the fires burn low and the sun enriches the chilled dirt. My first thought upon waking is my need for a plan. As I chew on another slice of bread, I spread my belongings out in front of me.

My gaze falls on the nanobook from Skelley Chase. Do I want to complete this? Do I want to fuel Skelley Chase's attempt to use me to boost his fame? I don't understand his motivation behind betraying me. I guess my story wasn't good enough without me risking death.

I hate him, but I can't stop the vision of Radicals falling off the cliff on this side. If I help Skelley Chase publish my story, maybe other Radicals will find hope—hope for survival and purpose. I need to do this for their sake, for my family's sake. They need to know I'm alive and I'm fighting.

The blame for our world's separation may fall on our ancestors' shoulders, but no one ever petitioned to take down the Wall—to renew the destroyed Earth. Did this separation kill the people who chose to stay on the West? Did we kill the Independents?

Then again, the Independents rebelled against government. They wanted to live in a wasteland. They used their own destroyed cities to start the Wall. Whatever happened to them on this side was likely deserved.

Still . . . what happened? It's possible to survive without a government, without electricity, and without technology, right? I'm doing it right now. These people stayed here for that very reason—they must be alive. Somewhere.

I must find the Independents. I want to see how they live *now*. Is it better than our structured system in the East? Do they have Clocks? Are they happy? Do they need rescuing? Could they help me rescue Radicals?

I look around the beach. I won't find anyone here. After encountering the wolves, I don't blame the Independents for avoiding this place. They must be further in the forest, away from the canyon.

I open my journal to record my thoughts. Seeing them in print may help me organize them better. When the nanobook turns on, the *Contact* bubble pulses red. I press it and a screen evolves with the title *Messages From:*

Below this is one pulsing bubble name:

Skelley Chase

I tap it. His message is short and rude.

-You're going to have to do better than that. Are you a writer or not? -SC

I imagine his bored smirk and press the reply button. "First, Mister Chase, I'm *not* a writer—you said so yourself. Second, since you programmed this device to send you everything the instant I try and save it, I have no opportunity to add to or edit my entries."

The nanobook scripts out every annoyed word, adding italics and capitalized print where necessary. I press the *Ss* since it's the obvious button on the screen.

His reply comes within seconds with a tiny *pop* sound like a soap bubble bursting.

-I see you're still alive and sassy. Say the word, "Save" or press S. The Ss button means save-and-send. -SC

I'd prefer a more offended response, but at least he provided me with some guidance. Seeing my journal entries now, they *do* look bland, especially when I think of my feelings at the time. I edit them and elaborate, inserting details. A chill runs through me as I describe the skeletons coating the canyon floor.

To spite the Enforcers, I mention the Newtons. Tears escape when I say the name aloud. I try not to think of the two little girls being eaten by wolves. Their fate is the hardest to handle. Mrs. Newton was more kind to me in the few months she lived on Straight Street than all of Unity Village has been in the entirety of my life.

Once finished, I press *Ss*. I pray my words are enough to show readers the horrors of the West thus far. Maybe even grow compassion for the Radicals, though they'll gain more insight from the emotigraphs than my writing. This thought reminds me of my thin emotigraphs tucked inside Reid's journal. How do I send them to Skelley Chase?

I fish them from between the pages and examine my electronic journal. A long slit lines one side—the perfect size for an emotigraph. I insert the short side and the nanobook sucks it in. It whirs for a moment, makes a *ding!* and spits the emotigraph back out. On the screen of my journal entry, the picture of my boot shows up alongside a small bubble saying, *Press purple button for emotigraph.*

The expelled emotigraph is now a clear silver. I insert and download the other emotigraphs to my journal, save them, and return them into a long slit in Reid's sentra. The sentra whirs and settles to silence after each one. I don't send them to Skelley Chase yet. They're too personal to give to someone who betrayed me.

I return to the *Messages* page to see if he sent me any further sarcasm. His name-bubble is still, floating messageless, but my eyes fix upon a new bubble. It pulses beneath Skelley Chase's with a single word in it:

Unknown

I frown. Unknown? Is it something new from Skelley Chase? When I press it, a single sentence shows up in what looks like handwritten script, nothing like Skelley Chase's flowing cursive.

~I'm currently rushed for time, but if you are alive, you may return.

16

I swallow a lump of cement and stare at the script. Return?

My fingers shake. I look around my fire haven, but nothing is different. How does this person know where I am? Is this Skelley Chase changing his mind? I peer back at the screen. I mustn't get my hopes up. Too nervous to speak out loud, I click the *Talk/Type* bubble and type a response.

~Who are you?

Blood pounds in my ears as I wait for a reply. Is it Mother? Reid? Who else knows I'm alive on this side? My nanobook releases a tiny *pop*. Unknown has written.

~You've survived! I did not know what the West held. Have you found any other Radicals? Are the Newtons alive?

I study the questions. My first impulse is to answer them, yet this person still did not reveal a name. It's not Mother—the questions don't match her character. Father wouldn't know how to use a nanobook. Reid might pull out technology like this. The curiosity behind the questions match his personality.

~Reid? My breath quickens. He *does* care. Did he know I'd survive? Was his faith in me so strong that his odd attitude at my departure was just a form of peace? Perhaps I've misjudged him.

Pop.

~Reid is your brother, right?

My entire body slumps. Not Reid. Not Mother. Not anyone I know because everyone who knows me wouldn't have to ask. So who is this stranger telling me to return? *~For time's sake, who* are *you?*

~My name is Solomon Hawke. I'm an Enforcer in Unity Village.

I let out a long breath. Hawke—the young, attractive Enforcer who escorted the Newtons. The one person who expressed true sorrow over my situation.

-You want me to return? Through Opening Three? How? When?

If I continue to rest here by the lake, I might be healed enough in a few days to climb back up that cliff. But the wolves . . . could I face them again? I'd have to.

-I'm the temporary Wall Keeper at Opening Three until the new one arrives. I can have it open until darkness falls. I know it's not long.

My heart sinks like a victim of quicksand. Not long? That's not even twelve hours. I could never return and climb the cliff in that amount of time, even if I found overhangs on which to rest.

-It's not enough, Mr. Hawke.

Every letter erases the residue of hope on my heart. I want to beg for a longer window, ask Hawke why he didn't contact me sooner, demand freedom, but something twists my heart like a wet rag. It's a pull to continue seeking. If I returned now, would I feel relief or would I feel like I missed out on my chance?

I escaped the wolves. I survived a fall from the top of a cliff. I stitched my own leg. I can't stop yet. I want to leave behind a story and show people what I've pushed through. Will Skelley Chase keep his promise to publish my biography after my Numbers run out?

Something nags at my mind. He never promised. He said he'd try. What if it's already published? I've been gone, what, three days? Four? Has it been that long already? Memory of home feels like a faded life of yesterday.

I pull *The Daily Hemisphere* from my pack and scan the table of contents on the side. I don't see my name, Skelley Chase's, or the word *Radical* anywhere. The same holds true for the three days before now. The only interesting headline is about new medical lenience from the government: *Flu Shots Now Available to Citizens with Numbers 6 Months and Higher.*

As far as I know, Skelley Chase hasn't published my biography yet—that, or the government is trying to hide it, but news and government have never been friends. They feed off each other's drama. The newspaper will spill anything the government tries to hide—including my survival across the Wall. I'll keep my eye on the news until something leaks.

A *pop* alerts me to a new message from Hawke.

-You're sure you can't make it? Have you seen the Newtons? How many people are over there?

His questions hold desperation, but I have no answers to satisfy him. I try not to dwell on the Newtons, but I can't help thinking the skull I tripped on was awfully tiny.

-I am the only one. I don't think the Newtons survived. I'm sorry.

My finger pauses over the *send* button. A sense of guilt brushes against me. Why did I survive when the Newtons died to stay together? Perhaps his offer of return was more for the Newtons than for me. Either way, I think I owe him an explanation.

-I survived by miracle alone, Enforcer Hawke.

A long pause follows my message. What is he thinking?

-I understand. I'm sorry, Miss Blackwater. Keep your NAB close. If I find another way to help you, I will.

I stare at his words. They are sad. Blunt. Like they're written by someone who's resigned himself to an aching heart for the rest of his Numbers. *-What's a NAB?*

-A nanobook. It's the device with which we are communicating. I must leave for now. Tally ho, Miss Blackwater.

His bubble remains still after this. Something in me sinks with disappointment. I enjoyed the momentary communication. I want to share with someone—share my pain of trying to survive. Instead, I remain alone. My communicators are a betrayer and an Enforcer.

Did Hawke replace the Wall Keeper whom the wolves devoured? What a sad death for the Wall Keeper after his many years of service. He was a Radical all this time. Or did he sneak through for his Goodbye? If he had control of the Wall, he could have skirted the system.

My fingers tremble around the NAB edges. I itch to contact Mother, but I can't trust Skelley Chase to convey a message to her. They share a secret. When Mother didn't come to my hearing, she'd been with Skelley Chase. What emotion painted her face when I asked her about it? Guilt? Nervousness? It had more to it than her just sewing a skirt for me. I wish I'd paid closer attention.

No matter. The less I'm vulnerable with Skelley Chase, the less power he will have over my family and me. Yet, I have to keep my family updated on my progress. They need to know I'm alive. I must keep them informed through Skelley Chase and my biography.

I sigh. Why do I feel so alone? Abandoned?

I'M HERE.

I jump at the words that enter my mind like fire. Did God speak or just implant the words into my consciousness?

You are *here.* I hope He hears me. *That's what I've been told. You're always here.* Mild comfort arises, but there's no response. I look up into the bright noon sky. *"Are* You here?"

Nothing in the scenery changes—no gust of wind, no booming voice, no earthquake. My comfort fades. I lean back on the dirt. Will I ever figure out how to talk to Him? Reid went through so many phases as his relationship with God progressed. He began by praying in old English, then moved to kneeling, then to standing with arms raised. I can't do any of that. It's not comfortable. I don't talk to other people like this, why must I talk to God like this?

Maybe that's why He's not listening, because I talk with Him as if he's a peer. He's God. Perhaps I *should* talk to Him differently.

I push myself to a standing position. *Almighty God, grant me Your— uh, Thy—presence and protection as I depart.* I cringe, both from stretching sores and my stiff request. I feel even more like I'm talking to a tree stump when I word it like this. "Sorry, You know it's all fake. You'll have to tolerate my incoherent babbling. Otherwise I'll never view You as a God I can talk to."

Upon inspection, my wounds look the same as last night. Though I'm a bit dizzy, I clean some of the dried blood off my stitches. The suture are still numb to the touch. The bandages are warm from hanging by the fires and soothe my injuries as I rewrap them. I've used half of Mother's small pouch of salve. My back wounds are more flexible.

A moment of rest passes. With my eyes closed, I block Hawke's offer out of my head. Focus. This is my chance to live the adventure bottled in every human's heart—to be part of something great. To save lives.

I return my belongings to my pack, loop my filled canteen through my belt, and survey the lake. The crackle of my dying fires is the only afternoon noise. A thin bank runs along the edges of the lake, choked by trees in thicker patches. It's best if I cross to the other side. These wolves need to be left behind.

My pack scrapes against my wounds as I slide it over my shoulders. With a wince, I tighten the straps and adjust my undershirt. I tuck my knife in the belt loop on my skirt and slip my NAB into a pocket on the opposite side. It is bulky, but no more uncomfortable than carrying my Clock around my entire life.

I follow the left border of the lake, toward the hills out of the canyon. The brush is thick and stiff, leaning over the bank. Branches snap instead of bend, rocks spill into the icy water, sent there from my disjointed stumbles.

The lake stretches around a bend in the shore. Rounds of ice float in the middle of its waters. In Unity Village, the ice is long gone by now.

The sun overhead is not as warm as I'm used to. The temperature here resembles late February more than mid-April—another side effect of the towering Wall. My blue watch says it's already noon.

Ten minutes pass before I reach the end of the lake. I scoop a few handfuls of water from the shadowed icy portion of shore. It tastes a little cleaner. I swish some in my mouth, rubbing my tongue over the film coating my teeth. Why didn't I bring a toothbrush? A pouch of baking soda for toothpaste? Soap?

Scrubbing with my finger makes little difference. I sigh. Leaving the boiled water in my canteen for later, I start up the hill. My calves burn as I reach a steep incline. I cling to brittle branches to hoist myself up. A bird screeches in the distance with what sounds like a sore throat. I get the feeling it's yelling at me to leave.

I reach a level portion of hill and stop, gulping for air, before attempting the next incline. My toes are numb and my legs throb. Bandaged or not, my wounds take a beating from the walking and the branches. I shiver from the echo of the fever that held my body captive the past few days. I shouldn't push myself.

Yes, push! The thought comes from my restless dragon. *It's about time.*

The lake rests a hundred feet below me. Across it, some forest, but in the distance the Wall stretches high from the top of the cliff, shadowing the scraggly treetops below as the sun passes over. It's less organized on this side—lumpy with cracks, vines, and moss crawling like diseases and tumors across its surface. It appears so close, even though I've traveled away from it. Are the wolves still at its base?

I take a deep breath and force myself to continue a little longer. I can't rest yet. I must build my stamina if I expect to find the Independents before I run out of food.

God will help me find them, right? He helped me survive the wolves and He's promised me the next five months and a handful of days. I don't understand why. I've never given Him much reason to prolong my life.

My thoughts drift back to Hawke. He wanted to rescue me. Maybe he's a rogue Enforcer. I smile at the thought. What would the government do to him? Smash his Clock? Send him across the Wall? I could use some company.

I shake my head. Silly daydreams.

The incline lessens and I eye my canteen, gauging my thirst. After my recent encounter with dehydration, I'm not anxious to repeat the incident. A tiny sip swished around in my mouth suffices for now, but the swallow torments me.

I devote several minutes to locating a shaded tree for an outhouse. I'm in the middle of nowhere with no sign of human life, but still keep a sharp eye when dropping my britches in the open. A spare wool bandage serves as toilet paper, which I then wrap with the clean remains, swearing to wash it at the first sight of water.

Why didn't I pack toilet paper? Necessities? I didn't plan. And now I'm understanding how much I love being clean.

Hours creep by as I trudge. The sun warms a little. I stop in a clearing and let the rays shine on my chilled face. My nose tingles when I scrunch it. I drop my pack on the ground and roll my shoulders. They ache from the small constant weight. My back itches and burns from the pack's movement against my sores.

Mother's banana bread is over half gone. My hunger screams, but I limit myself to a single slice. Thank you, God, for the bland density of cornmeal. I've never tasted bread made with flour, but it looks so much softer and more airy in the Upper City magazines. Father says people once used wheat in almost every meal—before the Wall, of course. Everything was different when the world was bigger.

I pull out the NAB. Both Skelley Chase's and Hawke's name-bubbles sit silent and unmoving. Why do I wish I had a message? They're both dangerous.

Not bothering with a journal entry, I unroll *The Daily Hemisphere*. I'm mildly surprised to see the numerous headlines again. Life in the East should have stopped now that I'm not there. Don't people realize I'm gone?

I look at the first headline I'd skipped earlier, hoping to dispel the forlorn feeling creeping into my heart.

President Garraty Proposes Controversial Law Adjustments.

President Garraty has been a good president as far as I know—complacent and friendly. At least we don't hate him. Yet I can't think of anything he's done. That's how the public likes it—no extreme changes. Our nation refuses to pursue flexibility. Why should we? We've survived this long without it.

I scan the article about the changes. One is placing a comprehensive age for the age-limit restrictions—voting, alcohol, smoking, driving, and processed food.

When Reid and I turned sixteen, Mother and Father threw us a party with chocolate-flavored corn cereal, vanilla pudding, a bubbly drink, and chewy meat rolls called hot dogs. I got sick that night and vowed never to eat processed food again, but when morning came, I returned to the cereal and bubbly drink.

The morning of my Good-bye marked the last day I'd tasted processed food. Did Mother eat the rest after I left? Did she think of me?

I put things away. Chills arrest my muscles. The sunrays have passed out of range and the sky is grey. I loop the buttons on my coat to keep it shut. My eyes grow heavy and a headache throbs. I'm tempted to lie down in this little clearing and sleep, but I've made little progress. The Wall is still visible in the distance and I want that stone monster out of my sight.

Time feels different on this side of the Wall. I look at the sleepy sky and then around the forest. Bugs have calmed their buzzing and spiders creep out on the trees. Dinnertime. I glance at my blue watch, unaccustomed to its presence. Spot on: six o'clock.

My salivary glands tingle at the thought of Mother's corn bread and lamb. Is she finding it hard to cook for two people instead of three? Did Reid stay home or return to Florida? What if he's not healing as well as we hoped? Does he worry I'm dead? He wouldn't know if I died.

I sit straight with a jolt. What if *he* dies and *I* don't know it?

In a moment of panic, I pull out my NAB and type a wild message to Skelley Chase.

~Is Reid still alive?

As I watch the screen, my body starts to calm. It wouldn't matter much if Reid died while I'm in the West. I can't return until my five months are over. By that point, I'll be a few days from death myself. Still, I release a breath when Skelley Chase's reply pops on the screen.

-As far as I know, yes. I'm not your family's keeper. -SC

I hoist my pack, but drop it from my shoulders as soon as I've lifted it up. My back aches. The sores have turned stiff and tender to the touch. I hang the pack over one shoulder instead and leave my clearing as I hear a distant clap of thunder. The sky darkens. Trees turn black as the setting sun steals the color away.

I make it another thirty minutes before exhaustion sets in. Every muscle aches with sickness. How long will it take before I can travel a full day at a regular pace instead of this slow, painful crawl?

Rain droplets splash on my head. Panic rises in my chest. It's almost dark. What is out here? What is watching me?

My breath fogs my vision and I tug my sleeve over my fingers. Should I start a fire before the rain gets too heavy or will the rain put it out?

The downpour increases and drives me under a wide tree. The branches are bare and thin; in fact, all the trees around me stretch tall like wiry soldiers. Dry cracks crawl up the grey-brown trunks and patches of crisp dried leaves still cling to the tips of the branches, mixing with the small spring buds. They won't block a single drop.

Dead leaves layer the ground, left over from autumn and rejected by the soil. Short evergreens dot the area, ranging ten to fifteen feet high. I sprint to the nearest one—at least I feel like I'm sprinting; it's more of a hobble. The rain pounds harder and the wind picks up. Lightning flashes, nearer now, and I spare a prayer it doesn't strike my tree.

My bandages are dirty, but they'll have to stay on through the night. I don't want to change them in the rain. If there's one thing I know about stitches, it's to keep them dry as long as possible. My flimsy thread won't hold my skin together for long.

I stomp down the yellow grass tickling my thighs around the pine tree and lay out my spare shirt on the forest floor, tucking it as far under the prickly branches as possible. The worst that will happen is a little dirt rubbing into the material.

I shove my pack beneath the tree, leaving out a strip of beef to gnaw on until I fall asleep. I peel off my coat and skirt then tuck myself under the tree on top of my extra shirt. Pines are thick, that's why they always have so many spiders—the rain can't disturb the webs.

The ground is prickly, but my bandages provide some cushion. I wrap my coat around my torso and spread what's left of my skirt over the rest of my body. It takes several minutes to convince my legs to bend enough to tuck under the blanket.

I leave my knife and NAB in my skirt pockets in case I need them in the night. The gale increases. I shove the beef in my mouth and tuck my head under my coat, trying to block the sound, increase the warmth, and ward the spiders away from my ears.

Goodnight, God. I don't know what to pray. I'm not sure if I can force out a 'thank You' for anything right now. I'm under a spider tree in a storm. *This doesn't feel like You're on my side. Did this need to be part of my calling? What is my calling again?*

The only response is silence.

17

000 . 168 . 07 . 00 . 55

I spend two days under the spider tree, curled in a stiff ball as the rain pours down. I cry some because I'm cold. Then I cry because I hate that I'm crying. I don't touch the sentra for fear that it might sense some of my despair and send it to Skelley Chase.

Wafting in and out. Fever. Delirium. Sickened sleep. My sores throb, but I don't change the bandages. My appetite is gone—maybe from sickness, maybe from prolonged hunger.

When morning dawns the third day on a clear, stormless sky, I drag my aching form out from under the branches. My damp clothes stick to my skin. My hair snags on pine needles. Hollowness eats the core of my body.

I manage to stand and look around at the wet forest. The rain shines on the leaves and everything looks greener. The next several minutes I stretch as best I can, then I leave this portion of forest, dragging my pack along the forest floor. Ten minutes pass before I can lift it onto my shoulders. One hour. Just one hour before I allow a rest.

My stomach shrivels with every foodless step. Reid's scolding voice drifts through my mind: *"You're getting too thin. You need to eat."*

I force a corner of banana bread into my mouth. The muscles in my throat spasm. It takes four tries to swallow.

The terrain continues upward. I stop several times to catch my breath, and heave a sigh when the land levels out. After forty-five minutes, I sink to the damp forest floor and let the chilled sunrays hit my face. The branches above are thinner. Tiny flowers mix with the green buds and leaves. It's spring in the West.

I pull *The Daily Hemisphere* from my pack. Nothing about me yet. I let out another breath. Reid is still safe.

The other headlines don't earn a single blink. Now that I'm not in the East, I don't care so much about what's happening over there. I won't live there again until the week of my death. What does it matter?

I reach deeper in my pack for the NAB's leather cover. My hand searches through tangled coils of rope until it finds the nanobook. It feels thicker. I pull it out. It's not my NAB, but my Bible. An instant pang hits me. I haven't opened my Bible during this entire week in the West.

A week? Really? I look at the blue watch. Sure enough. Thanks to the delirium and fever, six whole days disappeared from my Clock in what feels like the course of two. Panic flutters across my heart. How many weeks do I have left? I've done nothing meaningful yet. I need to find the Independents. They'll provide insight. Guidance . . . .

Something.

God? Are You there? Does He even listen? My prayers feel like a pious form of talking to myself.

I open the Bible and let it flop to an open page. I scan the page for divine guidance, but all I see are a hundred repetitions of the word *begat* surrounded by names I can't pronounce. I flip a chunk of pages to the right and stop when I hit what resembles a poem. It starts with, *"Pray then like this:"*

Wow, coincidence?

When I start reading, I hear Reid's voice in my mind: *"Our Father in Heaven, hallowed be Your name."*

I've heard Reid pray this so many times before, but never focused on what it meant. Is it truly instruction on how to talk to God?

"Our Father in Heaven, hallowed be Your name." What does *hallowed* even mean? Farther down in the poem there's mention of bread. "Give us this day our daily bread."

Mother's banana bread is almost gone. Maybe God will make the last slice regenerate every time I look away.

I read the five verses three times, repeating them in my head, and they stick like honey. For once, I'm proud of my memory. My peers used to say normal people don't remember words like I do. They called me a freak. Reid told me they were jealous, but I think they were snobs with a higher income. They had access to paper and didn't *have* to memorize.

Even with the verses now in my head, I don't like the formality of the prayer—I never have. *Hallowed* makes me think of Halloween.

I reword the passage and mutter it aloud. "God, help me figure You out. Do with me what You will, please give me food, keep me safe, and forgive me for whatever I've done wrong."

As I finish, I think of the Newtons and cringe. Regret sinks even lower knowing my punishment for helping them would have been exile across the Wall. I'd be in the same position I'm in—but they might be alive.

I shove the Bible back into the pack and locate the NAB in my pocket. Skelley Chase's message bubble pulsates with three new messages:

-*Are you still alive? -SC*

-*Send me an emotigraph. -SC*

-*Are you dead? -SC*

I respond with a terse, -*I'm alive, but sick. I think from wolf bites.* I follow this with my emotigraph from the cave. Time for a journal update.

4.22.2149 – 08:20

Slept under a spider-infested, short pine tree for two days through freezing storm. Sick, tired, and very very cold. Can't believe a whole week has passed already.

I send it to him at the same time I receive another message.

-*I'm relieved to see you alive, Parvin. I knew you had the perseverance to survive. It's admirable. -SC*

His niceness reminds me of his deception. Unsure how to respond, I close the NAB. Hawke's bubble remains still. I want to send him a message, to ask if he has any other ways to help me. But how can he?

In the containment center he pulled me away from Skelley Chase and the other Enforcers. He fought for me. Was his compassion for me or for the Newtons? I hope it was for me. I can't get his face out of my mind. He cared so much.

I abandon my hesitation and press his bubble. Hawke and I are separated by a number of walls—literal rock and stone, status, the law. It's doubtful I'll see him again. Why care if I overstep any bounds by contacting him? I've already overstepped too many legal bounds to ever warrant the title *innocent* again.

~I'm sorry about the Newtons, Mr. Hawke. I was their neighbor. I should have done something.

My stomach grumbles, sick and hollow. I stare at the NAB for several seconds. When a full minute passes without a reply, I force myself to drink some of my water then pull out the last piece of banana bread. My water pouch is down to its last quarter. I'm still within a full day's walk from the lake. I could return if I need to.

I smear Mother's caramel-apple butter on the bread and continue my walk, thoroughly chewing every bite. Still, it's consumed sooner than I'd like. The soup medley in my cloth will last a day or two.

God, help me figure You out. Do with me what You will, please give me food, keep me safe, and forgive me for whatever I've done wrong.

I take my time walking, but continue to move forward—wherever forward may lead. The morning air feels so different than afternoon or evening. Sounds echo. A bird sends out a loud chirp. At least five varied bird whistles answer it. It chirps again. Five responses. The exchange continues for several minutes until a harsh crow's cry interrupts.

The day drags and I grow tired of the forest scenery, even with the spring flowers coming. I force repeated steps in hopes I'll break from the trees to something new. The sun warms as it nears midday—or what *looks* like midday. I can't tell on this side of the Wall. How far have I come?

I almost forget about my watch. *11:04.*

Around noon, I succumb to a short nap. When I wake, a distant noise, like radio static, reaches my ears. The Independents?

When I scramble to my feet, a small *pop* comes from my NAB.

~There are many people who should have and could have done something, Miss Blackwater, Hawke writes. *~Do not carry the full weight of blame. Unity Village's form of enforcing is not how it should be. That's one reason I'm here, to help make things right.*

From his message, it seems he agrees I am somewhat to blame. *Not how it should be,* I read again, remembering Reid's journal. He said shalom was "the way things were intended to be."

A second message pops up. *~How are you faring?*

Not too well after his down-in-the-dumps response. I rein in my attitude and type, *~I am still alive, running out of food and water, and feel like I'm walking without a purpose. But God is still providing for me.*

I feel a little hypocritical with the last sentence. It makes me look so much more faithful than I am.

Hawke responds, ~*God is the ultimate Provider.*

I stare at his short answer. It's so generic, but people don't talk openly about God. It's too risky with the law against teaching children younger than eighteen a religion. Is Hawke mentioning God because I did, or is it part of who he is?

~*Miss Blackwater, if you need any further help, please continue to message. I may not be able to respond often. I'm sure you understand the limitations I face in being an Enforcer. I must remain cautious when reading and replying to your messages. Even though you are on the other side of the Wall, it is still my desire to help and protect you as true Enforcers should.*

It's the first comment from him that encourages me. ~*Thank you, Mister Hawke. Please refer to me as Parvin.*

I offer my name up as a gift—a gift for Solomon Hawke to step a little closer. It's such a new feeling to allow the crack of openness to widen. I like it.

~*I will. You may call me Hawke. I'm not a fan of anything "mister."* *Tally ho.*

I give him Parvin and he gives me Hawke? I *may* call him Hawke? I *already* call him Hawke. This is not a fair exchange.

Following suit from our first NAB communication, I respond as he did: ~*Tally ho.* I gather my belongings and walk toward the static sound. It grows louder and more distinct. It's not a radio, it's a river. I must not have noticed the gradual growl before my nap.

I meet a break in the confining trees to see the first beautiful sight on the West: rushing water weaving around smooth glassy rocks, reflecting the sun and sky in flashes. Tree boughs lean over the water, dropping new flowers and old leaves onto its shining surface like miniature fairy boats. The slope of the ground makes the river look like it's racing itself to the bottom.

With a delighted breath, I pull my sentra from my pocket and snap a picture. Then, I scoot to the edge of a log spanning the river. My feet hang above the moving water—the swirls, the curves, and the slow ripples beg for a swimmer. The water flows over a tiny fall, churning in green and white bubbles.

I remove my boots and bandages and step into the shallow. Goosebumps sweep up my legs followed by a harsh wave of muscle spasms. What is wrong with my body? Is it the wounds? With gentle movements, I rinse the injuries of blood and grime. My stitching strings are frayed. They might not last another day.

Across the river is a clearing on the bank big enough for a fire. I look around for stepping-stones. No luck. The dead tree is the only bridge in view and it's suspended over the steeper drop in the river. No problem. I have fair balance and the log is thick.

I stuff my bandages in my pack and hoist it onto my shoulders. If I cross while I still have energy, then I can relax on the other side.

At first, I try to walk across, but can't balance on the round surface enough to raise myself from my hands and knees. The water seems further down and the log is thinner than I expected. My knees don't fit side by side so I straddle the log and use my hands to scoot myself across, inch by inch.

My wounds stretch as I crawl on the log, making me wince. The rough bark scratches the inside of my thighs. My heart speeds up and my stomach flutters. I shake my head. I'm being pitiful. This is nothing like walking through a pack of wolves. Still, my stomach won't stop twisting.

Halfway across, my arms start to shake. Tiny black ants race through the bark cracks, reaching the other side without a hitch. If only I could shrink to their size.

Despite the padding of my leggings, my thighs grow raw with each scoot. This was a stupid idea.

I raise myself to my knees again to relieve the growing pain on my thighs, but the movement threatens my balance. I lurch to one side and shriek, dropping to my stomach against the bark. I grip the log tight with my arms. I don't move. I don't fall.

Pathetic.

The last half is less intimidating once I get moving again. By the time I crawl off the log, my thighs itch and burn. I barely remain standing on my shaking legs. Anxious to sit and recover, I collect broken branches and build a small fire. Not much dead wood is available, unlike the other side of the river, so I search for dry trees to stock up for evening. Some of the branches are still green and take a lot of twisting to rip them off their trunks. They'll smoke a lot so I burn them first, not wanting to smoke-poison myself when I'm sleeping.

I rinse my bandages and then boil them in Mother's teapot. I boil water three more times—once to clear any grime left from the bandages, again for fresh water in my water pouch, and then to make some of the noodles, corn, and beef Mother packed. By the time the third boil is ready for food, darkness has crept over the river, bringing with it a harsh chill. I pull my coat tight and whittle a piece of stick into a rough spoon. It looks more like a mini spatula, but it'll prove more useful than trying to drink soup out of the teapot spout.

As I slurp hot corn and noodles off my stick, I think of the verse Mother quoted before my Good-bye.

"He who began a good work in you will bring it to completion at the day of Jesus Christ."

I told her God hadn't started anything in me. Now I'm in the West and I'm alive, but so what? I'm not *doing* anything. I'm looking for the Independents by wandering around a forest. This isn't purpose, it's desperation.

"God, what do You have me doing?" As expected, He doesn't answer.

I force down half the soup through a tight and quivering jaw. Something's wrong with me, with my muscles. The fever still hasn't left my body. I try not to think about the pain or discomfort. I'm no healer. Even if I knew what my body is fighting, I can't fix it.

I can't fix anything.

All I can do is lie down and hope I wake up alive.

The next morning, I wake up cold. The fire is dead and the chill wind has a bite more bitter than the grey morning clouds. A black-and-white speckled bird stands on the rock by my bandages—a chunk of pale straw in her mouth. She cocks her head from side to side as if thinking, then takes flight.

With a groan, I toss the remaining green sticks onto the dead fire, arrange a small teepee of twigs, and sacrifice another match. It doesn't catch. I should have known better—it's live wood. I push myself up with a growl and pull handfuls of twigs and leaves from under a nearby tree.

A wasted match. Twenty-seven left. I light a fresh one, shield it from the wind, and let the flame play against the kindling. A small crackle starts and I blow on the embers.

Make that twenty-six.

Ten minutes allows the fire to gather real heat. Black smoke billows into the air. I step away and search for more dead sticks further upstream. No luck. When I return to the fire, the smoke has lessened. I place my pot of cold soup over it to warm, but when I try to eat I can barely open my jaw against the muscle spasms. I manage a few spoonfuls and then give up.

The grey clouds disperse. *God, help me figure You out. Do with me what You will, please give me food, keep me safe, and forgive me for whatever I've done wrong.*

Once my bandages are tied around freshly salved wounds and I've stuffed a roll of wool in the spout of my kettle to keep the soup in, I place my pack on my shoulders and walk into the forest. The kettle bounces from the strap of my pack, but nothing spills. For the first time since Skelley Chase betrayed me, my heart feels lighter.

Trees seem to have flowered overnight. Cream and purple blossoms dot the limbs and tiny yellow flowers cover the forest floor. Downy serviceberry trees spread their branches, dropping miniature white petals into my hair. I don't even mind their strange scent.

Walking is almost pleasant despite my sickness. The ground is more level, there's little underbrush, and the air is wet and crisp. Dew coats the patches of green growth and clovers around me. Moss grows thicker as I go deeper into the forest. The light hits it, turning the forest into glowing logs and carpet. The moss looks soft and spongy, but it's dry to the touch, bedecked with tiny ferns and shrunken green blankets.

I raise the sentra and snap an emotigraph, hoping the future readers will feel my calm and delight in the scenery. I move to a more sunlit area and lift the sentra once more. Such a glowing landscape can never be bottled, but I still try. I slide my finger across the button.

The air is split by a child's scream.

I jolt, snapping an emotigraph. My muscles shake and my mind panics. I shove the sentra into my pocket.

Who screamed? Why? Wolves?

I look around. The child screams again, closer. I cover my own mouth and stumble back. Movement from ahead startles me into a defensive stance. I fumble for my dagger. Bushes crash apart, and thirty yards ahead of me—

I see my first Independent.

18

She's paler than snow. Not just her face, but her tangled short hair, her thin bare arms poking from the sleeveless white shirt, the flash of her calves and tiny feet propelling her forward. Her small mouth is open in a gasp, her brows together. She can't be older than eleven.

The ivory girl runs in jerky motions, scanning her surroundings and the ground for footing. A layered pale pink skirt flaps around her knees. She hops to her left, still trying to run, but skipping and veering right.

I tense as she nears me. She looks up and does a double take, skidding to a halt. Her lip quivers. A moment passes before she releases an agonized yell and stumbles to her right.

Whatever she's running from makes me want to run, too. I inch behind a tree, but before I can turn away, the bushes part again and four grown men emerge. They run in a similar stilted manner, but their hops and dashes are more fluid. They all wear brown or black pants made from what looks like animal skin. Boots reach up past their calves. Two wear tied cloth vests and the other two wear no upper clothing at all.

They, too, are pale and white, like their blood has been drained from their bodies. One has chopped yellowish hair and a young face. The other three have long hair reaching past their sunburned shoulders. One is missing a hand. They carry no weapons, but the moment they spot the child they shout and hurry after her.

My fingers tear into the bark of the tree behind which I hide. *God, help her!*

She swerves toward me, her face scrunched. I hear a sob. Her skirt tangles around her knees. She staggers mere yards away from my tree as the man with short hair grabs her arm. Her shriek is cut short when he yanks her toward him. She tries to twist from his grasp, but he lifts a hand high and slaps her. Twice. Her head snaps to the side from the impact and her small form collapses on the ground. The other three men approach.

She sobs into the moss and I hear her muffled, "Please."

The other three men close in. With seconds to decide, I reach up and, with a harsh jerk, snap a small branch from my tree. It's thin and supple, like a switch. Mother and Father punished Reid and me with switches in our younger years. Though they only ever marked my backside, I have no doubt a swift swipe across the face will keep a grown man at bay.

All five Independents start from the sound. I step forward, ripping the leaves off the end of the branch. They stare at it. *God, help me!* I hold up my tiny dagger in my other hand. "Go away." I say this through clenched teeth, as if shooing a cat. My voice is shaky—anything but threatening.

The men straighten and the girl lies panting on the ground. A harsh handprint glows on her cheek. Her left eye is puffy.

The man with short hair takes a step toward me.

"Stop!" I raise my weapons and hop back.

His gaze rests on my switch and his eyes narrow. "You are the one," he says with a frayed voice. "You burned the fire by the river." He looks me up and down and his next words are hard. "You haven't atoned."

All four of the pale men move forward. I stumble away and my muscle cramps relax my jaw enough to let me shout, "I don't know you. Leave me alone!"

He doesn't stop his approach. I throw the dagger, and then curse my idiocy in relinquishing my good weapon. It tumbles through the air and the handle knocks him in the forehead. He stops with a jerk, eyes widening. A tiny cut lines his brow and a trickle of blood creeps down his temple. The color is stark against his white skin.

He growls and lunges. I manage one swipe with the switch before he grabs my wrist with one hand and my hair with the other. He yanks my head back so far, I'm sure my neck will snap. I whimper.

Multiple hands grab me, keeping a tight grip on my hair and pulling me forward. I trip to my knees and choke. "Let me go."

My hair is released. All my limbs are shaking when the man without a hand hoists me back to my feet. He loops a small cord around my right wrist and pulls it up behind my back like the bullies used to do. My shoulder is about to tear from its socket. The sores on my skin grate against my pack.

One of the other men rips the switch from my left hand and whips me across the face with it. I gasp at the stunning pain.

Oh yes, it hurts far more than on my backside.

He tucks the switch in his belt and grips my free wrist, digging his thumb between the two bones. Nausea hits my stomach. The man with short hair pulls the young girl behind him by the hair. She doesn't resist, but continues to cry.

"Please," she sobs. "Please, Black, don't punish me. I didn't mean to."

"You were warned." The man named Black—who is anything *but* black—gives her another hard yank.

We walk in the direction from which they came, weaving around bushes and careful to duck under branches. There is no path, but the men choose a winding route, walking on patches of moss.

"I don't know who you are," I repeat through the pain. "Let me go."

"You are a stranger who injured the land. Either you are dull-minded or your people did not educate you. Still, atonement is always made—even by the ignorant."

Atonement makes me think of Jesus, which makes me think of nails, blood, and drawn-out suffering. So that's my future?

I want to pray, but grind my teeth against the temptation. *I asked for Your* help! *You call* this *help?*

I think back to my prayer this morning—the rehearsed adapted poem. Part of that prayer was, *Do with me what You will,* but the other part was, *Keep me safe.* God seems to have forgotten that part. Why did I ever pray?

I absorb the forest scenery, trying to memorize our path. The moss is thicker and the trees thinner. We pass a tall tree stump with a round cage around its base. The cage is made of woven branches curving from the ground to the bark of the stump. A wispy baby tree grows new from the side of the stump. Moss and undergrowth crowd the spaces of the cage, but between the thin boughs, shadowed inside the cage, is a lump—a pale lump.

My breath catches. *God, what is this?* I look away, queasy. "My arm hurts," I choke, pulling against the rope and trying to distract my thoughts. Are those dead prisoners?

"It won't for long," Black says stiffly. "We are almost there."

The girl resumes her pleading. "Black, please take me to Father first. It was an accident. You *know* I care for—"

"Be silent, Willow," Black interrupts. "You hit bloom two weeks ago. We've had children atone a mere *day* after bloom. Remember Elm?"

Willow hangs her head. "Please."

I close my eyes at the sound of her high child's voice. She's pleading for grace. Will they listen if *I* plead for grace? I can't get those cages out of my mind. Desperation pounds the walls of my heart.

"Who are you?" I swallow the question I *want* to ask, *"What are you going to do to me?"*

"I'm Black. Who are you?"

"I already knew your name. Are you Independents?"

He shrugs. "We are albino."

Albino people? I saw an albino ferret once, sold for lunch at the town square market. I can't see if Black's eyes are red like the ferret's were. Willow's aren't. Hers are a very light purple.

"Do you originate from the people who chose to stay in the West?" Black doesn't answer, but I can't stop. "I didn't injure the land. The fire I burned was safely built right beside the river."

He holds up a hand. We step down into a thinned wooded clearing. Moss covers every inch of ground, dotted by small stone-stacked huts with woven, animal-skin roofs. Twenty dogwood trees cover the small village like umbrellas of snow. Each one is in some stage of bloom, white flowers stretching open and painting the air. They seem dwarfed and fairy-like beside the towering evergreens and oaks.

One wide pink dogwood sits on a raised knoll beside a clump of huts. Beneath it, a giant square slab of stone stands upright in the mossy ground, like a tombstone. Two small arches are carved from its base. I am led toward this stone.

When we reach it, my arm is released and I groan my relief. Before I can rub my shoulder, I'm shoved to the ground. Black removes my boots and pushes my feet through the two holes at the base of the stone. The freedom feels good on my sore legs—until heavy chain shackles clamp around my ankles on the other side of the stone. My socks are crooked and bunched beneath the shackles.

At least I'm sitting, though I'm uncomfortable and vulnerable.

The albinos disperse into different stone houses. Black drags Willow out of sight. They're leaving me unguarded. They're also leaving me with my belongings. Don't they fear I'll escape?

I wiggle my feet once I'm alone. The chains clank on the other side. My socks are still bunched. I can't see through the arches over my ankles and there's not enough room for me to squeeze a hand through to reach my feet. I push against the stone with my hands. The effort results in further pain through my already tortured muscles.

I gasp. My NAB. Maybe Skelley Chase can use his "I can do anything" power to help me.

I glance around. Some albino women mingle near the furthest house. Black and the other albinos who brought me here are not in view. I slide my pack off my shoulders and pull out the NAB. I go straight to Skelley Chase's communication bubble. I press the *Talk/Type* button and whisper a message while monitoring the village with narrowed eyes.

-I need help. I don't know what you can do, but I've been captured by albino Independents. They are going to make me atone for something. I don't know what that means, but I'm a captive.

I pull out the sentra and snap a picture of my feet shoved through the stone and then another emotigraph of the village. I send them both to him along with my message. I stare at the screen for several seconds as if that will hasten his reply.

Something churns inside me, sickened by asking Skelley Chase for help. Will he help me? What can he do, anyway? He doesn't know where I am. In fact, has he ever really been interested in helping me?

Hawke has. I should have considered him first. I send the same message to him, but tweak it a little.

-Hawke, I need help. I've been captured by albino Independents. I don't know what you can do, but they're going to punish me for something. Can you help me?

I reread the message. It looks dramatic and . . . desperate. "Send."

"Put it away."

I jump at the quiet voice and look up. A tall, half-naked albino man stands before me, bald, but with thick eyebrows and a smooth beard. Behind him stand Black, Willow, the handless man, and several other albinos.

I slip the NAB back in my pocket, just as I hear a soft *pop!* come from it. I dare not look at the response.

"What is your name?" The tall one asks. Inside, my heart lifts. We're off to a good start—they're not dragging me away to a tree cage.

"Parvin Blackwater."

"I am Alder. I help lead this town and I judge misdeeds. We shall discuss yours in a moment. Where are you from?"

"I didn't break any laws that I know of." Black glares from behind Alder, but I return my gaze to Alder. His face remains blank. "I'm from the East."

"There is no East," Alder says.

I look away. He might see me as an invader if I tell him, but my other option isn't very appealing. "I'm from the East side of the Wall." The atmosphere turns silent. "I was betrayed and sent across the Wall as a Radical for not having a Clock."

I catch the hint of a murmur from somewhere in the back of the small crowd. ". . . like the other ones. The woman . . ."

"Has someone else come through here?" My breathing comes in short breaths. "Someone from my side?"

Alder studies me. "How did you get here?"

"I climbed down the cliff and was attacked by a pack of wolves, coyotes, and bears, but got past them into the forest. I've been traveling for days trying to locate Independents to find guidance. I had no intention to break rules—"

"Yet you did. You need to understand our beliefs to know what you've done."

I don't *want* to know what I've done. I want to stay ignorant, believing myself innocent, but Alder doesn't care what I want.

"The destruction of the West side of this country gave us the opportunity to save what people spent their lives destroying." Alder watches me in a moment of silence.

Am I supposed to know what he means?

He continues. "Our lives are devoted to working and caring for this land, particularly the trees and growths of nature. They were mistreated and used at people's whims."

"But aren't they just plants?"

He narrows his eyes. "Nature is our equal. It relies on us for care. Mistreating this forest is like mistreating a child—both make you an inadequate caregiver worthy of punishment. We cannot care for all, but we do our best with the number of people we have."

I realize I'm frowning and staring. I straighten my shoulders and nod in nervous understanding, but his words don't sound right. "I thought God made this Earth for us to live in. It's supposed to be our home, not our master."

Alder shakes his head, his small smile seeming to say I have a comprehension deficit. Maybe I do. Most of my knowledge comes from what I've been told. But I can't help thinking this isn't what God meant.

"The Earth is not our master—it is our equal. It cares for us if we care for it. In attending to the trees and plants, we receive the same pain we inflict upon them. If we pick a flower, we pluck a hair. If we carve the bark, we carve our skin." He points to the scar of a tree branch carving on his right shoulder.

I squirm, imagining a knife scraping his white flesh.

"If we snap a limb, we give equally."

At Alder's somber words, the albino without a hand steps forward and holds up the stump. My blood runs cold and I stare, my jaw open. My weapon . . .

The switch.

All five Independents stared at me, wide-eyed, when I broke it from the tree.

"P-People mean more to G-God than trees do." My jaw grows tight. *Not now,* I plead against the muscle spasms. *I need to be able to speak in my defense.*

Don't they know God loves them more than He loves trees or flowers? Do *I* know that He loves us more? "Plants don't even have souls, right?"

"Our duty is to help the helpless." Alder holds up the switch that caused the long welt on my face. "This comes with personal sacrifice. Parvin, though you're unfamiliar with our laws, you've caused harm to the trees we vow to care for. You broke fresh branches by the river and burned them. You tore this limb from its trunk in the presence of five of our people. You've hurt the trees we love."

I look between the several unfamiliar faces and feel like I'm back in Unity square for my hearing. No one will listen. The albinos look mournful, like they need to punish me against their will. Or do they mourn for the trees?

"But this Earth is for *us*. Not the other way around. God doesn't have a personal relationship with the trees. His Son didn't die for the trees."

"We acknowledge no God," Alder says. "All are equal."

"But—"

Alder holds up a hand. "Black has presented your situation to us. We are distributing some of your atonement, but the remaining punishment is for you to have a single limb severed. Do you have a preference?"

"What?" My body recoils and I feel as though the chains tighten around my ankles. "This isn't right! You can't cut off one of my arms or legs. I'm not under your laws! You don't even know me."

Alder speaks over me. "It is not our intent to be cruel, we seek justice." He turns to the small crowd. "Please complete your duties."

Everyone turns and leaves. All except the girl from earlier—Willow. She stands several yards away. Her right hand is bandaged. Three small splints line her fingers. She stares at me with a tear-streaked face. Mini watchdog, I assume. I don't care. My heart pounds stronger than a miner's pick and I yank my feet against the shackles. They're too tight. I want to tear the flesh right out of them—that'd be better than losing a limb.

As Alder leaves, my NAB makes another sound from my pocket and I fumble for it. *Please, God, please. Help me!*

Willow hasn't moved. I have a note from both Skelley Chase and Hawke.

-I can't help you, Parvin. Escape if you can. -SC

Duh. Thanks, Skelley. Tears spring behind my eyes.

I click on Hawke's bubble and sniff hard. My hands shake. "Oh God, oh God, please, please, please."

-Parvin, I know where you are. Someone is on his way. – Hawke.

I cover my mouth with a trembling hand and look around. Who? When? Is he here yet? How did Hawke do it?

The albinos have been gone for five solid minutes—all except Willow. I still pull against the chains and push against the stone with my hands, but to no avail. I just need to wait for Hawke's man. Maybe it's Hawke himself.

I look around, anxiety building. Movement comes from among the stone houses. Four albinos walk my way, carrying different items.

"Help me," I hiss to Willow. Her eyes widen and she takes a step back. "I helped *you*. That's why I'm here."

She holds her splinted hand close to her chest and takes another silent step backward, as the other four albinos reach the base of the knoll.

"Leave me alone! I have more to explain." The movement of speaking sends my jaw muscles into a spasm frenzy and I can't speak for a moment. My NAB still lies on the forest floor beside me. Hawke hasn't sent anything more.

The albinos climb up the knoll, passing Willow.

"Leave me alone." My throat closes.

Alder holds a long silver axe. Black carries a giant bag over his shoulder, filled to bursting with something. A woman carries a bundle of cloth. She reaches me first and I scramble away as far as my shackled legs allow. The other albino with them—a hefty muscled man—pins my shoulders to the ground.

"No!" I struggle against his grip.

The woman removes the bandage from my left arm and ties a stretchy piece of cloth below my elbow. Seconds pass before my pulse races. The tips of my fingers go numb. Then my palm.

A tourniquet.

"Hawke, help!" I scream to the NAB, though I don't think it's on verbatim mode. My arm burns from the tourniquet. Black places the bag beneath my left forearm. It's full of something grainy—maybe sand or dirt. Someone removes the blue watch from my wrist.

They wait. I look at Alder. He holds my gaze.

"Please, Mister Alder! I'm not from here. God sent me here to find the Independents. To find *you*. Are you going to reward my journey with pain?"

I haven't yet viewed my journey as a calling from God, but maybe I will someday. For now, Alder might as well believe I have as much conviction for my adventure as he does for his trees.

My arm tingles. The woman says, "Look at her wound. Infection has set."

I can't see my arm, but I know from the last time I peeked that the stitches need to come out. Maybe they've already frayed and sunk into my skin. I use this to my advantage.

"I have many wounds from fighting the wolves," I gasp in a strangled voice. "I'm sick and had to stitch my own skin on my arm and my leg. I have burns and cuts. Isn't that enough to atone?"

Alder closes his eyes and takes a deep breath. "We are already showing you grace."

The man holding me down straddles me, using his weight to keep me pinned.

"Get *off!*" I arch my body.

Black wraps both hands around my left wrist and stretches my arm across the sandbag. I pull against him, but a muscle in my shoulder pops. Desperation builds like a shriek inside me. Every fiber flashes in frenzy.

"Alder," the tourniquet lady whispers. "Maybe we should wait."

"I am sorry," Alder murmurs. "I am so sorry for your pain." He steadies the axe in his hands.

I writhe against Black and the others. *"Mercy!* I'll do whatever else you want!" My tiny body causes no change in their iron holds. Every muscle strains in agony. I can't get free. "No! No! *No!*" Where is Hawke?

Alder lifts the axe. I've chopped enough wood in my lifetime to know what comes next.

"HAWKE!" I scream long and loud.

Alder lets out a loud grunt of effort at the same time a distant voice roars over the chaos. "Alder, stop!"

But no one stops.

19

000.166.22.27.37

The axe thuds into the sandbag.

A flash of shock sears my brain. Screaming drowns out all other senses—*my* screaming. The pressure on my body releases, but I don't move. My voice dies like a drowned kitten.

Confused shouting fills the cracks in the horrified air. My vision turns black. Someone brushes my hair from my face.

"Oh God . . ." Pain seeps like a stain into my body.

The shouts grow louder in my ears. Chilled words.

". . . tourniquet . . . too much blood . . ."

". . . shouldn't have . . . so soon . . . waited."

Black's enraged voice stands out from the others. "That was too close, Alder."

"Oh, no." The newest voice—a gentle male voice—comes closer. "Oh, no . . . no. Didn't you hear me say stop?"

My eyes close. With each agonizing thud from my heart, I sink further into the tar of shock. Hopelessness. Finally, I let myself drown.

000.166.08.01.22

I wake with a fever, long enough to retch onto my naked body. Voices. Flickering lights. Pain. My muscles shake like an earthquake. I need water. *Water.*

000.165.18.19.00

Confused. Choking. Someone hushes me. I mentally flail my arms at the spoon against my lips, but my body doesn't move.

Stop. I can't breathe.

Something small and solid rolls across my tongue. The spoon pours hot salty liquid into my mouth. Suffocating. I swallow.

A black abyss consumes my mind and sight. I scream. "Mother!"

000.162.23.06.44

The draped ceiling above is not my home, yet home is the first thought in my mind. My door should be to my right, my window to my left. I'm warm. What season is it?

I look around. Two windows let in light on each side of me, set into stacked stone walls. Rolls of cloth rest in leather ties above each one. A dark marble dresser rests against the right wall beneath the window. Not home.

What is this place?

Nothing comes rushing back. Nothing matches. I don't have a memory with this room. No one is here.

"Reid?" I say to the space. My throat burns. *Water.*

My eyes hurt with every blink. They're dry and grainy, like I've been crying. Even though I feel rested, I ache—an ache deeper than I ever thought could dig through my heart. I didn't know my heart had such a bottomless place to hold pain. The pain festers, writhing in agony, causing more and more ache with each movement. I try to place a name to the pain. *Sorrow?* Not fully.

Loss. Injustice.

My arm.

I raise both limbs in front of my face. On the right, my fingers spread apart, curling and uncurling. On the left is my bony elbow, connected to my thin forearm, connected to . . . nothing. My arm ends in a swollen lump of skin, held together with disjointed stitches. I gape at the two mismatched arms. I open and close my right hand. My left arm yearns to do the same.

I'm shaking.

Someone enters this strange hut and I lower my arms to my side. The woman is very pregnant and pale white. I don't recognize her face, but with her skin color come memories of Black slapping Willow, of the dogwood trees, of Alder saying he's sorry. A silver axe.

"My hand . . ."

The albino woman doesn't look up from the pile of furs she is sorting. "Be calm."

I turn my face away, placing the cover over my left arm. I can't look at it. I'm supposed to have two hands.

The cover slides off my limb. I glance up, angry.

"Your wound must breathe." The woman folds down the corner of the blanket. Her face is soft. Young with light pink lips and white eyelashes like snow.

"Where is my hand?" I resist the temptation to shout. I want it reattached, stitched back on. They stole it.

She turns away. "It is buried in the sky. Burned to ashes."

"B-Burned?" So many injustices run through my head, I can't decide which to proclaim. "It was *mine.*" Fire scorches my throat. My energy shrivels and I fight back tears.

I lie still, craving water. As if hearing my silent plea, the woman appears with a small stone cup. I drink without question; she refills without comment. The pattern continues until my throat feels restored. Then, as if my body can't handle the hydration, I cry.

The woman doesn't soothe. I don't ask her to. She leaves me alone and I close my eyes, imagining Mother here. I want my NAB to send her a message. I need her to come to me.

Mother, come help me. I swallow hard and instead turn to the only One I know is present. *God . . . help me.*

I'm not angry with Him. I don't know why. He allowed this to happen. Perhaps the anger will come later. Right now, I am so . . . alone. I need Him.

I need You. I need You. I need You. My breathing adopts the rhythm of my mindless prayer until I fall asleep.

I'm awakened by a new voice—a man's voice. When my eyes open, the light is dim and candles are lit. The man in the doorway is tall with shadowed features.

"Hawke?" I squirm into a better position. He turns. It's not Hawke.

"I'm Jude. Sorry I was late."

Late? I frown at him for a moment then close my eyes. *Too late to save me.*

A hand touches my cheek and my eyes fly open. Jude is at my bed-side. "I truly am sorry. Solomon's message didn't give me much time."

His eyes are a chocolate-raspberry brown, his skin lightly tanned, and a gentle upturn of his lips soothes my anxiety. He's the one Hawke asked to help me—the one who shouted for Alder to stop.

"Who . . . ?" I lick my lips. "Who are you? You're not albino." With the question comes a pinch of insecurity. Is this man an Independent or is he from *my* side?

Jude's hand slides from my face. "Hawke sent me to help you."

I squirm, relieving my limbs of stiffness. "He knows about this side? He knew what would be here and let the Enforcers send me anyway?"

"No, he's never been here. He didn't know. He sent me to help you." Jude bows his head. "I hoped Alder would stop."

"He didn't."

"My voice holds little power here." We sit in silence, looking at each other. My mental discomfort fades with exhaustion.

"Why should it, Jude?"

I look up to find Alder has stepped into the hut.

"You're not one of us."

Jude stands. "You say 'all are equal', yet belittle those of us from other cities. Don't get too used to leading, you're starting to contradict yourself."

"Don't get too used to speaking," Alder responds, coolly.

I recoil. Is that a threat? Do the albinos cut out people's tongues, too?

Alder sets a small cloth bag on a table by the bucket of water then kneels by my bed. I look away. How dare he come to me when *he* severed my hand?

"Parvin Blackwater." His hoarse voice cracks. This display of emo-tion draws my gaze to his face. Red lines the rims of his pale blue eyes. A tear slips down his white cheek. "Your pain grieves my heart." He takes my right hand in his and lowers his forehead to it. His tear wets my skin. "I hope that, over time, you will see the purpose behind this." A small sob escapes his choked voice.

I've never seen a man cry. Father's tears were silent at the train stop. I've never seen raw vulnerability like this, especially over *me*. Is he truly grieved? Maybe this is fake, but why would Alder feign such a thing? He's a leader.

I stare at his bent body. Tears from his grief drip off my hand onto the blanket. My own eyes burn. In this moment, I could forgive him. I want to comfort him. I reach over to place a comforting hand on his bald head, but see a stump. I can't place my hand on him. I don't *have* a hand.

The urge to forgive dissipates. "You'll be hoping for a long time." The hardness in my voice startles me.

He says nothing more, but remains bent over for another few seconds. Then he rises and leaves the hut. My body relaxes. I didn't realize I'd tensed. My eyes droop and I'm surprised by the sudden fatigue. Jude stands on my left. Candlelight flickers against his skin. I'm ashamed to look at him.

I tuck my aching stump under the covers despite the woman's instructions to let it breathe and close my eyes. I register pain in my arm, the sounds of my own breathing, and the movement of clothing as Jude walks out.

Morning wakes me next. Instead of an animal-skin roof overhead, my eyes open to the bending branches of a white dogwood tree. Flecks of blue sky flicker through the swaying blossoms. I am still in the same hut, but the windows and door are covered by leather squares. The roof is rolled back.

Something soft and wet pats my bare legs. I lift my head. The ever-present pregnant woman wipes my calves with a damp cloth. I realize I'm uncovered and still without clothes. I snatch the covers, but only my right hand catches hold. Angry tears burn my eyes at the uselessness of my stump. It tinges with pain from the sudden movement.

"What are you doing?"

She straightens at my barked question. Her face is both gentle and sorrowful. "Keeping you clean."

A full bedpan rests on the floor. My face reddens and, in childish fashion, I slump back against the pillow and pull the blanket over my head.

"This is common." The woman inches the blanket off my face. I hold tight with my right hand. "You are more alert every time you wake. You had many wounds and much tetanus sickness from the bites. Soon you will be able to walk around."

At these words, I notice my injuries from the wolves and my dive down the cliff side don't hurt. I feel my neck. The burn marks are smoother. I lift the cover and look at my leg. My stitches have been removed and resewn with thin fishing line.

"How long have I been here?"

"Today is your fifth day."

My heart hiccups and I lift my left arm. The blue watch is gone. "Where's my watch?"

"In your bag." The woman hands me a stone mug of hot broth. "Drink this."

Five precious days, gone. Stolen by these albino people who wanted my hand. What would they do to me if they knew Father is a carpenter?

I take the mug by the handle. Her other hand holds out three small white pills.

"What are those?" I reach out to take them, but jerk my left arm away with a start, surprised yet again by the stitched stump. I clutch the mug.

"Pain medication." She squeezes the hand around the soup mug. "The medicine in your system will wear off soon. These will help for the next several hours."

My throat is too tight to ask how she has something so out of place in a forest village, to ask why they were so rash to take my hand, to ask why they hurt me and now spend days healing me.

The woman touches my cheek. I look into her face. Her lower lip quivers. "How are you?"

Seeing her on the verge of tears pushes me over the edge. I shake my head and thrust the mug of soup at her. She takes it from me as my face scrunches. I hide it in my hand. Breath seems to have left me, replaced by angry, incessant sobs.

She pulls my hand down. "Do not hide." Her voice is choked. "Allow yourself to mourn."

"Why are *you* crying?" I demand with my first solid breath. "You have two hands."

"We are grieving with you."

I don't want to grieve. I want to rewind time and have my hand back. I don't want to cry—crying means I'm weak. Mother never cried.

The woman sets the soup down and climbs onto my bed. Startled, I scoot over. I lean away as she reaches for me, but she slips her arms around my shoulders and pulls me close. I tense. I hate her. I hate them.

I'm alone. Broken.

"Shhh." She says this though I made no sound. Her mother-like action, despite her young age, shatters my brittle composure. I bury my face into the crook of her shoulder. She moves the stray hairs from my cheek with the tips of her fingers.

I mourn the injustice done to me. Though she remains mute, her own tears drop onto her pregnant belly. I no longer feel alone.

Two days later, I'm as far away from crying as a butterfly is from the moon. My clothes are patched, cleaned, and returned to me, I've healed enough to leave the hut, and learned the pregnant albino woman's name: Ash. I think of ashes from a fire, but she says Ash is a tree. I'm not surprised. Everyone's name here comes from some sort of plant or tree except for Jude . . . and Black.

The most dramatic change is the dissipation of my sorrow. It's been replaced by something much stronger that screams for action: *anger*. I've had a long time to think about Alder's reasoning behind chopping off my arm. I clutch my Bible. We need to have a talk.

Jude meets me when I step from Ash's hut. "Good sunrise, Miss Blackwater." He wears a black wool coat with missing buttons and the collar turned up. His thick straight eyebrows catch every twinge of emotion as he surveys me. A small frown, a masked smirk, narrowed eyes, alert.

"Good morning, Jude. Where is Alder?"

Jude steps back. "Uh . . ." He looks around. "I can find him for you. It's a cool morning and it's your first time up and walking—"

"I'll find him, thanks." I leave Jude behind. I don't want anyone telling me to stay in the hut and rest. Nobody needs to be over-protective. I'm capable of walking for a few minutes.

I'm not weak. I survived having my hand chopped off and I'm done crying for the rest of my life. I'm *not* weak.

I weave through huts, ignoring the presence of other albinos tending small gardens in beds of moss. What's the punishment for uprooting a carrot, having a tooth pulled? Almost every house has rolled back the animal-skinned roofs to let the sun, breeze, and dogwood flowers into their homes.

I round a corner. Alder stands at a taut clothesline strung between huts, though instead of clothes he ties the feet of a headless pheasant to the thick length of twine. I stare at his two hands for a moment. Heat rises to my face. I can't even tie a knot anymore.

"What about animals?" I blurt. "You'll sacrifice *my hand* for the sake of a tree with no brain, blood, or breath, yet you kill and eat animals?"

Alder turns from the pile of dead pheasants on the ground. "Animals are not helpless—they have defense mechanisms and can fight for their own lives. Plants cannot."

I try to fold my arms, but bump the stitches on my left arm and cringe. "This forest is huge, what about the portions you *can't* take care of that other people chop down?"

"We do what we can with the people we have." Alder picks up another dead pheasant. "During the building of the Wall, my ancestors wanted to start over with a new perspective. They realized there is a link between the ground and humans we need to respect." He chops the pheasant's limp head off. The axe sticks in the log.

"Do all albino people think this way?"

"No, just as all black people don't think the same, nor all white people, nor anyone in between." He yanks the axe from the log.

"You're using wood for a chopping block." I gesture toward the block with my Bible in my hand. "Why is *that* accepted?"

"Because the tree from which this block came fell of its own accord. Its lifetime was over—ended by the wind or age, we don't know. It died. Now can we use it as we wish."

Blood drips from the severed necks of the pheasants. At a loss for words, I watch it splatter on the ground. Alder hangs a third pheasant to drain.

I look down at my Bible. *God, it'd be great if You could speak for me right now.*

Alder wipes his hands on the feathered body of a dead bird and gestures at my Bible. "From the stories I've heard, God destroyed the men on the Earth because they were corrupting it. One hundred and eleven years ago, people corrupted it again—turning it into concrete and stone. Your God used a single woman to destroy their creation."

"She was a terrorist. Her actions were her own and no one knows why she did what she did."

"Still, supernatural power didn't stop this space expert from directing meteorites into the Pacific and China. It brought tidal waves, earthquakes, volcanoes . . . your God didn't stop them. He seems more on my side than yours."

I roll my eyes. "God gave us Earth to *live on*, not just to die with forests of healthy trees. You had no right to cut off my hand." My chest tightens and I hide my stump behind my back. When I speak again, my voice cracks. "This is not how things are supposed to be."

I turn and leave him alone with his pheasants.

Jude sits by the door of Ash's hut when I return, bobbing his head and tapping his foot, though not humming. His hands whittle a small length of wood into what looks like a short whistle.

He stands when I reach him and rubs his ear. "How are you feeling?"

"Aren't they going to peel off your skin if they see you doing that?" I gesture to the whistle. Ash steps out of the hut as I finish my question. She walks past without a word.

Jude shrugs. "I was working on this before they knew me. It was a dead stick when I found it. You can't properly whittle anything alive."

"How do you know the albinos? Where are you from?"

"This is a conversation for another time, Miss Blackwater."

I step closer. "No it's not. I need to know." My heartbeat quickens. Hawke—an *Enforcer*—sent Jude to me. How many others are at

Hawke's command? Is there an army on this side that he could send after me? Did Skelley Chase know? And if Hawke has people here, how many others have minions on this side? "Are you an Enforcer?"

Jude allows half a smile. "No."

So, he knows what an Enforcer is. "Then what are you?" My muscles quiver and I want to sit, but I need answers. "I don't trust you."

His smile disintegrates and his fist tightens around his whittling knife. "I tried to save you and now you don't trust me?"

I stumble backward, eyeing his knife. "I-I just don't understand."

He lets out a sigh and holds up the whittling tools. "Can we talk after I finish this? I need to think." His gaze darts around the clump of huts. "I'll answer your questions. Just not here. Not now."

He sits and returns to his whittling as if I'm not present.

I turn my back on him. "I'll be back, Mister Jude, and I'll expect answers."

20

000.160.04.21.59

I lie under the pink dogwood tree on the knoll. The stone that held me captive during my amputation shines beneath the morning sun. This is the only pink dogwood in the village, as if stained by years of spilled blood. How many other people have been shackled beneath this gorgeous tree? How many screams for mercy have taken place on this knoll and not been heard? It's like the sacrifice of Radicals, but in a different culture. Why is the sound of a human voice ignored?

I fold my right arm behind my head for support and stare at the tree. Hundreds of blossoms curl out from the branches—white in the center and pinkish-red on the four tips. Even more buds still wait to open. The old joy I used to find when these trees bloomed is too buried to surface now. How can something so beautiful exist when my heart weighs so heavy?

I look over the village. No one seems to mind that I'm up here. This little haven is stunning—dark moss, flawless trees, scattered cottages, and sun that tingles the skin. A small pond rests in an indentation of the earth, reflecting the tall tree trunks and the blue sky. How can such a beautiful village be so dark?

"Are you going to do anything for us?"

I jump at the tiny voice and sit up. Willow stands on the other side of the dogwood, peeking around the bark. Her white skin has lost its bruise. Her lips are parted, allowing small breaths to escape. She's expectant. Staring with those light, stark purple eyes.

"Why should I? You didn't do anything for me." I close my eyes and force myself to tame my tone.

Willow wiggles her splinted fingers. "I took a broke finger for you. So did other people. Well, Elm took some toes, too. We distributed your atonement so you only had to lose a hand."

I allow no outward response to this, but my anger squeezes a fist around my emotions. I never asked them to do that. Why couldn't they distribute enough broken fingers to keep me whole?

"What do you want me to do?"

She shrugs and steps from behind the tree. Green vines from a willow tree are woven into the tiny braids scattered through her long hair. The tiny leaves poke between white strands.

"Why are plant strands in your hair?"

"A willow tree fell two days ago from the wind. Because of my name, I honor its death by attaching its legacy to myself." Her voice is feathery, like a musical chime heard on the street corners of Unity Village during holidays.

"People just come and go." She looks at me with a tilt to her head. "Why do they come only to go?"

"Who else has come here, Willow?"

"Lots of people. Last was a lady and a girl, but they didn't stay long."

I almost can't breathe past my hope. "Did they have names?"

"Newton-lady and Newton-girl."

They survived! At least two of the Newtons survived.

I lie back down to keep the sudden spring of tears under control. My voice comes out hoarse. "Do you know where they are?"

Willow shakes her head and her hair makes a soft swooshing sound through the air. "Gone now. Why did you come here?"

"I've been searching for Independents. I thought I'd find guidance from your village. I didn't know they would punish me for something I didn't even know was wrong."

"Alder says that's how we *learn* what's wrong."

I curb my urge to argue with the little girl. "How old are you?"

"Spring eleven."

"What's that mean?"

She wiggles her pale toes in the moss. "I was born in spring and I'm eleven."

I grin. "I'm spring eighteen."

Willow links her arms around the trunk of the dogwood and swings back and forth, pivoting on her small feet. Her splinted fingers are unable to curve around the bark with the others. She leans her head back so she's looking at me upside-down.

I reach out with my palm, allowing the tips of her woven hair to tickle my fingers. "Do your fingers hurt?"

"Not anymore. Ash gave me white pills for the hurt at first." She sucks on her bottom lip for a moment. "I cracked some branches on a new tree. It was my first accident since I hit bloom. I was afraid, so I ran away. Then I found you." Her voice turns soft and hesitant. "Were *you* afraid?"

I close my eyes. "More terrified than any other time in my life."

"Do you hate us?"

My anger boils at the instant mental flash of Alder and Black, but then I look at Willow. Her upside-down purple eyes watch my face. I don't hate *her*. I thought I hated the boys who called me "Empty Numbers" during my childhood, but the feeling I have toward Alder is so much stronger. Is *this* hate?

"I don't know."

Willow straightens, reaches around to the opposite side of the tree, and produces my pack of belongings. "Here you go."

"Oh, um, thanks." Did she go into my hut to get this? Why did she bring it to me?

"Welks."

"Welks?"

She skips down the knoll. "It's what Jude-man says." And she's gone, traipsing through the rest of the village and out of sight. I stare after her for a while—she was raised here and seems so opposite from Alder. Will his crooked beliefs turn her into an angry axe-swinger?

I use my teeth and fingers to undo the ties on my pack. My left arm aches with sickening pulses. I take a deep breath, keeping my eyes away from seeing the wound. The first item I pull out is my NAB. I've neglected it and Skelley Chase must believe me dead.

Sure enough, no less than twelve messages blink on his bubble. Hawke's bubble has three. I open Skelley Chase's, but don't read any of the messages; instead, I send him my own.

~I'm alive in a village full of albino people who cut off my hand. I'll send you a journal entry soon.

Hawke is a different story. I open the earliest message. It's sent the same time my hand was chopped.

~Parvin, did Jude reach you? Are you okay? Please answer me.

The next one is timed twenty minutes later.

~I am so . . . so sorry I didn't read your message sooner. I could have prevented this. I thought Jude would reach you in time. Thank God, you're not dead, but I doubt this brings you much comfort. I asked Jude to stay with you and protect you until you are well enough to leave.

His next message is shorter, but brightens my morning more than any other words could.

~Jude says you are faring well. I have taken the liberty to inform your family of the little I know regarding your survival. They miss you.

My family. What did Mother and Father think when an Enforcer came to their door? Did Mother think Hawke would take Reid away? How did she react when he told her my arm was cut off? What did she say when she heard I'm still alive?

~Thank you, I type while resting the NAB on the ground. *~You've brought me more comfort than I've received from anyone else here. I'll admit, I'm uneasy about Jude. How did you send him to me? How did he know where I was? Do others know where I am?*

I sit up straighter, lean against the trunk of the dogwood, and then record a new journal entry. It's the longest one yet and I go into as much detail as I can remember—the feeling of Alder coming with his axe, the muscular albino holding me down, the shock that I wasn't saved in time, the sound of Jude's desperate shout a moment too late.

A thin stream of emotional poison seeps out of my heart as I write, leaving me hollow, but a quarter-inch closer to healing. I finish the entry with my recent interactions with Alder and Willow and then take an emotigraph of the village. It can't capture the mixture of emotions inside me when I look over its beauty. I also take one of the shackle stone. I hesitate over the *send* button.

I ache. Skelley Chase is to blame. He sent me here. How can I confide this to him? I want to send it to Hawke instead. My heart feels safer with this mysterious Enforcer.

But others need to know about my story. My hurt can't be for nothing. They will see my bravery. My pain. People will feel for me, *with* me. I can't hold this all myself.

I send the entry and emotigraphs to Skelley Chase. He responds several minutes later with a single sentence.

~It's about time.

I hear his bored warble in my mind. The scent of lemon wafts from my NAB. I clench the cover so hard my fingernails leave crescent moon imprints in its leather. My story, my life, is just a deadline to him.

When did this thrum of hatred turn so solid?

A pop from the NAB steals my attention. It's Hawke.

~Parvin, Jude is no threat to you. He has been to the albino village several times. We keep close contact. He is the only person I know in the West. To my knowledge, no one knows where you are and no one else is in the West. I'll have to leave any other questions to Jude's discretion. His story is his to tell.

I don't know what to reply. Instead of calm, his message prods my anxiety deeper. Hawke avoided direct answers to my questions. Can I even trust *him?*

God, I'm afraid. I fold up the NAB. *I'm among strangers—dangerous strangers. I don't know who to turn to besides You. Are You still protecting me?*

I return to the cluster of huts. A small fire burns in front of Ash's and she sets an iron box with a long handle over the flame. In the breath I take to shout, "Hypocrite!" I spy the pile of coal feeding the flame.

I built a fire with wood and lost an arm. Ash builds a fire with coal and the world is her dinner table. Unjust.

"Did the Newtons have to atone for anything when they came through here?"

She glances up from the fire. "They did not stay long. I helped heal them of small injuries, but they left with the Ivanhoe traders."

"Ivanhoe?"

She hands me three white pills from a pouch on the ground. "Yes. We trade with cities for medicine, technology, or resources. The larger cities are far from the Wall, across the Dregs. Ivanhoe is the largest city in the West."

Ivanhoe. The name latches like a wood clamp to my mind. She opens the iron box, revealing a dinner of pheasant meat and a pile of strange blackened stalks.

"Cattails," she says.

I scrunch my nose and lean away, imagining choking on hairballs of cattail fluff. My family lived off the land, but we never thought to eat the cattails clogging our ponds. Even Harman, the Master Gardener, never included cattails in his wares. No, thank you.

I pick the pheasant off the breastbone and drink a small mug of cold soup. "The cattails are good with butter and salt." Ash holds one out.

"No thank you." I still visualize white fluff in my throat. "What do you trade with Ivanhoe?"

Ash sets a stripped cattail stalk beside the cooking box. "Feathers and animal furs mostly. Because we are the keepers of this stretch of forest, we also grant permission to gather dead-standing."

I discover what dead-standing means the next morning because it's the first sentence shouted at sunrise. "Awake! Dead-standing gathering!"

It's shouted once, but once is enough to rouse the entire village. Everyone leaves his or her hut with packs on their backs, boots on their feet, and an axe over one shoulder. Willow is among them. Her axe is short with a silver head like the rest. She bounces up and down on her tiptoes and looks up at a woman next to her who is dressed in similar fashion. She squeezes Willow's shoulder and plants a kiss on her forehead.

The albinos gather for a few minutes, dispersing different belongings and counting heads. Alder takes the lead and they leave the village in single file. At the rear, Black looks back at me every few steps. His eyes narrow, but his emotion behind the mask of anger is concern.

Not a word is said to me or Jude, who leans against Alder's hut, tapping his fingers on the stones like a drum. I look around. Are they leaving us alone in their village? Do they trust us to stay here? They continue walking, with Black glancing backward, until they're out of sight.

Ash steps out of the hut, drying her hands on her brown tunic. "Are you staying behind?" Jude asks her at the same time I ask, "Where did they go?"

I raise my eyebrows at him. "Obviously she's staying behind—she's pregnant."

Jude folds his arms. "*Obviously* they're going to gather the dead-standing."

Ash clears her throat. "Dead-standing are the trees that died from beetles, age, winter, and such. We gather dead-standing on the first of every month and float them down river to our village to trade or use. This keeps the forest from growing too dense or at high risk for fire."

The explanation is tamer than I expected. The word "dead"—and the way Alder walked out of the village with the axe over his shoulder—made me think of human beings, not trees. "How long are they gone?"

Ash shrugs. "A week. Sometimes two." I look at her bulging stomach. She pats it. "I'll be okay."

Three days later, as she cooks a hearty dinner, her "okay" transforms into contractions.

21

000.155.16.05.30

I've never delivered a baby. I've never had the desire to do so. The youngest newborn I've ever seen was a six-month-old with a scrunched face, and that only in passing at the Market one Saturday morning. I know nothing about birth! It sounds harsh, and looks complicated.

Ash doesn't ask for help, but guilt pressures me. I've slept in her house all this time. Where has *she* been sleeping? Why didn't I think of her well being?

"What can I do?" I watch her support herself on the side of the hut with one hand, holding her stomach with the other.

She takes several deep breaths. They grow deeper and longer, more relaxed. She straightens and smiles. "You say you have a God, so why don't you pray?"

Her voice is genuine and innocent, like she welcomes my beliefs but doesn't accept them. I chide myself. Prayer should have been *my* idea, but I'd expected something more from Ash. Something like, "Go make the bed," "Run for help," or "Give a shoulder massage." But pray?

Okay, God, I think, not feeling an ounce of His presence. *I don't know anything about babies or birth, but please let Ash live.*

Ash does a series of squat-stretches beside her hut.

And please make things go smooth so I don't have to help too much. I don't have the stomach to deliver a baby. I don't know what I'll do if Ash starts screaming. Where is her husband anyway? Does she have a husband? Do the albinos even marry?

Jude shows up as another contraction takes hold of Ash's body. She sinks down to her hands and knees and adopts another series of loud long breaths.

"Where have you been?" The moment Ash told us she was in labor, Jude ran off. I wanted to tackle him and scream, "Don't make me do this alone!"

"I've taken the liberty to boil some water."

My anger dissipates. "Good idea."

Ash chuckles from the ground and sits back on her heels. "Why?"

We lapse into an embarrassed pause. "Don't you need it?" Jude's cheeks redden. "I've always read it's important for births, though I haven't studied the topic."

I can't seem to remember why the water is important. For cleaning, maybe?

"Maybe for a bath," I suggest. "To help you relax."

Ash rises from the ground and walks around, hugging her middle. Jude and I watch her pace. After a minute, she puts her hands on her hips. "You don't have to watch me. This will take hours. Get some rest so you can be useful when I *do* need you."

Jude bites his lip, then looks at me. I shrug, though I want to do the opposite of "get some rest." I walk into Ash's hut.

From outside, Jude says, "I'll go, uh, find something to use as a tub."

Once I'm in the shadows of Ash's hut, I light more candles, using the one already burning as a starter. I glance at my left wrist, but then look away. There's no watch there. No hand. I close my eyes and take a long breath through my nose. Now is not the time to mourn.

I rummage in my pack for the watch. Two hours until midnight. I put it back inside my pack. Ash groans outside.

I can't go to sleep with her out there—the woman who provided the only true comfort I've received. I owe this to her. I will be the best imitation-midwife this mossy forest has ever seen.

I make Ash's bed and fluff the pillow. The marble, two-drawer dresser holds women's and men's clothing. I straighten, clutching a long nightgown that looks as if it's been traded for rather than made. Ash steps into the hut, panting. "I need your help changing."

I hold up the nightgown. "Does this work?"

"I just need to take these off." She points at the loose pants hanging to her knees and her loose belted top.

"Oh." Even better—a naked birth. It makes sense, but still . . . awkward. "Jude's out there, though."

Ash doesn't respond. Doesn't she care another man might see her naked? I untie the rope belt beneath her giant belly. Her boots are the most difficult to pull off. As we get her top off, she has another contraction. She slams her back against the wall of the hut and grimaces.

"Keep breathing," I whisper.

Her breaths come out in gasps. I avert my eyes and spot the small cloth bag Alder laid on the dresser when he visited me. Inside are hundreds of the white pain pills. I grab three and hold them out to her once her breathing relaxes.

"Take some of these, they'll help with the pain." I finally have something useful for her.

She shakes her head. "Those will slow down the process."

I try a different tactic. "Shouldn't you lie down?" I pat the bed, still looking at her as little as possible. "The covers will keep you warm."

"We have gravity for a reason. It helps transport the baby." She steps forward and squeezes my shoulder. "You are sweet and very innocent, Parvin." She reaches past me, grabs the nightgown, and pulls it over her head.

Peeved at the way she called me innocent, I gesture to the gown. "You don't have to wear that for me. Do what's comfortable."

"This is fine." We exit the hut and she walks around doing squats.

The things Ash does are foreign to me. Walking around? Squatting? No medicine? Mother gave birth to triplets lying down. We turned out fine . . . well, two of us did, at least.

Over the next hour, Ash's contractions increase in intensity. She continues her odd habits of squatting and leaning against tree trunks. How does she remain so calm through it all?

My heart beats faster when I think of the actual birth moment. I won't know what to do. I don't know when to yell, "Push!" I won't know what to do with the baby. When do I cut the umbilical cord? Is there a certain length it needs to be? Isn't there something important about the baby's lungs?

The entire camp is lit with fires in front of the huts. Each fire has a pot over it. I find Jude near Alder's hut, peeking under the lid of a pot. Sweat keeps his short hair stuck to his forehead, but he still wears his black coat. He looks up when I approach.

"Good midnight, Parvin. The bath is almost ready." He leads me to the back of Alder's hut where a one-man hollow boat sits like a giant walnut cut in half. "An unfinished coracle."

"It looks like a miniature boat."

Jude grins. "That's what a coracle is. It takes the albinos a long time to make them because they have to wait for a Willow tree to uproot or reach the verge of death before they can use its wood. Alder started this one a few days ago. I lined it with some animal skins to keep the water in."

"So are you almost done?"

"Just waiting for the water." He looks up with a start. "The water!" He rushes to the fire and pulls the pot off the coals as boiling water overflows.

"Check the others," he commands.

Before I can move, Ash's voice rushes through the night. "Parvin!"

I break into a run. She is even paler than her albino-whiteness and sits on the ground, leaning against the base of one of the white dog-wood trees. I fall to my knees beside her.

"I can't do this alone." She gasps, covering her face with one hand.

"I'm here." My stomach gives a nasty twist. *God, what am I supposed to do?*

"I'm afraid," she mumbles. "Is it supposed to hurt this much?"

As if on cue, another contraction steals her breath away. Her face contorts. I watch her chest for any rising or falling action. "Breathe, Ash." She doesn't. "Breathe!" She manages a small inhalation.

God, give me insight! Her grip tightens and my fingers go numb. I stare at her twisted face. *This is* not *how things are supposed to be.*

THIS IS BROKEN SHALOM.

There's His voice again. Or was it a sudden thought? Broken shalom . . . why did Adam and Eve have to ruin everything?

Ash is crying. Her tears, her pain, this brokenness eats at my soul. I never want to witness this ever again. I never want to *do* this.

"The bath is ready," Jude yells from afar. I wait until Ash's contraction ends and try pulling her to her feet.

"No." She waves me away. "I'll sit here."

"The warm water might help." Her body seems so tense. Relaxing in warm water ought to do something. Don't some people have babies in water? I sling her arm around my shoulder. *Lift with the legs, not the back,* I chant as my muscles scream.

"I don't know," Ash protests, but pushes herself up.

"It's not too far." I pray she makes it to the bath before another contraction. We take shaky steps. Running footsteps reach my ears as my knees threaten to buckle. "Jude, get her other side!"

But it's not Jude, and he doesn't do what I ask. Instead he lifts Ash off her feet and strides faster than I can walk toward the bath.

"Black." Ash buries her face against his chest. "How did you know?"

My mouth falls open as I follow. Black is covered in sweat and dirt, with a small wound healing on his forehead from my dagger.

His chest heaves with deep exhausted breaths. "I couldn't sleep and I couldn't get rid of chills. I just knew, Ash. I saw the fires when I got closer and my thoughts were confirmed." He plants a kiss on her forehead.

Everything about Ash's demeanor seems to relax. They reach Jude's bath as another contraction wracks her body. Jude stands beside the coracle with an empty kettle. He stares at Black for a moment, but says nothing.

Black tests the water with his hand before placing Ash in it, nightgown and all. I suddenly hope he doesn't ask why she's wearing a nightgown.

Even though the contraction looks just as painful, my nerves and heart are calmed. Black seems to know what to do. He cues Ash to breathe and even takes deep breaths with her to help pace her.

When her contraction ends, he grips her hand as she closes her eyes for breath. Sweat lines her forehead. Black groans. "This can't be how it's supposed to be."

Ash looks up with wide eyes. "Am I doing things wrong?"

He places a trembling hand on her face. "No, I meant birth. This pain . . . it just doesn't seem necessary."

"It's not how things are supposed to be," I blurt. "Your pain hurts God's heart like it hurts yours. His creation was broken by Adam and Eve's disobedience." I look at Ash. "This pain is a result of that brokenness."

My words sound preachy to my ears, but clarification sinks into my heart. Somehow, I understand another hair's breadth of God's character.

Black and Ash give no response to my mini sermon. Heat fills my face. What did I expect? Black helped chop off my hand—does he think *that's* how things should be?

Another contraction hits and I watch them for the next several minutes, thinking of Mother and Father. As far as I know, Father wasn't even in the room when Mother gave birth. Ash and Black, though, form a type of team.

I meet Jude's eyes. He looks somber, tired, but alive. We stare at each other for a long moment. He smiles. Warmth builds inside me, initiating a genuine smile back. It is strange, smiling again, like I'm not supposed to feel happy after everything I've gone through. It reminds me of when I laughed with Reid at our One Year Assessment.

Thinking of that life six months ago sucks away my smile and I break our stare.

"It's time."

"Time?" Black croaks, mirroring my own reaction to Ash's words. "You mean the baby's coming?"

Ash reaches for him. "Let's get to the bed."

Black puts one foot in the water to lift her out.

Ash's house is at least three contractions away. Can she make it before the baby comes?

They head in the opposite direction. I stare after them. *"Where* are you going?"

"Our house," Black responds, tense.

I point back toward where I've been sleeping. "I thought *that* was Ash's house."

"That's the healing house—" Black is cut off by a sharp inhalation from Ash. He moves behind her and supports her exhausted frame as she puts her hands on her knees.

"It might be better for her to lie down," Jude says.

"Get under her!" Black shouts at me.

Not having a clue what I'm going to do, I drop to my knees as the baby's head emerges. "It's here!" Shock—and a tinge of disgust—race through me.

Ash releases a gut-wrenching groan and I guide the rest of the baby free. I catch it in the crook of my left arm, avoiding my stitches, and stabilize it with my right hand. Everything is a mess of blood—the ground, Ash, the baby—but I can't stop staring at the small albino form in my arms. I turn the baby over.

"It's a boy," I murmur, using Ash's nightgown to wipe off the baby's face. Ash collapses against Black and they both sit down on the ground. I hand them the baby. "Where do I cut the umbilical cord?"

"Wait," Black says. "Wait until the baby gets all of the nutrients he needs."

So we wait and stare. My initial disgust melts away into euphoric wonder. My anger about broken shalom sees new light, new *hope*. Ash's pain didn't last forever. It resulted in a new creation.

I stare at the pale baby skin. *This* is how it's supposed to be. God hates broken shalom. He won't leave us in it forever. He plans something more for us.

I want it.

Everything after these silent minutes of awe and shock happens in a mindless fog. Black cuts the umbilical cord, the baby cries, Ash washes in the coracle, and they hobble into their hut. Jude puts out his fires, sets two pots of boiling water outside Black and Ash's door, then we both wash, go our own way, and collapse.

A windstorm hits that next morning. The flapping of my animal-skin roof wakes me, but I snuggle beneath the blankets, falling back asleep with the vision of Ash's baby in my mind. I never liked babies much, but for some reason, even though his eyelids were red and his skin an odd splotchy white, the albino baby left me stunned.

After two days of eating leftover pheasant, reading my Bible, and resting, I crawl out of bed and use my teeth to help squirm into my fresh extra shirt. Then I pick up Reid's journal. I haven't touched it since the cave above the wolves. Sickness and then the atonement have directed my mind elsewhere.

I sink back into bed, pulling the covers up high and crack open the book. Where should I start? I turn to the first page with writing.

09.19.2147, Time: 08:32

I've come to the realization that I will be the one to die on October 7, 2149. The Clock is mine.

The journal slips from my fingers and flops backward onto my lap, losing my place. I scramble to pick it back up again with my one hand. What . . . what did Reid write? How could he know the Clock is his?

I can't open the book fast enough. My breathing accelerates. There it is.

> *. . . The Clock is mine. So I've started a journal to record my last two years. It's a strange feeling, knowing I'm going to die. I've always felt an urgency to live my life, but now it's increased. I've decided to travel some more. I think I want to visit the Upper Cities in Florida.*

"But how? *How* do you know?" I shake the journal as if it will grow a mouth and share the answers.

"Parvin?" Jude calls through the doorflap in a quiet voice. "You better come out here."

With a harsh squeeze to the binding of the journal, I discard it for the moment and climb out of bed. I lift back the flap and meet Jude's eyes.

He looks over his shoulder. "We need to leave."

"Leave?" I look past him, but see nothing unusual. What about Ash and the baby? "Why?" I don't want to leave yet, and that thought frightens me.

Jude takes my hand and pulls me out of the hut toward the edge of the village. I'm startled by his touch, but even more startled by his careful quiet manner. "There."

I look where he's pointing. Far in the shadow of the forest march a line of albinos with trimmed, soaked logs on their shoulders. They're returning with the dead standing.

A vice clamps around my throat. Between them and us lies the pink dogwood, broken clean in two, blossoms scattered across the ground like tree blood.

22

"Did you do that?" I breathe.

He drops my hand. "Of course not. Do you think I want my head chopped off?"

I gulp. "H-Head chopped . . . off?"

"That's what they do if you kill a tree. Then they bury you at its base in a cage made from the dead tree's branches."

A blossom blows toward my feet, but I can't seem to move. The albinos are closer. My heart twists like a wrung rag. "It must have happened during the windstorm."

"Parvin, they're going to think we did it," Jude hisses.

"But we didn't." I straighten. "Black and Ash can vouch for us—there've been strong winds through the night."

"Do you want to risk that? Black held you down when you were innocent last time."

No need to remind me. Alder cut off my hand. If he thinks we killed their dogwood, he won't hesitate to kill us. "I need to get my belongings." My voice shakes. Maybe I can talk to Alder first and explain.

"I'll help."

I stumble across the mossy forest floor into the healing hut and throw my few possessions in my pack. Jude lifts it onto my shoulders. He is tying the flap shut when shouts drift from the direction of the knoll.

On a whim, I say, "Grab my Bible out of there."

"We don't have time."

Time. We're always running out of time—in the West and the East. "Please, Jude." I bounce up and down on my anxious toes as he fiddles with the flap. My hand rubs my throat.

God, oh God. You don't want us to die like this, do you? I'm acutely aware that God can and will do whatever He wants. *Please don't kill me!*

Jude thrusts my Bible into my hand. We sprint out of the hut and veer toward the edge of the village opposite the dogwood tree. I run into Black and Ash's hut before Jude can protest. They are both still in bed, holding their baby.

I halt, staring at them, embarrassed that I interrupted. Pushed by the gnawing pressure of dread, I ask, "How's the baby?"

"Hello, Parvin." Ash smiles, nestling the sleeping baby in her arm between the two of them. I think back to her care for me. She will make a wonderful mother. "Cedar is perfect." She strokes the baby's face. His closed eyelids are red as fire and his thin shock of hair looks bleached, even against his pale skin.

"You named him Cedar?" Poor kid.

"After the Red Cedar tree," she says. Black watches me with a stern look.

Jude steps into the hut without an invitation. "We're leaving."

Ash's lips part and she looks at Jude. Something in her posture weakens and her face falls. I speak in a rush, trying to word it in a less brutal manner. "The pink dogwood tree is broken, I think it's from the windstorm, but Alder might think we did it."

Black sits straight up in the bed, alert, like he's ready to spring after us.

"I want you to have my Bible." I inch toward the doorflap. "I know it's not what you believe, but the first part shows how God intended us to live on this earth. It shows life before brokenness. There's so much more in there you need to know. Please read it."

Ash's eyes are wide. "No. We can't—"

"You must! It's a gift. Thank you, Ash. I really—" but my voice won't let me finish. Tears well up. "Good-bye." I toss the Bible onto the bed.

Jude and I run out of the village. White dogwood flowers paint the forest floor, fallen from the storm. My footsteps crush twigs and plants beneath me. I hope I don't have to atone.

We crash through bushes covered in remnants of morning rain. Water droplets explode off the wet leaves, showering our faces. I wipe my face with my hand, opening my eyes as I run straight into an albino. He falls backward. I tumble to the side with a shriek.

Alder.

Another albino stands behind him, balancing the log Alder dropped. I scramble to my feet as a third albino parts the bushes behind me.

"The pink dogwood," he exclaims to Alder. "It's *dead*!"

I bolt.

"Parvin?" Alder shouts.

"Jude!" I push through thick branches and force my weakened legs to move. "Jude!"

He's there, holding out a hand for me. I grasp it like a lifeline and we run. Sounds of slapping leaves and cracking underbrush follow. I imagine Alder gearing up to hurl his axe straight into my fleeing back.

A young girl's voice yells from behind. "Jude-man! Parvin! I'm coming with!"

I slow my pace to make out the tiny form. Willow. Why is she coming? She has nothing to fear from the other albinos and we have no direction in our flight.

"Go back," Jude shouts at her. He's faster than me and pulls me along. I nearly trip as we break from the forest to a long stretch of plain. It's so bright, I squint and run even more mindlessly, no longer dodging trees.

A loud snap of wood breaks the air and I look back. Willow is on the ground, a small young pine tree split in half beneath her body at the edge of the forest. She throws a wild glance over her shoulder then stumbles after us.

"Willow!" Alder shrieks from the forest, kneeling beside the pine as she flees. Now we have to take her with otherwise she'll have to atone.

I am speed, running across this flat treeless ground. Free. Weightless. But the feeling is fleeting when the ground slants down and reveals a wide canyon cutting the ground in half, like a knife through a block of cheese.

"Where do we go?" I shout, still a hundred yards away.

"The bridge."

My running jolts my vision too much to locate the bridge.

"Jude-man," Willow screams.

Jude looks back and I stumble to all fours. My left arm crumples from the pressure on my wound and my face scrapes the weedy ground. The other albinos, including Alder and Black, exit the forest running.

Willow has a small lead and the gap is closing fast. Jude and I approach the edge of the canyon.

"Where's the bridge?" Hysteria slithers under every inch of my skin. The albinos still have their axes.

Jude points. "There."

Twenty yards to our right, a thick rope is mounted to the ground with metal prongs hammered into the dirt. The rope is strung taut across the hundred-foot gap.

"That's not a bridge! That's a rope!"

Jude skids to a halt, mere feet from the rope. He stares at me with what looks like anger and panic. "You can't . . . ?" He gestures to the rope. "You've never—"

I look at the rope and back to him, gasping for air. "Never what? Walked a tightrope?" I hold my fist over my eyes. "This—is—not—a—*bridge.*"

I face the albinos, helplessness building like a volcano. I'm now willing to beg in any manner, but Alder's history shows he doesn't heed begging. Maybe he'll swipe my head off before the first word comes out.

Willow reaches us and heads straight for the rope without a word. Already barefoot, she spends a careful five seconds transferring her balance from the ground to the rope. Once both feet are on, she takes long steps across, holding her tiny arms out as wide as they'll go.

I stare with my mouth open. She holds her chin high, staring at the other side of the canyon. The rope sags a little from her weight and her tiny toes grip the grains.

"Go, Parvin." Jude faces the oncoming albinos. "Crawl across the rope if you have to. Hand over hand."

It's too late. "I have *one hand.*" I can't let Jude die for me. He's only here because he tried to save me.

Willow is already on solid ground across the canyon, inching away from the edge with her eyes set on the group of albinos.

I stand between the rope and Jude like a deathly game of monkey in the middle. I'm the monkey. Neither of my prospects looks promising, but if I stay in the middle I'll lose.

The albinos will reach us in a matter of seconds.

Jude pulls something from the inside of his black coat. "Stop!"

Everyone freezes, including me.

"This is a gun." He aims a grey metal barrel at Alder's chest. His hands are steady, his jaw clenched, and his face set in firm resolve. No trace of his nonchalant character remains. The edges of his lips turn up in a grim smile. "It can propel a bullet into your body fifty times faster than you can hurl your axe."

My breathing slows, hitched to stunned trepidation. The air is frozen. The albinos are stock-still. Jude stares them down like a matador.

In this moment, I realize I don't know Jude. What little trust I had in him was because Hawke sent him, but even Hawke is a mystery. Trusting Jude was foolish. Rash.

Characteristic.

"Parvin, give me your knife and go." His voice is chilled.

My hand covers the sheath on my belt. "Why do you need my knife?"

"Give it to me!" He thrusts his hand back.

"Okay!" I'm so afraid he'll shoot someone that I hand him the weapon.

"Now *go*!"

Do I escape with the man with the gun? Each passing second screams *no*. I look across the canyon. Willow turns and runs away from us.

"Willow!" Black calls after her tiny retreating form. She keeps running. I would, too, if I had the opportunity.

"Be quiet," Jude barks. "She has a right to leave you if she wants. You said so yourself—she hit her bloom."

"She needs to atone," Alder growls.

I glance at the rope. It's this or a beheading. After Jude's threatening, the albinos are bound to behead me if I go to them now.

Alder opens his mouth again, but Jude cuts him off. "Say nothing."

Again, the silence hangs. Jude waits for me. I drop to the ground and inch my body onto the rope, upside down, clinging with my right hand. *God, protect me from these maniacs!*

Crisscrossing my legs over the rope, I scoot in increments. Every muscle quivers. My strength won't last long. I pray my pack is secured enough that nothing falls out.

I must keep moving. I can make it across. The bottom seems ages away, flooded with a murky cattail marsh. If cattails are growing from the bottom, the stagnant water is shallow—too shallow to break a fall.

Scoot. Scoot. The fibers of the rope dig into my skin.

"Turn and leave." Jude says to the albinos.

"We can't do that." Alder's voice holds no mercy. "Why do you flee? Guilt?"

"Don't shoot anyone!" Even though I hate Alder, I don't want to witness his death.

My fingers start to uncurl from the rope. I hook my left arm over at the elbow, but the pressure hurts my wounds. Queasiness sets in and I look away from the albinos. I continue to inch across. My back prickles from the space beneath me.

God. God. God. I should have faced the albinos.

My weak legs can't hold on. I'm half way across and whimper, "Jude." One leg slips off and a shriek escapes. *"Jude!"*

He looks over at me in a flash, keeping the gun leveled at Alder. "Hold on."

"She's going to fall into the Dregs, Jude." Alder's voice rises. "Parvin, come back while you can."

Why, so he can *behead* me? Even breathing is dangerous to my strength right now.

Jude inches backward to the edge and kneels down. Holding the gun up with one hand, he lowers the dagger with the other and saws back and forth on the rope—*my* rope.

"What are you *doing?"* The vibrations peel my fingers away.

"Grip the rope as tight as possible and don't let go!"

"I'm falling."

Alder gestures toward the canyon bottom. "You're dooming yourselves!"

Those are the last words I make out. The rope crackles and rotates on thin threads. Jude slips my dagger into his belt and the albinos start screaming. Some twirl stones in their slings. Alder raises his axe. Black steps forward, both hands extended.

Meanwhile, I grip the rope with my shaking hand. So much for not being the monkey.

Jude turns his back on the albinos and leaps spread-eagle off the edge. I scream. A stone zings over his head. He grabs the rope with his empty hand and the jolt of his weight snaps the remaining threads. We plummet toward the canyon bottom.

"Don't let go!" Jude roars.

The jolt of my stomach brings me back to when I dove off the edge at the Wall. Only that time, I wasn't at risk of being speared by cattails or shot by a deranged stranger.

The fall is not a smooth swing to the other side as I'd imagined. We freefall for several feet—just enough time to picture a horrific death.

What will death feel like?

The rope goes taut. My hold breaks from the jerk and I tumble through the air. My flailing limbs collide with Jude. The cacophony of screams, rush of wind, and explosion of a gunshot are doused upon my impact.

23

I land, flat as a board, and my lungs collapse. What felt like a brick road turns out to be the marshy water. The back of my head connects with the mossy bottom, but not hard enough to steal my consciousness. Water rushes into my lungs, carried by my ill-timed gasp.

My pack absorbs most of the impact, which is why every vertebra feels hyper extended. Hot tingling spreads through my body like scorching acid. I'm drenched. I can't move. My head is now held above water by my pack.

My breath returns in minute increments. "Help." A cough wracks my body into a sitting position.

The pain frightening me subsides into mere discomfort. I can conquer discomfort. Using my right hand, I roll over onto my knees. Green slime washes over my face as I disturb the water. I come up, gasping. Cattails surround me like a green wall. My eyes focus on a large locust mere inches away on the thick leaf.

Eww.

I stand with a groan and look up. The albinos are gone. The cut tightrope hangs on the opposite wall, twenty feet above my head. Blood creeps down my right arm. I broke several cattails, but each one pierced my body in thick gashes. I guess I've atoned for them.

The air seems oddly calm compared to the chaos moments ago. My right hand stings from a rope burn. I trail it in the water.

"Jude?" I weave through the cattails. Broken spines of old stalks hide under the water like brittle stakes. My rabbit fur boots are thick, but won't withstand the rough marsh bottom for long. "Jude?" A second parting of cattails reveals his body facedown in the marsh, black coat filled with a pocket of air. "No!"

I stumble forward, snapping cattails with my knees. I clench his coat by the shoulder and rotate him with a loud grunt.

"Jude! Don't be dead." I keep my left arm under his neck to hold his head above water. A purple bruise swells on his forehead and blood streams from his nose. I tilt my ear by his mouth, but I'm breathing so loud I can't tell if he's breathing at all. I hold my breath.

No sound meets my ears. No exhale touches my face. But his heartbeat is faint against my hand on his chest. *God, he's dying.*

I wasn't taught how to save anyone. I was raised to locate a Clock and look at the Numbers, but a quick scan of Jude's coat doesn't reveal a Clock bulge. Is he zeroing out?

He's not breathing. He needs air. My panic rises like an inevitable tide. We're surrounded by swamp. No place is flat enough to lay him out. I've seen a man thrust his fist into another man's abdomen when the second man choked on a boiled egg. I've also heard the boys in school joke about mouth-to-mouth.

Nothing funny about it now.

I adjust my knee to support his body out of the water as much as possible. I curve my right arm around to plug his nose, wiping blood away with my elbow. Then I lower my face to his.

Our lips touch. It's anything but romantic and I can't help feeling awkward. I send a long breath into his mouth. His chest barely rises. Marsh water touches my tongue, bringing with it the taste of aged fish.

I gag, but force myself to send another breath into his lungs, blowing harder. His chest rises higher. I stifle another heave against the green sheen of water covering his skin. It reeks. *God, revive him. Please revive him.*

Halfway through my fifth breath, his body convulses. I jerk back as he vomits on me. Instinctively, I dunk myself in the water. When I emerge, the smell reaches my nose and I struggle not to retch in response.

I peek back at Jude. He's breathing heavily. Coughs seize him with each exhale. I help him sit up and clean off his face with some swamp water. He looks around and spits into the cattails. Blood mixes with the water from his nose to his jawline. Neither of us speaks for a long moment. I watch air return to his body.

The sun flickers in my eyes with a water ripple. My dagger is wedged between two rocks, reflecting the light. Without mentioning it to Jude, I slip it into my sheath, feeling much safer with a weapon. *Thank You, Lord.*

"How are you?" Jude's hoarse voice is garbled by blood and a broken nose.

How am *I?* At the moment, hollow. I breathed out every emotion and reaction when saving Jude. Perhaps the panic devoured them.

I peek at him from the corner of my eye. Does he know I semi-kissed him? I avoid his gaze. We are alive. Neither of us should be. By God's continued grace, Jude breathed again.

Shame seeps into my soul as the swamp water laps against my side. Of course I'm alive. How could I allow myself to think I would die? Where was my wolf-walking confidence when I clung to the tightrope? I feared for my life, even though I knew—*know*—I won't die until October. My current survival is proof.

"I still have five more months." But I remember what Reid wrote in his journal. *The Clock is mine.* How in time's name, could he know?

Jude clears his throat and spits again. "You hab a Clock?"

"Don't you? I know you're not an Independent."

He wipes his face with his wet sleeve, tapping his nose tenderly. "I'b a Radical frob the East. Crossed id Canada."

I gape at his easy admission. I expected him to avoid the topic. Even more question marks and confusion pop through the soil of my mind like moles. I thought *I* was the only one to cross and live. Skelley Chase made it sound like I was doing something original.

A loud crunch sound and exclamation from Jude makes me jump. He holds his nose with both hands and a new gush of blood spurts down his face and clothes.

I look away, holding my breath.

"Ah," Jude groans. "Hopefully that helped and didn't hinder." His voice sounds clearer.

I look back at him. He holds a sleeve to his nose. It's less crooked. I shudder, thankful *he* broke his nose and not me. I wouldn't have the mental strength to pull it straight again.

"So you have five months left on your Clock?" Jude examines a scratch on his hand, not even looking at me.

"Yeah." Yes. Yes, I do. Reid didn't know what he was writing. He has no more knowledge about our Clock than I do. And it *must* be my Clock. Reid needs to live because . . . I can't be the survivor. I can't even accept the *idea* of outliving him. "So you're a Radical? Were you sent through the Wall as punishment?"

"Nah, I smashed my Clock on this side of the Wall. I snuck through."

"Are you Canadian?" How did Jude cross? *Why* did he cross? The Canada Opening is thousands of miles away.

He cocks a head to one side. "I'm from the USE and I've been here just under two months."

Two months? I've almost been here a month, yet I have a scrap of the confidence and naturalness he has in this wilderness. Perhaps he's used to living more in the wild. What are the odds I meet a man from the United States of the East and we have an acquaintance on the other side?

Jude stands up and shrugs off his coat. Underneath, a brown vest tied in the front covers a sleeveless frayed shirt patterned with black and silver. Something squirms on his bare right arm. Something alive.

"Look out!" I gasp, lifting my hand to hit the black and green snake.

"Calm down. It's my tattoo."

I pause. "But it's . . . moving." The snake is *in* his skin. The tattoo pauses then continues its pattern, coiling around his wrist and back toward his shoulder. My hand sinks back to my side. "How does it do that?"

His eyes light up and his speech comes out fast, excited. "It's made with flexible silicon light-emitting diodes that conformed to the shape of my skin. They're no thicker than a couple hundred nanometers each. It's combined with bioluminescent ink and programmable kinetic energy." He pauses as if waiting for me to probe deeper.

"I've never heard about it." Why couldn't he just say, *"It's paint acting alive inside my body."* His mixture of scientific words threatens to collapse my uneducated brain cells. I try a simpler question. "Where did you get it?"

"In Prime."

"The High City? That's somewhere northeast, right?"

He wrings the water out of his coat. "Of course. In New York, near the Canada border. You didn't know?"

His 'this-should-be-common-knowledge' attitude irks me. I straighten to look him in the eyes. "I've never been to a High City, Jude-man. The best I can do is read about them, but that doesn't mean you should treat me like a schoolgirl. I'm from a Low City—born, raised, and toughened like leather."

High-City status. So Jude is oblivious to struggles of people beneath him. I bet he's been raised behind hundreds of smooth glass windows, eating flour and processed food. Does he even know about the injustice done to Radicals in Low Cities? He'll probably think I deserved betrayal.

"Jude-man?" Well, he has his breath back. Now it makes more sense why Jude would know someone like Hawke. Did Hawke enforce in Prime?

The memory of him pointing the gun steady and intent at Alder reminds me I don't know this man. Yet here we are, trapped inside a boggy canyon bottom.

"So what do we do?" I bet Jude's never even *been* to a Low City.

A gust of wind blows through the canyon. I didn't notice the chill until now as the portion of my body out of the water grows goose bumps.

Jude rubs his bare arms. "Well, we're in the Dregs."

If this place has a name, it has a reputation. The albinos knew this— *Alder* knew this. They must have known we'd die down here. Why else would they refrain from throwing stones and axes at us?

I have five months. I can't die in here. "You got us here, don't you have a plan?"

"I warned you to keep a tight grip."

I wave my hand in front of his face. "This is all I have. I was already weak from crawling." There's that word again. *Weak.* "I mean, I was tired." An ache steals back into my emotions. I look away as if I can erase the loss of my hand from my mind.

"Tally ho. I'll try and find us a way out."

"Tally ho? Hawke says that."

"Everyone from a High City says that."

Hours pass and we find no golden stairs. At first, we go for the rope. Jude tries climbing, jumping, and putting me on his shoulders. We are still short a good fifteen feet. I take my wet rope from my bag and we try lassoing the end of the other rope. Jude's aim is as good as his manners. I'm not much better. The walls are impossible to climb, slicked smooth by years of rainfall. Small vines of purple and yellow flowers crawl down the canyon face, but they're too flimsy to hold any amount of weight.

"We'll head northwest." Jude leads the way up the canyon.

I can't tell the direction, nor do I care. What I *do* care about is the growing ache in my severed arm, the chill making its way to my bones, the shrinking sun, and the fact that we have two feet of cold swamp water for a bed.

"How will we sleep?" I follow him through thick patches of cattails. The water is at our thighs, too deep to lie down in and I don't like the idea of locusts crawling on my face.

"Are you tired?"

"Well, not yet, but we will be."

"You can't sleep in the Dregs. You can't hide in the Dregs. You can't drink the swamp water. You can't build a fire in the Dregs. You can't climb out of the Dregs."

"*I* will escape the Dregs," I snap, incited by his pessimism. "God's assigned me a purpose. I have five months left to my Clock, remember?"

"You base a lot of your life on your Clock." Jude sneers. "Try imagining life without it for once."

How can I tell him I've lived both lives—Clocked and Clockless—until a month ago? "You had a Clock once."

He swats a tiny blue dragonfly from his face. "And now I'm a Radical."

I'm viewed as a Radical, too. That somehow makes Jude and me a team. "Why did you destroy your Clock?"

"Personal reasons. My family wanted to sell it on the black market for specie, but I don't like the idea of Clocks running the world."

"Oh." I frown. "I didn't know people could sell them." So Jude has a High-City family that participates in an illegal economy. This still doesn't explain why or how he crossed.

"A Radical who has no Clock but wants one can buy it and pretend it's his," Jude explains. "Then he can enter society and receive the benefits his former Radical status denied him."

"I wonder if the government will ever figure out how to match Clocks to people after conception." I marvel at the idea of a secret world of illegal Clock holders. "Then the black market wouldn't be necessary. Anyone who lost or accidentally broke his or her Clock could just get a new one."

Do people in Unity have black-market Clocks? No one would ever know. Reid and I could have solved our problem years ago with a little extra coin.

"Jude, why did you cross?"

He turns away from me. "That's not your business."

Closed door. All right. He's entitled to his privacy, but he doesn't have to be so sharp about it. "I'm glad you crossed in Canada," I say, attempting to reinstate peace. "Otherwise you'd be dead."

"*You* survived."

"I had nothing to do with it." I wave my hand in front of my face as tiny gnats buzz in a growing group. "The West side of Opening Three was the top of a cliff. I either had to jump or starve to death in the Wall tunnel. I jumped off the cliff thinking I was diving to my death, but my rope got caught in the sliding electric door. It almost hung me." I rub the fading burn on my neck. "I climbed down the rest of the way."

My throat closes and I look at my hands—well, my hand and stump. I wouldn't be able to climb down now. Will I be able to climb back up the cliff to meet Skelley Chase in five months?

"Why would you think you were diving to your death if you have a Clock?"

"Well, it could have been my brother's Clock." I shrug. "It's complicated. Never mind."

"Tally ho." He faces forward, leading a path through the Dregs like a water snake. Sharp tingling crackles in my left arm. I stare at my stump, feeling, but not seeing my hand. I can't clench it against the pain. My lips tighten, tugged downward by the threat of tears.

I stumble.

Jude turns around. "Are you tired?"

No, I'm just missing a piece of me, inside and out. But he mustn't know that. "I need a small rest."

We walk toward the side of the canyon, but rest only comes in the form of a wall-sit. The mossy rocks on the bottom are too far down to sit on, unless I want the water lapping my nostrils.

Jude helps me take off my pack and holds it as I rummage through. Skelley Chase is probably furious with my limited journaling. He's going to have to get used to it because my NAB has been doused in Dregs water. I half expect it to be snapped in pieces when I pull it out, but High City electronics are sturdier than I expect. It unfolds like normal and the screen says in shaded blue letters:

Water mode initiated.

"Wow. It's still alive."

"So *that's* how you communicate with Solomon." Jude frowns. "And you're from a Low City?"

"Unity Village isn't underground, you know. We know about things like NABs." I press the start button.

He raises his eyebrows. "And moving tattoos?"

I roll my eyes and change the subject. "How do you know Hawke?"

"It's better for now if you don't know." He glances up at the canyon edge with a grim look. "It would have been better if you never even knew *me*."

"Why?"

He shrugs. "Never mind."

I lower the NAB. "You can't say *never mind*. I never asked you to stay in the albino village to look after me. You could have left and never known me."

A tiny weight tugs my heart into a pout. Jude doesn't want to be with me. Can I blame him? We're in the Dregs. We're enemies with the albinos. And I'm not exactly Susie Sunshine.

Jude's response comes out terse. "If not for me, you'd be dead in a cage at a tree base."

I lift my chin. "You're the one who wishes I never knew you. I'm not saying I'm ungrateful."

He folds his arms. The writhing snake tattoo bulges. "You're also not saying you *are* grateful. I tried to save you and you don't even acknowledge that."

I gape at him. He lets out a breath as if he's irritated.

"I *am* grateful." I force my voice to work, but I'm lying. His praise-seeking attitude just sucked my gratitude right out. I'm thankful for his effort, but the truth is he didn't stop anything from happening. I'm still handless.

I, however, saved his life mere hours ago, and he's yet to utter an ounce of thanks. He vomited on me and I didn't complain. I look down at my arm and swallow. "Can we keep going, please?" The sooner we're out of the Dregs, the better. Then we can go our separate ways.

Jude pushes off the canyon wall. "Tally ho."

I walk with my head down, following him with peripheral vision. I take several deep breaths to calm myself, but only fill my lungs with fishy air. How did we end up angry and distant? I don't know Jude well enough to be at odds. Why do I care if he enjoys my company?

I turn my focus to the NAB still in my hand. It takes a moment of finagling to balance it on my left arm so I can tap the screen. I enter my journal and record a new entry in a low voice so I don't have to type.

"I'm no longer with the albinos," I speak to the screen, watching the letters flow out one by one. "Jude and I fled when we saw the pink dogwood tree broken in half. We didn't want to be blamed and killed by the albinos."

Jude glances over his shoulder. I look up, but he faces forward again before we can make eye contact.

"I'm recording a journal entry," I explain, sensitive to his judgment. He snaps a cattail out of the way.

I enter as many details as my mind recalls, more for my sake than Skelley Chase's. I want to remember this time—the most traumatic weeks of my life. I speak Willow's name and scan the canyon edge. Where is she? Does she know how to survive on her own?

God, please protect her. I don't know why she tried to come with us, but please keep her safe.

My journal entry ends with our plummet into the Dregs. I whisper the portion about saving Jude's life as soft as possible so he doesn't hear. Why do I feel ashamed? Maybe Jude doesn't realize I saved him.

I leave the entry with all facts except Jude's history. It's not mine to tell. I don't want the world reading about him since I don't know why he crossed. Maybe he's a victim of the Enforcers.

I gulp. Maybe he's a convict, escaped from a prison. I stare at the back of his head. Maybe he's *killed* people.

No. Hawke sent him to help me. I can at least trust Hawke . . . to an extent.

I send the entry to Skelley Chase and notice Hawke's bubble pulsing when I exit the journal page. I click it with a stomach-flip, visualizing his shadowy blond hair and light olive skin—the sharpest recollection of his looks I have.

He sent the message yesterday. It is short with little flair, but makes my heart lose its breath.

~I'm glad you're safe with Jude, Miss Blackwater. He will take good care of you. By the way, today I saw your name in The Daily Hemisphere. *The world knows who you are.*

24

000.154.20.13.23

My biography is published.

The announcement stands like a resolute stamp of finality four scrolls down *The Daily Hemisphere.*

> *Author Skelley Chase, best known for riveting biographies like* Blood Numbers *and* Sweeping Death's Doorstep, *stunned the world with his newest release,* A Time to Die, *about a Radical girl who was sent across the Wall and still lives.*

My story is known. I can't erase it. According to the date at the top of the article, it's been known for two days already. A shiver sweeps down my body and my stomach coils like a snake in a knot. Skelley Chase published it early. Is Reid still safe?

I'm taken back to the East with a single inhale. Scenes flutter through my mind like a flip book: the library displaying my book as the newest biography, the Lead Enforcer seething about my accusations against the justice system, Trevor Rain realizing he unknowingly supported and funded Skelley Chase's plot, Reid being questioned about his Clock . . . maybe even denied a job or hospital care.

I think of the bullies—Dusten Grunt chanting "Empty Numbers". When he reads my biography (if he can read), will he think I'm desperate or brave? Which do *I* think I am?

Mother's voice echoes through my mind: *Impulsive.*

I *am* impulsive. She was right. My impulse led to where I am. But so did God. It all connects to my prayer on the hospital floor.

The scenes sweep out of my mind like dust under a rug, brooding until they are unearthed later. My present surroundings return with one slow blink in a swirl of green cattails.

I stand alone in the Dregs, holding *The Daily Hemisphere* with my right hand. My pack hangs over my left shoulder and the NAB rests by my feet underwater—dropped and abandoned in the flurry of nerves.

Jude is a short speck wading through green water far ahead. He doesn't realize I stopped. Irrational anger clenches my throat. I don't yell for him. Why should I call him? He doesn't seem to care if I'm left behind.

I scan the next paragraph of the article, unable to spur my legs into forward motion yet. My chest feels empty except for my heart pounding like a bell clapper.

> *Told with nuggets from her point of view,* A Time to Die *introduces us to Parvin Blackwater, a girl from a Low City with a bland past except for the secret she and her twin brother kept from the world.*

My stomach lurches at the sight of my name on screen.

> *Born with a third brother as an unexpected set of triplets, the Blackwater children outnumbered the required two Clocks in the household at birth. After one Clock zeroed-out, taking a triplet with it, Parvin and her brother remained half-Radical, never knowing to whom the remaining Clock belonged.*
>
> *This time out, Skelley Chase transcends his previous pattern of biographying by following Parvin Blackwater's continuing story. He will offer the new biography to fans in X-book form with weekly installments following her miraculous survival on the West side of the Wall, including emotigraphs and journal entries.*
>
> *Is Mr. Chase leading a revolution in the way X-books are presented, or exploring a new format for a unique case of survival? Mr. Chase hastens to say he has nothing against the current or previous forms of biographies, in fact, he intends to publish another one within the next three-months of an already zeroed-out High citizen. Some question his desire to write about the living when he's only ever scripted stories of the dead, but Skelley Chase remains unphased.*

"My writing proves I'm an expert in life and death. If someone doubts, then they haven't read A Time to Die, *which is, in fact, about both."*

I stare at the end. The article seems more about Skelley Chase than me. Proof, again, that this biography is still about his "good story" and I'm just the tool. But even though I want to remain bitter, I can't deny the fact he's proven himself. He published my biography. Granted, he broke his promise of waiting, but my story lives.

I tuck *The Daily Hemisphere* under my left arm, pick up the NAB, and send a hurried reply to Hawke.

-Is Reid still okay?

I shove the NAB into my pack. Once I'm put back together, I continue my slow trek, avoiding the sharp stalks beneath the water and fighting for balance against the moss. I return *The Daily Hemisphere* to my right hand, unable to put it away yet. I want to read every word of the article with a magnifying glass.

"Oy!" Jude stands far ahead by a bend in the canyon. He throws up his arms. "Why are you back there?"

Defiance stiffens my muscles and I lift my chin. I continue to walk, giving no response. My initial impulse is to shout, "You've noticed, then?"

"We have to keep going," he says once I reach him. "There's no time for you to meander along. I don't know what food you have in your pack, but I have nothing. We need to find a way out as soon as possible or we'll starve."

"I wasn't *meandering.* And I have nothing in my pack. I didn't have time to grab anything." Once I start defending myself, the words roll out like tumbleweed down a hill. "You're the one who dragged me out of the village without preparing. You're so focused on the plans in your head you can't even notice if I'm stopped behind you. I could have passed out and you wouldn't know until I drowned. *You* got us down here by sawing the rope and flailing a gun and now you turn to *me* to provide food? I guess saving your life wasn't enough."

I got carried away. Again. It's strange how easy it is to vomit my frustration on Jude. Where has my filter gone?

Jude bows with a sweep of one arm and a hard look. "Lead the way, ma'am."

"*I* don't know where to go."

He straightens and wipes a trace of blood from his nose. "You have two choices—forward or back the way we came."

I roll my eyes and try to fold my arms before I remember my stub. Instead, I look away. "I'm not leading." *I'll stand here all night if you want, Jude-man.*

He turns around, rubs the back of his ear with two fingers, and we travel in silence until darkness falls. By this point, my anger subsides enough that I ache for simple friendship, yet every time I imagine saying, "I'm sorry", my voice disintegrates. It doesn't help that his prior words and actions send the message that he doesn't want me with him. I shouldn't have lost my temper.

I've never had much of a friend. Reid was always my go-to. Now that I'm faced with the prospect of sharing bits of life with someone else, I'm rudely aware of my lack in friendliness. Even more pressing is the *desire* to share. I want someone else to know about me in a real way. My biography ought to do that. Maybe Hawke will read it.

The stars come out and our steps through the water turn slower and slower. Instead of imagining a bed to sleep on, I dream of a flat cropping of rock or beach on which to collapse. The darkness makes me jumpy. Anything could be watching us from the canyon edge. What lives in these waters?

Jude's head droops ahead of me. I wish he'd offer to carry my pack. It pulls against my shoulders forming muscle knots like mini boulders. He has only his coat. Doesn't he have belongings?

"So tell me your story." He rubs the back of his neck.

I fold my arms to keep warm, lodging my stump under my right bicep. My lungs shrink and my breath quickens. Excitement seeps like molasses. He wants to know about me. Do I want to share?

Yes, my mind whispers. If I'm allowing strangers in the United States of the East to read about Parvin Blackwater, I ought to share with the man who did *try* to save my life. And, he's waving a white flag of reconciliation.

"I have a twin brother." I choke a little on the conflict between pride and desire. "We were born as triplets, but our older brother, William, died right after birth." My explanation of our single Clock is far less eloquent than the paragraphs Skelley Chase formed at the start of my biography. Still, Jude seems to follow along with little prompting.

"I started writing an autobiography in my Last Year to defend the lives of Radicals. They don't need to die." My voice catches as faces flash across my mind—faces now gone and dead. Eaten by wolves.

"Then what did you do?"

He doesn't even realize I'm struggling. I push through the story of meeting and trusting a biographer. I can't bring myself to say Skelley Chase's name—it's like acid on my lips. "The biographer betrayed me, so I proclaimed myself a Radical so Reid could continue to receive medical care. My village sent me across the Wall."

Facts. Limited emotion. It's like I'm sharing the shell of my story. I'm not inclined to give Jude the raw portions—fear, loneliness, betrayal, worthlessness . . . *weakness*.

"Why didn't you choose relocation? There are plenty of other cities that house registered Radicals."

"That's not an option in Unity." I turn my face away to block out the memory. Betrayal. "Unity Enforcers don't register Radicals. The trial is supposed to give the impression Radicals have a choice, but Unity Village is so close to Opening Three the Enforcers just send Radicals through. I think they do this in more places than Unity Village. Maybe even all Low Cities."

Jude is silent for a long time. Does he see how this is wrong or does he have a similar mindset to the Enforcers? "So you're on a pilgrimage now."

"Pilgrimage?"

"It means you're on a quest to something sacred."

Quest. Pilgrimage. These words light flares of hope inside me. "But I don't even know where I'm going."

Jude shrugs. "It's not based on what you're doing, it's dependent on your mindset. A pilgrimage is about following *despite* not knowing the answers. Maybe this quest you're on can stop Enforcers from sending Radicals through the Wall. How many lives could you save?"

"That's what I tried to do with the biography." I look away, pondering his words. Is there a more tangible way I can help Radicals? Am I following God's call to pilgrimage? What *is* my mindset?

An image of staring at Ash's freshly birthed son flows into my consciousness, bringing with it strong hope. God wants something more for me. He won't leave me in this broken shalom.

"Maybe I'm supposed to find the Newtons." I glance up. "They're a Radical family I know. The Albinos said they went through their village. I want to find them."

"I know the Newtons. They adopted a Radical child from an orphanage near where I lived. The law took away their High-City status because of the girl. Solomon escorted them to your village to help them settle in."

I shake my head. "It's bizarre how many people we both know. I never would have expected to even *meet* someone from the East on this side." I stumble and land on all fours in the water. Jude stops. "Sorry, I'm tired."

I try to push myself up, but my left arm crumples under the pressure. I wince and Jude hauls me to my feet. I'm both warmed and shamed by his help.

We stand there in silence, slimy water dripping down my neck. I shiver. Jude looks around and I know he's thinking the same as I am: how will we sleep?

The wind picks up, rustling the unseen darkened cattails. The sound of their long stalks bumping into each other sounds cold and intimidating. The gnats, locusts, and dragonflies have long since gone to sleep.

"One of us will need to rest," he says. "Otherwise we'll both collapse once we're weaker."

I cringe at the word *weaker*. I won't collapse. I'll be the last one standing, no matter what. "What do you suggest?"

"What if you lie down in the water and I pull you by your pack? I'll keep your head above water and you can try to rest."

I wrap my arms around my middle. "I'm already freezing." The idea of submerging myself in the fishy gunk when I'm shivering in the darkness sounds as pleasant as walking with the wolves.

"I guess we'll keep walking, then."

"Thanks for the thought."

"Welks." He rubs the back of his ear again as if scratching away an itch.

The night feels endless in the silence. At first, I watch the moon creep higher in the sky, but my neck grows increasingly sore and I succumb to staring at Jude's back. Crickets and frog croaks grate on my nerves.

Hours creep by, taking bites of my sanity with them. Even when daylight comes, the sleepy sand in my eyes keeps me squinting. Pimples dot my upper lip, brought on by sleep deprivation. I habitually rub my fingers over the spots, hoping a moment will come when I find they've disappeared.

By noon, I speak. "I need another break, Jude."

I don't tell him my pack feels like a boulder or that my legs are numb and heavy from the water. I don't want him to know I want to collapse. My injuries have piled on my body like barnacles over the past few weeks. They scream for attention.

Jude's hand flies up to swat a bug from his temple. "What?"

"I *need* to *rest.*" The least he could do is look tired.

"Lie down and I'll pull you along."

This time I don't argue, though the water still causes a perpetual shiver. I release a chilled breath as my body sinks into the murk. Jude grips the two straps of my pack with both hands and I lean my head back on the lump of belongings. I've accepted the fact the items inside will be wet, no matter how hard I try to keep them dry.

My body is buoyant, even though my boots drag against the bottom. A sense of freedom comes once my weight leaves my feet. I close my eyes and force my muscles to relax against the cold. Small waves lick the back of my neck making me shiver. The slimy water creeps through my clothes like long water worms, filling my boots and separating my numb toes. I'll never be warm again.

I allow twenty minutes to pass before groaning, "I can't sleep."

Jude continues to walk. I twist to my feet. The movement jerks him backward. He looks at me with raised eyebrows and I wince at the two black eyes from his broken nose.

"Didn't you hear me?" The Dregs are so silent it's hard to imagine he's not ignoring me. "I can't sleep."

"I was listening to music."

I roll my eyes. "How?"

"My tune-chip."

My sluggish brain runs the word *tune-chip* through my mental process three times before I ask, "What's that?"

"A chip that plays music matching my mood." He folds his right ear in half. I squint through the shadows beneath his hair and see an undefined black spot in the crease between his ear and his skull.

Music. I rarely hear music. The county building played music in every room of the building—soft wordless music that doesn't spread an ounce of inspiration. Boys in school would sometimes carry small pocket music players, but they always wore cordless headphones so I never heard the songs.

"I can't hear it." I wrap my arms around my dripping form. How nice for him that he's been entertained by melodious art while I've listened to mosquitoes nibble my ear hairs.

"Of course you can't." Jude releases his ear. "It's surgically programmed in my brain. You think I'd force the whole world to hear my mood?"

The concept is so bizarre I stare at his head for a moment as if I'll see wiring. Is half his brain made up of electronics? How can music be implanted? "I didn't know they could do that," I whisper. What mood would his music reveal at this moment?

Sunlight accentuates his frown. "I didn't think about you having to deal with the silence." He looks past me in his own wave of thought. "Wow. I'd hate that."

"Silence? There's a lot of sound. Wind, the lapping water, bugs and things . . ."

He shakes his head. "I can't think when it's quiet like that."

Weird. What must it be like to be so used to hearing music that the sounds of the world are distracting?

"You still tired?"

I nod, forcing my drooping eyes to blink instead of close.

He turns his back to me. "Hop on."

"A piggyback ride?" When's the last time I had one? "Won't this hurt you?" I climb up with difficulty.

"You're not very heavy." For once I'm thankful for the comment on my size.

He has a firm hold as the canyon slopes down and my backside dips beneath the water. Wrapping my arms around his chest and resting my head on his shoulder feels acutely intimate, which may be why I'm so calm.

I drift off, watching the cattails pass by and listening to the sound of his rhythmic breathing.

Who needs music? I think in a sappy stupor.

When I wake, it's dusk. A cricket chirps, awakening the other dusk insects. Jude is still walking, bobbing his head to his tune-chip. He must be in a happy mood. I strain my ear right next to his, but catch no whiff of melody.

We're still in deeper water and my legs are numb from the pressure around his waist. Soreness crawls up my spine and my neck pops when I straighten it.

"I'm so cold," I croak.

Jude lowers me into the water so I can stand. "Try walking again. The movement will help."

My stomach rumbles with a stab of pain. "Are you hungry?"

"Yes."

No other speech passes between us. No use thinking about food without a solution. *God, please get us out of this canyon,* I pray. *Must my time be wasted in this place deserted of people? Bring us the hope You showed me during Ash's labor.*

Thinking of Ash reminds me of my Bible. What if she and Black burn it as heresy? The albinos have no faith in God. But they have to see that their life isn't how things are supposed to be. How can they not see this? Where does *their* purpose come from? Do they even feel the pull for more?

I need more than what they have to offer. Protecting trees while partaking in purposeful mutilation will never fulfill me, even if they hold a unity I've longed for within my village. I can't be part of their purpose because it doesn't look like purpose at all. I *am* on a pilgrimage. As Jude said: a quest to something sacred.

A quest to shalom.

Thirst drags drying saliva down my throat, but my water pouch is empty. The departure of the sun brings shadows once again, leaving the water with a black sheen. When I can't see all the cattails, bugs, water-spiders, and slime on the surface, it's easier to imagine the water being clean. How bad would it be for us to drink it?

The disgust I had when we first fell in the Dregs isn't as strong any-more. It takes only an hour of dry mouth and the memory of dehydration with the wolves to scoop a handful of water to my lips.

I've slurped half of it before Jude slaps away my hand. "Don't drink that!" His voice echoes against the canyon walls.

"Don't shout!" My hand stings. "I'm thirsty."

"This water isn't clean."

I shake my head. "Would you rather die of dehydration than drink a little dirty water?"

Jude lets out a huff. "Cities dump their waste and refuse into the Dregs. You could get seriously sick."

My mouth seems to shrivel up at the idea of what I might have put into it. I have nothing to say, but I don't doubt Jude will be drinking from the Dregs by sunrise.

Morning comes as pleasantly as the raising of a guillotine. Grey clouds grow stronger with the rising of the sun. I'm sick of living and Jude looks like a nauseous clown. His eyes are puffy and the black beneath them is turning to greenish yellow. Around two in the morning, I'd tried dragging him by my pack like he'd done to me, but I lasted an hour before my arm felt like a searing iron. I don't even know if he slept, but the momentary rest seemed to invigorate him.

Our hunger takes precedence once the sun shines its muted warmth on our skin between the dark clouds. Jude plucks a locust off a cattail and bites it in half.

"Eww!" I recoil. I force a swallow to rid my mouth of the imagined crunch of locust.

"It's food." Jude pops the other half in his mouth. The legs are still squirming. "Men of God ate locusts in the Bible."

"You can't listen to bugs, but you can *eat* to them?" I shudder. "You are strange, Jude-man. *Strange.*"

Jude releases a one-beat laugh at my joking tone. I squeeze a green cattail stalk as we push through. "The albinos ate these." I *so* hope he doesn't suggest I eat a locust.

"I know. They're delicious with salt and butter. Taste a lot like artichoke."

"Do you think we can eat them raw?" If only we could somehow make a fire.

He responds by snapping a stalk. "If they're green. Never eat them once they've turned brown."

I follow his lead and pluck off a cattail head, checking to make sure no grasshoppers are hiding on it. All clear. Without allowing myself to question, I bite into it.

The center is hard as a rock, so I nibble the green fuzz around it. The texture is stiff and stringy, with little hairs like a peach. Raw, there's not much taste to them; either that, or I'm distracted by the fact it feels like a miniature animal in my mouth. I still eat three of them.

"They're much better cooked," Jude says after his fourth one.

"I would assume so."

He chuckles and I smile, desperate for an ounce of hope. My ounce turns into an avalanche when I glance up at the brightening edge of the canyon. A person stands on the albino side, a hundred yards away.

I grip Jude's arm with a gasp. "Look."

The person is tall and scans the Dregs. From this distance, it looks like a man wearing copious amounts of traveling gear. Maybe he has food. And water! He might even have a rope.

Jude squints. The man spots us and waves.

"Jude! He can help us."

"Hey!" The man jogs up the canyon toward us. His voice is a tiny pinprick of sound, but settles like gold aloe on my heart. He waves again and Jude waves back.

"Hello!" I shout.

When he reaches us, he's panting. "Hey! Jude and Parvin?"

"Yes!" I exclaim, but Jude steps forward, holding out a hand to silence me.

"Who are you?" His tone is cool.

"Willow sent me. A little albino girl. Do you know her?"

Jude relaxes. "Yes, where is she?"

"On the other side of the canyon. I saw her a day ago. She asked me to find you. Do you need help?"

"We need food and water." My stomach clenches at the thought.

Jude laughs, relief clear on his voice. "We need *rescue*. Do you have a rope?"

The man sets his giant bag on the ground and rummages inside. It's all black and looks very official. "Here." He tosses us a silver canister. "To hold you over while I dig out my rope."

The canister lands short with a *plop* and both Jude and I trudge forward to retrieve it. Inside are half a loaf of bread and three small cooked potatoes. What a savior!

I look back up. "Thank yo—" The words die on my lips as the stranger takes aim with a sleek sniper pistol. Before I can register the explosion from the weapon, Jude is struck by a bullet.

25

000.154.04.45.00

Thump. The impact sends Jude tumbling backward.

In a state of panic, thought comes to me clearer than a polished window.

Jude is shot.

I am next.

I dive under the water and propel myself toward a clump of cattails, trying to drag Jude with me. Adrenaline steals my breath. These bushes won't stop a bullet. We're like cougars trapped in our own den.

I come above the water for breath, tense and praying, waiting for the bullet to find me. *God, please protect us.* I know I won't die, but the placement of this bullet could mean the death of many other things—movement, thinking, consciousness, personality, walking . . .

Splashing startles me as Jude flails in the water.

"You're alive!" I reach for him and he grabs my hand like I'm his only hope. *Thank you, God!*

I pull him toward me and glance at the cliffside, terrified of seeing the barrel of the pistol again. But the stranger is gone, and his weapon with him.

"Time to go," Jude hisses, yanking me to my feet.

"Where's the shooter?" I remain in a crouch. "Is he hiding? Don't move!"

Jude pulls me up the canyon anyway. "Come on, Parvin."

It's hard to flee when we're in a death cage. Bullets could beat us in any race, but, as we run through deep water, none seem up for competition. The air is calm. No gunpowder explodes from the canyon edge.

"The food!" I slow.

"No time."

But I'm not willing to let it go. We run a few yards before I look behind at the tin still floating, half-filled with water.

I turn back.

"No!" But Jude makes no move to stop me.

I dump the water from the tin, shove the floating potatoes back in, and run with forced movement back to him. Jude's panic seems to have lessened, but he's paler than Willow.

I gasp. *Willow.* That man said he found her. Did he kill her?

Blood flows from Jude's upper right arm. He's shaking. Once he moves forward again, he stumbles.

"Stop." I lay my hand on his shoulder. "We need to make sure you're okay."

I lead him to the wall of the canyon, where he leans his back against it and squeezes his eyes tight. Blood blocks me from seeing the severity of the wound. I rinse it with some Dregs water. Jude doesn't protest. In the brief moment when the blood is thinned with water, I see the hole above the crook of his elbow, interrupting the fluid movement of his snake tattoo.

"God . . ." He puts his hand over his face. "O God . . ."

I can tell by Jude's voice that he's praying. I keep my own voice calm. "It'll be okay."

He just shakes his head. His shoulders move in small jerks like he's crying but won't let me hear.

An ache threatens to clinch my beating heart. *It's okay, Jude. I'm here.*

I unwind the bandage from around the wolf scratches on my left arm. They're almost healed now and no longer need covering. I rinse them in the Dregs and squeeze the wad of cloth against my chest to wring it out. Then I wrap his upper arm.

He groans. "What will I do? He didn't kill me."

"Thank God, then. You'll heal. I know you will. I'll get you out of here." Get him out of here? What am I saying? How will I get him out? I can't even get myself out.

His left arm grips my wrist. "Your dagger." He looks at me with his red-rimmed black eyes. "You have to use it to get the . . . the bullet out."

I step back. "I can't do that."

"You *have* to!" He straightens.

I stumble away. "No!"

His ferocity leaves him in a flash and his hand covers his anguished face again. I finish the bandage with trembling fingers, tucking the end into a fold since I can't tie it. I steel myself to be strong.

"It's okay." I take his hand. "Let's keep going. God will give us a way out."

Funny how, when someone else is cracking, my faith seems to bloom. I know God will get us out because I'm going to live five more months. He also kept Jude from getting shot in the head. We *will* get out.

In a brief moment, Jude's hand slides out of my grasp and his fingers touch the side of my face. I look down, unsure why he's touching me. His hand moves to my shoulder and pulls me into a tentative hug. He's trembling.

The tension flows from my muscles and I release a thick breath. He sighs, too, and then takes my hand again. We push onward with renewed energy and multiplied questions.

I lead, and we both scan the canyon edges for movement. My heart continues to pump so fast I feel sick, but I'm strong—assigned to protect Jude. I will be strong for us. For him.

I squint at cracks in the canyon wall, trying to locate a hiding place in case the shooter returns. This worries me most. If he reappears, we are still helpless trapped targets.

Jude calms after an hour, but I hesitate to ask him the many questions running through my mind. Why did this man shoot Jude and leave? Did he really encounter Willow? If so, did he kill her or just use her information? Is she on his side? Was all of this a conspiracy?

Jude didn't seem surprised by the shooter. Why would this man let Jude live if he'd decided to shoot him? "Jude . . . who was that man?"

He trudges in silence. I look over at him and he just shakes his head.

"You expected to be killed. Why is someone after you?"

"No, Parvin," he says in a choked voice. "I didn't know. I don't . . . I need to think a while."

I bite my tongue. "Okay." Storm clouds rumble overhead, sending gusts that shake the cattail stalks. Our coats do little to protect from the increasing chill. Jude clutches his arm and moans every few minutes, making me wish I had white pills to ease his pain.

The rain starts in small sheets. I know enough about the weather to accept that this will be the most uncomfortable day in the Dregs. If the clouds have built in the morning, they will likely last through the day and night. But I can't stop the scratchy squeal that comes out of my throat. "Water!"

Jude and I split the soggy bread and potatoes, hoping the digestion will keep us a little warmer and more energized. Then I hold out the canister to gather rainwater.

I'm still confused by the provided food. If the shooter intended to kill us, why sacrifice his food? Then again, Jude said the man chose not to kill him.

For a wild moment, I wonder if the food is poisoned. I swallow hard and turn to Jude. He pops the last bite of his potato into his mouth. I suppress my suspicion. If the food is deadly, it's too late to get it out of our systems. Besides, no matter what Reid wrote, I hold to the belief that *I* still have five months.

The sky darkens so much it looks like evening and the rain grows to painful drops. The canister is full in minutes and we slurp the cool liquid in relief. It coats my throat, soothes my stomach. I can't get enough.

But Jude makes me slow down. "You'll be sick if you drink too much."

"Okay." We fill the canister again and then close it. Jude shoves it in my pack for later.

Now that we are no longer thirsty, the storm turns into less of a blessing. It's cold. Hard. Loud. *God, is this necessary? Do You see us at all, or do the Dregs keep us from view? Where is Your protection? Calm this rain!*

The storm roars louder and louder, like a rushing river. My arms shake, though whether from cold or concern, I can't say.

"Jude . . ." My voice quivers and I reach back for his hand. "The storm is too fierce."

"What?"

I turn so he can hear me better. His hand is pressed against his wound and he's shaking like a shaved cat in winter. I long more than ever for Ash's white pills.

I repeat myself as loud as possible. "The storm is too fierce! Maybe we should stop!" He's in a lot of pain. We should definitely stop.

But what good will stopping do? That won't alleviate the rain or his suffering.

His lips move, but I hear no response. He's looking hard into my face and gesturing with his free hand, but I might as well have cotton in my ears.

Suddenly his hand grips mine, crushing my fingers. I jump and jerk my hand away. He stares past me with dilated eyes. I spin around, expecting to see the shooter on the canyon edge, but instead I have a single second to register an eight-foot wall of water barreling down the canyon.

I have no time to take a breath. It slams us to the floor like a train. Broken cattail stalks jab my cheek and forehead. My lungs burn as water fingers tear my body in separate directions. Sticks slap me. I tumble.

Up! Up! Up! My mind screams and I thrash against the torrent. I break the surface and, in my desperation for air, gulp two lungfuls of water. Before I can cough it out, a sweep of water shoves me under, throwing me about like a leaf in a tornado. My chest convulses, wanting to cough and breathe at the same time.

A fist of water slams my body into hard rock. I push away from it with my feet, battling it like a boxer. The force propels me upward. In the moment my face meets the air; instead of taking a breath, I retch. Then comes the oxygen—sweet, sublime oxygen.

I seem to have undergone most of the thrashing and now ride the flood with my one good hand, like a bull-rider. The waters propel me back down the canyon Jude and I spent so many days traveling up—back toward the albinos.

Why, God? Why must this flood undo all we've struggled for?

My coat and pack snag this way and that on nothing but force. I fight to keep them on my body. Already a weak swimmer, I kick madly to stay afloat. My left arm flies through the water with each paddle, useless and thin.

I slam into the bends of the curvy canyon like a rag doll. No matter how I fight, I'm under the will of the devil water. It tears my boots from my feet one after the other. My hair swirls around my neck and sticks to my face, blocking my sight. Bandages around my calf loosen and tangle my legs together.

When I round another corner, something slams into me from behind, knocking my forehead against the canyon wall. Fingers grip my hair and an arm wraps in one of my pack straps.

Jude.

Even in the midst of drowning, relief provides another gasp of air. We are linked. He'll help us. He's a survivor.

His kicks are forceful and keep us above water, though we're still subjected to the whim of the flood. His hand releases my hair and a moment later it wraps a rope around my middle.

"Help me!" he shouts.

We spend several seconds underwater, allowing the flood to hammer us as we fumble with the rope. I don't know how it manages to wind its way around us both, but Jude kicks us back above water and yells, "Okay!" in my ear. I trust he considers it secure.

After another curve, we slide along the right side of the canyon where the water is a little slower. I hate the helplessness consuming me as I watch my own strength fall short. My life is out of my control. If the flood continues to flow much longer, I'll surely drown. Already, my body aches with exhaustion.

Without warning, we stop with a jerk. The rushing water flows over my head. I can't breathe. The rope tightens with a pinch. We're snagged on something. It's going to drown us. Jude is screaming one word over and over. I can't make it out.

My body pounds against the canyon wall like a wild fishing bobber. I push against the smooth stripped rock with my feet until my head gains more height and I take a decent breath. Jude is still screaming and I make out his word.

"Cli . . . ! C . . . mb! *Climb!*"

I glance behind me to see what he means, but water douses my face. I reach back, groping the slick canyon wall for handholds.

His shout changes. "R . . . pe! Climb . . . ope!"

What rope? Then my hand finds it—a grainy, thick, woven rope to which Jude clings. We're at the beginning where we first fell into the Dregs. The water's risen so much we can now reach the cut tightrope anchored to the top.

But *climb?*

God, this strength is beyond me!

I grip the rope tight and pull myself toward it, against the pounding water. My muscles quiver. I gain a few inches of height— enough to gasp a full breath, but my arm shakes.

Jude plants his feet against the canyon wall and pushes. His body suspends above the water like a board. He is free of the torrent, but we are still tied together. I cling to the tail of the rope with limp muscles. My stump slides helplessly when I try to use both hands.

Stupid arm!

Jude releases the rope with one hand, grabs my elbow, and pulls me higher. "Put your arms around me!"

I kick against the wall to position myself, but the current sweeps my feet away again and again. The rope around us is too constricting. I can't maneuver.

Throwing control to the wind, I wrap my stump around Jude's chest and release the rope. In the moment when I fall, I grip his coat with my right hand and manage to hold on. The rope holds us tighter than my flimsy muscles.

I guide my feet above the water and onto the side of the canyon. Then Jude climbs. Hand over hand he ascends, walking up the wall. I cling to him, shuffling up the wall behind him like a vertical piggyback ride.

His entire body trembles. Blood flows again from his arm. The bandage is gone. Any second, he'll fall.

God, strengthen him. If ever I needed a miracle, it's now.

My legs burn and my arms fill with weights.

One more step.

I'm not breathing, riddled with confusing emotions—desperate, painful hope for freedom and sickening fear of the flood.

Just one more step.

My foot slips an inch. Jude stops the ascent. *Keep going*, I urge. His body moves, feeble and spent.

"One more!" I gasp.

Jude flops an arm over the slanted, water-smoothed edge. He pushes. The rope goes slack. Our feet flail and I link my leg on the rope mount. Sheer survival adrenaline—and possibly the nudge of an angel—hoists us over.

At last, our bodies drag in the first burning breath of freedom.

26

Time does not exist. Only survival pounds louder than the thunder.

Breathe.

Rest. The inches of flowing water caress our depleted bodies. Muscles turn to churned butter. Hypothermic chills are as mild as a bout of hiccups compared to the preciousness of existence.

We pant like beached trout, too tired to flail, to put more space between the edge and us. Even the idea of Jude's gunman can't prick my brain into worry. Let him find us. Let him see what we've done.

We've survived.

I've survived. I'm not weak. *God is not weak. God sees us.*

Hours or minutes may have passed before the chills force us to move. I don't know; I didn't keep track of time. My arm buckles when I push myself to my hand and knees. I hold my stump to my chest as a wounded dog might. Jude sits back on his heels and unties my rope from around us with quivering arms.

We crawl in a broken daze, dragging ourselves to higher ground until the water isn't sweeping around us. Rocks scrape off our soaked, wrinkled skin. Mud coats between my fingers. We crawl like powerless children, fighting for nonexistent strength.

At last, Jude collapses at the base of a tall smooth rock. I lie down beside him, desperate for any ounce of body heat. The rain turns warmer. Our clothing drips on our chilled wounds.

Jude pulls me against his shivering form with his good arm. Dreams of drowning steal my consciousness and I remember an old story of a girl selling matches, freezing in the snow as she dreamed of a fire.

Fire. What delight the sizzle of fire would be to my ears.

Crackle. Snap. Burn.

My face warms. My stump stings from cold. My body trembles. Hours weave between my veins, tempting me to relinquish my hold on life.

Pop! Wood hisses, reminding me of a winter morning at home. Cinnamon oatmeal in Mother's giant bowl. Warm mugs. Smoky warmth in the air.

My eyes flutter open to a blast of heat from a small flame. Sparks sing into the air from the jab of a stoking stick. I squint against the heat, seeking clarity.

A red face. White, tangled hair. Purple eyes.

"Willow?" I push up on my elbow. Stones seem to fill my head. It rocks side to side as I try to keep it balanced.

Willow comes around the fire, holding a charred stick. She kneels by me. Her face is splotchy red with peeling skin along her cheeks and nose. Sunburned. "Are you warm yet?"

I shake my head. The movement disorients me, so I lower myself back to the ground. How did she find us? What time is it?

"Keep sleeping." Her soft voice returns me to slumber.

Each time I wake through the unknown hours, the crackle of fire meets my ears. Sometimes Willow is there, sometimes she's gone. Sometimes the sky is light, sometimes it's dark. Sometimes food roasts over the flames.

I wake enough to eat roasted gopher. "How did you do this?"

It's early morning. I don't know what day. Jude is still sleeping. Has he woken at all yet? The blood in his arm has clotted and turned a dark red color, almost black.

"I've been burning dead sticks. I search hard for them. I have no coal."

My first taste of warm, cooked meat elicits a moan. Willow hands me a small pouch of water. Her splinted finger sticks out from the others—splinted for my sake. What made her sacrifice for me? What is making her help us?

"I filled yours with rain water, too." She gestures to my water containers on the ground.

"Thanks."

"Welks."

She watches me eat, as if expecting something. I have nothing to offer. I want answers. "Who is the man you sent after Jude and me?"

She frowns. "What man?"

"A man found us in the Dregs. He said you told him to find us. It was right before the storm. I thought . . ." I bite my lip. "I thought maybe he hurt you."

She shakes her head before I finish. "I've been alone since crossing the Dregs."

I release a long breath. There's no reason for her to lie . . . unless she's on the shooter's side. "He shot Jude."

She cocks her head to one side. "With a sling and stone?"

I spit out a thin gopher bone. "With a *bullet*. From a gun."

Her eyes dart to Jude and back to me. "The hole in his arm?"

"Yes."

Her sunburned face turns pale and concerned. "It's deep," she says in a shaky voice. "I think he will heal, but he groans a lot when sleeping. It must hurt very badly."

As if to confirm her statement, Jude rolls over with a pitiful whimper, wrapping a muddy hand over his wound. Willow takes a small step toward him as if to comfort, but stops with a quivering lip.

Her distress calms my irritation. "His wound stopped bleeding. It may be painful, but he climbed a rope out of the Dregs, pulling me with him. He'll be fine."

But will he?

She sits cross-legged on a small stretch of animal skin. I continue staring at Jude. Unable to stop myself, I ask in a quiet voice, "Is Jude a bad person?"

Willow rotates a second gopher on a stick over the fire. "Alder doesn't like him, but that's because Jude-man doesn't agree with how we live. He says it's unpractical. He doesn't like customs, so he's always making suggestions to Alder on how to change them. I like him, though. He's come to our village three times now."

"Why?"

Willow shrugs. "Because I asked him to come back and tell me stories. He reads many tales to Elm and me from a small electronic square—stories about a warrior who killed a giant with a sling like mine, a hairy man who ate grasshoppers, a young queen who saved the world . . . ." A blush enhances the color of her sunburn and she turns the gopher.

I wiggle my eyebrows up and down. "You *like* Jude."

Instead of looking bashful, Willow glances at Jude, then glares at me. "Jude-man's my friend. I graft with Elm."

I hold up my hands in defense, ignoring the sight of my invisible left hand. "I didn't know."

Asking what "grafting" means and who Elm is seems unwise, so I remain quiet, but it sounds like an albino betrothal of sorts. I peek at Willow. She's so little. Spring eleven. Already betrothed?

What would it be like to be betrothed? I cringe, imagining myself standing in a white dress across from Dusten Grunt and his hairy knuckles. Who would Mother and Father choose for me? They'd have better taste than to pick Dusten, right? They chose each other, after all.

My mind flits to Jude. Reid might like Jude. Would *I* like Jude?

Willow interrupts my thoughts by waving a flaming gopher on a stick. "Still hungry?"

I jerk back. "Um . . ." We should save some for Jude. My fingers are greasy. It doesn't taste very good. My stomach is churning. "Yes."

She slides it off the stick with careful fingers.

"How did you find us?" I pop off one of the gopher legs to release some of the heat. Gopher oil drips onto my skirt. I try to calm the nasty twist of my stomach.

"It was an accident. I headed back home—to atone, but the rope was cut."

"I thought you wanted to come with us."

"I do now that I found you. I want to see new places. I'm tired of people leaving without giving me stories or showing me something new. You're the first stranger to atone. Tell me a story from the other side of the Wall."

I shrug. "I don't have any stories."

"Yes, you do. What's over there?"

"Piles and piles of chopped up trees." Her eyes shrink to slits and I smirk, pretending to poke her with the gopher stick. "Okay, not really. We have houses, people, brick sidewalks . . . boring stuff."

She huffs. "Everywhere has that. What did you do when you lived there?" Her small mouth breaks into a shameless grin. "You didn't fight much, did you? Black captured you faster than a falling petal."

I glower at the fire.

She must take my silence as an answer because she moves on with another question. "What's in your bag?"

My bag lies by the fire, the rope still tangled around it like a vine. Mud covers the bottom half, meeting dense patches of wet cloth.

"I'll show you." I unbuckle the flap with Willow's help so I don't have to muddy my teeth. First out is the NAB. Willow's eyes widen and she turns it over and over in her hands.

"Did you get this from Ivanhoe?" she breathes. "It's like the one Jude-man has, but bigger."

That name. Ivanhoe. Ash called it the largest city in the West. She said the Newtons might be there. "No, it was given to me."

Next is my box of matches. The wood box is still in good condition, but the sliding top is open. Six matches remain. I dispel my concern. Willow can make a fire without matches. Maybe Jude can, too. They can teach me.

I take out my watch and toss it on the ground.

"Why don't you wear this?" Willow picks it back up.

I hold up my stump in response. Why draw more attention to my severed arm than I need to?

"Wear it on your other arm."

"I don't *want* to wear my watch on my other arm! I want the right to put it on my left without worrying it will slide off." My heart wilts. "I want my hand."

Before she can talk again, I dig deeper into my pack. My wool socks and handful of underwear are in a wadded mess, still soaked and covered in dirt. I close my eyes at the idea of wearing fresh undergarments.

I set them aside, away from Willow. *The Daily Hemisphere* is in a stiff roll in my pocket. I laugh at the irony. The flash flood takes my boots, but doesn't empty my pockets?

I wipe the mud and green Dregs grime off the electrosheet with my skirt. Willow's jaw drops when I show her how to turn it flat. While she's preoccupied, I reach in and pull out a thick wad of heavy, water-logged paper. My stomach drops before I even see it.

Reid's journal.

The cover corners are curled and soggy. Pages fold in on themselves. It's still dripping. I crack it open with a crying heart to see blur after blur. A few words link together in short sentences, but otherwise it's ruined.

"Oh Reid," I whisper, gripping the pages. Water trickles out. I'm an idiot. I'm not used to having paper, so I didn't think of what the

Dregs water would do to his journal. An emotigraph slips from the pages into my lap. I sniff.

"Oh"—Willow notices the journal—"what happened?"

"What do you think happened?" I toss the journal aside. It lands in mud. "We were in the Dregs." I grab the loose emotigraph and push myself to my feet, walking away from the fire.

I struggle to place one foot in front of the other. Why wasn't I more careful? But who knew we'd land in the Dregs? Still, I could have pulled it out and dried it as we traveled.

No. This was inevitable. The flash flood would have destroyed it in the end. Now I'll never know why Reid thinks the Clock is his.

I stop and cover my face. Do I even care about Reid anymore? Or Mother? Or Father? I crossed the Wall and seem to have shoved them out of my mind. I've focused only on myself. If I cared, I would have read through Reid's journal first chance.

"What was I supposed to do?" I shout to the sky. "How could I have prevented this? Do *You* have an answer?"

I don't wait to hear if He does. I pace, tapping the stiff emotigraph against my hip. Since crossing the Wall I've just reacted by clinging to survival. But mere survival holds no purpose. I refuse to believe God created us to just get by, so where does that put me?

My thumb rubs Reid's emotigraph button. I hold the sheet up. It's a picture of the sunlight streaming through the new lattice window at home. Mother's fresh spreads sit on the windowsill with small price cards, not yet snatched by the morning sill-traders.

What was Reid feeling when he took this? I lick my lips and press the button.

A mental wall leaps into my mind, blocking my current emotions. Like the flash flood, new ones slam into the corners of my heart. Remnants of fading sorrow precede a sweep of thick hope and jealous excitement. My heart swells with conviction. *Something great can be achieved.* The hope, excitement, and conviction stir faster. Faster. I gasp and my walls disappear, letting the flood mix with my own emotions, leaving a tiny almost invisible wisp of regret.

"Wow." I breathe in short gasps, organizing the confusion in my mind. The emotions don't fit with my circumstance, but even their shadows feel good. Reid's conviction is the strongest feeling tingling my nerves. He felt helpless, but he *knew* something great could be achieved. By me?

I press the emotigraph again. The several seconds of emotion pass, leaving me gasping as they did the first time. His hope and conviction *had* to be for me. They must be. My thumb presses the button again, welcoming the prick. I close my eyes, soaking the emotions in—welcoming them into permanence. This time, when I emerge, the conviction almost feels like mine. Maybe I *am* convicted. Reid thinks I can achieve greatness. I can. I must! I have the potential.

My finger rubs back and forth over the button. I fit my thumb into the indentation. One last time.

PARVIN.

I twitch, dropping the emotigraph. God's voice echoed in my spirit, not my ears, almost like *feeling* my name come from Him.

I stare at the emotigraph beside my feet. "Sorry . . ." Why do I feel the need to apologize?

Like a whisper caught in the breeze, I sense a calm hush. SHHH . . .

I breathe. Reid's emotions fade into memory, taking the conviction with them. I guess it wasn't my conviction after all. It all came from the emotigraph.

For the first time since stomping away from Willow, I notice my surroundings. I stand in a graveyard, only it's more than a yard. Thousands of headstones stick from the ground like petrified mushrooms, leaning this way and that as if bent by the wind. They stretch in every direction for miles, marking raised lumps of ground; some are tall carvings of wood, others are hewn stones, some have a pile of rocks. The most common grave markers are rough crosses.

The sight overwhelms me. Each of these markers represents a human. My toes tingle, thinking of a lifeless body six feet below me. I've found the cemetery of the world.

Who buried everyone? I allow a chill to take its course over my body. Who died? I reach out to a tall gravestone beside me for balance. It's one of few with an engraving.

J. F. H. IV
2004 – 2030
"A young man whose soul knew the years were limited
yet pushed him to great purpose and compassion."

It takes several seconds for me to remember they didn't have Clocks back then. How did his soul know? What does my soul know? Is that what spurred my restless dragon?

I need to sit, but I don't want to sit on the ground. Maybe it's because of what may lie beneath me. I lower myself onto the headstone. My skirt sways and something in my pocket clatters against the rock. I pull out Reid's sentra.

With a trembling hand, I raise it up and take a picture. The emotigraph comes out. The sad picture of tiny stones doesn't capture the magnitude of this burial ground. I don't think it could, even if I took a hundred more.

I rest my hand and stump in my lap and stare. *Who are these people?* I barely think the question before answers spill in from my banks of logic—the dead. The ones killed by the terrorism.

I've never grasped the gravity of our world's history. Present day in Unity Village was all I knew, but in school history I heard about the woman who studied and worked in space technology. She directed two meteors into our planet—one in an ocean called Pacific, and the other in a place called China. She left no note of explanation and died under her own act of terrorism. An earthquake joined repeating tsunamis and chains of volcanic eruptions. The bodies beneath me may have suffocated from ash, drowned in water, been crushed by rubble.

I push a fist against my stomach, willing it to calm as a vision of flesh scorched by lava pierces my imagination.

This isn't how it should be, God.

Thousands of graves marking thousands of lives—so much focus on death. Did the gravediggers spend their lives just serving the dead? How many Numbers ticked away for the sake of carving headstones no one would read?

As I stare at this scene, I decide I don't want a headstone when I die. I don't even want to be buried. I want to disappear—save that chunk of earth for people to live on. This land I stand on is worthless now. No one can build a house here. No one can plant gardens or start a new village. Is that what the people buried beneath me would have wanted?

Earth wasn't intended to hold only dead bodies.

I stand. *God, I need to live.*

Swelling passion mixes with panic at my still dwindling Numbers. I can't keep reacting. I need to *take* a step. "Use what's left of my life for something worthwhile," I whisper. "Guide me on Your pilgrimage. And God . . . please forgive me for wasting my life."

I return to the campfire where Willow sits with Reid's journal open before the flames. She turns each page slowly, letting them dry a little.

I flop down beside her. "You don't need to do that."

"There's a lot of writing that's not blurry. You might want to keep it."

Several sentences are intact on the current drying page. "Are you reading it?"

Willow shakes her head. "I don't read."

I relax, watching the methodical flip of pages. The next time I have a pen, maybe I'll write messages to Reid on the blank pages. I may have missed what he wanted to tell me, but I can use his own journal to write to him, to tell him *I'll* be the one dying, and that I'm proud of him.

For now, though, it's time to take a step. God destined me for greatness. It's my own conviction this time. I look into Willow's sunburned face, hesitant to share my recent idea. Should I think on it longer?

No. No more waiting.

"Willow, what do you know about Ivanhoe? I want to go there. I want to find the Newtons."

27

"We're not going." Jude sits up from his spot, leaving a body imprint in the ground. His voice is hoarse and only now do I realize he's been sleeping at the base of a headstone. His face is covered in bruises turning green and sick yellow.

"Jude-man!" Willow exclaims. "You are awake. Want a gopher?"

He forces a stiff grin. "I'm glad you're safe, Willow. And yes, I'm quite hungry."

I bristle from his first comment. "Why can't we go to Ivanhoe?"

"Why do you want to go?"

I fumble over my words, trying to reorder the clarity I felt moments ago. "Because I have five months left. I think I can find answers in Ivanhoe. And the Newtons might be there."

Jude's jaw tightens and he raises his eyebrows.

"I've never seen a city," I finish, feeling stupid.

"I think you're being impulsive," he says. "Ivanhoe is far away—"

I jump to my feet. "Don't tell me I'm impulsive. You don't know me. I'm not asking you to come." Why does he act as though I'm dragging him along with me? Doesn't he know he can leave at any time?

He looks away with a nonchalant shrug. "Tally ho."

I return to my spot beside Willow and say, rather forcefully, "Tell me about Ivanhoe."

It turns out Willow knows rumors of Ivanhoe, but has never been there. Still, her eagerness surges as she talks. "I think people there live in a castle of sorts, created from ruined cities. When they come to trade, they bring a lot of medicines and technology. No one trades for the technology items because we don't have much use for them, but they're very interesting."

She tosses another pile of dead sticks onto the fire. "They are fun to bargain with and almost always turn it into a competition. They like to compete. The man in charge of Ivanhoe is supposed to have done everything possible in life. People go there from all around the *world* to ask him questions. He knows everything."

My ears perk at this. Someone with answers. Answers can bring guidance. The more we talk about Ivanhoe, the more my assurance builds. This is where I must go.

"What type of technology?" Jude raises his head from his brooding position by the headstone.

Willow shrugs. "I told you, we never trade for it. You could ask the man in charge."

"Do you know how to get there?" Jude asks.

Willow and I grow silent. Her smile fades and pride sickens my insides. "I can find my way."

"It's in that direction." Willow points behind her, toward where I came from.

No mountains line the horizon for me to mark in my mind. Even the hills strewn with headstones block the canyon and albino forest from view. I couldn't even return to the Wall if I wanted to without help.

Jude smirks. "What direction is that, Parvin?"

Mockery. It breaks through my defiant pride and squeezes my emotions. Tears burn and my throat closes like a pinched straw. He's just like the boys in Unity Village.

"That's West," he says.

I keep silent, staring hard into the flame and trying desperately to quell my hurt.

"Do you know how far away Ivanhoe is?"

"No!" I turn to glare at him. "Why are you trying to crush my motivation? You've offered me no good alternative, so stop being a jerk."

Great. I've sunk to name calling. Another reason for him to look down on me. Why do I always know how I want to act, yet let immaturity dominate?

"What can I expect from you, Jude?" Despair overtakes all other emotion. "I thought we were going to stick together, but you seem to have your own plans. I need to know if we're a team or if we're going to split ways."

The late morning air is silent except for the windy licks from the fire. Willow hunches over Reid's journal, avoiding looking in our direction.

"I'll go to Ivanhoe with you." Jude's voice is low and tense. He stands and walks away with hunched shoulders. He runs a hand through his hair then lets it slide down to his side.

I lean backward until I'm lying down and cover my face. "God . . . I thought this was what You were telling me to do. Why do I feel like I blundered it all?"

We remain among our small section of gravestone hills for three more nights. My urgency to travel builds inside my chest, but I don't argue. Willow tends to Jude's wounds, and I allow the built-up soreness to seep out of my body. The gashes from cattail stalks turn stiff now that they're out of the marshy water. My legs itch from the growing hair and healing wounds. I wish I had a razor.

Ticks and mosquitoes seem to like my dirty smell because I'm constantly plucking them off me. I indulge in fond thoughts of smooth, clean clothes hanging in my closet in Unity Village. They don't smell of sweat or fish. They have no holes. Blood stains haven't marred their colors. I used to think them crude creations from my inexpert hands. Now, they seem like masterpieces.

Willow scoots around the gravestones over the course of the days to keep in the shadows. Her sunburned face peels and she picks at the dry skin with her small fingers. I catch up on the news. Another article in *The Daily Hemisphere* announces Skelley Chase's newest release of a journal entry continuing my biography X-book. It doesn't say which journal entry it is.

-Send me my biography X-book, I write him through the NAB. *-And send my profits to my family.* This last request is an afterthought. It's only fair I receive some of the profits since this is my story.

I stare at Hawke's name bubble several times over the course of the three days. He hasn't sent any more messages, but I want to send him one. Maybe asking him a question will ensure a response.

The message page is as blank as my thoughts. As Willow talks to Jude, I whisper to the NAB. *-Did you read my biography?* It's the best I can think of and connects with his last message to me.

Willow tosses me my water pouch and I surprise myself by catching it with my good hand.

"Who are you writing?" Jude crouches by the fire.

I don't want to admit I'm writing Hawke, but why not? Why should it matter if Jude knows or not? "Hawke," I finally say.

He looks into the flames. "What were you saying?" His voice is terse.

Now *that's* not his business. "Asking a question."

"I can answer your questions. You don't have to bother him with them."

My throat grows tight. I never thought I might be bothering Hawke. He never seems annoyed. I add, *~Do my messages bother you?* to the message. "Send."

In an effort to show I do care about Jude, I make a sling out of one of my bandages and help him fit his arm in it. I resist the temptation to run my fingers over the path of his snake tattoo. I've never looked at a man's muscles before. Does my fascination with his make me shallow?

Don't be silly. God made muscles. I'm admiring His creation. Still, it is strange to think about muscles right after I sent Hawke a message. An odd section in my stomach feels sick, deceitful, as if I'm somehow being disloyal to one of the two men helping me.

I slip my NAB back into my bag. "Jude, are you ready to leave?"

It's ironic that now I've entered my last few months of life, I have the opportunity to start a new—albeit short—life with all the things I wanted: travel, remembrance . . . and maybe even love.

We spread dirt on the fire and trudge deeper into the graveyard. Willow helped me stuff my socks with balls of my rinsed underwear for makeshift shoes since my boots are still at the bottom of the Dregs somewhere. The prickles of sagebrush and stiff grass still pierce the soft fabric, but they're better than barefoot.

She cups her hands over her forehead like a hat brim as we travel.

"Here." I hand her *The Daily Hemisphere,* unrolled.

She shields her face. "Thanks."

"Sure." The sun seems harsher on her skin than mine, even though we're both burned. I think of Hawke's light skin. I bet his pale olive color would tan nicely under this sun.

Bah! First Jude's muscles and now Hawke's skin. What's the matter with me? I'll be dead before I see Hawke again. I'm thinking like this because they're the first two men who haven't bullied me.

So then, why *not* allow my heart to dwell? Since I zero-out soon, the risk is brief. If my emotions are crushed the disappointment will only last a few more months.

This idea sticks in my mind. Hawke doesn't mock my short Numbers; instead, he strives to help me through them. My ticking Clock didn't defer him from showing me kindness. He's even sharing information with my family.

But where does Jude fall in all this? God placed me with a man my age with whom to travel. He's from the East. He's mildly attractive. Is this God's way of presenting me with a man of interest?

My heart doesn't seem ready to welcome in Jude yet, though I'm open to his attempts if he wants to try. He *did* save me from the flash flood. I'm still in awe over the strength he showed to pull us out.

That evening we settle among gravestones and sagebrush. My legs ache and I imagine a long foot massage from Mother. I gently rub the tight area of skin around my stump. My hand was cut off two and a half weeks ago, but my discomfort grows. Waves of sharp pain course down my left arm, all the way to my nonexistent fingers.

Willow presses the outside of her water pouch against her burned face. She scrunches her nose with a wince and moves the pouch. Jude settles down cross-legged, pulls out his unfinished whistle, but returns it to his pocket, rubbing his wounded arm.

We don't build a fire. We don't eat. Again, my stomach grumbles. I'm so useless. Tomorrow Jude or Willow will catch an animal. Maybe *I* will kill something and prove myself capable of surviving.

The next morning, Jude presents Willow with a wide-brimmed hat made from woven tumbleweed. He wrapped portions of it with his own shirt to cushion her head. She stares at it with a frown.

"It's a tumbleweed. It was already dead, blown by the wind, and with no roots or green."

With hesitant movements, she takes the hat. "Thanks."

Jude laughs. "Welks."

He looks different when he laughs. Little creases curve inside his cheeks, shaping his sun-beaten skin into a sign of joy. I'm transfixed until he turns away. Now, instead of his face, I stare at the bare torso hidden only by his vest.

I squeeze my eyes shut. *God, You know this is unusual for me. What's right? What's wrong? I've never had thoughts like these before. Am I sinning?*

No one taught me how God looks at attraction. All Reid ever said when he gave me my ring was, "Don't you let a man touch you until you're married."

I'd blushed and muttered, "Of course not."

Did Reid mean intimacy, or did he mean holding hands? Touching tattoos? Brushing cheeks with fingers?

I sigh. *He's not here to judge me, so what do I think? What do* You *think, God?*

The day grows so warm I shed my skirt and stuff it in my pack. Jude flops his coat around his neck. Willow seems content in her full clothing, which keeps her skin covered. She often reaches up and touches her hat with a smile.

"You know"—I catch up with Jude—"maybe Ivanhoe is part of my pilgrimage."

He glances over at me without moving his head and looks annoyed. "Let the pilgrimage change *you*. Don't try and change *it*."

I frown. "What do you mean?"

"If you're not letting yourself be changed, can you even call this a pilgrimage?"

"*You* called it a pilgrimage."

Jude lets out a long breath. "I mean you're trying to lead instead of follow."

Disapproval. I should have known. My intent in bringing up Ivanhoe again was to try and convince him it's a good vision, but he's telling me to follow.

"I *am* following. I think God wants me to go there." I force my voice to remain strong as I talk about God. It's time I master my weak faith. "Besides, God doesn't want me to be stagnant. Aren't I supposed to make decisions, too? I want to find the Newtons."

"How do you know they're in trouble?"

"I don't. I hope they're not. I just want to find them, to see them and make sure they're okay. Their story can inspire every other Radical facing death."

"Tally ho."

Silence returns to our marching band. I don't break it, but a small loathing grows toward the phrase *tally ho*. It shuts down conversation.

I consider my own question. *Am* I supposed to make decisions? Or should I wait until I know God has told me something? Have I ever known?

No. So then how do I find out God's plan for me?

I log this question into my memory. I'll ask the leader of Ivanhoe. The man with answers.

We drink a lot of water to combat the heat. I request sever.. ...... to maintain stamina, growing self-conscious. Jude ...d W...... seem to need to stop. Do they expect me to keep up w.

Willow weaves between sagebrush, avoiding step.... bushes or flowers. It looks exhausting, like she's walking tw..... as she has to. Still, she has more energy than I do.

Why can't my legs keep going like theirs? Why do I crav.... moment we stop to sleep and they never seem to desire rest? I feel sub-liminal pressure from both of them to have endless endurance.

God, this is Your plan, right? My conviction when standing among the tombstones is nothing more than a memory now. *I have to believe it was from You. You're still guiding me, right? Or was that impulse? Is Jude right?*

My NAB sends a muted *pop* from my pocket. I drop behind Willow to read the new message and walk without drawing Jude's attention.

~*Good noon, Miss Blackwater.*

I fight a grin. Hawke.

~ *I did invest in your X-book. Though you were forced across the Wall against your will, great things are still happening in your life. You are brave to share them. I dare to hope your story might cause some change in the processing of Radicals here in the East, in the Low Cities.*

I reread this first paragraph. He thinks great things are happening in my life? Like what, my survival? Nothing I've done so far would con-stitute as great in my mind . . . except maybe helping Ash give birth. But Hawke thinks I'm brave. The corners of my eyes smart.

His sentence about changing the processing of Radicals strikes a chord in my memory. Jude said something similar. They both believe I can do it—they believe in me. What if I let them down?

I take a deep breath. Hawke's reply continues and I relish the long message.

~*Your brother, Reid, is safe for now. When your biography revealed the secret of your Clock, Reid was placed on house arrest with your parents until the end of the Clock. And no, your messages do not bother me. Much of your hardship I consider my fault for not stepping forward and standing by the* correct *laws of Enforcing. I'm here for you. Tally ho.*

My heart sinks. So guilt drives his messages. Even his compliment of my bravery seems tainted now. His "Tally ho" at the end has a note of finality to it. It reminds me of Jude's harshness. I don't respond.

Skelley Chase hasn't sent a reply, so I reach back and slide the NAB into the opened flap of my pack. It's harder to move my feet forward when I want to sit on a stone and let my heart fall out.

The only change in scenery over the course of several days is when we hit a wide cracked black road, winding into the distance as far as I can squint. Grass and weeds crawl through the cracks and painted lines fade from its weathered stone skin.

"Blacktop," Jude says. "Or asphalt. Highway. Freeway. Pavement. It's what people drove cars on when they ran on tires."

He talks as if it's old-fashioned, but I've never seen a road so smooth. "The Enforcers in Unity Village still drive cars on tires. I rode in one."

"Really? Strange."

"Low City, remember?"

We walk on the blacktop a few hours, but it increases the heat. We leave it behind to veer straighter north. Headstones and crosses still outnumber the sagebrush, hills continue to roll, and the sky is cloudless and full of heat. Dirt, sweat, and grime waft from my skin. I ache for a bath and position myself downwind from Jude and Willow, though they don't smell any better.

Willow kills rabbits with her sling. When we stop for the night, she cleans them, Jude builds a fire, and we eat them. Every day she kills at least two more. For the first time, their overpopulating habits are in our favor, though I grow tired of their meat. We use a couple skins to replace my torn, muddy socks and fill up our water pouches at a small stream. Willow inspects the wood Jude uses for the fires and the land is deprived of even more tumbleweeds.

On what seems the hottest day during my time in the West, we crest a hill and find a gentle flowing river below. It's wide and smooth and the banks are soft. I drop my pack and wait to see if Jude and Willow run in so I can follow suit. Jude slips off his boots and rests his feet over the bank. Willow wades in. I join her, clothes and all. She lifts cool water to her burns and I scrub the dirt off what skin I can decently expose.

We refill our water pouches and return to the bank. Jude holds out his good hand when I approach. He's on his feet. I don't respond fast enough, so he takes my hand and steps into the water. He starts humming an upbeat tune, inserting, "Da da dums" and "Oom pa pa, oom pa pas." He twirls me.

I can almost imagine the music playing through his mind. It's difficult to spin in knee-deep water on slippery stones, but Jude's hand is firm.

I laugh.

The dance doesn't last long, but each second siphons off a little despair. He takes his injured arm out of the sling and ends with a dip. His arm convulses and almost drops me. With a grunt, he lifts me and helps me onto the bank, favoring his wounded arm. I wring out my hair, but let my clothes drip dry. Refreshed. My body longs to sit here and let the breeze cool my damp skin.

Jude sits beside me and leans back on one elbow. Willow dunks herself in the water. I eye him with a fluttering stomach.

He danced with me. Why did he want to dance with me? Did I look foolish? The show of affection was soothing. Perhaps Jude will say something about dancing with me. Perhaps I should say something.

"Don't go to Ivanhoe."

I glance at him sharply. Our dancing fun disappears from my mind like a dried puddle on a hot day. I look at my lap. "Where would you have me go, Jude?"

He shrugs. "Let's find somewhere new."

Let's? As in *us?* He still wants to travel with me. He doesn't want to leave me behind, but he doesn't want to travel where I'm called. "Ivanhoe *is* new to me. What don't you like about it?"

He is silent for a moment, staring hard at the river. "I've never actually been there, but I know the way. I've seen it. I don't think we should go to the largest city in the West and bed down. He . . . would expect us to go there."

"The shooter won't find us in Ivanhoe." I hoped the topic would come up again. Jude's been hit with more than a bullet—he's infused with fear and not admitting it. I remember his terror in the Dregs. His shaking. His entire persona of strength shattered. "It's the largest city in the West, you said so yourself—he'd be well pressed to spot us. We'd be in more danger in a smaller town."

Jude helps Willow out of the water then lifts my pack onto his back. He tromps up river. I scramble to catch up with him.

"He'd expect us to go there, Parvin." He hoists my pack higher. "It's easy to hunt someone who doesn't belong. We can't blend in. We should keep moving."

"For how long?" I ask, in a smaller voice and gesture to my pack. " You don't have to carry that for me, by the way." He makes no move to take it off and I'm secretly thankful. "Why would the shooter hunt you? He left us in the Dregs. Maybe he thinks you're dead."

"He knows I'm not dead."

"Then why did he let us survive?"

"I don't know." He answers too fast, like he's worried and his response is to appease my curiosity.

I lay my hand on Jude's arm. "Who is that man who shot you?"

The scuff of Jude's boots on the dusty ground takes over the conversation. My hand slides back to my side. His eyes stare at a memory, vacant yet focused. After a long minute I whisper, "Jude?"

"I'm thinking," he barks.

I will myself to be patient. Behind me, the swish of Willow's sling is followed by a scurry and *thunk*. Another rabbit down. She ties it to her belt by its hind legs to be skinned and cleaned tonight. My stomach roils. Mother's banana bread feels like a year ago.

"He's an assassin," Jude says at last. "He's sent from the East by the Citizen Welfare Development Council."

"The CWDC?"

"Yes, also called the Council. It pairs with the government to develop security and well-being for USE citizens."

"I know what it is. But they're supposed to be on our side—the citizen's side. Why would they hunt you?"

"Because I have information they want." He looks at his feet. "I was an inventor. I created something they wanted and decided not to give it to them."

"What did you invent?"

He pauses for a long time. Is he annoyed? Will he even answer? "You can't know." Before I can ask why not he cuts me off with a single word. "Yet."

Yet.

He's asking for patience. Maybe this is hard for him—a vulnerable topic. Can I be patient? I look up at him as he stares at the dry sagebrush-covered plains and find myself nodding.

Questions swarm in my mind like hornets. Jude said the assassin didn't kill him on purpose, so why did he shoot Jude? Why is Jude still afraid of the assassin? One clear thought makes its way through the swarm: The USE is much more involved with this side of the Wall than our government lets on.

"I guess it's okay to go to Ivanhoe, as long as we're careful when we enter and leave. We will need food and supplies soon anyway. But let's not stay too long."

"Okay." I try not to sound too excited. "Just long enough to find the Newtons."

Jude digs his hand into his pocket. "Go see how Willow is doing with her rabbits."

With a deep breath through my nose, I obey. Jude must need a moment to himself. What must it feel like being hunted?

I bite my lip, thinking of my single journal entry to Skelley Chase about Jude and me in the Dregs. I wish I could take it back. I wish I'd kept Jude's name out of the whole thing—or used a fake name.

I pull my NAB from my skirt. Maybe it's not too late. Perhaps Skelley Chase hasn't published that journal entry yet. I balance the thin booklet on my stub and click Skelley Chase's pulsing message bubble.

–Here's your X-book. Keep up on that journal, you're leaving me dry.
-SC

My X-book. I tap the small link. A stunning cover with a dogwood tree the color of blood holds the title starting to define my life.

A Time to Die
By Skelley Chase

I squirm. Shouldn't my name be on the cover? I squint closer, seeing if it's in finer print, but a shout from Jude startles me.

"Writing in your journal?" He yells much louder than needed to reach my ears.

"No, I'm—" I look up and my voice seizes.

He's stopped walking and faces me, unmoving. His eyes are wild and his lips are pressed into a tense line. "You never said those entries are broadcasted to the entire nation!"

I halt, too, and attempt to clear my throat. Willow stands beside me, looking at Jude with wide eyes. He's scaring her. He's scaring *me*.

Jude takes three long strides and hits my NAB from my hand. *"Stupid!"*

I stumble backward, now truly afraid.

"*You* led the assassin to us. Those journal entries told him where we were. Your selfish desire for the world to know your name caused *this*." He jerks a finger at his shot arm.

My face grows hot. I can't bring myself to apologize. His hands clench and I could swear the snake on his arm silently hisses at me. Jude's eyes are wide and red-rimmed. He raises a fist. I tense, but he turns away and grabs two handfuls of his own hair, allowing the sling to slip off his shoulder.

"You have no idea what you've done," he grinds through gritted teeth.

"If you would have told me—" I jerk back when he spins around.

"You can't blame your idiocy on me." Saliva gathers at the corners of his mouth. "You lack the ability to think of others before your own impulse."

His words are like a whip. My restraint snaps. I shove him.

My stump crumples against his chest and he barely sways. What I don't expect is for him to shove me back. His hands hit me like two impenetrable rams, striking my shoulders with the force of a cannonball. I fall backward and my knees buckle against a gravestone. I land hard, stiff sagebrush branches piercing my skin. The impact knocks my breath out in a painful cry. My stub screams for attention, shooting zings like newly sewn sutures.

"I'm *not* taking you to Ivanhoe. Not if you're announcing it to the world."

Everything in me wants to curl up and cry. Where is compassion? Where is grace?

Willow kneels by me, crying. "Is your arm hurt?"

I shake my head and glare after Jude.

I hate him.

28

Campfire is hell contained in a pit of stones. We add wood. Willow cooks the rabbits. Hell-smoked rabbits. I decline dinner. My appetite still lies behind the headstone over which Jude pushed me.

No one has spoken since his outburst, but all of us have thought. Anger and hurt war within me. Each procures a different desire—one makes me want to scream at Jude and the other makes me want to cry until he comforts. But he won't comfort.

The sound of him gnawing on rabbit bones slides down my nerves like a potato peeler. I hate him. I *hate* him. I press the button on my sentra over and over, shoving the same emotigraph back in every time it's expelled. I care not about recording my emotions, but the prick feels good, like I'm releasing my anger.

"Parvin, I'm sorry."

At Jude's quiet words I slide my narrow glare from the flames to his face. *Sorry?* That's not good enough. He doesn't look at me. I wait. He gives no further elaboration—no *why* behind the sorry. Is he sorry I'm with him? Sorry he shoved me? Sorry he got angry?

He looks up. "Did you hear me?"

My glare diminishes. "Yes." Then, when the awkward pause of expectation grows too weighty, I say, "Thanks."

He doesn't say "Welks." Instead, he prods the fire. "We'd better rest." He stretches himself out on the ground.

Rest for what? He said he's not taking me to Ivanhoe. I watch him for several minutes. He lies on his back with his good arm over his eyes and his foot tapping to an imaginary beat. It looks like a happy one.

My internal anger reaches a low boil. How can he sleep when we are so divided? How can he leave me alone and listen to his music?

How can he feel happy and content? Doesn't he care about what he did? Doesn't he care about frightening Willow and me?

Willow won't look at me. She's avoided speaking or sitting beside either of us since the argument. What does her albino culture do about arguments? Maybe they don't argue, they just amputate body parts.

My left arm still throbs from the impact of my fall. A tight squeeze wraps around my nonexistent hand, pulling. Pulling. Why do I feel it? It's Black holding my wrist again, stretching my arm against my weak struggles; holding it for Alder to sever.

I retrieve my NAB, glancing at Jude as the screen adapts to the darkness. Part of me wants the glow to wake him—to evoke another quarrel. At least the boiling beneath my heart might lessen. What changed between our calm talking and his outburst? How did he discover the assassin was my fault?

Was it my fault?

He doesn't turn over. As I set the screen to typing, a flashing message across the top of the screen catches my attention.

10% energy, please charge . . . 10% energy, please charge . . .

Charge? I never imagined the NAB would run out. How do I charge it? I haven't seen electricity anywhere in the West.

I look at Jude again. He'd have the answer. He must have a NAB of his own—how else would Hawke have contacted him when I needed help? Maybe my emotions will lessen enough by morning that I can ask him for help. It's doubtful.

The moon rises higher in a clear night sky. I vent my emotions via typing onto the NAB. I don't know where else to put them. God feels too far away, Skelley Chase is too untrustworthy, and Hawke is friends with Jude. I record my anger in a journal entry. I'm careful to press the *save* button so it doesn't send to Skelley Chase.

When I finish, I return the NAB to my pack. The fire consists of embers. I ought to place more wood on it to keep us warm through morning. As I tie the flap back down, a distant low whistle reaches my ears—a sound completely out of place in this graveyard wasteland.

I sit straight with a start, my hand clutching the strap of my pack. Silence stretches and I scan the darkness. There. A flash of electric light miles away. Another deep whistle.

A train.

I leap to my feet, disoriented. A train in the West? *Here* in this wasteland where we're scraping for survival? The light flashes over another distant graveyard hill. Closer.

The Independents have trains.

Jude's foot no longer taps. Willow is curled with a small fur pelt over her skinny body. I need to catch the train, if only for information—to read its name as it passes by, to see if it's passenger or cargo, to gather another scrap of information.

Willow will be too slow to run with me. I need to go now, before Jude can tell me not to. Before Jude wakes up. They'll wake in the morning and I can share my new information. Maybe he'll be proud.

My gaze narrows. *Who cares?*

I hoist my pack on my back, unsure of what may come in useful and not willing to waste time searching through it right now. Then I run, for all our sakes, but mostly for mine.

The running is freeing—like I'm in charge at last. I'm taking action. I race forward to intersect the train. The whistle sounds again, louder. It's fast. Much faster than me. It will wake Jude and Willow soon, despite Jude's brain music.

Headstones jump out at me like ground shields, stilting my pace. They form short rows in spurts, but no permanent order organizes them enough for me to run full out. Even though it goes against every scream of adrenaline, I slow my pace so I don't bash my shins.

The train whistles from my right, like four different harmonies off key, screeching its approach.

Forget bashing my shins. I break into a sprint. My pack thwacks like dead weight on my spine. My rabbit furs slip and twist on my feet with each pounding footfall. A rock pierces my sole. The train light crests a bridge over the river we've been following. Three headlights form a triangle, their conical beams revealing the tracks ahead of me on a raised length of pyramidal ground. I can get there.

Breathe. A rabbit fur tears and flops around my ankle. My pumping arms screech like the approaching whistle. Stinging irritation presses like a glove of needles on my stump. I tighten my remaining muscles against it. The rumble of the train vibrates in my chest. The tracks glow under the dim stars.

My shins collide with a cement headstone.

With a shriek, I career forward as my disjointed sprint steals my balance. Loss of control. Arms out. My stump shines in the train's headlight like a mutilated wave good-bye.

I crash, headfirst, onto the tracks.

My cheekbone smashes against the vibrating rail, jarring my teeth. Despite the shock, I maintain enough reflex to pull a foot up and hurl myself off the tracks. The train flies past like an arrow.

I flip onto my back, fighting for air. Leaning back on my elbows, I stare up at the hurtling beast. My loose hair flies around my face like a windstorm. Unable to read a single word on the shadowed paint, I gape. The high hiss of metal rims on railroad ties scrapes like a sharpened knife on my pounding heart. The ground shudders with exhilaration.

Thrill. Hope. It's all contained in the speeding train that almost claimed my shaking, very human, very fragile body.

Lights flash by in small square windows with rounded corners. Drapes cover some. Others are open, letting the internal glow shine out. The power behind the locomotive rolls my nerves like underground thunder.

A passenger train. A passenger train now screeching against the rails with a new sound. Brakes. It's stopping.

The intensity of my heartbeat is almost painful. I struggle to breathe. My cheek throbs, but excitement douses the pain. I crawl to my knees and push myself to my feet. The end car passes me with a receding whiz, pulling me after it as if hooking me with a fishing line.

I jog beside the tracks, fighting the limp in my burning shin. The train places more distance between us, all the while slowing. Slowing. For me?

It stops. I continue to jog. My every nerve trembles with wary excitement. I reach the end car as an orb of light bobs through the darkness toward me. When the bearer of this odd lantern nears, I make out facial features.

It's a woman, mid-fifties. Her short hair is smooth silver—dyed, not aged—and curled in a heavy side part over to her left. Her prominent cheekbones, thin curved eyebrows, and pursed rose lips stand out against her cool skin. She wears dirty overalls rolled up to her shins, a baggy green shirt, and floppy shoes. She's not albino. Is she from the East?

"You're alive then?" Her voice is low and creamy, contradicting her irritated look.

Flustered, I close my mouth to swallow. "Yes," I gasp.

"Is that your intention?" Her voice holds tinges of a British accent. I frown. "What?"

She drops her arm, holding the orb by a triangle handle. "Is it your intention to be alive or was your stunt on the tracks an attempt to take your life?"

"Take my life?" I hate that I don't understand. "How would I take my life? I still have four and a half months."

She rolls her eyes and waves her free hand in the air. "Never mind. Where are you headed? Make it quick."

"Ivanhoe." Finally! A response that's not a question. "Where are you from?"

"Ivanhoe." She jerks her thumb to the train. "Hop on. You got trade?"

So she *is* an Independent. My tension lessens. "Trade?"

"To. Pay. Your. Way." She keeps a calm low tone, but speaks with crisp enunciation.

"No."

She shrugs and lifts the lantern again. "A trade collector will mark you down for Ivanhoe credit. He'll explain the details if you're willing to work." She turns away.

I stumble forward and grab her shoulder. "Wait, what am I supposed to do?"

"Get on board." She raises an eyebrow and jerks her shoulder from my tense fingers. "I'm on a tight schedule. We have five minutes per stop and a thirty-stop maximum. You're number twenty-four and we still have five hundred miles to go. There may be more pick-ups ahead."

I gesture into the blackness with my stump. "But two others are with me. I need to get them."

She raises both eyebrows this time and looks down at me with a degrading appraisal. Her eyes stop on my severed hand and a tiny frown brings her brows together. I slide it behind my back, tensing. Why didn't I keep it hidden?

With a breath, she seems to recover herself. "Then you better wait for the next train."

"When will that be?"

"Two weeks for my line. You can travel south and meet up with the *Kansas Rail*. It runs a shorter line and you should be able to catch it next week."

Weeks? I have only twenty weeks left. Can I sacrifice two, maybe three weeks of my last Numbers to wait for Jude and Willow?

I must. I can't leave them.

The conductress leaves me in the dark, heading back toward the engine. I step back and stare at the train. Now that it's stopped and the moonlight hits it, I make out the dark yellow paint spread over the metallic beast. Small dents dot the shell, mixing with grease and stains. The top of each car is capped with silver metal and a railed walkway lines the bottom of the cars. *Ivanhoe Independent* is painted between the two.

Ivanhoe.

The conductress and her orb are gone. I step back from the locomotive as groans announce its intent to continue. Desperation pounds my sternum. Five hundred miles. Jude never told me Ivanhoe was five hundred miles away. It will take us at least three weeks to reach it on foot, maybe even a month. Could we even gather enough food to last us that long?

The thought of Jude plates my heart with steel. He's not taking me to Ivanhoe anyway. Why should I go back to him? He hit me.

"Don't you let a man touch you . . ." Reid had said. Was he also considering moments of violence? I never thought a man would want to hurt me.

Jude never committed to traveling with me and I never committed to him. I owe him nothing.

God, You told me to go to Ivanhoe. The train clamors into motion, inching forward, crawling along the tracks with whines and deep croaks of machinery. *You brought this train for me. Can there be any clearer message?*

"Wait." I reach out to the train and glance back toward the direction from which I ran. If I shout, Jude won't hear me. He has his music. Besides, he wouldn't run here fast enough. If I leave, Jude will be angry . . . but he won't find me. He won't go to Ivanhoe. He doesn't even want to. He wants to be alone.

But do I want to leave him?

I walk along the dirt as the train gains speed. Should I go? Can I venture out alone again? I remind myself of Jude yelling at me, of him pushing me down, not caring he hurt me. He called me stupid. Selfish. *Impulsive.*

I reach up, wrap my chilled fingers around the metal railing, and hoist myself on board. Something inside me shudders—a weak nervousness. I'm going. Going to Ivanhoe.

My first city.

I stare into the darkness, conflicted, but paralyzed with thrill. I *have* to go. I need to find the Newtons. Soon Jude will realize he went too far when he pushed me. I'm protecting him by leaving. I can submit journal entries at my will and the assassin won't be able to follow Jude because I'm no longer with him. Jude can go where he wants, safely.

My breath comes in gasps. I clutch the rail. Wind generates goose bumps on my tired skin. The train reaches running speed. If I'm going to change my mind, it needs to be now, while I can still jump off.

Sick doubt prods my conscience. I imagine Jude waking and finding me gone. What will he think? Will he regret his actions? Consider it his fault? Will he worry about me?

I hope so, I think savagely.

Maybe I should stay. What am I doing leaving Jude and Willow so I can progress on my own? What's three weeks of traveling?

I step to the edge and watch sagebrush fly by. The jump will hurt.

But it's *three weeks* of traveling. God said to go. Jude and I are safer apart. Obedient. I'm being obedient and I'm already on the train. I step back, safe behind the rail.

I've made my decision.

I look forward, toward the engine, toward the mystery. Onward to Ivanhoe.

A pale ghostlike form pushes through the tar of blackness ahead. Barefoot. Wild and stumbling.

Willow.

She sees me and releases a throaty scream. "Parvin!"

Ice clenches my breath.

"No! Parvin!" She races toward the train.

I bolt down the railing to the end, cursing myself. How could I think only of Jude? How can I leave Willow alone with him?

"Willow, here!" I reach over the railing at the end of the car by the steps, straining to stretch my slim body.

"I can't!" She sobs, as the train passes her. She staggers after it, but grows smaller. "Don't leave me!"

My own tears threaten to join hers. "I'm sorry." How can I explain? I *have* to go.

But she wanted to go, too. With me.

"I'm sorry, Willow!" I call back to her. "I'm going to Ivanhoe! Follow the tracks!"

She crumples on the rails. "Jump off!" Her voice is nothing more than a washed out echo.

"I can't," I whisper as her ghostly form is swallowed by the night. I didn't think fast enough. I didn't think. Something kept me glued to the train.

Now, it's too late.

29

000.143.10.51.20

The warm interior of the *Ivanhoe Independent* welcomes me, but my soul remains chilled.

Willow.

Lines of brown bench seats, big enough for two people, flank each side of the car, facing forward. Each one is empty. Light orbs, like the one the conductress held, hang from the center of the ceiling in a long line. Cold metal floors chill my exposed foot.

I wrap my arms around my middle and walk into the next car. More empty seats line the sides like café booths with tables between them. I don't know what I expected—Independents cheering me aboard while they sit drinking hot chocolate?

No one is here.

Chills creep up my legs like iced fingers. I wish I wasn't alone.

Willow.

I open the next door and step across the shuddering enclosed walk-way between cars. This one has a narrow hall with olive curtains along both sides. The orbs expel dim light. A snore crescendos over the deaf-ening train. Sleeping quarters. I've always wanted to sleep on a train.

Some of my guilt recedes into interest. I look from curtained bed to curtained bed and sneak a peek under one of them. A snoring gentle-man lies on his side with his lips sticking out like a lazy fish. I walk on, embarrassed that I peeked.

I pass more occupied beds until I reach three open ones, curtains still tied back. Three. One for each of us. I close my eyes and curse myself.

God, strike me dead now. Forget about my Clock. I hate myself.

The aches of my body flair in anticipation of lying down on cloth, on a mattress. I look down at my clothes and back at the folded white bed sheets. My own blood, scrapes, and dirt stand out with a shout against the possibility of touching something clean. I glance around before sniffing my right armpit. I cringe and suck in a breath through my mouth.

One of these beds is for me. I'm a passenger. They can't kick me off for being dirty. I'll take the lower bed. The other two open bunks are too high for a girl with a stump arm to climb into. Willow could've slept above me.

I drag a hand over my face, envisioning her small form crumpled on the tracks. Abandoned. By me. Has she ever seen a train before? She was so excited about Ivanhoe.

I let out a long breath and drop my pack onto the foot of the bed. A hiss meets my ears from my left. I pause, tense.

"Pssst."

I look over and start. A woman with wheat-blonde hair in a side braid stares down at me with smeared eye makeup. She smiles, revealing sleepy bags beneath her eyes and splotchy skin.

"The showers are two cars up." Her sleep breath hits my face with the strength of a rhino.

I step back. "Thank you. I've been traveling."

She looks me up and down, her eyes lingering on my stump then taps her nose. "I can tell. It's so much nicer sleeping refreshed."

I can't remember the last time I went to sleep refreshed. Showers. I know how they work, but I've never seen one before. Leaving my pack on the bed, I take my extra shirt, a wad of remaining underwear, and untie the curtains to claim my spot. I then proceed through another sleep car into the shower car. Four wooden stalls on the right say, *Men* and four on the left say, *Women*. Ahead are toilets with curtains around them. Toilets.

They tremble from the harsh clatter of the train, but the cold metal still feels like a luxury. After relieving myself, I enter the first shower stall. More cold grey metal lines the three walls, surrounding a spout above my head. A knob below it has an *H* and *C* for what I assume are 'hot' and 'cold'. Beside that is a small digital clock covered in plastic.

A clear sealed box hangs on the shower wall. With careful maneuvering, using my teeth and good hand, I extract myself from my layered clothing and stuff it all in the box. It feels strange being unclothed and I double-check the latched door. Then I turn the knob to the *H*.

Ice water spews from the spout into my face. I leap back and slam against the door. It stays latched. The clock above the temperature knob blinks a number countdown from six minutes. By 5:23, the water is hot and glorious.

A sigh escapes my throat and I soak in the water for a full minute before scrubbing the grime from my skin. My bashed shin is already swollen and turning purple. It's numb to the touch.

This is so much easier than heating the kettle over and over again. If I get enough specie from my biography, maybe Mother and Father can invest in a shower.

A large bottle labeled *SOAP* with a dispenser sits in a holder beside the glass box. I use my elbow to squirt liberal amounts into my hand. The left side of my body gets much cleaner than my right, since I don't have a left hand. I rub my forearm up and down, hoping to spread the soap that way. Scrubbing my extra clothing proves even harder so I kneel and use my elbow to hold each piece against the floor while I brush soap over them.

Tired, discouraged, and grateful tears mix with the shower water, confusing me. I should stop crying, but no one's here to see me. No one will know.

Six minutes end far too soon and I try to restart the shower after the water turns off. It doesn't work. I even wait a full minute, but the water won't return. With a reluctant groan, I dress in as few of my dirty clothes as possible, slipping into fresh, but wet, underwear, leggings, and top. Everything else smells of campfire—something I didn't notice before. Touching the clothes leaves my hand smelling the same. It reminds me a little of home.

I return to my bed. Has Willow ever had a shower? Has she ever heard of one?

"God," I groan. "I'm just obeying You." But I can't blame Him. He said go to Ivanhoe. He didn't say when. "Jude wasn't going to take me anymore." I bite my tongue. Jude apologized. Maybe his apology meant he *was* going to take me to Ivanhoe. He should have said more with his 'sorry'.

I lie in my curtained haven and think. Instead of the anger and conviction I felt about leaving Jude behind, I now recall the other things he's done for me. He saved my life during the flash flood in the Dregs. He saved us from the angry albinos. He *tried* to help me when the albinos cut off my hand.

He said sorry.

Why couldn't I remember *those* things when deciding to board? But my decision wasn't based on leaving Jude. I don't want to travel by foot anymore. I don't want to sleep at the base of headstones or pick ticks out of my skin, or swat the bugs seeking my sweat anymore. I don't want to spend my Numbers traveling.

He danced with me, I think, growing more despondent. *I made him laugh. He carried my pack. He said he'd take us to Ivanhoe even though he didn't want to.* Will I ever find out what he invented that angered the Council?

I shouldn't have left.

My NAB blinks 7% energy. I don't want to talk to anyone right now, but I need to. I need to contact Hawke for help, but can I expect help when I've deserted his friend?

~Hawke, I left Jude and Willow. I boarded a train going to Ivanhoe. It's for the best. Jude and I had a . . . disagreement. The NAB picks up on the hesitation in my voice. I leave it.

~ It's not safe for us to travel together anymore.

Should I elaborate?

~Apparently he got shot because of me.

Was it my fault?

~I think if we're separate, he'll be safer.

Do I really?

~I need to find my own way.

But I don't want to be alone.

~Lastly, my NAB is saying it needs to be charged. How is that done?

Will Hawke see why I left? Will he see that part of my decision was for Jude's safety?

I place the NAB back in my pack, trying to stifle the scent of lemon still attached to its cover. I don't know how it lingers after all the Dregs water. I'll write Skelley Chase his new journal entry tomorrow. He'll like this one.

I roll onto my side and breathe in the softness of the pillow. It smells clean—soapy clean. I haven't smelled something clean like this since home. I inhale again and imagine the scent of sawdust mixed in.

Father . . .

A fierce desire to go home flares in my soul. Simplicity was another life—one where I didn't feel guilty or tired or hunted. A life where I could sleep in and didn't have to wonder if I'd find water that day. A life of sewing and new clothes and fresh wool socks on a polished wood floor. No bleeding feet, no scarred legs, no rope burns, no aching muscles.

NO PURPOSE.

My eyes pop open. Him. God. That was Him putting a thought in my head. *God?* I reach out with my mental fingers. *You're here with me? Did I mess up? Are You disappointed?*

The clarity of God-infused thought doesn't return, but I know He's here. He reminded me He's giving me purpose.

"He who began a good work in you will bring it to completion . . ."

I'm on a train headed to Ivanhoe where I'll find answers. I've fought for survival and clung to faith in His promise of life. He's promised me four and a half more months . . . and I'm spending them abandoning my two companions. What must they think of me?

Fighting the emotional nausea, I pull the fresh blanket up to my chin and curl my head beneath it. Sooner than I expect, my body and mind relax into oblivion.

Morning is announced by a crewmember mere hours later. "Breakfast, seven to nine!" He taps his hands on the safety rails of a few beds and continues down the car. "Breakfast seven to nine!"

I tumble out of bed at the thought of food consisting of something other than rabbit meat. My mouth waters in wistful memory of Mother's cinnamon oatmeal. I pull my pack after me and head through the washing car, barefoot and self-conscious.

A line has already formed in front of the women's showers. Misty hot water and the aroma of soap fill the air. I feel out of place, clothed and dry, but the food car must be ahead.

Sure enough, the next car holds a long table on each side. Chairs are nailed down at one, facing the flyby scenery and the other table is laden with covered food dishes. A crewmember stands at the door, but says nothing when I cross the threshold. His eyes flick to my wrist and then he stares determinedly out the window.

"Do I just help myself?" I ask, fighting the threat of misery. Will people see me as half human? Handless? Will anyone look at my face anymore?

He bows. "Of course. Sit where you like."

I walk down the food table like a dragon surveying its treasures. The meal is not elaborate, but it's enough to make my stomach twist in a greedy knot. Scrambled eggs covered in cheese, boiled red potatoes, sliced apples, and thick flat rounds of bread. I pick one up. It's light and floppy. Beside it sit two lidded glass tureens of gravy. The gravy is a dark amber color and almost see-through.

"What is that?" I ask the crewmember, pointing to the gravy.

"Maple syrup." His eyes pause on my left arm again. "Uh . . . for your pancakes."

I cover my stump with the floppy bread, fighting the warmth crawling up my face. Turning away, I return to the syrup. The pancakes must be the floppy bread. Mother makes something similar, but we call them corn patties and eat them with butter.

I spoon a drizzle of syrup onto a plate and taste it with my finger. Sweet. *Very* sweet. When's the last time I had anything sweet? A couple spoonfuls later, I sit down at the opposite table, alone in the food car with plans already to return for seconds. To my surprise, I only eat half a pancake and my eggs. I stare at the remaining sticky bread made with precious flour seldom seen in Unity Village.

"Are you finished?" The crewmember reaches for my plate.

"Yes, but"—I grip the plate with my hand—"I'll—I'll keep this for now."

He frowns and his lips twitch as if he's about to say something. I look away, staring hard at the passing tombstones. *Leave . . . please leave.* I can't let him throw away my pancake. It seems unjust when Jude and Willow are still eating rabbit meat.

When he walks away, I fold the pancake in a thin cloth napkin and place it in my pack. A different crewmember approaches me as I replace the flap over my pack.

"Ma'am?"

"I just wanted to save—"

"Are you last night's pick-up?"

I blink. "Excuse me?"

He sits in the chair beside me. A bristle mustache lines his upper lip. Crinkles between his eyebrows hint at several years of frowning. "You were last night's pick-up at two in the morning?"

"I-I believe that was the time." I tug down the flap of my pack. He pulls a pencil from his pocket and unfolds a piece of paper. Black lines create columns down the length of the sheet. Half of them are filled in with tiny pictures and writing I can't read.

"I'm the trade collector for the *Ivanhoe Independent*. You are traveling all the way to Ivanhoe, I presume?"

"Yeah."

He makes a little smack sound with his tongue and scribbles on his paper.

"Name?" He doesn't look up.

"Do you have an extra pencil I can borrow?" I blurt.

He glances at me with a frown, making me feel like a purple thistle in an alfalfa field. Without a word, he hands me his own pencil and pulls a new one from his pocket. "Name?"

"I'm sorry." I fight a growing unease. "Why do you need my name?"

His scowl meshes with his many wrinkles. "I set up trade-pay. The conductress informed me you have no trade." His eyes flit to my stump and linger there. "You will have to pay for your current passage when we reach Ivanhoe."

"Pay with what?" I mentally search through my pack. Is there anything of worth in there?

"With *time*." The man sighs, and I wipe my hand along my skirt pocket as if I can clench my Clock. "I have a list of vendors and traders who pay the train line for workers. I will set you up with one of them until your passage debt is paid."

Why did I leave my sack of money at home? "How much is my debt?"

"We run a day-per-hour charge. Since you boarded around two in the morning and we'll arrive at Ivanhoe around ten . . ." he squints in the air. ". . . that's eight hours, so you'll work for eight days."

My muscles slacken with a stunned shiver. "E-eight *days*?"

"That's how it works, ma'am. Unless you've got trade."

My brain sinks into a sludge of injustice. "You can't take eight days from me."

His wrinkles harden into a firm glare. "You boarded the train with the knowledge you'd be using Ivanhoe credit. If you don't pay it you get yourself locked up until you have a change of mind." He must notice some sort of horror on my face because he softens his tone until he sounds a little more like a grandfather. "It's not so bad. They don't make you scrub floors. You can learn a lot under a trader. It's commitment-free apprenticeship."

His words don't make much sense to me, but my heart withers at his gentler manner. "I don't have a lot of time."

"How long will you be there?"

"I-I don't know." I haven't thought past *getting* to Ivanhoe.

"Why are you going?"

Sound confident. Think of a sure reason. "I need questions answered from the city leader."

The old man's laugh carries a sharp bite. "You want to see the Preacher? Who are you that he'd answer your questions?"

I gape at him with mounting exasperation. "I'll keep my information to myself, thank you."

Preacher? Willow never said the leader was a preacher. Maybe, in Ivanhoe, religion is common. Maybe they don't have laws against raising children in faith like they do in the USE.

The trade collector rolls his eyes and returns to his paper, poising his pencil over a new line. "Give me your name."

I pause long enough so he looks up, then lift my eyebrows and respond in as cold a voice as I can muster, "Parvin Blackwater."

"Age?"

"Eighteen."

"City?"

"None."

He writes nothing nor does he look up, but his fingers tighten on his pencil. "I'll inform you of your assignment options when we reach Ivanhoe." He tucks his pencil into a pocket and folds up the piece of paper. "Keep in mind you are not permitted to enter the city proper of Ivanhoe until your passage has been paid in full." With that, he walks away, my glare ushering him out the carriage door.

I rest my head in my hand, allowing the rhythmic clap of the tracks to jolt my body. A week of work. I boarded the *Ivanhoe Independent* to avoid wasting my last weeks. Now I'm paying for my rash action.

I should have jumped off when I saw Willow.

My NAB sends out a *pop* from inside my pack. With a heavy, leaden hand, I pull it out and view my message from Hawke.

-I'm afraid this may have been my fault. I informed Jude that your X-book journal entries mentioned him so he might need to caution you against how that information might be used. It was inevitable the assassin would find him, whether you sped that process up or not. Do not blame yourself.

-Your NAB should charge with the exposure to sunrays, either from the actual sun or a sun-port. It should take an hour to charge. This should last you up to a month. Stay safe. Tally ho.

Hawke's message leaves me feeling worse and I'm not sure why. The NAB now blinks:

. . . 2% energy, please charge . . . .

The sun outside shines parallel to the direction of the train. I make my way to the end car and step outside onto the same railing on which I watched Willow shrink into the distance. Now, the only things in the distance are the curve of the shrinking blacktop, giant white windmills, and the last of the dotted headstones. The ground looks so much flatter without the crosses and arced markers interrupting its pattern.

Morning sun illuminates the locomotive's yellow paint. I sink to the shuddering ground with my NAB on my lap, leaving it open to the rays. The scent of lemons swirls in gusts with the wind. I turn my head away, trying not to breathe it in.

Skelley Chase caused all this. He forced me into the West. He published my biography and journal entries early. He's making a game out of my life, and now I'm endangering Jude and Hawke.

I lift my chin with pursed lips and scowl at the sunrise. Going to Ivanhoe was the right thing to do. I'm alone again, as it started, as it should be, as I've always been. These people are toying with my decisions and emotions, interrupting my focus. Who cares what Hawke thinks? Who cares what Jude thinks? Who cares what Skelley Chase does or what Willow feels?

I never asked for any of it.

I'll travel to Ivanhoe, work a week, and then demand answers from the Preacher. He'll tell me how to find out God's plan for me. He'll tell me what the Independents need. He'll tell me what to do and I'll do it with every ounce of energy for one hundred and thirty-five days, five hours, and thirteen minutes. And then . . .

Then I'll die.

30

Ivanhoe.

The city glints beneath morning sun like towers of jewels, stretching tall from the flat, laurel green sagebrush plains. The puffy-cloud sprinkled sky shines blue in a way that contrasts the polished metal in perfect beauty. A brown boxcar train passes along the outside like a morning commuter.

Ivanhoe's definition of *city* is far superior to my limited Low-City imagination. I doubt even a High City could compare. Futuristic factories and buildings are cut and pasted into scrapbook architecture. Some buildings are square grey boxes and others are cylindrical towers with domed tops, ringed with staircases. In the center of my limited view arcs a giant spherical building, like a marble the size of a city. From far away, the exterior appears smooth, but as we get closer I see pop-out structures, bridges, windows, ladders, balconies, and upraised tunnels. People on the train have told me it's the heart of the city and it shimmers like a nugget of silver.

My brain doesn't have the capacity to absorb my awe. I went from wolves and stone huts to . . . this—a new era. Modernity in the West. Does Hawke know about this? Does Skelley Chase or the Council?

I could stand before this city for a month straight and remain stupefied. How could Jude see this and not enter?

The sun bursts from between clouds and warms my face, finishing the scene by submerging me in feelings of grandeur. I unleash my sentra, determined to capture this moment and keep it all to myself, but something nags my subconscious: A desire to share this with someone.

It's too much wonder to handle alone. Three names wander unbidden across my mental path of loneliness.

Mother.

Hawke.

Jude.

I sigh. *Click. Click. Click.*

As I slide the sentra back into my pocket, one of the emotigraphs flies from its precarious place between my fingers. I slam my stub against the others, pinning them to my splayed hand and shove them into my other pocket. The free one swirls in the wake of the train, a lost jewel. Someone will have a surprise if they ever find it. Do Independents know about emotigraphs?

The *Ivanhoe Independent* curves around the city until we're on the other side of the sphere. The tracks slope into a carved path, blocking the rest of the city from view. We enter a dark tunnel where the air slides between the rough walls and my precariously perched body. It smells like earth.

I hold tight to the railing until we slow, emerging into a station with a tall ceiling. It's long with an ascending tunnel out the other end and multiple platforms, some occupied by small trains.

We bend to the right, passing the other trains, and glide into a mini station of our own in a separate underground chamber. By this time, we've slowed to jogging speed and the platform passes beside me, littered with stains, footprints, and dirt. My feet are still bare. I'll pull out my needle and thread to patch the rabbit skins once I have a moment to process. For now, I return inside where I encounter the trade collector. He must have been watching me through the window.

"Gather your belongings," he says with his wrinkled frown. "And follow me to the collection post."

My belongings are already gathered so we stand until the train stops. I follow him off the back of the train. Everyone else seems to know where to go.

I've never seen building walls so tall—the closest comparison is the county building in Unity, but everything about it is unfriendly. This station, this city, is *worn*. I'm a stranger stepping into a broken-in sweatshirt. It smells different, feels different, but carries a welcoming feeling of use.

Ivanhoe and I were meant to meet today.

The pockmarked cement chills my feet despite the warm air. I follow the confident trade collector into a box building. The interior is covered with postboards lathered in bits of paper with no words, but several pictures and symbols. If paper is used so flippantly here it must be less expensive than in Unity Village. That, or everyone is rich.

A man leans against the wall beside the postboard with the most papers. He is in his early forties, with baggy eyes and a receding hairline that explodes into a tremendous russet afro. He's dressed in faded jeans, floppy sneakers, and a suit jacket over a T-shirt. When he sees us, he steps forward and holds his hand out to the trade collector.

"Good day." His eyes flit to me and back to the collector. "Have ye a debtor?" His voice is low, but with a clear accent I've never heard. What accents are in the West? Is it rude to ask? "I'm needing short-time help. My apprentice is off after injuring herself. She's on home rest."

"We'll have to see what she wants." The trade collector jerks his head toward me. "You aren't the only option today." He plucks a length of paper from the postboard beside the afro man. The stranger jumps at the ripping sound and looks at me again.

"Are you on here?" The trade collector puckers his lips.

The afro man shuffles over. "I am." He points. "There, now."

"You're this human symbol?"

"I am."

The trade collector looks up. "Wilbur Sherrod, the couturier?"

"It's Sher-*rod*, not *Sher*-rod." Wilbur gives a nervous laugh. "And I never could pronounce that last word."

The trade collector looks up. "But it's your title."

Wilbur shrugs. He turns to me as if obligated to explain himself. "I'm a fashion designer for the Preacher, the military, and the Barter-Combat Arena."

I straighten with a skipped heartbeat. "Designer? Do you mean clothing?"

"In a way." He steps forward and takes a breath, but the trade collector cuts him off.

"Miss Blackwater, there are three other trade options: the bookbinder, the game designers, and arena servicing. Do any of those sound of interest?"

I look from Wilbur to the trade collector, already feeling more comfortable with the clothes designer who talks strange. "I-I don't really know what they are."

Wilbur Sherrod scrunches his nose and shakes his head as if the other traders are nasty options on a menu.

"Actually," I say on a quick breath, cutting off the might-have-been-a-nice explanation of each trade. "I think I'll go with Mr. Sherrod."

Wilbur tucks his chin with a wide grin and turns to the collector. "Good! Let's settle up, then."

The men scratch numbers and messages on the trade collector's endless provision of paper. I don't bother to decipher their mutterings. What will I be doing with Wilbur? He said he's a clothing designer of sorts, but he doesn't look it.

My own sewing kit is in my bag. Won't he be surprised I can already stitch neat hems and patterns? But in the moment I allow the thought to excite me, my elation plummets like a convict tied to an ocean weight.

I look down at my hands as if the sight will be less painful, but my stump is still there, tingling like a simmering kettle. There's no way to guide the fabric with one hand. I can't line two cloths up together. I can't even thread a needle.

"Are ye coming?" Wilbur asks from the doorway, shattering my frozen state.

I'm lost, like I need to pick something up—my heart, maybe. I can no longer sew. I look up at Wilbur. He stares, oblivious to the internal collapse of my single life-long passion.

"Just follow me."

I obey with a high wail in my ears. Did Wilbur see my arm? Does he know I can't sew? He didn't ask. Maybe he doesn't even want me to sew. Maybe I'll be a cleaner—the one-handed girl who disposes of scraps and snipped threads while everyone else turns patterns into masterpieces.

"Have ye ever been Ivanhoe before?" Wilbur leads me through a set of doorless arches into a train station filled with benches, clocks, and echoing voices. The ceiling stretches upward with long windows and a pointed peak. In another life—an older life—it could have been a cathedral.

I shake my head, but realize he's not looking. "No," I choke.

"Hmm." He sounds disappointed.

The enormity of Ivanhoe helps displace the stiffness from my mind. The exit deposits us onto a sidewalk level with a smooth black street like the blacktop Jude showed me. Pedestrians walk along the paths, but most people are riding bikes of all sizes, colors, and styles.

Tandem bikes carry what look to be couples and friends. A woman steers a bike with a sidecar holding three children. Men with coats and ties clutch their bags while sitting on the handlebars of someone else's cycle. A mechanical contraption rotates like a moving rubber band up and down the outer wall of the train station, moving parked bicycles into the air, out of the way.

On the road, people pedal and weave between long, snakelike cars, shouting hellos or screaming warnings. The cars look like boxcars from a train and all follow rails in the ground. Their motorized movement creates a cool static in the air like a rushing river.

With each step, my lungs fill with inhaled excitement. I'm finally . . . *somewhere.* People are here. Life is here. "Your cars are enormous."

Wilbur steers me through the mayhem with surprising ease and without accident. He looks around as we reach the other side of the street. "What cars?"

I roll my eyes and gesture to the grey, green, and black boxcars zipping up and down the street like caterpillars. "*Those* cars. The giant metal machines right in front of us."

"They're motorcoaches." His 'r' sound stands out in each word, distinct.

"What is your accent?" I ask on a whim as we walk across a large grassy square filled with groomed dirt paths, lampposts, and dogwood trees. Swarms of people weave through the dogwoods, leaving the paths as they please and tromping on the fallen petals. I almost miss Wilbur's answer in my awe.

"I have Irish."

Something out of place clicks with a red beacon of confusion. "Irish? But Ireland is on *my* side." Is Wilbur another secret escapee of the East?

"Yer side? Where're ye from?"

I swallow hard. "Never mind."

We leave the square and approach the base of the Marble, as I've christened it. It is even more magnificent up close. Parts of it consist of glass, wood, metal framing, and smooth bridges sticking out like wayward strands of hair, connected to nearby buildings.

Pillars line the base as if the entire structure rests solely upon their stalks. In the center of the Marble's flattened base, through the pillars and covered in shadows, is an enormous glass cylinder. This cylinder appears to be every person's destination, including Wilbur's.

A mass of multicolored people swarm under the shadow of the Marble—black people, white people, Hispanic people, Asian people, and . . . albino people. They stand out like glowworms and I marvel at how different they look with makeup and typical clothing. They can't all be from the forest, can they?

People approach the glass cylinder from the other side of the Marble, too. I ignore the feeling we might be squashed any moment when the pillars collapse like toothpicks.

Four lines form around the cylinder, each in front of a curved sliding door. Wilbur and I join a line and I get a closer look. The cylinder is a vast elevator chute. Every two minutes, one of the four doors opens to allow the rhythmical entrance of roughly thirty people.

A quarter of the cylinder shoots up through the cemented underside of the Marble. Thicker pillars circle the cylinder as added support to the base. Wilbur and I are the last to squish into the elevator and I'm closest to the door. I look for the buttons, but smooth glass wall stares back. The elevator moves on its own, gliding in a smooth ascent.

My heart falls through the floor. We rise through the center of the Marble and I'm hit with an overwhelming amount of brown—brown storefronts, brown signs, wooden flooring, and subtle earthy walls. The base floor of this foreign system of life is filled with so many shops and people I can't possibly discern their contents.

All floors open to the inside of the Marble, made of encircling rings around the inner edge of the sphere. Their levels contain shops, signs, hallways out, house fronts, and stairs to the floors above and below. Various trees grow inside, showering petals onto the floors beneath.

Nauseous. The sphere is hollow and we seem to be rising to the very top of it. I'm almost flying. The elevator moves so smoothly yet the rest of the world so quickly I close my eyes and take a deep breath, feeling the heat of bodies behind me. I've never been this high in my life.

A strange pressure pulls me not to reveal my naivety, to blend in, to act as though I've been in the Marble hundreds of times and ridden this elevator every day. I close my mouth, just noticing it's hanging open. I wiggle my toes against the glass. Will I leave sweaty footprints behind? Have other people noticed my feet? My stub? My shabby appearance?

I stand taller, as if I can mask my differences.

A woven rope net obstructs my view for a moment, spread like a giant spider's web over the sky of the Marble. It descends beneath our feet as we climb. The Marble walls curve closer together and our elevator slows to a stop.

The doors open and I step out onto an enormous round platform only to instinctively reel back. I collide with Wilbur. He releases a nervous laugh and pushes me away.

The platform is suspended from poles connected to the Marble's glass and metal ceiling. Though the areas of ceiling glass are tinted, the sun shines through onto a scene horribly familiar.

Tightropes.

Not just one tightrope across a single canyon, but twenty, spreading from my platform to the top floor walkway in each direction. Every rope connects to individual pole mounts from the ceiling, stretching across space. What baffles me further is how each person from the elevator takes a brief moment to transfer from the platform to a tightrope of his or her choice, then walks across at a decent balanced pace. Some carry bags or walk behind their children. A couple even shares morning gossip as they cross to the left level.

Some tightropes are thicker than others. Some curve beneath a person's weight and others remain stiff and taut. Everyone wears thin, pliable shoes or no shoes at all. The last of my worries are my bare feet.

I scrape a teaspoon of voice from my windpipe. "I-I can't tightrope walk."

Wilbur gestures to a loose rope to my right. "We've a slackline."

I shake my head and look at him. His baggy eyes are wide and his prominent cheekbones accentuate his thin lips. He glances around as if fearful others are watching us. "If we return to the ground, we'll need climb the stairs to reach the t'irty-t'ird floor bridge. Ye never crossed on rope before?"

"No." My voice sounds shrill even to me. "Does everyone here know how to do this?"

"Everyone except crawling infants and the disabled."

I peer down, my eyes blurred against our incredible height. "How do *they* get to the thirty-third floor?"

"They're carried or they use the rounding elevator, but ye must qualify fer a pass." He looks me up and down. "And ye won't qualify. Ye'll need to cross the nettin'."

"Netting?" I spot the woven net we passed in the elevator four stories below us. The crooked squares and knots anchor around a platform around the elevator chute similar to the one on which I stand.

"I t'ink crawling will be best for ye. I ain't going carry ye."

Crawl across netting in the middle of a new city where everyone above and below can see me? Of course. "You said something about stairs?" My voice is a hoarse whisper now.

Wilbur shakes his head. "Ye'll take the netting. Ye're my debtor and we haven't time for the stairs. Hurry up now."

My comfort in choosing Wilbur as a trader ignites into blazing frustration. I'd rather do anything than cross that netting in front of thousands of spectators, but he's right. I'm his debtor.

"How do I get there?" I ask in a cold sharp voice.

Wilbur looks up with a scowl. "Ye can jump or take the ladder."

"*Jump?*"

He walks around the platform as another filled elevator approaches. A bolted wooden ladder with thick rings descends from the edge of this platform down to the netting platform. "Ye head that way." Wilbur points to left. "I'll meet ye there. Hurry now, the elevator is opening."

I walk to the edge of the ladder, scoot onto my bottom, and swing my legs over the side. I'm tempted to take my sweet time to irritate Wilbur, but he's already transferring his weight onto a thick tightrope, holding his floppy shoes in one hand. People pour out of the elevator. I close my eyes, hungering for invisibility.

Turning onto my stomach, I descend the ladder, using my left elbow and my right hand. It takes only a few rungs for my elbow to incur the start of a bruise. At least now I'm out of view from the crowd on the platform, but every passing elevator sends curious eyes to my missing hand and my plight.

My heart delivers painful beats as I descend into the daunting openness of space in the middle of the Marble.

"God." I force myself down rung after rung. "I deserve this after leaving Jude and Willow. I suppose You're just humbling me." My anger melts into shame. "I deserve this. I'm sorry I do things wrong."

The rope net wobbles and sags when I crawl onto it. I use my knees, elbow, and hand to work my way across, off-balanced and watched. I try not to focus on the whir sound when elevators pass. I don't look down to see if anyone is looking up, but all my insides seem to have fallen out of my body, leaving shaking nerves behind.

Wilbur offers no hand of help when I reach the solid outer walkway. "There we go," is all he says as I straighten. He leads me up a set of stairs and into a dark arched tunnel out of the Marble. "Ye aren't allowed to leave the Core until ye finish with me. The trade collector said ye have eight days. I may need ye a little longer, but that's up to ye."

I have no interest in being in this man's presence a second longer than I must, even if it *does* involve sewing. Why am I never free? The only time I had control was while fighting a pack of wolves and starving on a lakeside.

Wilbur Sherrod walks through a dark door leading to a hallway and into a large round room. One side of the room holds long tables with thin upright screens. A single person sits before each screen, not looking up when Wilbur and I enter. On the other side of the room is a black steel machine with wires connected to a giant glass box large enough to hold an elephant.

"This is my design studio. Each maker crafts and programs my patterns."

I glance around. "Where are the sewing machines?"

"Construction takes place in that box."

One of the makers looks up from her screen. "Sherrod, where ya been? Your fire piece is finished."

"I'm after findin' a debtor." Wilbur gestures to me. "She's of small size. I t'ink she'd make a good blueprint." I want to ask them to please tell me what's going on, but Wilbur pushes me with the lightest of touches toward the glass box. "Now then, step inside so we can blueprint ye."

Numb, I walk to the glass box. At some point this will make sense. I just need to act as if I understand until I really do.

I lift a black handle on one side and pull the door open. It unseals with a loud squelch. The glass is heavy and thick. Once inside, the door closes of its own accord and latches. My breath freezes.

The makers and Wilbur stare at me like I'm a specimen in an experiment—a creature observed, like my trial in Unity Village.

Lights blare in my face. I squint and step back, but they surround me from top to bottom—red, green, and bright blue lasers poised on my body, quivering. I think of Jude's assassin, aiming like a sniper. I'm gripped by a mad fear of being shot by a thousand bullets.

As soon as I take a breath to shout, the lights turn off without so much as a *click*. I don't ask if I'm free to go, I just turn to the door and push. It doesn't budge. I glance at Wilbur, who steps forward and opens it.

Silent but shaken, I exit the box. Shrill whining comes from the giant metal machine behind it. Something forms at the base of the glass cube, like sand particles building on top of each other, melding into a solid shape.

The figure builds from the ground: Scraped feet, shins marred by nasty scars—one swollen with a plum bruise ringed with muted chartreuse—scuffed knees, thighs, fingertips on only the right side.

As the human body forms from miniscule granules, iciness trickles from the top of my head straight to my stomach. A stump appears with old stitching scars.

Mutters from the makers join the soft whirring.

My body. *My* body is forming inside this glass box. The copy of me is covered by a thin, skintight black leotard from hips to shoulders. I've never worn something so form-fitting in my life.

I grow hot, seeing my body displayed before these people. The tip of my head finishes, leaving a wide-eyed tight-lipped expression on my copy's face. The machine even includes the bruise on my cheekbone. The created Parvin doesn't move, breathe, or blink. It's a lifelike mannequin.

"Blueprint complete." The female maker taps spots on her screen and rotates my exposed body. The whirring stops. She smiles at me. "Strange to see yourself, isn't it?"

I don't respond. Strangers are eyeing my body like it's a piece of fabric waiting to be cut. All my flaws are exposed. My stump. My bruises. My thin stick form. My ribs poke through the fabric, giving me a ghostly appearance.

Wilbur's eyes are on me. His eyebrows form a frown and his face twitches as if he's on the edge of speaking. He clamps his lips shut, then opens them again. "Perhaps I should've asked ye first."

"Perhaps you should have." My voice comes out so deathly harsh I surprise even myself. I've never spoken that way to anyone—not even Mother, but I'm glad my body can produce a tone strong enough to convey my internal horror. "But why should you?" I continue, silent as a striking snake. "I'm your *debtor*. You can do with me as you wish, right?"

I back away from the box. Away from Wilbur. Away from my exposed mannequin. I feel dirty. Used somehow. Weak. Ignorant. Tears burn my eyes.

Wilbur seems paralyzed. His hands splay as if he's wondering whether or not to reach out to me. I turn on my heel, my chin held high, and stride from the circular room.

Once in the hallway outside the entrance door, I lean against the wall, gripping my stump to stop it from shaking. My entire body quivers. I'm overreacting, but this knowledge doesn't stop me from sinking to the floor, tucking my head into my knees, and covering my head with my arms.

Who do I turn to?

No one. I can't contact Reid. Jude is gone. Mother would demand strength. No one.

ME.

I take a deep breath and let it out through my nose. *Where are You?* But again, He goes silent. For the first time, I regret giving my Bible to Ash. I want more of God's words, but a handful of verses cling to my memory bank. I should have read more.

I draw from the one verse that always seems to enter my mind when I doubt: God is completing what He started in me.

A deep, shuddering breath fills my body with renewed confidence. I'm dying in four and a half months. What's a little embarrassment? I chose to come to Ivanhoe. I stayed on the train even when I found out I had to pay with my time.

I slide back up the wall.

I can do this. I'll make my own decisions, be in charge of my reactions. It doesn't matter how others see me. In writing my biography and continuing the journaling, I've *chosen* to be watched by strangers. No more fighting it. It's time to own it.

I'm not weak.

Wilbur Sherrod enters my hallway. We stand in silence, looking at each other for a moment.

"Ye're my debtor." He picks at the dead skin surrounding his fingers. "Don't leave again wit'out my permission. Otherwise, I'll need return ye to the trainline."

"Listen." I force my voice to lose some of its hardness. "I'm not from Ivanhoe. I'm not even from the West. I'm from the United States of the East—the other side of the Wall. I'm going to be *dead* in four and a half months. If I'm going to be your debtor then you've got to teach me, not use me."

He nods, maybe hoping I won't cry, leave, or freak out.

But I count it as an agreement. "So what's my job?"

He breathes an obvious sigh of relief. "Test the outfits."

"How do I test them? Just wear them for a day and see if they're comfortable?"

"Depends which one ye're wearin'. We've four untested ones—Fire, Balance, Nuclear, and Blizzard."

I shift my weight and glance back toward the dark room. "These are *outfits?*"

"They are. Which one do ye want first?"

31

Monday sweeps the silent weekend out of the way and I choose my first outfit: Balance.

Balance sounded the least lethal, and it's time I learned to tight-rope walk. The metal machine created the Balance outfit to the exact measurements of my mannequin with the single press of a button. When I asked Wilbur about sewing machines and real material he said, "Everyt'ing is software. This machine rearranges atoms to our specifications."

"So you can *print* a fully-designed dress if you wanted?"

Wilbur smirked. "Printin' a dress. What a quaint notion."

I no longer fear being asked to thread a needle. Wilbur's design studio doesn't even use them. Any skill at hemming is useless when perfection can be programmed.

Wilbur leads me along a long corridor into a new room similar to a warehouse. Around the edges are glass cubicles with screens and people inside. In the center rests an enormous rectangle enclosure with cement walls and a single black door.

My mannequin stands by the door wearing Balance. It's a thin, silver, jumpsuit clinging to every form of my copied body. The left arm disappears in the left sleeve, but the right hand is dressed in a matching silver glove. I lift the extra material on the left arm and let it drop. It's light as a leaf.

"Do people wear these when learning to walk the tightrope?" I watch as Wilbur attaches what look like small freckle stickers to the base of my skull.

"It has not'ing to do wit that. It's created to balance emotions. This will help soldiers t'ink more clearly during stressful or life-t'reat'ning situations."

He gestures to the grey cement building in the center of the warehouse. "This is where interactive scenes are monitored and created. Before ye can test any outfits, I need a baseline. We only need baseline ye once. It's the hardest part. Ye'll go in one scene wit'out any outfit to monitor and record yer negative emotions, physical strengt', natural reactions, and tolerance. Then ye'll wear the Balance suit and enter another scene. Hopefully we'll see a difference wit' the emotions."

We stand before the large black door until a short woman carrying a metal tube joins us.

"This is the simulologist," Wilbur says.

She pulls a small syringe from the tube. "Here's the reactor." Her voice is throaty, like a man's. She reaches for my left arm, but I curl it to my chest.

"What is that?"

She looks at Wilbur. He raises his eyebrows, so she says, "The reactor is a harmless substance that causes the simulation effects to feel real. Once the scene is over, all feeling and pain will dispel."

"Pain?" I shoot a look at Wilbur. "What am I doing again?"

"Ye'll go into a simulated scene that builds off yer fears and reactions. The reactor is the only way to record yer true responses to situations."

"What sort of scene?"

"Ye can't know." He huffs. "It'll affect yer response."

I pinch my lips together and hold out my arm, wishing I could clench my invisible hand against the prick of the needle. I jump when the needle punctures my skin. Pressure churns my stomach as she pushes the unknown liquid into my veins. The simulologist's eyes flit to my stump and stay there the entire time it takes her to inject the reactor.

I stare hard at the black door. What will I meet on the other side? The simulologist said pain. Wilbur mentioned my fears.

What *are* my fears?

Too many to count.

Suddenly I'm utterly convinced this is not a good idea.

The door turns a glowing red and Wilbur sends a thumbs-up to a person in one of the glass cubicles.

"She's ready." The simulologist puts a cap over the reactor needle.

"Go on with ye, then." Wilbur bounces on his toes.

I stare at the door, swept back to my moment in the East when I stood before the Wall. Again, I face the unknown. Is my nervousness coming up on their data sheets already? Without knowledge, there can be no control.

You're protecting me, right God? I remember the Bible prayer from the beginning of my travels and pray my adjusted version. *Help me figure You out, do with me what You will, please give me food, keep me safe, and forgive me for whatever I've done wrong.* I add a little mental emphasis on the *keep me safe* portion.

The door has no handle so I flatten my hand against the red surface. It looks hot, but it cools my sweating palm. I push. It opens without a sound.

The room is dark. The beam from the closing door illuminates a stretch of long polished floor covered with millions of holes no larger than pinpricks. With the *thump* of the door shutting, I stop walking. My breath echoes in black space.

What's in here? It's too dark to tell if anyone else is present. Will a video screen show up soon with the scene? Should I sit down? What sort of pain did they mean?

I take deep breaths. The idea of pain doesn't concern me too much. My body has grown into a toughened, albeit emaciated, mass of resilience. I think I can handle—

A child screams.

I flinch and my heartbeat explodes. *"Willow?"*

Her scream continues, guttural under wetness in her throat. It rings around me. Instinctual terror prepares me for the pounding approach of wolves, coyotes, and bears.

The scream dies, coated in despair. "Where are you? Willow!"

All sound stops and a gentle white glow builds fifteen yards ahead of me. I squint, trying to locate her. The light brightens, dented by tendrils of darkness. Then I see the hearing platform from Unity Village, as weathered and threatening as always.

Nine people stand atop it in a chained line. Willow is first, then Reid, Mother, Father, Jude, and the Newton family. An Enforcer stands behind each one. Sound cuts in as if someone removed muffs from my ears.

". . . are reported of being Radicals." The voice is deep, like the black Enforcer who sentenced me to the wall. "Can anyone vouch for their Clocks?"

"I can!" I try to shout, but even though my mouth moves, no sound comes out. I try again. Nothing.

Panic thrums through my skin. I attempt a step forward, but the crowd below the platform is so thick and unmoving, I can't squeeze between a single pair.

"If no one can vouch for their Numbers, then these nine Radicals are sentenced to crossing the Wall."

"No!" I scream with my muted voice. I shove against the people in the crowd. They might as well be statues. But I must fight. I must reach my family, the Newtons, Jude, Willow . . .

I must save them. No one else can.

My pushing and fighting accomplishes nothing. When I look up again, the platform is empty and the line of my family and friends disappears into the shadowed darkness.

I sink to my knees, gasping for breath. What can I do? Run after them? Appeal to the Lead Enforcer? Find Solomon Hawke?

A loud series of clicks breaks the eerie silence. I raise my head.

A line of Enforcers face me with guns leveled at my face. Behind them is an endless crowd of people, all with blank eyes and plastered smiles. Watching me. Waiting for my death.

I don't search their faces. Instead, I close my eyes and wait. What will it feel like when the bullets hit me? Pain. Shock, but I won't die. I still have four and a half months left. I must stay calm. Strong. I must push through the pain for the sake of other Radicals.

Lights blind as if someone lit a thousand flames in my pupils. I take a sharp inhale and blink. I kneel on the cold floor of the vast square room. The silver walls are also speckled with billions of miniscule holes.

Memory hits me with embarrassing orientation. Simulation. Scene. Not real. How did I forget?

Though the walls are solid, I feel watched again, like an animal in a cage. The exit is to my right, the door still closed. I force myself to my feet, stride to the door, and push it open with both hands.

Wilbur Sherrod stands on the other side.

"Well, you have a morbid sense of humor!" I want nothing more than to curl up in my bed and let my emotions settle. He lifts the hair from my neck and peers around me. I jerk away from his touch and push him in the chest. "Don't *touch* me."

His floppy sneakers make him stumble a few steps. He looks at me with eyes wide with . . . is that terror? "The simulations are started by simulologists, but they progress according to yer fears. I told ye this was the hardest part."

Does he think this excuses him? Everyone watched me. They didn't care that I was going to die. I was just their *experiment*.

"May I examine yer transmitters?"

I stare at him, not even trying to understand.

He delivers a feeble wave toward my face. "The stickers ye have on yer neck."

The simulologist woman comes around the corner next. "Are they secure?"

Wilbur looks at me, hesitant. With a huff, I pull my hair up and turn around. I try not to cringe at the scrape of his fingernails on my skin. "They were secure."

The simulologist tilts her head with an eyebrow raised. "Well, Wilbur, it seems you have some fascinating data." She ambles away without further explanation.

I turn to Wilbur as my heightened emotions subside. The shaking lessens. Why I am I so angry right now? How did I lose myself in such a short scene? It felt so real.

So, those are my fears. The conviction of the people I care about, helplessness, and being killed under the eyes of impassive onlookers.

"Weren't ye afraid?" Wilbur leads me back into the hall toward his studio.

I snort. "A child's scream, the death of everyone I love, and a firing squad? Who wouldn't be afraid?"

We enter the studio. "But ye weren't afraid of dyin'?"

I shrug. "Well, I don't die for another four and a half months."

He stops and faces me, rolling his shoulders beneath his coat. "That's the second time ye've said somet'ing like that. How do ye know?"

I let out a long breath. What must his mindset be without the understanding of Clocks? "I'm from the East, remember? The other side of the Wall."

"I t'ought ye weren't being truthful."

"I don't lie. We have Clocks over there. The Clocks tell us how long we have to live."

"How do they know?"

I rub my neck, trying to erase the residue of the simulation stickers. "Some mixture of prediction and linking with the growth of a baby. Each woman has ovachips in her body to detect conception. Then the Clock starts ticking and everyone knows how long the baby will live." I throw up my hands. "They just know. The government sends them to us. Do you know what a government is?"

"I've heard of the government on yer side."

I squint at him through my wayward bangs. "You have? How?"

"The Preacher. He's on the United Assembly."

The man with answers. The sooner I meet the Preacher, the better. "What's the United Assembly?"

Wilbur shrugs and resumes his walking. "The leaders who meet from the East and West. That's all I know."

It's time to start my list of questions for the Preacher. First up: What is the United Assembly? Another link between the USE and the West? How much does my government know? "Well as soon as I'm done working for you, I'm meeting with the Preacher for answers."

Wilbur stops and faces me. His eyebrows collide in a frown and he bites a side of his bottom lip. "Ye t'ink a week of work will get ye a meeting?"

I plop my hand on my hip. "Why shouldn't it?"

He looks at the ceiling and shoves his hands in his pockets. "Ye won't make enough trade tickets in a week. Ye need at least t'ree."

"Three trade tickets? What are those?"

"Not t'ree trade tickets, t'ree *weeks*. Trade tickets are the payment we use here. Ye don't get any unless ye work extra for me. Right now, all yer earnings pay off the *Ivanhoe Independent*."

Work extra for Wilbur. More time as a guinea pig? Another simulation? Weird suits? I never should have boarded the train. Before I can think up a comment, one of Wilbur's makers steps out of the room of design.

"How did the suit work?"

I glare at the box in the middle of the room.

"We didn't test it yet." Wilbur turns his back on me. "I need to t'ink." He walks past his makers to his private office, leaving the rest of us behind. His maker looks stunned, as if it's the first time Wilbur hasn't shared everything on his mind.

I back away. "I'll just return to my accommodations," I say in a quiet voice, wanting them to hear me, but also trying to avoid opposition.

The room Wilbur assigned me is more like a cubby. A porcelain sink with its own plumbing juts from the right wall, and a dresser with two drawers rests beside it. A door off the left wall leads to a toilet stall—like the outhouse at home, but with a flushing handle. Thankfully, it doesn't smell.

The bed is a heavy mattress stretched on a thick window seat. My window faces away from the Marble over the sparkling city of Ivanhoe. I'm sleeping on top of the world. Last night I watched plethoric bicycles and motorcoaches transport dozens of people on the smooth rails below, wondering what Wilbur Sherrod had in store for me once the weekend ended.

I didn't expect the simulated scene. A nightmare. Did I really have some sort of control over it?

I understand the fear of not being heard—of being voiceless and ignored, but why do I hate being watched? How can I dislike this when my biography is spread across the East with my continuing story? *That* doesn't bother me, yet the box in Wilbur's studio, the simulation, the albino atonement, the town square in Unity Village . . . all included being watched without mercy by people who don't *know* me. I was alone. Trapped.

It's the sense of helplessness that I hate—of weakness. I was helpless to save everyone on that simulated platform. No matter what I did, Reid and everyone else were condemned.

I can't bear the idea of him dying and me living, but what if the Clock *is* his? What if he knows something I don't? What would that mean for me?

"It can't be his." I speak to the empty room. "I can believe just as strongly that it's mine."

My NAB lies on the crisp white pillow where I left it this morning, hoping it would lap up some sunrays. I re-read the message Hawke sent me last night.

~Good midnight, Miss Parvin, (although it may not be midnight when you read this.) I can write only at certain times to keep my correspondence

with you confidential—basically, to avoid getting us both in trouble with the Enforcer organization.

~You are in my thoughts quite . . . often. I run through idea after idea on how to help you, but none come to me. Sending Jude to you was my best attempt, but that seems to have backfired. Will you forgive me?

~I've spent time with your family, sharing what I can of your X-book with them. The more I get to know them, the more I wish I could have known you better . . . sooner. You are missed on this side. But we are all proud of you.

I still don't know how to respond, but the message leaves me light-hearted, as it did the first time I read it. I like the idea of a man risking something to help me, to talk to me, and to help my family. Even if he's out of ideas, he's still trying to think of some.

Skelley Chase's bubble has been still. The lack of concerned messages leaves me wondering. Does he still care about my journal entries?

Last night I went through a week's worth of *The Daily Hemisphere* articles and saw small announcements of my new journal entries being posted to my X-book. Despite having the X-book, I haven't read past the cover page.

Are people reading my story? Are they asking questions? Is anything changing with the Radicals? No one replies to *The Daily Hemisphere* announcements. I could be famous or invisible. I'm not sure which one I want. These past weeks have left me with robust doubt that my biography will convey what I want it to—it won't in Skelley Chase's hands, anyway.

Now that I've found the Independents, I might find new purpose away from my old life. Perhaps it's locating the Newtons or helping Wilbur Sherrod with his suits. Maybe it's finding out information from the Preacher to share when I go back.

Go back.

The thought sits in my mind like a sour bite of fruit. Swallow or spit it out? The East lies like a dead past life. Just the idea of traveling again wearies my soul. Returning is like stepping back into the shoes of drab life. I'll return only to die.

So why should I return?

The question feels rebellious as I stare at Skelley Chase's name on my NAB. He'd hunt me himself if I dared stay in the West. But that's not reason enough to return. I don't care about offending him.

If I return, I need to bring something back. Something that will cause change.

SHALOM.

I jump and look around the room. "I heard You," I whisper, drenched with instant giddiness.

I'm starting to love when God lodges thoughts in my head. They come in my own voice, but they're so far from my own doing that I know it's Him. It's such a delicious form of guidance.

As my giddiness subsides, I think on the word He implanted. Shalom—wholeness and completeness in Him. The way things were intended to be. Hawke wanted shalom in my village.

I sink down onto my window bed. I want shalom. I want things in my life to be the way they were intended to be. How were they intended to be?

A harsh knock startles me. I jump off the bed and answer the door. The short plump simulologist woman stands before me. She glances up and down the hallway before speaking in her throaty voice. "I know those people in your simulation."

"What people?" I'm still thrown off by her presence. Did I do something wrong in the simulation?

"The two on the platform. They are my neighbors."

My brain struggles to make sense of her words. "I'm sorry, I'm still unsure who you're talking about."

"The woman and child. The Newtons. I live by them."

32

"Will it be the same nightmare?"

Wilbur pulls the second silver Balance glove over my stump and considers my question.

I can barely contain my excitement. The Newtons are alive. And I get to see them in four days. They live outside of the Marble, but I'm not allowed to leave until my train debt is paid. Any irritation or dislike about working for Wilbur Sherrod is nothing now that I know Mrs. Newton and one of her daughters survived.

Somehow, it feels like I saved a life. Even though I never vouched for them and never helped them, it gives me hope that other Radicals have survived.

I have a friend on this side . . . someone who's been where I've been.

Wilbur drops his hand away from the glove. "It's a simulation, not a nightmare. Parts of it might be the same, but ye've already been in once. Ye know what to expect, so the simulation will change according to yer new fears and reactions."

"Okay." I shake my left arm and the empty fingers on the glove flop back and forth. The Balance suit fits my body tight from neck to ankles and rests light like an extra layer of skin. I ignore Wilbur's examination as he walks around me, surveying the fit of the suit. He has eyes only for smooth seams and programmed quality. He's not looking at anything more.

The door glows red. Willow screams in my memory and I resist taking a step back.

"Go on, then," Wilbur says, just like yesterday.

Without allowing time to overthink, I push through the door into the blackness. My breathing rebounds off the silence when the door closes. My heart tries to pound, but something reminds it to be calm. Steady. Instead of blood, it's pumping sweet, amber honey. Smooth.

Breathing comes easier. I anticipate Willow's scream. I wait. Calm. The suit is working.

The floor drops out from beneath me. My stomach lurches to my throat and before I can react, I land in a bone-crunching heap inside a thick glass box. It's small. Tight, like an upright coffin.

I manage to stand in the cramped space. The top of my head brushes the top of the box. The glass is clean and smooth, resting on the hearing platform.

Here I am again, in front of my village. Their eyes are blank, white, unfocused and uncaring. Among them stand Mother, Father, Reid, and Hawke. Instead of panicking, I take even breaths.

"Parvin Blackwater is accused of wasting her life," a bored voice warbles from my left. My head snaps toward the sound. Skelley Chase stands beside me in an Enforcer uniform. He tips his green fedora when our gazes meet.

"Let me out!" I pound a fist against the glass. It's thick. He turns back to the crowd.

"She's a Radical with no purpose, no merit, and no accomplishments."

The honey in my heart catches fire and I can't seem to recover my senses. I'm being sentenced again, but it's unjust. I *have* accomplished something. Some of my people must know this.

"Exile her!" someone from the crowd cries. It sounds like Mother.

"Send her back across the Wall." That's Father's voice.

"She's not worth saving," Hawke says. "Bury her alive. Let her spend her Numbers in the ground!"

"No." I moan as hope slips out of my heart. Don't they love me? As the thought settles, a foreign wave of calm hits me. My despair is halted. Frozen. Something deep inside me says, *You're not thinking straight.*

That's right. I'm in control here. I'm strong.

Skelley Chase steps in front of my glass box and gives it a hard shove. I scream as it falls backward off the platform, into a fresh grave. Reid throws the first shovelful of dirt over me.

"Reid!" But the glass stops the sound from reaching him.

A giant clod of dirt lands on the glass above my face. My view is blocked and all I hear are the loud thuds of dirt and rocks. I take four deep breaths and exhale my nerves. I'm fine. I'll be fine. They'll finish burying me and then I'll escape. I'll explain everything to them. There's no need to panic.

Lights explode around me—beneath, above, in the air. The glass coffin, dirt, and people disintegrate into shadows. I sit up and look around. My heart and nerves are quiet and placid, not angry or surprised like last time. I take a moment to recover reality and push myself to my feet.

When I exit the room, I allow Wilbur Sherrod to take off the freckle stickers one by one.

"Please give a verbal report," he says.

I stand straight. "I don't know how, but . . . but I remained calm even when I was terrified." I peel the silver glove off my right hand with my teeth. "Um . . . I still knew I wasn't going to die, I just needed to endure the attack for a moment."

"So how did the suit work?"

I shrug. "Great, I guess." Even though my emotions felt stifled, the suit fascinates me. I felt . . . strong. Powerful, even. I was in control of my emotions. The suit now feels like a protective shield instead of a torture device. I almost ask Wilbur what the next one will be—*when* it will be.

"Ye can go to your room and change. Bring the outfit back wit' ye to my office and I'll ask ye more questions then."

"Okay." I turn to leave, taking deep breaths even though my body is telling me I don't need them.

Wilbur reaches out as I pass by and pats my shoulder. "Well done."

000.134.01.03.18

Mrs. Newton hugs me so tight I can't breathe. I don't mind.

"My dear, dear, girl."

The only words that escape past my tears are, "I'm so sorry."

She leans back. "Whatever for?"

I study her face, drinking in the memories of Straight Street, of Unity Village. Her hair is tied back with a light blue handkerchief. Dark blond strands stream around her pink cheeks.

"For not helping your family. I saw the Enforcers in front of your house, I should have said something."

She shakes her head and takes my hand. "It was not your doing. Even our dear friend, Enforcer Hawke, couldn't help us. And he tried everything." She dabs a tear from my cheek with the sleeve of her shirt. "Come, let's sit down and catch up."

Catch up. It sounds so . . . normal.

The entry of Mrs. Newton's house is made of swirled marble flooring, which melds into a dark plank wood. We enter the living room where muted brownish-pink walls meet a cloudy blue ceiling. Lines of windows stretch from floor to ceiling with long cream drapes, tied back to let the sun in. A short glass table rests in front of a framed fireplace. Around it sit two single black plush chairs and a poofy couch.

"Elaborate, isn't it?"

I shake my head. "How did you get this house?"

She sinks to the couch and tugs me down beside her. My body relaxes into every fold.

"The Preacher—the leader of Ivanhoe—donated it." Joy builds behind her words. "When Laelynn and I arrived in Ivanhoe via train, we begged an audience with the Preacher. He rescheduled his own wedding to meet with us the next day. In our meeting he asked what I needed. I said we wanted to start a new life. He gave us this house and a year's worth of trade tickets.

"Wow. I haven't used trade tickets yet. Are they like regular money?"

"Yes, but it's all done through bargains. Bargaining is competitive, and if people don't come to an agreement, they can challenge each other to a match in the Barter-Combat Arena."

I lean back against a thick green pillow. "Today is my first day out of the Marble. I'm still learning the culture."

She leans forward to brush my hair out of my face. "Parvin, why are you here? You weren't a Radical were you?"

So I share my story—every teensy little ounce starting with the bullies of my childhood, then vouching for Radicals, and meeting Skelley Chase. I talk about Reid's accident, Jude, the shooter, Hawke, Willow, and the albinos. "Until I entered their village, I thought I'd killed your entire family with my silence. But the albinos gave me hope. They said you were alive. That's why I came here."

By the time I finish sharing my dreams, my renewed hope, and my failures the sunset is glaring through the windows. Mrs. Newton never interrupted me. Not once. She listened and held my hand, delivering small squeezes during the emotional parts.

"So what are you going to do now?"

I shrug one shoulder and let my head plop onto the back of the couch. "I want to talk to the Preacher. I want to see if he can do anything about the Radicals coming through Opening Three."

She pauses for a moment. "Will you stay with us, Parvin?"

The question startles me and I lift my head. Mrs. Newton stares at me with a light smile, blinking hard. Her lashes are wet.

"St-stay?"

She gives a sharp nod. "Live here, with me and Laelynn."

My eyes burn and my thinking falters, interrupted by emotion. Live with Mrs. Newton and Laelynn? Like a family?

I lurch forward into her arms, crying.

000.133.04.43.31

-*Dear Hawke,*

-*I found the Newtons. Mrs. Newton and her adopted daughter, Laelynn, are both alive. The Preacher gave them money and a beautiful home. I'm staying with them.*

-*You didn't fail. Mrs. Newton expressed that she knows you tried your hardest to save them. She called you a dear friend. She is happy, even though her family has been broken. She's happy, Hawke.*

-*So am I.*

000.120.05.25.02

My NAB rests on my bed by the window to catch the sunrays. My most recent journal update blinks, unsent. I turn away from it and dress in a flowy pullover black dress with concealed pockets—a gift from Wilbur because he hated my clothes, even once they were clean.

The front of the dress reaches just above my knees, but the back brushes against the top of my calves. Light beading covers the bodice, but the sleeveless shoulder straps are simple sheen fabric. I told Wilbur it looked like a maternity frock.

"Stop giving out that ye don't like the dress, Parvin. If ye hate it, find a belt or wear yer smoke-clothes."

A wide belt made a world of difference, and Wilbur even provided matching calf-high boots with soft soles for tightrope walking. I still won't try.

After latching the belt, I return to the NAB. It's the most thorough update I've penned, but something in me doesn't want to send it. That last sentence . . . should I erase it? I read over the entry for the hundredth time.

06.09.2149 – 08:00

My three weeks in Ivanhoe have continued similarly to the rst one. I've accepted Wilbur Sherrod's invitation to continue evaluating the effectiveness of his designed out ts. I've gone through Balance, Blizzard, Fire, Intellect, Brawn, and Noir.

The simulations aren't as terrifying anymore, although being immersed in a sea of re felt very real. I choose to test the suits that affect my physical state more often than those testing my emotional state.

Mr. Sherrod pays me daily with trade tickets for my extended work since his apprentice is still out of commission (he won't tell me why.) His social capabilities are limited, and I've come to accept and understand this about him. Somewhere inside, there's a caring and human side of him. I know it.

He's still intrigued at the idea of not fearing death. He says things like, "We never know when the time will come."

No one here has Clocks. It's strange, but they all seem so free. They're not focused on time. I wish the East could function this way. Wilbur explained that the word suicide means people end their own lives. I'm glad we don't have suicide in the USE. It sounds like it carries a lot of sadness.

I'll have to bargain for a visitation with the Preacher. I'm curious about the United Assembly. It sounds like the Preacher meets with leaders from the East (and maybe the rest of the world?) He may even know President Garraty. What hasn't our government told us about the West?

Ivanhoe feels more and more like a new home even though there's so much to explore. I almost don't want to return.

"Send," I say with a stiff voice. No more thinking. The entry is honest. Real. That's what everyone wants, right? But what if Mother and Father feel betrayed by my attachment to Ivanhoe? Will they be hurt if I don't return? After all, we already went through the difficult Good-byes.

My room in Mrs. Newton's house is small and quaint. I have my own bathroom and my bed is big enough for at least two people. The carpet is thick and massages my feet every time I take off my shoes.

I leave my room with a pocket full of trade tickets. They're made of sturdy green paper that can't rip and each has a tally mark on it. Some people bargain by the number and others bargain in fractions, the risk being guessing how many tickets a person is carrying. I tried to carry only one ticket with me one day, but somehow people just knew and no one would trade.

Today I carry all my tickets—a round fifty. I'm bargaining for a meeting with the Preacher.

"'Bye, neighbor!" Laelynn calls from behind her closed bedroom door.

I giggle. "By Laelynn!" She always knows when I'm leaving and never lets me go without a farewell. She's also decided that *neighbor* is my official name.

I ride the motorcoach to the Marble. Motorcoaches are free for the people of Ivanhoe, compliments of the Preacher. "Lovely dress, Miss Blackwater," the motorcoach driver says as I step off. "Have a good day."

"Thank you, Peter."

As I take the elevator to the first floor of the Marble, I feel . . . pretty. Maybe I'll impress the Preacher. My belt is a notch loose to try and make me look like less of a waif, but after three weeks of solid meals, I'm pleased to see my form filling out more than ever. My legs aren't so twiggy, my scars are fading, and when I flex, my arms reveal puny but noticeable muscles.

Reid would be proud.

The elevator doors open and I step out. The ground floor is covered in vendor booths set on clay flooring. People mill about and bargaining shouts fill the air. Signs and pictures hang from each booth or wall mounts. A wooden sign with a carving of an oval colosseum hangs over a stone-arched hallway out of the main floor. The Combat Arena. I still haven't seen a competition—too busy working.

No one walks in or out, which indicates no matches are taking place. Part of me sinks.

The Visitation booth sits on the opposite side of the market, marked by a wooden sign of two stick people with a dual arrow between them. Every sign is in pictures with no writing.

The trader woman is a short albino with straight dyed silver hair and a flat nose. She wears thin yellow disc earrings and snowy blue mascara. I gape at her and she lifts an eyebrow.

"Hello." I give a meek smile. "Sorry I stared. I've only met albinos from the village in the forest."

"*Albino* isn't considered politically correct anymore, you know."

I look around. "I-It's not?"

The trader woman shrugs. "I don't care, but it comes off as a little rude. Some people don't like it. I could call you whitey and we'd be square."

I scrunch my nose. "Whitey?"

"You're white aren't you? Not as white as *me* of course, but I don't pick the labels."

"Sorry." I look down. "There aren't any albino people where I come from."

"Where ya from, little one?"

"East." I bite my lip and hurry on. "How do I meet with the Preacher?"

"We can trade for a visitation." There is unmasked eagerness in her voice. "But he's not accepting questions until July fifth."

"That's four weeks away!" My excitement fizzles to a pathetic ember.

She shuffles through some papers. "He's done it again, you know."

I shake my head. "Done what?"

She leans forward with a look of distaste. "Gotten married. This is his sixteenth wife, and she's *young*."

My jaw turns slack. "What happened to the other fifteen?"

"Oh, he's still got them."

I make a face. "Isn't that illegal?"

She waves a hand. "We let the Preacher do what he wants after all he's done for us. Besides, he did it to form an alliance with a coastal city. That's why I expect he wants another bride. Everyone knows Kamea is his wife of *love*. All the rest are alliance wives."

My mental image of the Preacher dips into poisonous black sludge. Sixteen wives? He can't possibly care about them all. Do any of them feel loved? Does *he* feel loved? It sounds like brokenness to me—broken life, broken marriage, broken relationship.

Broken shalom. It's my thought this time, instead of God's, and it feels right. My mind approaches conclusions that resonate with what He's been teaching me the past few months. I'm proud I recognize the broken shalom, though my heart sinks when I think what the Preacher is missing out on.

"I can give you a visitation on that first day." The vendor sits back, returning to bargain mode. "You won't be the first in, but a nice afternoon visit should suit you, yes?"

I perk up. "Sure." Four weeks aren't bad as long as I have a sched-uled visit. I can explore Ivanhoe and spend time with Mrs. Newton and Laelynn. I can work with Wilbur and earn more trading tickets. I've come to enjoy testing out the suits. Pushing through those simulations is empowering. I feel strong, despite my missing hand.

"Well?" the trader pressures. "What are you wanting? A plea for change? Proposition? Does your visitation deal with Ivanhoe's well-being or is it personal inquiry?"

"Uh . . . I want to ask him some questions about life."

"Personal inquiry. What's your starting go?"

I slip my hand into my pocket and grip the trading-tickets like I used to clutch my Clock. "What do people usually start at?"

She grins. "You think I'll be honest?"

"I don't know."

She sighs and leans on her elbows. "All right . . . em, how about ninety trade tickets and an item of quality?"

"Ninety?" My yelp draws the stares of passers-by. I instantly regret my outburst. A few people pause in their go-about-mornings and inch closer.

The trader lifts her icy eyebrows and chuckles. "Outside your range?" She rubs her hands together. "Hit me."

It'll be another week before I have anything close to ninety trade tickets unless I borrow some from Mrs. Newton. But I have to try.

"Thirty." I'm reminded of the time bargaining Mother and I used to exchange.

"Ah, a wide field." The trader seems to lap up the moment. "This'll be good." More people shuffle into my peripheral vision. I lift my chin with an impersonal air as she comes back with a haggle. "Em, ninety-five *without* an item of quality."

"You went up!" Several people laugh, and I try to join them but any real humor is muffled by my indignation.

"I took off the item of quality." She gives a little pucker of her glossy lips, almost as if she's playing with me.

"Fine." I give my tone a sarcastic lilt. "Thirty *with* an item of qual-ity." I hope my blue watch counts as an item of quality. It's one of the nicest things I've ever owned.

"Seventy."

The growing crowd lets out a communal, "Oooh," of mock drama.

Someone cheers. "You get 'er, Rangell!"

The trader, Rangell, is alight with amusement, basking in the attention. I grow more and more uneasy. These people seem to know her. They're on her side. I can't win.

With a deep breath through my nose, I make the daring leap. "Fifty."

She folds her arms on the booth counter. "And you're still offering the item of quality?"

"Yes."

She rests her chin on one of her hands. "You're at your end, aren't you?"

My hopes plummet as the onlookers chuckle. At me. I don't respond.

"How badly do you want this visitation?"

I clench my hand and teeth. She's not mocking, but I feel a rise of injustice at being denied something I need for the sake of this woman's haggling enjoyment. "Badly."

"Then, let's take it to the Arena."

I step back. Chills sweep over my skin. A buzz lingers among the watching crowd. I rub my palm on the outside of my dress. "I'll just come back."

The people groan. "Aw, come on," someone shouts, but I'm immune to the pressure. I haven't even watched a match. I don't know what a competition consists of.

Rangell leans back. "I'll remember you, Whitey. Don't think I'll start as low when you return."

My embarrassment hardens into anger. So, she's a dirty bargainer. I could take her down in an arena. People would see my stamina and strength. I'm strong. She'll lose. Maybe it'll be a first for her. People will ooh and ahh and groan at her humiliation.

"Fine. To the arena." I don't even finish my sentence before everyone behind me cheers with hand slaps and open thrill. My anger extends toward them, too. Their delight comes at my expense, at my shame. And, more than likely . . .

At my defeat.

"My apprentice will meet you or your battler of choice at the arena next Wednesday." Rangell raises her voice so no one can miss the time. She glances at a chart nailed to the wooden wall of her booth. "Noon is free. My apprentice will see you then."

My anger settles into a stone. She's not even bold enough to fight me herself?

She eyes me with a gentler look. "Be clear you know how it works. If you lose, I still get your fifty and item of quality. If you win, you leave a rich lady with a visitation in your pocket as well as your fifty little trade tickets."

I give a curt nod, turn on my heel—

And walk straight into Jude.

33

000.120.03.57.44

My sharp gasp paralyzes my shocked nerves.

Run!

Jude doesn't even allow the thought to transfer to my muscles. He pulls me to his chest, tight. I'm trapped. Helpless. I can't flee. He's too strong. I'm his captive.

Weak.

His hands turn gentle as they move across my back, holding me less, but inviting me to remain here. It's not force. It's a hug. Jude is *hugging* me?

"I'm sorry I damaged your trust, Parvin." His voice is calm. Genuine.

I look up. We're close enough I can see the dust in his dark hair, smell the campfire on his clothes, see his roughly shaved facial hair.

He's sorry.

Regret. Shame. Fear. Anger. Surprise. The emotions sift through my bones, leaving painful chunks behind. "It's okay." I feel as though he robbed me of *my* apology. I'm humbled.

Blast him.

Jude gives a strained grimace, then releases me and returns his injured arm to the sling I made him so many weeks ago. Willow stands behind him holding her woven hat brim in her hand. Her eyes are hollow and the sunburn on her face is now a splotchy tan. She stares at me with marinated anger.

My throat constricts. I need to ask her forgiveness. I can't. Jude already said a sorry. Will she think mine's just a repeat?

I see her form crumpled on the tracks, screaming for me to return to her. Ghostly. Abandoned.

"I'm sorry, Willow." Why does it sound mechanical? I *am* sorry. I've been sorry for weeks.

The apology doesn't penetrate her cold silence.

"I'm sorry," I say again, louder.

She breaks the gaze. "Okay." It's small and tight and only makes me feel worse.

She and Jude carry fur pelts rolled and tied with slips of leather. A set of young deer antlers hang from Jude's belt.

"How long have you two been here?" The remnants of Jude's hug no longer feel comforting or gentle. I grow awkward. Confused.

Jude lets his good hand fall from my shoulders. I hadn't realized it was there. "Two days."

"Why are you even here?" Did he feel the need to follow me? Protect me? Find me? I don't need help. He shouldn't be here.

"I said I'd take you to Ivanhoe." Jude points to Willow and then me. "*Both* of you. And someone needs to fight in the Arena on Wednesday."

"You also said you *wouldn't* take us to Ivanhoe," I retort. "I'm still writing in my journal." He might as well know. "And *I* will compete in the Arena. It's my bargain."

He takes my arm and leads me away from the Visitation booth. "Let's go see the Arena, then. Willow and I discovered it yesterday."

I slide my arm out of his grasp. I was trying to protect Jude by leaving him. Now he's followed me here as if I'm his daycare ward.

I can fight on my own.

Our footsteps echo through the arched hallway until we emerge into an oval clearing with a ceiling six stories high. We stand at the top of an amphitheater. In the space between the descending rows of seats, stretch ropes. I close my eyes and release a horrified breath.

Slacklines, tightwires, flat belt-like ropes, cords of metal, wound cloth rope, thin lines, thick lines, ropes at every level. Above our heads, below us, slanted downward, and straight across. A rope-course without a safety net.

Two people are suspended over one of the lower ropes, a boy and a girl no older than Willow. The rope swings from side to side, but they both hold their balance.

"Stop *doing* that," the girl shouts on one end.

"That's what they do during actual combat." The boy moves his body even more with the sway.

"I'm going to fall!"

"Then that means I win."

At the peak of a sway, the girl leaps off the rope to a flat belt rope a few feet down. She lands with one foot in front of the other and grabs a metal cord nearby to steady herself. The change in weight steals the boy's balance and he careens off to one side, landing hard on his shoulder on the sandy floor.

I gasp and take a step forward.

The girl points at him. "Ha! Fooled you! I win!" She looks up and our eyes meet. Her laughing stops and she lowers herself to a rope below, then to the ground, and grabs the boy's arm. "Come on. No more practice, we'll get in trouble."

He looks up at us, too. They grab each other's hands and sprint the opposite way through a tunnel exit.

Jude is looking at me. I wish he wouldn't. My words and thoughts fall short of coherence.

"May I compete for you?"

I shake my head. "I can do this." He turns toward me, but I maintain a stiff stance staring ahead.

"Let me compete for you."

I spin to face him. "*Why?*" Here it comes . . . the deluge that flows from my helplessness. "Why should you compete? Why did you come here? I left you for a reason. Your assassin might be here, and if you go in the Arena he'll shoot you again. Do you think coming to my aid will change the fact you attacked me three weeks ago? You expect me to trust you? What do you want from me?"

My face is warm and vision blurry from the gush of breath. Jude stares at the ground, his hand cradling his slung arm. "What should I answer first?"

When I don't reply, he pushes on. "I want to fight because I know how to tightrope walk and you don't."

"That didn't stop you from forcing me to crawl across the Dregs."

"Look, Parvin, you're being—" He stops, though his tone has intensified.

What? I'm being what? Why doesn't he say it? I ache already and his rejection is escalating it. He should just finish his accusation.

With a lurch of effort, he drags his voice back into a sea of calm. "I didn't mean to hurt you. I didn't mean to let my anger go that far."

"It's the fact your anger *can* go that far that bothers me." If it happened once, when might it happen again? What might I do to make him snap? I don't trust him. I don't *know* him.

Willow stalks forward with folded arms. "Jude-man came here so you're not alone. He wants to be with you."

"Willow," Jude says in a tired voice, sliding a hand over his face.

"He's not afraid of the assassin. We want to help you find your purpose."

"We've been through a lot together already." Jude extends his hands in surrender. "Don't you think God introduced us for a reason?"

I stare at him. His *us* is more personal than just our threesome. He's intent. And my mind has the audacity to wonder if he's right.

Us.

Jude and Parvin.

I don't think I want him to leave. In fact, I'm glad he came after me. I want to give him a second chance. With this, his goodness returns to my memories. Rescuing me from the Dregs, giving me a piggy-back ride all night, dancing with me. Relationship. Shalom.

"Okay, you may fight for me."

000.113.01.27.00

Wednesday afternoon ushers a ring of onlookers into the amphitheater. They spread like fire ants surrounding two dying grasshoppers. Willow and I find a seat half way down the amphitheater while a small group across from us chants, "*Rangell! Rangell! Rangell!*"

"She's not even fighting," I fume to Willow. "She's sending her *apprentice*. Wuss!"

"You're sending Jude-man," Willow points out.

I glower. "Hush. He volunteered, for time's sake."

Willow's attitude has thawed this past week as we've lived in my small room together. She's still angry, but the raw hurt of this child doesn't run so deep it can't be overturned.

Mrs. Newton was gracious enough to open her other spare bedroom to Jude. It feels strange, all living in the same house—like cutouts from different sections of my life are being pasted together.

The combat commences with little flair. No announcer. No music. Just deafening cheers and two limber figures stepping out on platforms attached to the highest rope.

"One only has to knock the other off, right?" Willow asks.

There's nothing 'only' about it. Jude transfers his weight from platform to rope, six stories from the ground, both arms extended despite his healing gunshot wound. If he falls . . .

I shiver, imagining myself up there. "Yes. To the ground."

Rangell's apprentice steps on the rope as well. Her red hair is cropped like a newborn bird's. She wears tight black shorts with a long-sleeved spandex top. Jude heads toward the middle. She stays on the edge. He hesitates, watching her.

She starts bouncing the rope, absorbing the upward movement with her knees. The effect hits Jude like a tidal wave in the middle. Two solid bounces steal his balance and fling him into the air. He floats suspended for a mere second, twisting to face the ground. Then he plummets.

His outstretched hands miss the rope by a full foot. The next tight-rope down clotheslines him, throwing him into a spin. Somewhere between Willow's scream and me covering my eyes with a fist, Jude grabs a rope and stops the fall. He hangs by one hand.

His weight pulls the rope down, releasing a small handle on wheels near the mount in the wall. It glides down the rope toward him. He stops it with his free hand before it runs over his fingers.

I couldn't have done this. Even if I learned to tightrope walk, I have one hand and little strength. A single fall would have defeated me.

The apprentice descends from rope to rope, lowering herself to a hanging position until her toes are above another rope, angling a different direction.

Jude shuffles his hand and then, with one bounce, releases the rope and grabs the hanging handles. He zips down the line, slowing to a stop below the apprentice. She rubs her hands together and prepares for a leap.

Jude stills, his toes mere inches from a slackline. When his feet are positioned, he releases his hold on the handle above and sinks onto the loose wire. He wobbles and throws out a leg to gain balance.

I don't breathe.

His stability returns as the apprentice swings from a rope above, lined up for a collision. Jude ducks. She misses him, but flips like a gymnast.

He grabs her ankle as she swings by again. Her force pulls him off, but his weight rips her fingers from the rope. They both fall. She snatches another rope like a trapeze artist mid-flight, but Jude plunges through the remaining tangled web. The thud of his body on the sandy bottom hits my chest like a sledgehammer.

He doesn't move.

Willow's on her feet. The apprentice lowers herself to the sand with a cool look of victory. The fire ants cheer. Willow and I run down the amphitheater steps into the sand.

The apprentice nudges Jude with her tiny bare foot.

His neck is broken. He's dead. He's in a coma.

"Just a knock-out," the apprentice says when we reach her. The crowd is already leaving. Does no one care he's hurt? "If he doesn't wake in ten minutes, go fetch a med."

Willow sinks to her knees. Jude's face is in the sand. She angles it out so he doesn't breathe in the grains.

The apprentice waits.

I look up at her, hating her slim gymnast figure. Hating her master. Hating this arena.

"Fifty trade tickets and an item of value," she says.

"I'll bring them by," I spit out.

She shakes her head. "We had an agreement, even if the end result is dirty."

I can't argue. I pull out all fifty precious trade tickets. "I'll bring the watch today or tomorrow. I didn't bring it with me." I thought we would win. After all, Jude was fighting. He's a man on the run, a tightrope-walker, a fighter, a survivor. I didn't expect him to lose.

I stare at his unconscious body. He failed me. I'm out of trade tickets. I can't meet with the Preacher. Was this Jude's plan? To lose on purpose?

The apprentice leaves.

Jude groans. His eyes open in a confused frown. He raises a shaking hand to his head. "Was I knocked out?"

"Yes," I snap.

Willow leans over him. "Does anything else hurt?"

He lays silent with a frozen frown for several seconds. "Was I knocked out?"

Willow and I exchange a glance. *"Yes."* I stifle growing concern. "Does anything else hurt?"

He shakes his head. His fingers comb through his hair. With a small tweak of his ear, he grows stiff. He folds his ear again.

"My tune-chip is broken."

I snort. "Welcome to the world of the normal."

The next several days are difficult for us all. During the day, Willow tries to swap some of her furs for trade tickets. I monitor Wilbur Sherrod to see if he has created any new outfits to test. When he has none, I run errands for him in return for minimal trade tickets.

I quash my hopes of exploring Ivanhoe until Jude recovers. For now, he needs our care. Jude spends the days in his small room, dizzy and nauseous. His vision is blurry and he's always tired. When a med visited she said Jude had a concussion and needed to rest his mind.

He repeats questions and doesn't remember things I say, but I enjoy taking care of him in what I hope is an attractively bossy way, not that he'll remember. I tell him to rest, to sleep, and I make sure he has food. Sometimes I brush hair from his forehead for no reason other than the fact he's sleeping and doesn't know I do it. My fingers always tingle after touching his skin. I don't know if this response comes from the fact I'm touching Jude or the fact I'm touching a man's skin in general. It creates an aching longing in me.

Mrs. Newton helps when she's not out selling bread. She examined Jude's bullet wound one day and shook her head. "It's amazing this never got infected. In fact, I can't think of a single reason why it *wouldn't* get infected." Her eyes meet mine. "It may not be a bullet, Parvin. You ought to ask Jude about it when he's healed."

Jude sleeps a lot. I spend some of that time on my NAB. It's my duty to inform Hawke that the friend he sent to me has been injured. Hawke's responses are all business.

–How is Jude's memory? Ask him questions from when you first met him and see how well he remembers them. It is important that you monitor his memory. I'm sorry he lost the competition. Sometimes his ambitions are beyond his skill. Your messages and journal entries about Ivanhoe are enthralling. I wish I could be with you, discovering the mysterious west and

gathering trade tickets. I have a knack for bargaining. I think I'd do well in Ivanhoe.

I stare at his words. When he says, "I wish I could be with you," does he mean me or our group? I tilt my head to the side and reread the sentence as if he's speaking just to me. I grin. It's hard to imagine this tall Enforcer wandering around Ivanhoe. I'd like to see him bargain with Rangell.

But as I think it, my smile fades. Jude is back and now I feel uncomfortable communicating with Hawke. Soon, I need to think through my feelings and decide what's right.

It takes me a week and a half to return to the visitation booth to deliver my blue watch. Already, impatience has been stirring up my restless dragon. The longer it takes me to meet with the Preacher, the longer I don't know my purpose and Radicals continue to die in an anti-shalom world on the other side.

I'm surprised to find Rangell at her booth. I assumed she'd halt work on Sunday. I'd planned to leave the watch for her to find.

"I wondered if you were skipping out on me," she says when I approach.

"No, I've been caring for my friend, who your apprentice concussed."

Rangell raises her eyebrows. "Jem didn't concuss him. He fell. *Anyway*"—she waves her hand—"I'm sorry he has a concussion. That sand doesn't cushion like we all hope it will. I keep telling Arena maintenance we ought to change it to water."

Lacking energy to argue or small talk, I hold out my blue watch. She reaches for it, but I pull it back with an abrupt thought. "Before you accept this, may I tell you my story?"

She huffs once through her nose. "Your story?"

"Yes, I want to tell you why I need to meet with the Preacher."

She rolls her eyes. "Thrilling."

"It won't take long." And before she can protest, I jump in. It's a condensed version. I omit almost everything about the Clocks and focus on the Radicals. I don't know what made me speak, what gave me the boldness. But something's changed. I'm not ashamed of my story. I'm not even ashamed of my missing hand, even though Rangell seems to be.

"Albinos did that to you?"

I wink. "You know, it's not politically correct to call someone *albino*."

Her bottom lip quivers and I reach out with my good hand. "I need to speak to the Preacher to save lives and maybe to even recreate unity between your side of the Wall and mine. Will you help me?"

With a hard sniff, she raises her eyebrows and attempts to give me a look of indifference. "So you want me to just give you a meeting with the Preacher for free?"

"Yes."

"Do you have any idea what that costs?"

I stifle a grin. "I'd assume somewhere around fifty trade tickets and a blue watch."

Rangell laughs, losing her façade. "Nah. You keep the watch. I don't like blue."

34

000 . 087 . 02 . 22 . 53

It's time.

Questions will be answered. Guidance will be gained. I don't expect the Preacher to have every answer I seek. After all, he's a human. He understands the fear of wasted life. But he's *done* things. People revere him. *I* revere him, and we haven't even met yet.

The welcome room on the thirty-third floor is hexagonal with tall carvings on each flat wall. Sunlight streams from a domed glass ceiling onto a polished orange stone floor. Wooden benches rest against three walls, facing the tall wooden doors into the visitation hall.

Three other people sit in the room with me: a mother, her young son, and a weedy looking man with spotted bristly facial hair. The doors into the Preacher's visitation hall are open. His voice is soft and muffled, but I can't see him. I'm too nervous to peek. I rub my left arm, trying to disperse the tense feeling lacing my severed wrist like a bracelet of flames. Why doesn't the tingling go away? My hand is gone—doesn't my arm understand?

The others in the room stare at my missing hand. I'm the handless girl. It defines me. I used to think it showed me as weak, but when I think about where I've come—where God's taken me and what I've survived—it's a testament of His strength.

He helped me survive the albino atonement, crawl out of the Dregs, travel to Ivanhoe, and admit my fears during Wilbur's suit testing. I've never been the strong one, but as I wait to meet with the Preacher I realize I never *needed* to be the strong one. My missing hand reminds me that *God* is my strength.

The tall walls around me are covered in words. I stand up and step closer. The quotes are sections of Scripture.

Blessed are the poor in spirit, for theirs in the kingdom of heaven.
Blessed are those who mourn, for they shall be comforted.

On it goes, each verse beginning with "blessed". The verses are familiar. They don't make much sense to me, but I continue to read until my eyes alight on one near the bottom.

Blessed are the peacemakers, for they shall be called sons of God.

I stare at the word *peacemakers* and think of the word that's plagued my mind since I entered the West.

Shalom.

I brush my fingers over the words. *Blessed are the shalom-makers, for they shall be called sons—and daughters?—of God.*

I walk to the next section of wall and realize it holds the same verses in a different translation. The peacemaker verse is much longer in this version. As I start to read, a voice interrupts my thoughts.

"What are you doing?"

I turn around. The young boy stares at me. His mother watches as if waiting for an answer.

"Reading." I glance around the room. Then I remember how rare it is to see actual writing in Ivanhoe. Usually there are just pictures.

"No you're not."

I frown. "Yes, I am." I gesture to the verses. What does he see on these walls? Is he illiterate?

"I don't hear you."

"I was reading in my head."

The bristle-faced man speaks up in a creaky voice. "How do you expect others to hear it when you do that?"

"I-I'm sorry. I didn't know I was supposed to read out loud."

"I've never seen anyone read without speaking," the mother says in a polite tone.

I tighten my hand around my pulsing wrist and turn back to the verse. Why do I do everything wrong? And always in public? My desire to read is nonexistent, but I push myself anyway. This must be normal in Ivanhoe.

I start in a soft voice and grow louder as I go. "You're blessed wh-when you can show people how to cooperate instead of compete or fight. Th-That's when you discover who you really are and your place in God's family."

I scan the verse again and whisper it this time. "You're blessed when you can show people how to cooperate instead of compete or fight . . ." Jude and I fought, but then he came after me, seeking reconciliation. Does this mean he's blessed? "That's when you discover who you really are and your place in God's family."

By the time I finish, I no longer care what my three listeners are thinking. I sit down and ponder the verse, repeating it to myself until it's in my memory. Is this what it means to be a shalom-maker? Could I show the East how to cooperate with Radicals?

The talking from the hall of the Preacher stops. A squat young man walks out. I scan his face for signs of emotion. He looks passive. His eyes flicker to mine, then to my missing hand. Once he's gone, I wait. No one comes to get me. I look around at the others. The mother and man watch me. The little boy squints at the verses on the wall.

Do I just go in? I was here first, so I rise to my feet. I don't expect the Preacher to come for me. Deep breath. Chin high. My soft boots whisper against the reflective floor as I stride toward the hall. I cross the threshold.

The visitation room is an enormous rectangle. Piles of pillows surround a large black leather sofa straight ahead of me, but no one sits there. Small fires of different colors lick the air from random squares in the floor. Purple, green, blue, orange, and red.

"Good afternoon." The low voice catches me off guard to my right. I turn.

The Preacher lounges in another pile of pillows, propped on one elbow. He's middle-aged with short black hair and a triangle goatee. His skin is a dark Mediterranean brown veiled by a sheer black button-up shirt.

Even lying down I can tell he's tall. A dwarfed brown table stretches in front of him, holding several bottles of wine and three glasses. One glass is full.

Behind him sits a woman with long dark hair, a blue dress as flowy as loose flower petals, and heavy bracelets on her thin wrists. She massages the Preacher's shoulders with brittle fingers and spiked red nails.

One of his wives?

"Hello." Should I bow? My questions roll in my mind. Which do I ask first?

The Preacher stares at me, looking amused and bored at the same time. He runs his hand through a small green flame flickering between two pillows. It doesn't burn him.

His eyes are as stark green as the fire, catching the light from the windows behind me, shimmering like lake moss. He's waiting. Again I feel like I'm expected to know what to do. Does he know what I've sacrificed to stand before him?

I have no time or patience to be intimidated. Jude and Willow are waiting. My soul is waiting. "What is the United Assembly?"

He takes a sip of wine, not breaking my gaze. Once he swallows, he rests his free arm on the table. "An assembly of world leaders who gather yearly."

"Why?"

"To discuss the directions our nations are taking."

His answers come smooth as silk, as if nothing surprises him. The woman behind him weaves her painted claws through his short hair. He doesn't react. I rock back on my heels. "What countries do you meet with?"

"All of them."

"The USE?"

"The United States of the East is under the leadership of President Ethan L. Garraty." He says this as if to prove he knows exactly who I am, where I come from, and all the workings of the East.

How much does he know about the USE? How much does the USE know about the West? Is my venture on this side for nothing? "Do you know about Clocks?"

He raises an eyebrow. "Yes."

"Do you know that people without them are thrown across the Wall to this side? They're called Radicals."

"Yes."

I gape at him. "Do you know the Radicals *die?*"

The Preacher raises himself up to a sitting position. The woman behind him, no longer able to reach his head, slouches with a pout and whines, "Oh, Lemuel . . ."

So, the Preacher has a name. *Lemuel.*

The Preacher levels his gaze. "I do not believe your purpose in seeing me was to test my knowledge."

I hold eye contact with determination. "No, but . . . the USE leaders use their Wall as unjust punishment."

"*Their* Wall?" he asks with a tilt to his lips. "You think your side controls the Wall? Think about which side *built* it." As if doubtful I'll reach the conclusion myself, he points at his black-silk-covered chest. "We let the East use their labeled openings at their will. Meanwhile, we use it for many other things.

"I don't care if your ancestors started the Wall. I don't care *whose* Wall it is. My point is, people are *dying*. Does that matter to you?"

"Yes."

"Why don't you stop it?"

He sets his wine aside and tilts his head. "I cannot stop death."

"Opening Three is atop a *cliff.*" My voice nears shouting. I take a calming breath. "You can build a net or something. A ladder."

"Why me?"

"Because you're a leader. You hold people's respect. You can do what you want."

He lets my response rest in the silence for a moment. "I hear you are staying with Mrs. Newton."

"Yes." Is he trying to change the subject?

"She is from your side as well, correct?"

"Yes."

He takes a long calm breath. "They are your people. Can *you* not help them?"

I grip my left arm with my right, then clasp them both behind my back. "What do you expect me to do? I have no money. No resources."

"What if you *did* have the money and resources?"

"Well, I . . ." What *would* I do?

"Miss Blackwater, I offer to you and your delightful hostess my resources." He spreads his hands out in front of him, as if tossing invisible gifts at my feet. His wine sloshes. "I run Ivanhoe." He chuckles a little. "Actually, I run a lot more than that, though many would not admit it. I do not have the time to take a camping trip to the Wall. *You*, however, do."

"No, I don't! I only have a few months left."

"Ah." He lifts a finger. "There it is."

I eye him with a scowl. "What?"

"*Time.*"

I step back, cringing. "What about it?"

The Preacher—or Lemuel, as the whining woman called him—leans back. The woman wraps her arms around his chest and toys with the buttons running down his silk shirt. "It's laid claim to your faith. It's restricting your actions."

I hold his gaze with a determined stare. "My faith isn't in time, it's in God."

"Then why are you hesitant to help your people? Why do you insist on pawning off the hard jobs to others? Tell me"—he leans forward again—"what is your purpose here?"

I fumble for an answer. "To ask you questions. And to help Wilbur Sherrod with his work."

He shakes his head with a patient blink. "As much as I relish discussing Wilbur Sherrod's skill with design, I must redirect you. Why are you *here*? In the world. The big picture."

I stare at him. He stares back, waiting, calm. I'm ruffled. "A-Actually, that's one of my questions for you. How do I find out God's plan for my life?"

"He doesn't have one."

My head jerks. "What do you mean? He's God. Doesn't He have a specific purpose for everything? Everyone? For me?"

At this, the Preacher laughs. *"Purpose?"* he asks when he takes a breath. "Life is meaningless."

Anger just short of panic threatens to block my throat. "No, it's not. He has a plan, I know it."

"What is it?"

I throw my arms up. "I was hoping you'd help me find out. Is it to save Radicals? Write my biography? Start life over in Ivanhoe? Keep Mrs. Newton company? What is it?"

"Tell me, are you a pregnant virgin?"

My breath seizes and I'm in front of Trevor Rain again, answering whether or not I've been kissed. It's so embarrassing I struggle against the urge to laugh. "No." I shake my head. "I mean, no, I'm not pregnant, but yes . . ." I swallow. "I'm a . . ."

He spares me. "Have you spoken to a burning bush?"

My eyes narrow. "Are you mocking me?"

"I'm just pointing out that if God has a specific plan for your life, He'll tell you like he told Mary and Moses. But the disturbing truth is, you have to *decide* what you want, just decide it with prayer."

I stand limp. Defeated. "I don't know what I want."

"If you were in a ditch with your life seeping out of you, what's the one thing you'd want? What do you want *today?*"

I stare at him, but my imagination lowers me into a ditch surrounded by Reid, Mother, and Father. What would I want?

I'd want to save Radicals.

"In the end, life is meaningless," Lemuel continues. "Go eat what you want, indulge in drink, don't worry about deaths, and reward yourself for your work. None of it matters in the end."

"How can you say that? Everything matters. People in Ivanhoe look up to you. They admire you for all you've done."

He shrugs and takes a long sip of wine. "What does it matter, leading a self-sufficient city, donating my own riches, peacemaking between forgotten countries, or designing a culture to keep people healthy? I've gained nothing. When I die, this will all be left to a stranger. He could be a wise man or a fool, yet *he*—"

The Preacher throws his glass so it shatters against the wall to my right. Both the red-nailed woman and I jump.

"—will be master of all I worked for, all I created with my wisdom. He, who will have toiled over *none* of it!" He pours another glass of wine and toasts me.

Wine spatters the ground, but the Preacher doesn't seem angry anymore. He's calm, surveying me and offering a gentle, but distant smile to his woman.

"What about shalom? Being peacemakers, *shalom-makers*. It's on the wall outside of this room. Aren't we supposed to help bring shalom to the world? Make things how they were intended to be?"

"What's the point of bringing shalom to the world when the world is going to end?"

"So I should do nothing?"

He waves a hand to the door. "Go enjoy your labor. Eat your fill, drink to your desire, and remember God while you're young before you age and hate your life."

He dismisses me with a cut in attention, turning to the woman and acknowledging her with a small kiss.

I stand, mute, staring at my betrayed hope. When feeling returns to my legs, I stumble out of the hall, my mind consisting of no insight and all frustration. The Preacher gave me nothing but questions. I sacrificed weeks of time for his wisdom and now I'm left with the message that life is meaningless.

It can't be. It's not. "It's not meaningless!" I shout, bringing myself back to reality and startling a short shopkeeper with black hair and crossed eyes. He bustles away from his wares and crouches behind his desk.

It can't be meaningless.

That's what I get for seeking answers from a man. *Well, God, You've made your point.*

By the time I reach Mrs. Newton's house, I'm sweating, tense, and determined to spew my thoughts to Mrs. Newton, Jude, and Willow. They'll affirm God has a purpose for life—at least, Jude will. They'll understand my despair.

I open the front door to a scene that stuns my fuming. Jude sits upright on the couch in the living room, his head in his hands and Willow stands beside him, her ivory face streaked with tears. She looks up when I enter.

"What's wrong?" I step forward.

"Jude can't remember my name." She releases a shuddering inhale, wiping a tear away with the back of her hand.

I look at him. "What?"

"Yes I can!" He lifts his head from his hands and slams his arms down on his knees. His sling lays abandoned on the floor. He looks at Willow with a mixture of anger and exasperation.

She stares back with growing tears.

His face contorts and his mouth moves as he reaches out with a hand as if her name floats on the air. Slow seconds tick by. His fingers curve together like a claw. Willow lets out a wail.

Jude releases a roar and grips his head again. "I *know* it."

I step forward and kneel down, concern turning my heart into a fluttering alarm bell. "Do you know my name?"

"Yes," he gasps, straightening, looking at me with wide eyes of disbelief. "P-P-Puh." He squeezes his eyes shut. "Pay . . ."

"Parvin," I whisper, aching with him.

He nods and blinks several times. It doesn't hide the red around his eyes. "Parvin," he murmurs back. "Parvin and Willow."

35

000.086.16.15.09

"Parvin."

I open my eyes and meet Jude's eyes above me. He shakes me. Jude knows my name. Jude is touching me.

I sit up.

"Want to see the sunset?"

My first instinct is to say no. In Unity Village I avoided the sunset because its rays glowed behind the Wall, but we're in the West. The Wall isn't blocking the sunset here. And this is the first time Jude has asked me to do something with him. My stomach flips. He desires my company.

It's odd being woken for a sunset. The day feels backward, like it should be starting not ending. My anxiety and meeting with the Preacher stole my energy and, after Jude's odd struggle with memory, I slipped into a desperate escape from reality.

Thoughts are foggy as we take a motorcoach to the Marble and then climb the endless stairs to the top floor. Shops are closed. The hollow sphere is stiff with silence—a sleepy evening of families gathered together.

Jude walks toward the web of ropes connecting to the center elevator platform. My stomach sinks. "Jude, you know I can't tightrope walk. Why didn't we take the elevator up to the platform?"

"Because I want to show you something." His eyes crinkle a little and something deep inside me shudders in a delightful way. "Piggyback ride?"

My delight dies a horrified death. I glance from him to the ropes. "Across *that?*"

"Yes." He reaches out for my hand.

"You'll fall." I take his hand. It's warmer than I expect. Then again, I've never held someone's hand. Not like this. Is he nervous? Why am I nervous?

"There are nets. Besides, you haven't seen me *really* tightrope walk before."

I tilt my head, playfulness basting my emotions. "That's true. I've seen you dive off a cliff with a gun in your hand and then get a concussion from a gymnast."

He laughs, but turns his back to me and crouches down. "Come on."

I climb on, pulling against his clothes with my right arm to gain leverage. I feel rebellious being so close to him. What would Mother say?

I smirk.

"Grip tight with your knees and wrap your arms around my shoulders." He steps toward one of the tighter ropes.

I close my eyes and take a deep breath, trying to dispel the memories of him falling from rope to rope in the Arena. That was different. He was fighting someone.

He transfers one foot from platform to rope. I grip him with every ounce of quivering energy.

His body is tight beneath me, his arms outstretched. One foot on firm ground, the other on the rope. My heart pounds. Can he feel it?

At least I know we won't die. I'm still at eighty-six days.

With a soft push, he brings his other foot onto the rope. We teeter. I bite back a squeal and grip even tighter. The less I move, the more stable he'll be.

"The hard part is over." He releases a long breath. Foot over foot, we advance.

Somehow, I'm not as frightened as I thought I'd be. He's secure. Controlled. The progress is slow. Sweat gathers at his temples. I inch my arms down a few centimeters until I feel his heartbeat.

Quick. Excited. Focused.

We reach the elevator platform. I slide from his back and my joints groan in relief. We both release a gush of nervous laughter.

"Not so bad, was it?" I say.

His laughter settles into a grin. "Tally ho."

I walk around the platform with a sense of empowerment. With Jude, I can go anywhere. I'm no longer trapped by my inability to tight-rope walk. We've discovered a solution.

Jude stops at the other side of the elevator chutes and looks up. I follow his gaze until my vision alights on a steel ladder stretching from the high ceiling of the Marble and connecting with the wall of the chute. The bottom rung is above my head.

"Up we go." Jude lifts me by the waist without so much as a warning.

"Wait!" I grab the highest rung with my right hand, wrap my left arm around it, and pull my weight from his arms. He guides my foot onto the bottom rung.

"Go on. Sunsets don't wait." His voice holds a hint of a smile. It's so different from his clipped strict tones, I don't argue. I like this side of Jude.

I climb with little difficulty. My right arm is strong from taking the effort of my left arm every day. The ladder shakes a few rungs as Jude hauls himself up. The square hole in the ceiling leads into an empty, domed, glass room with an arched floor. Jude climbs through moments later. He leads me across and through a small tunnel opening to an extended wraparound balcony of sorts.

The door closes behind us and warm wind blows my hair around my face. I used to hate my hair loose like this. Now I wonder if Jude likes it. I allow my eyes to slide to my left, hoping for a glimpse of his thoughts. He's watching me. Expectant.

I look out over Ivanhoe. We stand atop the city. My breath leaves me at the sight of orange-tinged glass towers casting shadows from the sinking sun. "Wow."

Jude's smile widens. I look at him, half-wishing I had my sentra, but thankful I have this moment all to myself.

We sit down and lean against the Marble roof and I glance at him. "How did you find out about this place?"

"I have a knack for observation. I saw the ladder, so Willow and I explored while you worked with Wilbur."

A frown threatens to steal my joy. He came here with Willow. I'm not jealous. How could I be when she's such a little girl? But I wish, somehow, Jude experienced this moment with no one but me.

Okay, I'm jealous.

The sunset is silent. Does it bother Jude? What would his tune-chip be playing right now?

I sigh. It broke because of my gamble with Rangell. Jude suffers because of my desire to see the Preacher. I should tell him I'm thankful he's here. I should tell him it was an accident. I should tell him . . . "I'm sorry I left you and Willow."

"It's okay." He looks at his hands.

Why do I wish he'd say, "It wasn't your fault"?

My emotions weave in and out, carrying strong whiffs of nostalgia and hope followed by despair and guilt. I wish they'd settle. I wish my mind would clear. I wish I knew what to say, to think, to hope.

"Parvin, I wanted to watch the sunset with you . . ." Jude twists his hands together, then takes a breath and forces them to still. "But I also wanted to talk with you."

Oh good. Talking. He had purpose in bringing me up here. Purpose beyond a romantic sunset.

Romantic? Was it romantic to begin with or am I creating the mood? I force myself to respond. "Okay. I'm listening." His intentionality brings a warmth of leadership with it.

"I told you I'd tell you about my invention."

The atoms in my body slow in tense anticipation as if, by decelerating, I'll hear him better. Tingling tickles my ears. "You don't have to if you're uncomfortable."

"I want to."

"Okay," I say before I offer another escape.

He flicks his hands, palms up, in a defenseless way. "It's hard to know where to start. I've never told anyone the full story."

"Why are you telling me?" What's special about Parvin Blackwater?

His voice hardens again, like thoughts I'll never know pour steel into his blood. "Because it's time for someone to know."

Just someone?

He lets out a breath. Neither of us watches the sunset. "Have you ever been to a USE orphanage?"

I shake my head. "No."

"I have." His tone is low, soft like a whisper. Something about it makes me sad. "Almost all the children in the orphanages are accidental Radicals—children of dead Radicals or irresponsible parents. They never get adopted. Why would someone adopt a child without a Clock?

They might be evicted like the Newtons were. The child could die any day."

A hollow cavity deep in my chest turns cold as I imagine hundreds of children waiting in a stone orphanage for an adult to show them interest. "What happens to them?"

He shrugs, but not in an unknowing way—in a helpless way. "They grow up, leave the orphanage, and live as Radicals. No jobs. Homeless. No health care. Stealing. Starving. Getting involved in the Black Market . . ." He looks away from me and speaks so soft I almost don't hear him. ". . . Dying."

Shadows creep across Ivanhoe, bringing with them a chill appropriate to the conversation topic.

"My family and I couldn't handle knowing the lives the children would have once they outgrew the orphanage. We all got involved in some way. My father entered a Black Market form of health care to help them. My brother became an Enforcer to try and relocate children to Radical families. And I . . . I went to school to study history, biochemistry, and nanotechnology.

"I started purchasing old Clocks from the Black Market and fiddling with them. Learning how the chips inserted into women detect the conception of a child. Eventually . . ."

He goes silent.

I tense, waiting. What came from his experiments? "Eventually what?"

"This is hard for me, Parvin!"

I shy away, drawn back to his flashing anger amongst the headstones. What if he hits me again? The pounding in my heart accelerates. I'm helpless up here. No one could aid me if Jude got angry. The railing around our balcony is short. He could push me over. I imagine myself plummeting toward the concrete ground, bouncing off the uneven sides of the Marble.

Stop, I bark at myself. I'm escalating a one-time incident for which Jude already apologized.

Jude takes a deep breath, oblivious to the dramatic swing of my imagination. "Eventually . . . I invented a Clock that can be matched to a person *after* conception. Adults. Kids. Anyone at any time in life."

I gape at him, frozen in a stunned silence. He looks up and gestures at my face. "I know, right? Enormous breakthrough! It can change the world." He doesn't sound happy.

My mind reels. "You can match Clocks to . . . *anyone?*"

"Yes."

"After birth?"

A pause. "Yes."

My breathing is constricted. "This is huge."

"I know."

Possibilities flood into my brain like a water-pump. "There would be no more Radicals. No more stupid ovachips. No more people thrust through the Wall. Everybody could be matched with a Clock if they accidentally destroyed theirs. People wouldn't have to die." I grab his hand. "Reid could have a Clock after mine zeroes out! He could still get medical care. A job. A life."

"Parvin . . ."

His voice holds a warning, but I don't want to stop. The hope in his invention continues to drown me. "Jude, you're incredible! How did you create it? Did you test it? People like the Newtons could return to Upper Cities if they got new Clocks. There would be no more evictions."

His fingers tighten like pincers around mine. "Parvin!"

I yank my hand away. "What?" I'm angry. He's going to crush my hope, I can tell by his tone. This is the invention he said he kept away from the government. He doesn't want people to have it. I don't want to hear why.

"That's what *I* thought, too." He tries to soften his voice, but it doesn't soften my heart. "I received permission to test the Clocks on some of the children at the orphanage. It would give them a higher likelihood of being adopted, even offer a better future once they left the orphanage. So I presented it to the council of my city."

He avoids my gaze. "They showed it to the Citizen Welfare Development Council I told you about. The CWDC wanted to see completed research. I brought some of the orphans with me and matched Clocks right before the Council's eyes. The Council congratulated me. They mentioned a lot of possibilities—fame, honor, awards, wealth, anything. They said they'd get back to me with decisions and thoughts for the future."

"That's great."

"Yeah." He releases a humorless laugh. "Great."

I lean toward him, straining to see his face in the shadows. Muscles in his jaw tighten and loosen, like he's trying to crush memories. "What is it?"

His pulse pounds the soft skin on his neck, growing faster. "All the kids' Clocks were short, just a teaspoon of months left for each of them, give or take. I wished I hadn't Clocked them. Once I did, then I saw that most of them would die before me. I loved these kids."

Jude closes his eyes. "The CWDC did a few tests of their own. They went to the orphanage—*my* orphanage—that first inspired my invention and took the children with whom I'd already matched Clocks. They wanted to test if my Clocks were accurate."

I can't bring myself to inhale. The word *test* instills a deep fear as I watch Jude process these memories.

"They starved several of the children, tried drowning or poisoning others." His voice shakes. His body shakes.

I'm shaking, too. Nauseous. Sick. Helpless. I can't breathe.

Jude grips the front of his black coat with both hands and knocks his head back against the Marble. "None of the children died before their Clocks," he croaks, sucking a breath in through his teeth. "Medical miracles. My invention was perfect. Too perfect." He shakes his head and sniffs. "But . . . the kids were never the same after that testing."

I touch his shoulder as hard burning pinches the back of my throat.

"Some of them," he rasps, taking his hands away from his coat and looking at me, "stared vacantly at nothing, like they had no soul left." Jude grits his teeth and the tears behind his eyes pool so high I can't see his irises. "Others were brain dead or crippled. Then they *did* zero-out, right on time with their Clocks—the Clocks I gave them."

With a thick voice, he gropes for words and points a shaking finger at his chest. "I d-did that. I-I caused that t-to happen."

"No, you didn't." I tighten my grip.

"Yes, I did!" He closes his eyes tight. I force myself to stay close to him. "I could have conducted experiments with more control. I shouldn't have shared so much information with the Council. Maybe, if I hadn't Clock-matched the kids, they wouldn't have died."

"You can still help people."

He shakes his head. "No. I started rethinking, weighing the pros and cons." His breath quickens and strength hardens his voice.

"Clock-matching would give the government more control. People wouldn't have a choice to be a Radical or not."

"No one *wants* to be a Radical."

"That's not true. Some people don't want to know how long they'll have. That's heavy knowledge and the government would start making even more decisions based solely on a person's Numbers. It's pushing the country in the wrong direction. We need to try going backward to the life before Clocks when decisions weren't based on someone's time."

I shake my head, horrified. "No. We *need* these Clocks. Reid needs a Clock. I've watched people die to the Wall all my life because of injustice. That must be stopped!"

He doesn't seem to hear me. "Clock-matching needs to be a choice, just like being a Radical. Both need to be accepted. One can't dominate the other. That's why I kept my invention. I never shared *how* I matched. That is the one decision I'm proud of." He straightens and glances over the city. "That's why I'm here, Parvin. I took the information and ran." He looks at me and his face turns into a cool mask. "And . . . I need to tell you something."

My heart squeezes my blood to a standstill. "What . . . do you need to tell me?"

"I smashed my own Clock—you know that—but . . ."

Chills sweep my skin.

He slumps against the wall. "I still remember my Numbers and . . . and I think you should know . . . I zero-out soon."

My world falls upon me like the darkness stealing our sunset. I can't move. His voice echoes in my mind like a holler from a mountaintop.

Zero-out . . . zero-out . . . zero-out . . .

My voice doesn't work. I can't even muster a whisper. My mouth forms the words, "How soon?"

Jude squints and scans my face. His grip tightens.

I take a shuddering breath and my voice breaks. "How soon, Jude?"

He stares, and, for a brief moment, his chin quivers. "Please . . . please don't ask me."

36

"Mrs. Newton?" The creak I heard at her bedroom door turns into shuffled footsteps down the hall. My eyes are heavy and the mug of coffee warms my hands. I haven't slept all night.

Jude has Numbers.

I've grown up around people with Numbers. Everyone had a Clock, but I've gotten so used to the idea of Jude's mystery time I started to imagine he had indefinite Numbers.

Mrs. Newton peeks into the kitchen wearing a thick tan robe that reaches all the way to the floor. "That *was* you. Good sunrise, Parvin, you're up early." Her tone is kind, but her brows crease. "Is everything okay?"

"I need . . . help." My voice trembles on that last word. "A lot has happened the past few days and I need to talk to someone."

"Of course. Do you mind if I grab some coffee?"

"No." It's like my mornings with Mother . . . only kinder. The memory pinches.

She sits across from me with a steaming ceramic mug and takes my hand. "What's wrong, dear one?"

If I don't start speaking now, I won't be able to. "My meeting with the Preacher yesterday didn't go too well. He told me life has no meaning. Then I came back and Jude took me to see the sunset and to talk. He remembers his Numbers. He wouldn't say what they were and . . . I don't know what to do. The way he said it sounded like he'll zero-out any moment. Why would he tell me that? What good does it do?"

She releases a long breath. "Maybe he was trying to prepare you."

"But . . . he can't die. I was just beginning to wonder if we were going to develop a relationship in my last days."

She tilts her head and smiles in a sad way. "Oh Parvin, why would you let this stop you?"

I gulp a swallow of coffee. It's weak and too hot. What can I say? That I don't want to commit to something that's sure to tear my heart into pieces? "I . . . don't want to lose him."

Her thumb rubs across my clenched knuckles. "Losing people is a part of life. But you must love them as deeply as you can before you lose the chance."

Choked emotion stills my heart. "I don't know how to love."

She allows a soft laugh. "Love is a choice. And, while you may not notice this yet, you've already chosen."

A burden crumbles from atop my heart. I have? The way Mrs. Newton says this sends the message that she's proud of me. She's happy for me. I think . . . I think I may be happy too, despite the recent dampenings.

"And the Preacher was wrong, you know. Life isn't meaningless."

"I know. I was discouraged."

"Did nothing good come from your meeting?"

I look out the window. The sky is lightening with the sunrise. It's not red yet, just a cold pale blue. "I realized I'm a fool for seeking answers from a man. God's been with me all along and He's the only one who can guide me with true answers."

Mrs. Newton leans back, sliding her hand from mine. Is she uncomfortable? I guess I don't know where she stands with the whole God-thing. Is she afraid I'll indoctrinate Laelynn with my beliefs?

"Um . . . and the Preacher offered me his resources, whatever that means. I think it was more of a joke. He suggested *we* help the other Radicals sent through Opening Three."

She meets my eyes with a startled glance. "We? You and me? But what can we do?"

I shrug. "I don't know. I'm not even going back to that side before I zero out."

A door down the hall opens. Mrs. Newton and I clamp our lips shut. Footsteps head toward the bathroom, then toward us. Jude steps into the kitchen. "Good sunrise."

"Good sunrise," we reply.

His eyes are weighed down by sleeplessness. Heavy. Dark. I stare down at the table. What will he see in my eyes if I look at him? What might I say?

"May I join you?"

I stand. "Actually, I was going to go change. I have a simulation with Wilbur today." My room is my safe haven and I close the door with a soft hand. I pick up my NAB and open the journal button. It's time to let Skelley Chase—and some others—know where I stand before I say good-bye and focus on life in Ivanhoe.

"I don't know what I'd do if I returned to the West," I whisper to the journal. "Ivanhoe has become a type of home for me. I'm comfortable here. It will be a nice place to zero-out. I'm not coming back."

After sending it, I click on Hawke's contact bubble. This will be a much harder message to send.

~Hello Hawke,

~Let me start off by thanking you for all the help and encouragement you've provided since I met you. You have been an unexpected friend.

My throat tightens, but I continue on.

~It's time for us to say good-bye now. I'm not coming back to the East. I'm staying in Ivanhoe until I zero out. Jude zeroes out soon, too, I think. I'm realizing . . . I may love him. Or I may be on the road to love. I'm not sure. I've never loved anyone before. But I cannot communicate with you anymore. I think it upsets Jude, it confuses me, and it's not fair to any of us.

~I will miss our communication. A lot. Which is why I must stop it. It doesn't feel right for me to continue it. After this message, I am deleting your contact information. Please don't reply.

~Farewell.

000.086.02.21.04

I enter a simulation in Wilbur Sherrod's newest suit, Inkling. It stimulates the activity of my brain and helps me use more brain cells, which should stimulate deeper thinking in the face of problems.

"This one's a bit different." Wilbur pointed to a round light on the underside of my wrist. "When this starts blinking, ye have one minute before the suit needs rechargin'. It's a new feature."

The simulation begins with me standing at the top of the cliff in the doorway of Opening Three. I'm assaulted by the memory of falling. I look out over the wide expanse of space, glancing at the plateaus a hundred feet to my left and right. If only I could reach them instead of climbing down to the wolves.

"We have to jump, you know."

I spin around. My insides freeze. "Reid?"

He's tall with disheveled hair. Solid. He opens his arms. "My little Brielle."

I launch myself into his embrace. "How did you find me?"

"Followed you through the Opening." He releases me and brushes back my hair. I smell his scent of forest and travel. It's been so long. "Now, we need to jump before the door closes."

I turn back to the cliff. "No, we can climb down."

"What's the point? The wolves are down there."

"I know how to get past them."

He comes up beside me. We stand shoulder to shoulder. "And then what, Parvin? Then what do we do?"

I know what he's asking and a hollow chasm opens in my stomach. Where would I take Reid if we survived? And not just Reid, but the rest of the Radicals coming through? Even if they all walk through the wolves and survive, they have no place to go.

"You see? They need your help." He stands on his tiptoes and spreads his arms wide, inches from the edge.

"Stop." I grab his arm. "What are you doing? I'll help you." The moment I say the words *I'll help you*, ideas blast into my mind like a flash flood. One after the other, so fast I can't even separate them to focus on a single thought. Visions of bridges, tight ropes, safe houses, helpers, stairs, ladders, maps, parachutes, Wilbur's suits, Hawke, the Newtons, the Preacher, resources.

A blinking light catches my eye, stifling the flow of ideas. My wrist light. What did that mean again? I let go of Reid's arm to hold the light closer. He leans forward and falls in slow motion.

"No!" I scream, reaching for him. I catch his arm and he yanks me off the edge as the door closes on my foot. We hang there, suspended. My joints stretch.

"Let go," he grunts. "It's my Clock, Parvin. Let me die."

"No!"

The lights in the simulation room blast away the scene. As with all the other simulations, reality comes swooping in and stirs my emotions with a rod of ice.

This one was bad, yet exhilarating at the same time. I didn't realize how much I missed Reid. I didn't realize how many ideas I could have in such a short course of time. I need to leave. I need to think.

I walk out.

Wilbur removes the stickers. "Report?"

"The suit worked. Wilbur, it was amazing. I had so many ideas. So many thoughts on how to save Radicals and somehow cause some change."

"So it was good?"

I roll my eyes. "Yes, but it'd be nice if you made the suit last a little longer."

He shakes his head. "There are too many rules fer this one. This suit is only fer unique users, otherwise people can get addicted."

"I guess I'm lucky I got to test it, huh?"

"Yes, ye are." He claps his hands together. "I'll get the reports from the computers. Ye can be done fer today. Return the suit to the lab."

I do as he says, contemplating my interaction with Reid while riding the motorcoach to Mrs. Newton's. There it was again, Reid claiming in my subconscious that the Clock is his. I can't continue to ignore this possibility.

If I *do* survive the Clock, what would I keep doing? I would have indefinite time. I could save more lives—help Radicals using one of the billion ideas that zipped through my mind during the simulation.

When I come to Mrs. Newton's house, dressed again in my own clothes, neither Jude nor Willow is here. A sigh of relief escapes me. Laelynn skips into the entry. Her blond hair is a ratty mess of clips, curls, bows, and a paper crown.

"Neighbor!"

"Hi, Laelynn, where's your mom?"

She points to the kitchen. When I enter, the warmth of cooking hits my face. "Mmm, what are you making?" I peek over Mrs. Newton's shoulder. A pot is filled with what looks like white maggots and vegetables.

"Rice."

I scrunch my face. "Is it food?"

She snickers. "Yes, it's from China. Just because they got hit with a meteor doesn't mean they disappeared. Apparently the East has been missing out on some great trade."

"Interesting." I set my shoulder pack on the floor and wrap her in a tight hug. "I've had an idea!"

She places a lid over the pot. "For what?"

"Helping Radicals." I don't bother explaining my simulation. Instead, I launch into my flowing thoughts. "The Preacher gave me access to his resources, and I intend to take him up on that offer, whether he meant it or not. We can send some builders to the Opening to make a bridge from the Wall to the plateau that you and Laelynn crawled to. We can create a station of sorts with travel equipment and a map to Ivanhoe or the *Ivanhoe Independent* line. Then instead of Radicals dying or fighting for survival, they can step into a new life. Like what you and I have! What do you think?"

"Well, I love the idea of saving lives. Then no one would have to fall off that cliff . . ." She trails off. Her fists clench.

I reach for her. What does one say? None of my words can bring back her husband and daughter.

She shakes her head. "I'm fine. It's tragedy, but Laelynn and I are still here."

She meets my gaze. Something in her eyes sends a message of strength. I always viewed Mrs. Newton as soft—much softer than Mother. But now I realize they both carry a unique strength. Maybe it's mother-strength.

"The Radicals will need a place to stay when they reach Ivanhoe." She raises an eyebrow and a grin creeps onto her face. "I've been thinking of this a lot lately—how to help other Radicals who come along. There's a mansion up for purchase on the other side of the Core. It would make a perfect halfway house."

"I *knew* it! I knew I could count on you."

We're going to do it. We're going to save lives.

000.079.23.07.33

A week passes with no word from Hawke or Skelley Chase. I relax and grow more confident in my new goal. I purchase and copy maps of the

West for the Radicals while Mrs. Newton meets with the Preacher. She has special access to him, I guess, because of his initial help. I'm glad she doesn't have to bargain for a meeting and waste trade tickets. Willow hunts outside of Ivanhoe so she can trade furs to help us with our quest.

I share my plan with Jude. It's strange speaking to him with the new knowledge I have of his Clock. The topic doesn't come up again, but I feel guilty for not treating him better. If I'd known about his Numbers earlier, would I have stayed with him and Willow when the train came? I want those weeks back. I can't seem to remember the conviction I felt when I left them behind.

I've given up thoughts of Jude's invention helping Radicals. The one time I brought it up, he said, "People are allowing themselves to place time above life. If we make life without a Clock more common, people will be more open to adopting the children."

How could I argue when Laelynn—physical proof to his argument—stood in the other room? Jude is so passionate against sharing his invention. I'm glad God gave me a new idea to save Radicals. Besides, problems on the East aren't my concern anymore. My new life is here, in Ivanhoe.

Jude and I talk a lot more. I'm more patient. Every time I feel like losing my temper with him, I remember he may zero-out soon. I don't have time to argue with him, like how I never had time to argue with Mother. I always should have sought more patience. Now is my second chance.

I still haven't revealed my feelings of possible love. What would I say? "Hey, Jude, I think I possibly love you."

Oh yeah. That'll impress him.

One morning, the sun rises behind thin clouds, burning away the light drizzle that welcomed the dawn. I wander down into the living room and curl up on the sofa. I pull Reid's journal out of my pack on the floor.

My eyes smart. I hold it close. It smells nothing like him. In fact, it smells old from the Dregs water. Fishy. I haven't looked through it since I found it thick with water and now I want to see if I can decipher any of the blurred entries. It's too hard to stare at smudged pages and know I'm missing out on so much of Reid's life. I've only scribbled notes on the first few pages.

As I'm on the brink of cracking it open, my NAB lets out a muffled *pop!* I contemplate ignoring it, but curiosity urges me find out who sent the message. Part of me hopes it's Hawke, but another part—a stronger part—hopes it's not. I don't like being conflicted. And if he can't accept my silence, I will have to be harsher. I don't want to be harsh.

I slip the NAB from the folds of my shoulder pack. Still lemon-scented. Yuck. When I open it, I breathe a relieved sigh. It's from Skelley Chase. Is he angry I'm not returning?

~Parvin, can I count on you or not? Have you read The Daily Hemisphere *lately? People suspect you're not real. They think I created you. If you don't return, there's no proof any of your survival matters or exists. Is that what you want? -SC*

I haven't touched *The Daily Hemisphere* since Jude arrived in Ivanhoe. Maybe that's why life in the East feels like a distant whisper. I've immersed myself in life here. It's become my new home, but his newest message irritates me. It's not my job to convince people I'm real.

But why are people doubting? Do they think I can't do what I've done? I type a quick reply, too tense to dwell on this new information.

~Mr. Chase, I'm not returning. I'm sorry. This is my new home. You of all people know my time is limited. I have new things to do on this side while I can.

How could people think I'm not real? They have my emotigraphs, my pictures, my . . . story. Does this mean they're not doing anything to help Radicals? Maybe that's their excuse—it's too hard to fix the Radical system, so they write me off as a fake.

Skelley Chase's response arrives and I tap the message bubble so hard a jolt of pain zings up my finger.

~Parvin, you've turned rather unreasonable and selfish. You really want to do this? Neglect your family? Go back on your readers? Go against our agreement? More Radicals will die if you don't return. You'll never be remembered. – SC

His message encourages me, which I'm certain wasn't his intent. He doesn't know I'm going to save Radicals on *this* side. He can't see the stacks of maps and instructions I've handwritten. He can't see the bridge sketches Jude helped me make.

I'll be remembered on *this* side. And my family will remember me. They'll know I tried. I was called to save lives in the West.

~Yes, Mr. Chase. I'm doing this.

He's going to have to accept the fact he can't have everything he wants. He can't control me any longer. I hardly finish my motivational thought before he responds.

-I can't let you. People on this side need to know you're real. This X-book we've created is powerful and I can't let you hinder that with your selfishness. If you don't return before the end of your Clock, then I will have your brother killed.

37

000.079.06.19.44

Have your brother killed . . . have your brother killed . . . have your brother killed . . .

A scream builds in my throat. I barely manage to clap a pillow over my face before it escapes. When I stop screaming, I'm breathing hard. My brain is fumbling, juggling the implications. The horrors.

He couldn't kill Reid . . . could he?

Oh yes, he could. He can do anything. He knows it. He knows that *I* know it.

But can Skelley Chase control death? Can he control the Clocks? The scary thing is . . . I feel like he can.

What do I do? I'm thousands of miles away. I can't help Reid at all. I can't even send Hawke to help my family because I deleted his contact bubble. Maybe I should ask Jude to contact Hawke for me.

Yes, that's what I'll do.

It takes all my energy to stay on the couch, waiting for Jude to wake up. I should go wake him, but he's still healing from his concussion. Darned rest. He needs it. But . . . this is urgent.

I'll give him five minutes.

I look at my blue watch. Skelley Chase gave this to me. The rat. The slimy evil snake. *God, why would you let this interrupt my vision? Would you let Reid die like that?*

But why would Skelley Chase kill him? Is my return so crucial to his own plan? What do I have that Skelley Chase wants? He already has fame. He already has my story.

I can't wait five minutes. I leap from the couch and run to Jude's room. "Jude!" I pound on his door with the flat of my fist. "Jude! Jude! Wake up."

The door flies open. "What is it?" Jude stands shirtless wearing only his pants. His snake tattoo weaves around the bullet wound near his elbow.

"It's Reid. He's in danger. I need you to contact Hawke and ask him to get Reid out of Unity Village. Ask him to get my whole family to safety. Hide them."

Jude tosses on his shirt and grabs a tiny NAB from his windowsill. We walk into the living room and I collapse back onto the couch.

"Why can't you contact Solomon?" he asks, typing away on his NAB.

I clutch Reid's journal to my chest. "Because I don't have his contact information anymore." He pauses in his typing. "Please, Jude, send the message."

He types for a long time, then we are forced to wait for Hawke's response. Jude sits on the ground by the fire and closes his eyes. I crack open Reid's journal, more for the hopes of distraction than any information. Sunlight flickers from a passing bird.

I flip page-by-page, making out single words like *adventure, Parvin,* and *school*. At one point, the word *Florida* stands out three different times. I squint at the watery words in between and make out what look like his first thoughts of traveling to Florida.

The next several pages are almost blank from the Dregs water. Another word starts cropping up. Soon it's written so often I can't imagine what words were in between it.

Tawny. Tawny. Tawny.

Tawny is a color, but he capitalizes it every time he writes it. On the next page, I find broken sentences.

. . . can't bring Tawny home . . .

I think Parvin . . . like how . . . Tawny is.

Tawny sounds like a person or a pet. Knowing Reid, it's probably a person. It's probably a girl. Despite the temptation to deny this, I know it is. She must be. It would explain his desire to be in Florida.

My nerves burn. So he deserted me for this Tawny girl? I turn the page with such ferocity the corner rips. On this page is taped a photograph. The colors melt together and I make out fuzzy outlines of two people. I squint as hard as I can, but no clarity comes to me.

I bet it's a picture of him and this Tawny girl.

Wanting more pictures, I flip to the back of the book where a conglomeration of pictures and emotigraphs clog the binding. The emotigraphs don't bleed, so I start with them. First is a picture of the ocean, but the next captures the faces of Reid and a girl, as if he held the sentra out to take their picture.

Wary, I press the emotigraph button and I'm floored with joy. Hope. Whimsy. Similar feelings to when Jude showed me the sunset.

The emotions shatter like a smashed windowpane and I gasp, trying to breathe again. I've never imagined Reid happy like that.

I scrutinize Tawny. She's maybe a year younger than us. Her hair is shoulder-length golden blond with dark streaks and the perfect mixture of curly and wavy. It frames her oval face as if a stylist spent hours sculpting it. Dark eye makeup lines her eyes, bringing out the smile crinkles. Teeth: straight. Lips: perfect pink. Eyebrows: trimmed. Skin: smooth.

I don't like her. Why is Reid's arm around her? Who is she?

Tawny.

I flip to the next emotigraph and grip it so tight, the small sheet bends. Tawny stands in the center of the picture, her hair half up with flawless makeup. Long earrings dangle to her bare shoulders.

My mouth drops open in horror. The rest of her body is covered in a white wedding gown made of gathered lace, outlining her skinny curvy body, revealing every angle, until it flares out at her knees.

She poses like a model with a little smirk that doesn't reach her eyes, but shows off her lipstick. She doesn't look happy. I flip the emotigraph over, not daring to press the button. Black words line the top, written in Reid's jerky handwriting.

4.02.2149 - Tawny Blackwater. Our wedding day.

Married. My brother. My triplet. On our eighteenth birthday. A Wednesday. Who gets married on a Wednesday?

I throw the emotigraph like a Ninja star across the room. It bounces off the fireplace mantle and lands near Jude.

"Are you okay?"

My skin is being ripped from my bones. "My brother's married."

He looks at me for a moment with a small frown. "I didn't know you had a brother."

I blink twice. "Yes, you do. You just wrote Hawke about him. Reid, remember?"

"Reid?"

"Yes, my twin."

Jude looks concerned. He picks up the emotigraph. "Who's this?"

"Reid's *wife*." I suck deep breaths through my nose. "And *don't* press the emotigraph button."

He stares at the picture. I want it back. I want it away from his eyes. I don't want him looking at Tawny while I'm in the room for comparison. We're a set of unbalanced scales and I'm the faulty side.

"She's pretty," he mutters.

I jump up and snatch it from his hands. "She's *married.*"

"To who?"

Throwing my arms in the air, I release an exasperated huff. "To *Reid.* My brother."

"Oh yeah."

I force myself to crush down my overwhelming emotions. Jude looks lost. "Do you really not remember my story?"

"Of course I do. I remember Reid now. He's in trouble and Hawke's checking on him."

I reach out, hesitant. "Jude . . . you're forgetting things."

His shoulders sag. "I know."

"Are you resting enough? Your concussion was pretty tough and stress causes the symptoms to flare up."

He nods.

"Any response from Hawke?"

"Not yet."

I face the window and allow my thoughts to claim control again.

Reid is married and he never told me. Did he think I wouldn't accept the fact he got married? How could he do this without me? I would never take such an important step without my family around to celebrate with me.

Tawny.

I look at the emotigraph and see a stranger—a pale-skinned, half-smiling, kissed-my-brother stranger. Does she even know about me?

About our family? Does she want to meet us? Does she know I'm going to die?

She looks like a man-snatcher.

Pressure builds inside me, turning into pain. *How could he, God? How could Reid live such a different life and not share it with me?*

Now I *have* to save Reid. He has a wife.

Thoughts of the past week weigh me down like spring mud. I've entered the seventies and everything is crashing around me. I thought Mrs. Newton and I were starting something great. Now what do I do? What if Hawke can't help Reid?

Then there's the issue of our Clock. Reid is so convinced the Clock is his, but I know it can't be. Why would he get married if he knew he'd die? It doesn't make sense. The Clock is mine. I can't let Skelley Chase kill Reid.

The Preacher said life is meaningless. Reid is married. Jude is going to die. Do I go back?

I rest my head against the arm of the couch, allowing it to bang harder than necessary. The jolt is refreshing. I have a sister. The thought is unbidden, but inevitable. I've had a sister for almost five months and I didn't know it. A man-snatching sister.

So that's why Reid gave me his journal. Maybe his entries explained why he kept her from us. That's why he left me at our One Year Assessment. He was returning to Florida to marry Tawny. They were married five days before his train accident. Did they have a honeymoon?

My stomach churns at the idea of my brother honeymooning. Neither of us ever dated. I never had a chance to. Reid never seemed to want to—he always had something more important to do like travel, study, and explore . . . or was that all a façade?

God, where do I go from here? How do I become a shalom-maker? The more I strive the more I'm sledge-hammered with surprises. Do I even have time?

I look up. Jude is staring at me. "Solomon replied."

I breathe heavy through my nose. "What did he say?"

"Reid is being held in the containment center until you return. The rest of your family is under house arrest."

"No! There's no way he could have confined Reid so fast."

"He?" Jude says.

"Skelley Chase." A sick wave hits my stomach.

"Skelley Chase?" Jude gives me a quizzical look. "I know that name."

I curl my legs up beneath me. "Yeah, he's a famous biographer."

"Oh." Jude's eyes droop as he stares at the fire. "I think I know him from something else. I'm not sure."

I'm nervous about Jude's memory issues. Maybe his concussion is the start of his death. Perhaps he's losing his memory because there's fluid build-up in his brain or interrupted blood flow. I can't help worrying something more than a simple impact jolted his mind.

"Jude?"

He turns toward me as if pulling out of a deep thought. "Yes?"

"I don't know what to do. I don't know how to save Reid."

"We're gonna have to brainstorm."

Brainstorm. It reminds me of Wilbur's suit and our plan to save Radicals. Mrs. Newton has gathered plenty of resources and even a promise from the Preacher of a mansion to use as a halfway house. The only thing we haven't secured is a force of men to send to the Wall. Builders.

But what if I go?

What if *I* return to build the bridge and set up the survival station? I'd still be furthering our purpose *and* I could save Reid.

But what about Jude? I peek at him, sitting by the fire. His dark hair is longer, getting into his eyes. I can't leave him. Then again, I don't know his Numbers. Do his outlast mine? I may have to watch him die. Can I do that?

He rubs his ear. "It's so quiet. I can't think straight. I don't know what I'm feeling."

I forgot how much he hates silence. He relied on his music to inform him of his emotions. "Jude, why is the Citizen Welfare Development Council trying to kill you if they want your information? Why would that assassin shoot you?"

Jude shrugs, but avoids my gaze. I continue to stare at him and he releases a pent-up breath. "I think he's trying to retrieve my information. All of my invention formulas are up here." He taps his temple. "That's why they're safe. But my wound hasn't gotten infected, and that makes me nervous. There are certain chips that can be shot into a person for pirating. Those chips have a solution coating to protect from infection. I'm wondering if there's one inside my arm."

"A chip?"

He nods, but doesn't expound. "I've been trying to survive long enough to die."

What a horrible purpose. How can he continue to breathe, smile, or laugh knowing he's doing so to breathe out another second of life? "You won't ever give them the information, right?"

He turns hollow eyes to me. "Never."

I rub my stump as a tingle sweeps across the scars, then I retreat to my room where I lie facedown on my bed and pray for the longest amount of time I've ever prayed. I share my fears about Reid's death, Skelley Chase's blackmail, Jude's memory, and Mrs. Newton's and my plan to save Radicals.

"Please, please help us save lives. Please help me save lives, starting with Reid's."

I sit up. I'll go to the albinos for help—they live a few days away from the Wall entrance. They might assist me in setting up a system of survival for the Radicals. If I share my hopes, will they listen?

Alder will want to chop off my head the moment he sees me. Daring rashness swirls in my mind, the same feeling that urged me to walk through wolves. He can't touch me. Not if I get there soon enough with plenty of time left to my Clock.

Anticipation drums through me. I must do this. For Reid. For the Radicals.

For Me.

I bite my lip. *Yes. For You, God. Does this mean this is Your plan?*

The Preacher's words float like a loose ribbon into my consciousness. "*. . . the disturbing truth is, you have to decide what you want.*"

Decisions. Impulse. Is there a difference? *Okay God, I don't know how accurate the Preacher's words were, but I'm going to make a decision. I just . . .* I breathe through my teeth to combat the threat of unwanted tears. *I just want to decide with You. Please bless me and guide me as I return to the East.*

I don't want to leave, but that is the beauty of it. I don't want to leave yet I am choosing to. This gives me strength and confidence. I'm sacrificing for the sake of others. This step brings the same terrified calm I had when I declared myself a Radical to save Reid.

This is right. This is me. This is my purpose.

-You win, Mr. Chase, I type. *-I'll come back.*

His response comes within seconds. *-And you'll continue to send me journal entries - SC.*

I throw the NAB onto the bed and then enter the living room. Jude and Willow are playing a game on the ground with cards Willow won through trade. She's been bargaining like a master ever since she arrived, winning items for cheap and selling them for more. It's her pastime, yet I'm at a complete loss as to how she acquired the skill.

They look up. "Hey." Jude smiles. "I like that dress."

I look down at the belted black frock I've worn all morning. Did he not notice it earlier? "Thanks."

"Welks."

"I need to leave," I blurt without so much as a warning.

Willow's head snaps up. "You're leaving?"

I soften my face when I meet her gaze. "Yes, Willow. I'm going to earn a train ticket in the next few days and then return East."

"Why?"

I kneel on the ground beside her. "The Radicals need me and I'm going to save my brother. In fact, I plan to talk to your people and see if they'll help me."

Jude stares at me. His thick eyebrows form a crease of concern. "They'll chop your head off."

"No, they won't." I'm surprised by the calm in my voice. "Not if I get there soon enough. My Clock still has seventy-six days. They can't kill me."

He releases a dismal laugh. "Putting your faith in the Clock again?"

"You do the same thing," I counter, on the defense. I've made him angry. Doesn't he realize this is something I have to do?

"I don't *think* by the Clock. I still live as if it doesn't matter. My faith is in *God*."

"You don't mention Him very often."

He rolls his eyes. "Neither does the girl wearing a cross ring."

The cards lie limp on the ground, like my strength. Will I ever make a decision that doesn't produce friction?

"So you're deserting us again," he says.

A deep breath brings no peace, but I say what I know I must. "If you choose to stay in Ivanhoe then . . . yes, I guess. If that's how you want to see it."

"Tally ho."

I throw up my hands and, with them, my caution. "I don't understand that saying, Jude, but it's driving me crazy. Does 'tally ho' mean 'good-bye' or a period at the end of a conversation? Is it an expression of frustration? What is it?"

"It's an expression to say 'okay' or . . ." He struggles for the right words. "Or a comfortable ending to a letter or conversation." He shrugs. "People in High Cities say it. Sometimes I use it to convey 'you win' or 'I give up'."

"So you're giving up on me?"

Silence rings between us. I bet Jude's tune-chip would be screaming right now. He doesn't blink. He doesn't speak.

"Good to know." I grip the hem of my dress. "Now I won't get my hopes up."

"Hopes up for what?"

"A relationship!" It's out of my mouth before I can catch it. Winter frost replaces my breath and I stare at him, my face warming. The following silence is so stunned, I doubt Jude's tune-chip could have created a matching song.

A muffled squeak comes from Willow.

"A relationship with me?" Jude speaks in a low voice.

I can't bring myself to answer, but my silence is answer enough. Jude watches my hand. I watch his face. It's passive. Deep in thought?

It doesn't matter what he thinks. I'm leaving.

Then his lips tip upward. The smile grows until his teeth show and he lifts his head, looking into my eyes with a vulnerable display of disbelief. A hesitant laugh issues from him, like an escaped bubble of joy. He reaches forward and takes my hand and stump in his. His fingers wrap around my left arm and slip between the fingers on my right hand.

A chord deep inside me, never before played, touched, or heard, trembles. We sit like this for a paused moment. Willow bobs her head from side to side, gathering cards and shuffling them while she hums. I don't know about Jude's tune-chip, but her humming matches my mood perfectly.

Happy. No . . . *more* than that.

Utter, complete joy.

38

"I still can't go with you."

Jude's low words break the moment.

I pull my hand and stump from his hold. "Why not? Is it because of your Numbers?"

He shakes his head. "Parvin." His voice is rough, forced from his body. "I *can't*."

I cover my face as I'm hit by how much I hoped he'd come. He doesn't want to be with me as much as I thought. "I can't do it without you, Jude." The words taste like vinegar, but I must plead, despite my desire to drown beneath a defiant mask. "How will I eat? How can I cross the Dregs? I still can't tightrope walk."

Maybe it's because death is so close for both of us, but Jude seems to fear things he won't tell me. I believe he wants to come. Why won't he? He didn't want to come to Ivanhoe in the first place, yet now he doesn't want to leave?

I look up through my tears and try to wipe them away. He doesn't look at me.

"I'm doing this for your orphans, too, you know." This statement gets his attention. His head snaps up and his eyes hold hardness—a challenge for me to finish my thought. I force my tears to abate and plunge on.

"Where do you think they'll go once they grow up and leave the orphanage? They'll plummet off that cliff like everyone else." I lean forward and force myself to place a calm hand on his shoulder. "You can still help them. By helping me."

He stands, jerking away from my hand. "Tally ho, Parvin. You win." He leaves the room.

I don't feel like I won. I feel like I killed something inside of him, like I've placed shackles around his limbs from the moment I asked Hawke to send me help. But I don't have time to regret. Instead, I move forward . . . for the sake of shalom.

000.069.22.25.51

I approach Wilbur Sherrod after a successful simulation testing his newest suit, Vitality, intended to keep a person awake twice as long as an average adult's capabilities and to strengthen the immune system. I yawn while I relay my report. When he gives his nod, I speak up.

"Wilbur, I'll only be here another week."

His plastered awkward smile droops like melting wax. "Ah now! Ye don't like the work?"

I raise an eyebrow. "Of course I like the work, but I'm earning money for two train tickets East."

He pushes his hands in and out of his pockets. "My apprentice will be returnin' in two week's time. Ye can't stay that long?"

I shake my head, though his pleading makes me want to concede. "I'm sorry."

He waves a hand at me. "It's fine. Ye been better than I expected."

I raise my eyebrows. "Thanks?"

His floppy shoes slap across the smooth floor as he walks away. I'll miss seeing his funny giant afro every day.

The time inches by with slow seconds ticking like death drums. I stop looking at my watch at the end of each day. I can't control the Numbers. Willow bargains for our train tickets when we have enough trade. She returns with three tickets and extra food.

"I'm coming, too."

"But . . . they'll make you atone," I say.

She shrugs. "It is our way of life. I can't leave Elm . . . or you." We hug and she squeezes me around the middle, tight. I love this little girl. Even though she's prepared to atone, I'll talk to Alder first. Perhaps grace is to be found.

The morning before the train leaves, I pack my belongings into Reid's freshly cleaned bag. It's more full than when I first arrived.

Wilbur gifted me a new set of boots and the Vitality suit as a good-bye present. He didn't look happy to part with it, but gave my shoulder an awkward pat. "Be sure the people on the West see my work."

I roll it up with plans to use it only when I need to. There's no point having extra energy when my travel partners have regular stamina levels.

"Train gets into the station in thirty minutes." Willow hands us our tickets. They're stamped with a picture of the *Ivanhoe Independent*.

Jude shrugs and picks up the new pack Willow brought him yesterday. It's not very full.

"Let's go," I say.

Jude's been oddly silent the past week and I've avoided him as well. Neither of us talked about my proclamation of interest. I already question myself. Do I still want a relationship with Jude? Does he dislike me now that I've confessed?

We exchange long hugs with Mrs. Newton and Laelynn.

"Tell Solomon hello from us," Mrs. Newton says to Jude, then turns to me. "Parvin, I know that our pursuits to save Radicals will work. The Preacher will send building supplies to the last train stop near the Wall. It should take a few weeks. I'm still trying to convince him to send some builders."

"Thank you, Mrs. Newton."

She wraps her arms around my shoulders and mumbles into my hair, "You dear, dear, girl. If you live . . . come back to us."

I just nod. Jude tugs me out of the house. Willow hugs my left arm, trying to comfort me.

We cross the street with the creeping motorcoaches and bicycles. I bid a silent farewell. The train station rests with an odd quiet preceding the evening rush that'll arrive within the next hour. We enter the side station for the *Ivanhoe Independent*.

"Willow, you'll love this train." I'm about to redeem the wrong I did when I left her alone on the tracks. "There are showers and soft beds so you can sleep while the train is still going. They serve breakfast with floppy bread cakes and syrup."

I close my eyes and sniff as if I can smell the food. The whistle erases my visions of breakfast as the *Ivanhoe Independent* comes into view. It takes a moment to slow in a rush of blurred yellow paint. The metal groans with relief when it stops. People pile onto the platform.

Jude sucks in a sharp breath and grabs Willow and me by our shoulder packs. We knock into each other and Willow shrieks, "Ow, Jude-man!"

"Hush!" He drags us from the platform.

I look over my shoulder, toward the train. A tall man clad in black lifts a large travel pack from the train's luggage compartment. He hands some form of payment to the trade collector, then looks up.

The assassin.

Our eyes meet in the split second before Jude drags me around the corner. I turn my back on the train and run with Jude. We take one of Willow's hands in each of ours and half-carry her, half-drag her with us.

"Jude, he saw me!" I tense against the expectation of flying bullets.

"Okay."

We run outside as a motorcoach barrels across the road. I wave and veer down the road after it. A bicyclist yells at me and I jump back onto the sidewalk. With a grunt, Jude follows. The motorcoach stops and we topple inside.

We drop to the floor between two bench seats as it rumbles away. Jude and I hold Willow's head down until several minutes pass. I don't peek out the windows, even though my nerves create the sensation of the assassin breathing down my neck.

Jude doesn't meet my eyes. His lips clench in a tight line and his eyes narrow. He straightens and sits on one of the cloth seats. Fumbling with my pack, I do the same.

Willow makes herself heard. "What's wrong?"

"The man who shot Jude is here." I meet his eyes over her head.

"We have to leave the city tonight." His voice is low and colder than iced steel. "On foot. We can't take the train." He meets my eyes for the first time. "If he saw you, Parvin, he knows we were intending to take a train out of here. And"—he rubs a hand through his hair—"he knows I'm with you."

"So he knows we're returning to the East." I fight the rising bile in my throat. "On foot it is, then."

The albinos are six hundred miles from here. The train would have taken us to the East Platte River in fifteen hours, then a few days of walking and we'd be there. Now my Clock is reduced by three more weeks.

God . . . don't You care about my Numbers?

We ride the motorcoach until the sun's light mourns with the twilight. We exit at the edge of the city on the opposite side from the train station. The air is silent on this side. All bikes are parked, locked, or hung from mounts.

We creep out toward the plains, ducking out of the shine of street orbs. Buildings meet sagebrush like a stiff shadow meets light. I jump at each snap of a branch and animal sound. Jude strides with unhindered purpose like an alpha male, not jumping, not stopping, and not speaking. What's going through his mind?

Do I want to know?

I look back at Ivanhoe as we crest the distant hill that will hide it from sight. Pure white shining dots line the buildings and circle the Marble like stars adhered to metal. Already, I want to turn around. Three weeks of hunger, chill, soreness, travel, and fear are my finale.

By late morning, Ivanhoe is no longer visible on the horizon no matter the size of hills we ascend. We lie on our stomachs behind stiff desert grass until the *Ivanhoe Independent* passes, taking a piece of my heart with it. We should have been on that.

I lower my face in my arms. *God, why did You hinder us?*

"We can't know if the assassin was on the train watching for us, or if he stayed in the city." Jude rises from the ground. "Our best option is to continue traveling out of sight of the tracks."

The days grow identical. Scenery stays the same and chill creeps into our bones as August days bookmark each footfall. Four days crawl into nothingness before we enter the barren stretch of headstones. Already, my back aches and Jude takes my pack from me, heaving it on top of his own new one. We don't start a fire, but eat the last servings of bread, crackers, and dried meat Mrs. Newton sent with us.

Sometimes when we eat, Jude reaches over and holds my left arm as if he's holding my hand. My face warms every time. I don't want him holding my hand—or arm—out of obligation or pity. It kills the romance in his gesture . . . if it's romance at all.

Several nights in a row, we sleep inside the hollow stalks of fallen white windmills. They're warmer than outside with the three of us end to end. Willow sleeps near me for warmth. Every night I curl into my own ball without making eye contact with Jude. I'm afraid of what I might see—of what he expects. He's mentioned God, but what does that mean to his life? His actions? Living for God is radically different than our cultural norm . . . if he's serious about it. People are rarely serious.

"Are you two going to graft?" Willow asks several days later as Jude helps me over the thin end of another giant fallen white windmill.

"What do you mean?"

"Grafting means spending the rest of your life together. You be each other's mates. Have babies. Be companions." She squints up at me.

Jude chuckles. "Neither of us has much life left, Willow."

"You told me once that you'll graft with Elm," I say. "How do you know? You're so young."

"I'm given my grafting partner at my bloom ritual."

I purse my lips to one side. "*Given?*"

"Elm will become my husband when we decide to graft."

My eyes narrow. "How old do you have to be?"

Willow shrugs and adjusts her tumbleweed hat. "It's whenever we want."

"But what if you like someone else? Someone instead of Elm?"

She scrunches her nose. "I don't. That's not fair to anyone. Everyone has their own grafting partner. If I don't want to graft, I don't have to, but then Elm will be ungrafted, too." She shakes her head. "That's not fair to him."

None of this grafting seems fair or right. Willow's so little. Grafting sounds a lot like marriage allowed far too early.

"No, Willow," Jude says ahead of us. "We're not going to graft."

I sidestep a flat headstone. "Jude, when do you zero-out?"

He responds by taking my hand. His skin feels so foreign, yet thrilling. The message sent through our touch ignites a desire for permanence. I want to zero-out with my fingers laced between someone else's.

Handholding grows less convenient as our energy levels decline and I start to anticipate when we can break apart. I don't want to be the one to do it, but the longer we touch the more tension pours into my muscles. We finally separate as we round a headstone. My hand feels cold without his palm on mine, but it's comfortable. I don't understand the relationship hierarchy. Is Jude expecting something after holding hands? Maybe a kiss?

Do I want to kiss Jude?

Do I want to die unkissed? I roll my eyes. Does kissing hold any weight in my current purpose right now?

Kissing seems to be the last thing on Jude's mind as we travel and I find myself grateful. I don't want to think about it. It makes me act strange around him. Uncomfortable.

Rabbits are scarcer on our travels back. The chill in the air drives them into burrows and they aren't breeding. I never thought I'd crave their meat again until we sit around a small fire chewing bark for dinner. My stomach aches for real food. Even Willow is hungry enough to suck on fresh leaves from the sparse bushes we pass.

"We're close to the albinos," Jude says. "A few days away if all goes smoothly."

I glance at the blue watch I succumbed to attaching on my right wrist. I'm at the end of the forties. Forty-two days and somewhere around nineteen hours. The past few days have been spent deep in thought about how to present my case to the albinos. If they resist, I don't have a back-up plan.

God, I invite you into this. You created me to save lives. Help me. I want to follow You. "Jude, do you think the albinos will try and behead me?"

He throws a stick into the fire. "Why would they do that?" When he looks up, his face holds genuine curiosity.

I wait for him to remember. He continues to stare. "Because of the pink dogwood."

"Oh yeah." He looks in the fire again, but his voice is tired. His eyes narrow as if trying to freeze the fire caught in his gaze. "I don't think they'll behead you."

My ears perk and I lean forward. "Why do you say that?"

"I think Ash and Black vouched for us." He folds his arms together and leans back against a headstone.

My heart rests in ease. Maybe the albinos *will* listen to my proposition. "That would make our goal so much easier. They might be more receptive. There will be a higher chance of protecting your orphans from the Wall."

"I don't have any kids." He picks a bug off the piece of bark he then puts in his mouth.

Taken aback, I struggle for words, "I know you don't have kids. I meant the orphans you tried to save with your invention."

"My invention . . ." he repeats. His face screws up as it did when he tried to remember my name.

God, why is his memory fading in and out like this? "The Clock-matching, Jude. You *have* to remember this. It's part of your story."

His eyes widen and he looks up with a jerk. "I'm forgetting, Parvin." His breath quickens. "I pulled the memory back, but it's being sucked out of my brain."

"That doesn't make sense."

He stands and slings his pack on. "Get up, we have to go."

Willow looks up from her cross-legged position on the ground and groans. "My feet hurt, Jude-man."

"I'll carry you," he says without pause. "Come on, Parvin."

I stand. "You're not making sense, Jude. What's going on in your head?"

"That's the problem, I don't know how long anything will *be* in my head. I'm losing my memory. It's the chip in my arm. It's stealing my memories. Get up, we have to go."

"Okay." I rise on wobbly legs. My empty stomach cries out.

We douse the fire and I change into my Vitality suit, away from the others. We're all starving and he wants to march through the night.

I couldn't do it without the suit. With every passing hour, I thank God for Wilbur's generous pride and creative brain. We're also making better use of my Numbers. Jude carries Willow piggyback style, seemingly immune to fatigue.

The next night we sleep because Jude doesn't have a stamina suit and Willow is a walking rag doll. When I finish building the fire, Jude sits beside me. I start when he places both hands on either side of my face, but I don't draw away.

"Parvin," he says in a gentle voice. "I need you to do something for me."

"Okay." What could he want? Is he going to ask me to change my mind about my mission? Maybe he wants me to go to the albinos alone. Maybe a kiss . . .

"I need you to sterilize your dagger and dig the chip out of my arm."

I jerk back. "Ugh, no." Embarrassed by my reaction, I take a breath. "I can't do that, Jude. I can barely kill animals."

"You have to," he says through clenched teeth. "This is important. I need it out."

He needs me. "I don't think I could even find it, Jude."

"I heard you stitched yourself up." He grins.

I look at him, eyes wide. "How did you hear about that?"

"Solomon told me."

Solomon Hawke talked to Jude about me? He *bragged* to Jude about me? A flicker of warmth hits me, having nothing to do with the fire. If I don't help Jude with this, I'll let them both down.

I brush my fingers along his upper arm where his wound is. He sucks in a breath. I think it's from my touch, even though his coat separates the contact of our skin.

"In the morning? When there's light?" What am I saying?

"Tally ho."

I close my eyes, forcing myself to breathe. I can't do this. But I must. We don't know what damage that chip is causing.

Morning brings a chilled nose tip. No amount of snuggling beneath my shredded skirt ushers in warmth. I sit up, bleary-eyed, and that's when I remember. My dagger. Jude. The chip.

Light rain sprinkles like glitter, enough to look beautiful yet chill my soul at the same time. I can't even hear it. I pray my hands don't shiver while I use my dagger.

Three attempts get the fire smoking despite the water already soaked through the bark. I warm my hands, allowing the growing crackle to wake Jude and Willow.

By the time their puffy eyes blink open, my dagger is sterilized. "Are you sure you need this done?" Maybe Jude's rested brain will speak more logic.

To my dismay, he nods, but doesn't take his eyes off the knife. Did Father imagine the dagger he gifted to me would be used for surgery?

"Remove your jacket," I say in a quavering voice. What am I doing?

He obeys with a tense shiver. It will be hard for him to relax when it's this cold, but maybe it will help with the pain. Goosebumps sweep down his bare skin.

Skin. I have to pierce it.

His tattoo weaves around his muscles, interrupted by the wound.

Wound. I have to open it.

Somewhere inside Jude's upper arm is a chip . . . or maybe just a bullet. How will I find it encased in so much blood?

Blood. I have to touch it.

I imagine my fingers drenched in the color of the Numbers. I look back up. My heart enters a vacuum, tension and emotions suctioning together until breath is an imagined luxury. "Do you zero out today?"

I have to know. I can't be the one who kills him.

"I don't think so." He frowns. "I mean, no. I don't."

"Are you forgetting?" How can anyone forget his or her Numbers?

"No. I remember," he rasps, still looking at the dagger.

"It's warm." I approach him. *God, I can't do this.*

I press his shoulder down until he's flat on his back. Willow scoots next to him and brushes hair from his sweating forehead. She places a thick stick in his mouth. Always thinking.

I poise the dagger over his closed wound. It's still red and raw. "Are you sure—"

"Yes."

In one breathless moment, I force my arm to act against every instinct and slice into the wound. Jude roars and I jerk my arm back. Blood drips from the knife.

"I'm sorry," I pant. "Oh, Jude, I'm sorry."

"Keep going!" he yells as Willow places the stick back in his mouth.

Chip. Chip. Chip. I look at the wound. It will take more pressure. I've only made a minor incision. As tenderly as I can, I press the knife-point deeper into the wound. Jude's back arches and he grunts, clamping down on the stick. The bark cracks.

"I'm sorry," I repeat, pushing his skin to the side with the blade.

I can't see a thing. Blood is everywhere in different shades, coating my hand. I need more fingers. "Willow, pull apart the wound."

Obedient. Fearless. Her white skin enters the mess. Blood splatters her knuckles. Dark. Red. Stench.

I gag. Deep breath. Vomit.

I just manage to turn my head toward the dirt when the little bit of bark I chewed yesterday comes up, followed by repeated dry heaving. Jude wheezes. I gasp for air.

"Come on, Parvin."

Willow's sharp command straightens my back. My stomach is empty, still, the smell of blood makes it churn. I place the dagger back into the wound and move it around, hoping to feel the knock of a bullet or chip. Jude's hand tangles in my skirt.

"Breathe," I say, but internally I'm screaming. What is the dagger touching? Bone? Tendon? Chip? If I'm not careful, I'm going to carve out a crucial piece of Jude's body. "I can't see anything."

"Come on, Parvin!" Willow's voice is intense. Adult. Determined.

"*You* do it!" I shout, losing my head.

Jude writhes on the ground and screams. "Stop!"

I lean back on my heels with a gush of breath, flinging the dagger away and cupping my hand before me, trying not to drip blood. I need to wash. Where's the water?

Jude sits up, trembling. "This was stupid. I don't know how I expected you to find it."

Stung, I inch away from him and rub my hand in dirt. I tried.

Willow dampens a rag and wipes his wound, then bandages it. I continue coating my hand in dirt until I no longer see or smell the blood.

"Let's keep going." Jude pushes Willow's bandaging aside. "Save the water. I'll be fine. We'll be with your people in a few days."

I follow, defeated, like a dog trying to please its master after it's misbehaved. Jude doesn't speak to me the rest of the day. When he sets down his belongings, I sit across from him, avoiding his gaze. A deer comes into the open, followed by a tiny spotted fawn. She sniffs the ground and lifts her head, chewing.

"Look." I touch Willow's arm and trust Jude to hear.

The doe's ears and nose perk into the air at the crunch of our movements. She stands stock-still, then lifts a foot and stomps on the ground. After a second, she does the same with her other foot, twitching her tail at the same time. It looks like some sort of signal. After repeating this process, she walks away with stiff steps. The baby follows her, imitating the regal movement.

"I'm sorry," Jude whispers before a gunshot splits the air. The doe drops to the ground, dead. I gasp. "Let's go clean it," he says. "We need the meat."

Rabbits were one thing, but this . . . "She had a fawn."

"The fawn will live."

The baby steps near its mother to sniff her, but the approach of Jude and Willow startles it away. A flash of tiny hooves, an upright tail, and the fawn is gone. I sit by the fire, defiant, as they gut the deer and drag a portion of its carcass toward the fire.

"Will you at least help us skin it?" Jude's voice drips contempt.

Weak from lack of food and the morning's effort at surgery, I follow directions and pull the skin back as Willow and Jude slice the connecting tissue. Nothing on the beast looks edible to me. Which part is meat? What's fat?

Blood soaks into the ground. I close my eyes and turn my head away, reminded of Jude's wound. The deer smells old, like bugs lived in her thin hair. Jude cooks the meat over the fire. My stomach compels me to fill it. I must eat. My lack of hunger is a trick. I'm empty inside.

The deer is gamey and tough. Even as I chew, I smell the doe, I smell Jude's blood. My appetite writhes in the back of my throat, turning up its nose to the idea of food, but I can't function on my emptied stomach.

I chew. I gag. I chew more, praying for tolerance.

And that this journey will soon end.

The next evening, we reach the Dregs with wrapped deer meat swinging from our packs. The tightrope is repaired, stretched across the boggy canyon as a bridge. I'm drawn back into our narrow escape from drowning, from starvation, from assassination.

Jude sets his small pack down and pulls out cold cooked deer. "We'll go tomorrow."

"We need to go in early morning." Willow sits and crosses her legs. "They leave for dead-standing tomorrow, Jude-man. It is first of the month."

September first. Thirty-eight days. A nervous glacier begins its descent inside me, freezing my insides. There's no time.

"We'll get there before they leave," Jude says.

I feel out of place. Part of me wishes I hadn't begged for Jude's help. The albinos are angry with him. What will they do when we return? When does Jude zero-out?

Morning dawns and I'm the first awake. I nudge Jude and Willow before the sun breaks. "We need to go."

The new rope across the canyon is taut and stable. I hop on Jude's back, as we did in the Marble, only this time there's nothing exciting about it. He grimaces, trying to hold his arms out to steady himself. I shiver with uncertainty, dreading another fall into the Dregs. What if we fall in again? I might zero-out in there. *God, help!*

Jude teeters at the halfway point. I shut my eyes and let my teeth grind on my nerves. Several seconds of balance pass as he fights for stability. It takes us over three minutes to cross. When Jude's second foot lands on firm ground, his arms flop to his side and he bows his head.

I do the same. *Thank You, Lord. We couldn't have done that alone.*

Willow follows and we all walk, attentive to every sound, toward the forest edge. Leaves flutter in an array of gold and green. Autumn is early. We push through the bushes. Blood pounds in my ears, blackening my vision.

Then I see the line of albinos, gathered with axes and traveling gear. Alder stands in front. We stop at the edge of the village clearing, careful to stand on the moss instead of gardens.

Alder sees us. His mouth gapes open. "Willow!"

The other albinos turn. What do I say? What do we do? I look to Jude for guidance. His arm is above his head, fingers resting on a thin aspen branch. He's silent as Alder approaches. Other albinos walk toward us. I scan the faces for Ash.

"Willow, you haven't atoned." Alder strides forward. Willow darts behind me. She grips the straps of my pack. I plant my feet as Alder advances.

"Leave her alone, Alder," Jude shouts. "Or I'll break off this aspen branch."

Alder halts mere feet away from us. His gaze flits from Jude to the thin branch in Jude's grasp. He shakes his head. "If not for the expense of the aspen, I would enjoy delivering your atonement, Jude."

Jude sets his jaw. "Well, I think I have a compromise for us then."

Alder pulls his axe from his shoulder. "And what is that?"

"Let me take Willow's atonement."

Willow and I gasp, but before we can protest, Alder nods.

"Granted."

39

000.038.06.50.09

"Jude!" I grip his wrist. "No!"

The albinos converge like a three-pronged pitchfork—some to the tree, some to Jude, and some to me because I'm screaming in his face.

He allows the albinos to grab his hair, his clothing, his skin in their fists. His masked face is void of concern or care, reminding me of my new understanding of the word *suicide*.

I push against the albinos dragging him from my side. "No . . . wait . . ." Sobs interrupt my mania. White hands hold me back. Fingernails bite my frigid skin. "Jude." Why won't he answer me? "Jude!"

Before a single thought can convert into sane clarity, Jude is chained to the stone slab beside the broken pink dogwood trunk.

"Don't kill him," I beg as two burly albinos stretch him over a sandbag. "Please!" I lurch forward, fighting with energy I've never known before. I'm immune to the nails tearing my flesh, the hair ripping from my head, and the screams in my ear.

Jude yells, too, but doesn't struggle. He shouts some sort of instruction, but to whom? Me? His face turns red from straining and even from my distance I see sweat lining his temple.

Alder raises the axe, white muscles rippling over his back. His grip tightens on the handle.

"Alder, *stop!*" I yell, just like Jude did so long ago. "Kill me instead!"

Alder pauses and glances over his shoulder at me for a breathless moment, but like last time, he releases a mighty yell and swings the axe into the sandbag.

A strangled scream joins the chaos. My scream. I fall to my knees, gulping for air. Hands release me. My tears wet the moss with splashes of smashed diamonds. My stump screeches like a train rail in agonizing memory.

Jude's body is limp. The albinos move him. A trail of blood marks their path.

I rise and stumble to reach him. "Jude . . ." He's groaning. His right arm is severed just above his right elbow. White bone is exposed.

They carry him to the healing hut. I slump to the ground, shaking. Willow lies on her side a few yards from me, sobbing freely. Her mother kneels over her, brushing her hair back. Alder cleans his axe in the small pond denting the mossy ground.

I want to kill Alder.

I want to save Radicals.

I can't do both.

God, help me choose the right one.

Three albino healers stay in Jude's hut around the clock. As far as I know, Jude is still alive. The albinos don't leave to gather dead-standing. Instead, as the days pass, they leave small gifts of hot broth or cooked meat. Each time a gift is left, a healer retrieves it and brings it inside.

I sleep out on the moss. Sometimes Willow stays with me. We watch the healing hut together, waiting for news. They burn Jude's severed arm over the coals. The snake tattoo writhes against the flame melting the dying skin. They burned my hand like this.

Internally, I am at war. I want to be angry with the albinos. I want to hate them, but Jude chose this. He took Willow's atonement and I can't fault him or them. Their ways are unusual to me, but Jude saved Willow in the only way he could.

I must accept that. I can't let it distract me from what I must do at the Wall.

Two women and one man settle on the ground outside of the healing hut. "We are mourning," Willow says. "We mourn until he returns to full consciousness." She looks down at the ground. "No one wants Jude-man to be in pain. Many of us have atoned and understand the pain."

"Did you do this when I was in there?" I ask in a thick voice.

She nods. That explains Alder's apology. Did he truly hurt with me when he cried by my bedside? Did all the albinos mourn?

"The branch I broke was the same size as that pine tree. Why did Alder only cut off my hand?"

Willow pokes the damp moss. "We dispersed your atonement, remember? I offered three broken fingers, Black gave two broken fingers, and Elm gave some broken toes."

"Black took some of my atonement?" I don't bother to hide my surprise.

"He is a good man. He's *scary*"—she releases a timid laugh—"but still good. My grafting mate, Elm, is Black's brother. Many girls are jealous." She throws me a wicked grin.

I look at the hut. The day is cool and all windows are rolled shut with tied animal skins. Will Jude wake with the same hollow feeling of loss? Does he even know what he's done? Everything will need to be relearned. He may not even be able to tightrope-walk anymore. People will define him by his loss.

Maybe he doesn't mind because he knows his Numbers are short. Or maybe he doesn't mind because that's who he is. My missing hand doesn't ever seem to bother him. He doesn't define me by this weakness.

I squeeze my eyes shut and release a sigh. While he heals, I must make use of the time here. I must speak with Alder. After that, I will find Ash and see if they read my Bible.

Shalom meets anti-shalom when I enter Alder's hut, clenching my hand so tight, my fingernails bend backward. His hut is larger than others and filled with furniture made from stone or metal. He sits in a chair beside a small fireplace. Coals hold a low flicker. He watches me assess his home.

"I'm not a hypocrite." His voice drops like a stone into my forced calm.

I move my gaze to the ceiling and take a long breath to avoid a defensive retort. *God, I need Your patience.* "Neither am I. When I first came here, I told you I believed God put people above the plants and animals. I have returned to you to ask for your help in saving lives."

He eyes me and crosses one leg over the other. "How?"

I force myself not to look at the empty chair in front of him. I'm not welcomed to sit. Does this mean he views me as a lesser equal? Does it mean he won't listen? "People are sent across the Wall to this side as an execution. Most of these people have done nothing wrong. They die because the Wall opens to a cliff and they have no choice but to jump off. I am returning to build a bridge or means of passage from the cliff to safety. I hoped you and your people could help me."

Alder looks into the coals for a moment. The warmth doesn't reach me. I bite back a shiver. Finally, he speaks. "It is not my responsibility to fix the harm your side causes."

"Not even if it saves innocent lives?"

He glances up. "Can you vow that every life taken by that Wall is innocent? You said yourself you're a Radical. Even you had to atone. What further harm will ignorant Radicals bring to our forest?"

"I will leave them instructions on how to reach the *Ivanhoe Independent*. I'll tell them to stay away from your forest. They won't come anywhere near you."

"I don't wish to take that risk."

We stare at each other. "Alder." I now know my words won't dent his shell, but perhaps they will fester in his mind and someday blossom. "God created you and your people for relationship. You were meant to bring shalom to the world—we all are. Shalom means how things *should* be, the way God intended things."

Alder opens his mouth, but I hold up a hand. "I've seen your heart for the land God created. You are caring for the Earth, just like God commanded man when He created us. You have right intentions, but they're imbalanced. People—*your* people—should be first priority. Be a leader of shalom."

His mild smile remains plastered and his eyes are thick barriers. "Thank you, Parvin." His posture is stiff and his fingers curl around the arm of his chair. "I hope your left wrist has healed sufficiently." A reminder and a dismissal. His heart is as cold and hard as his furniture.

I leave the hut as my wrist tingles from my renewed focus. I broke laws in Alder's village. My words hold no weight. But these didn't feel like my words.

God, I spoke Your words, I think. If Alder won't listen to You, what am I to do now?

I come to an abrupt halt, running into a tall woman. "Ash!" Cedar sits in her arms, resting his head against her shoulder with a yawn.

"Hello, Parvin," she says in her soft calm voice. Her white hair curves elegantly over a red and blue plaid scarf wrapped around her neck. "I am returning this."

She holds up my Bible. With a gasp, I snatch it and hold it to my chest. "I've missed it."

She looks at me with a faint smile. I step back to return appropriate distance between us. My heart pounds. Is this my answer to prayer?

"Did you read it?" Ash's facial expression doesn't change, but she shakes her head. My throat tightens. "But . . . you had it for months."

My voice alerts Cedar. He looks around until his eyes alight on my face. Ash rests her free hand on my arm. "We can't read, Parvin. None of us can. We have no use for it."

I look at the Bible. *God, why didn't You let me know?* All these months I could have been reading, learning, and growing. Instead, my precious Bible sat untouched among illiterate people.

"The Jude-man talked of God when he first came," Ash says. "And you must think He is very important if you left us your precious book. We are still interested. We have heard of God before. Sometimes, when I am with the trees, I feel a power larger than myself. The Earth is so intricate, we've often wondered how it came to be."

"We?" I'm unable to keep the disheartened note from my voice.

"Black and me."

"Oh." I glance back at Alder's hut. Could I ask Ash for help instead? Maybe she and Black will understand more than Alder.

She steps forward. "Will you read it to us?"

"The Bible?"

She holds my gaze. Hers is neither eager nor expectant. I look at the leatherbound book. It's not very worn. I've never even read through the entire thing.

"You don't have to read it all, just read what you deem important. At least until the Jude-man is well."

What I deem important. Who am I to pick and choose? *God, I don't know enough about Your Word to do this.* Yet, as I think this, I know I must read. My time is short. Before me stands an opportunity to be a shalom-maker.

"I'll read to you." I have nothing to fear. The words are written for me, I don't need to know answers. I just need to read out loud. Like in

Ivanhoe. "And I'll teach you how to read, so you can keep going where I leave off."

Over the next two weeks, I meet in Black and Ash's hut. There's something different about reading the Bible aloud. It tastes like a new flavor on my tongue. Something comes alive. I can't stop myself from doing voices for certain Bible figures or adopting a dramatic tone at intense moments. Some stories are known to my listeners. Others are new.

At the end of each reading, I teach Black and Ash a few letters from the alphabet. If they seem willing when I need to leave, I hope to leave my Bible with them again. Maybe they'll learn enough to read it on their own.

Black stares into the coals almost the entire time I read. He never asks questions, never stops me, and never looks at me, though when I finished reading the creation story, he nodded as if internal questions just met answers.

Ash's questions come in soft inquiries, like, "Why did God create an evil tree?"

My answers draw from my logic, but emerge with God's blessings. I've never been asked questions about the Bible before, but somehow my thoughts enter fresh clarity. "The tree itself wasn't bad, it served a purpose. The tree was a symbol of obedience and free choice God gave to Adam and Eve."

We read through Exodus before I skip to the New Testament. Ash and Black listen to the story of Jesus and don't stop me. I grow tense. Does any of this make sense?

"Jesus spent his life showing people shalom." I lower the Bible because the light has grown too dim to read any further. "He lived to show us the way things should be and He died to empower us to do the same. He atoned for *all* of us."

"Like what Jude did for Willow," Ash says.

I take a deep breath. "Yes." I avoid Black's emotionless gaze. "I, too, am trying to bring shalom to the world. I die in three weeks." I force my voice to remain strong. "I can't allow people to continue dying when they are sent to this side of the Wall. Will you help me save lives?"

Ash nods, but stops when she sees Black shaking his head.

"What can we do?" He looks at me. "Alder said he won't help. Will we go against our village leader?"

"I don't ask you to welcome others into your village. I ask your help to keep people from dying. Building materials are arriving from Ivanhoe at the nearest train stop in three weeks. By that point, I will already be on the other side of the Wall." I don't want to say I'll already be *dead*. "Help me build a bridge, a rope ladder, *something*. Jude and I aren't here long enough to do it ourselves."

I bow my head and let my forehead fall into my palm. I still have hope, but I feel like a clogged sink. I can't seem to say what boils inside me. This is my purpose, but I can't do it alone.

God, I need help!

A hand tips my chin up. I lift my eyes and meet Black's gaze. Instinctively, I jerk back. His hand lowers to hold mine. "We will do what we can. It will not be much."

Cedar cries and our evening reading is broken as Ash moves to feed him. I stand. How much do they risk by helping me?

When I exit the hut, I see Willow and Elm skipping into the darkness. It's not the first time I've suspected them of sitting outside while I read. Did they hear my plea for help?

I return to my patch of moss. The weather has grown colder and a sack of coal rests on my small lump. I grin and look around. Willow peeks from behind a hut. When our eyes meet, she ducks back into the shadows with a giggle.

"Thank you," I whisper.

Several minutes later, I curl beside my small fire, dwelling on the past two weeks. My time continues to tick, but death no longer frightens me. I'm leaving something behind—something God inspired. Tomorrow I will visit Jude to see if he's well enough to continue.

If I must, I will leave without him.

40

Death swept through the healing hut and came out empty-handed, but not before it replaced Jude with the body of a wraith. His autumn-tanned skin is bloodless and stitches spike like rose thorns from his purple-bruised upper arm stump.

His hollow face pushes out a strained grin when my eyes reach his. "Do I look that bad?"

I rub my left arm, stiffening against the flow of phantom pain crushing my nonexistent fingers. "How are you?"

"Cheered."

I perch on the edge of a cold metal healer chair. "Cheered?"

He gestures to his shoulder. "It's out."

A shovel of guilt digs a hole deep inside me. "I'm sorry I couldn't find the chip."

Jude shakes his head and sits up. The blanket slips from his bare chest and I remember how I was naked when I recovered in the healing hut. Heat tingles against my cheeks. I stare at his face, trying to focus.

"I never should have asked that of you. I'm sorry, Parvin. I'm certain it was a pirate chip in my arm, inserted to download and electronically transfer my memory."

I sit back with a frown, curious but not surprised to hear another High-City term. They mix electronics and flesh together like a daily dessert recipe. "But that chip was in you over four months. Wouldn't we have noticed your memory problems earlier?"

"Ah"—he wags a finger at me—"I installed protection before crossing the Wall. That's why I could fight for memories that seemed to be seeping out."

I'm struck again by how little I know about Jude. Tune chips. Clock inventions. Moving tattoos. Protection against pirate chips. Rich boy. People in Unity Village can't even afford paper. "What sort of protection?"

He shrugs then sucks a breath through his teeth. "Electronic implant. It guards against mental theft. You'd be surprised how often theft happens, especially for people who use Testimony Logs."

This conversation is cycling down a different road than I anticipated. "You're speaking High-City language, Jude-man. I'm still trying to understand a pirate chip." Do I want to understand or redirect? My heart pounds like a resilient itch for action. I need to get to the Wall. I need to get to Reid. I have less than three weeks.

Jude touches my face and I snap back to reality. "What's in your head, Parvin?"

Okay, redirect. "I'm leaving. Ash and Black are helping me save the Radicals sent through the Wall. I don't have much time left. When they're ready, I'm going." I take a shuddering queasy breath. "I'm here to say Good-bye."

His fingers still brush my skin. Warm. Friendly. "Good-bye? You don't want my help?"

I lean back, severing our physical connection. "*Can* you help?"

"Yes!" He sits straighter and I tug his blanket higher with the pretense of making sure he's warm. "Parvin, you were right about the orphans. I can't desert them. I want to help you. I want to stay with you!"

A calm steals through me at the grasp of his hand. We're united. We're on the same page, sharing the same goal, and unified through the desperation of shortened Numbers.

"What about you zeroing out?"

He stares at the end of the bed a long time. "I don't think that's important."

My heart pounds. "Then tell me when your Numbers end." Do I want to know? Can I bear it?

"I can't."

"Why not? Why won't you tell me?" Why can't I handle not knowing?

When Jude speaks next, his voice is low and relaxed. "I . . . I don't remember. The pirate chip got that nugget of info."

My hand jumps to my throat. "It did? You can't remember at all?"

He shakes his head. "But my Clock doesn't control me, Parvin. The Numbers hold no power unless you let them."

"But . . . if the pirate chip took *that*, it could have taken anything."

"I know."

I take a deep breath through my nose. My voice comes in a whisper. "What if I lose everyone, Jude?" Jude's Numbers are coming to an end and I don't know them. Skelley Chase is threatening to kill Reid. Can I stop any of this?

"So what if you do? Our life is nothing, Parvin. It's short. You're going to lose people. Me. Maybe Reid. Maybe others. Either way, the separation's going to come, whether it's you dying first or us."

Choked emotions still my heart. "I'm not strong enough to handle it all."

"It's not your strength that matters."

"I know, I know. It's God's strength, or something like that, right?"

He uses his left arm to adjust his bandaged right over the covers. "Well, when you say it like that, I can see why you doubt."

"Why would He want me to lose everyone I love?"

His lips turn up in a sad smile. "The problem is, you still see it as loss. You won't be losing me. You won't be losing Reid, if he's the spiritual guy you say he is. We'll just be separated for a time. God has longer plans for your life than he does ours."

This spiritual teaching has gone on long enough. "You keep talking as if both you and Reid are going to die. Like there's no hope!"

"You shouldn't be placing hope in our lives, Parvin. That's my point. I don't know the answers or the future, but your confidence and hope need to be in God."

"Can we stop talking about this please?"

"Okay, so what *do* you want to talk about?"

Good question. Anything other than the death of the men I love. "Tell me more about your mental protection."

Leaning back on his pillows, Jude speaks with a new surety. "I had it installed after the betrayal of the Council. It worked against the assassin's pirate chip so well I didn't even suspect he hit me with one. I think the trouble started with my concussion."

"Your tune chip broke. Maybe your protection broke at the same time!"

"I think it got damaged. That's why I was able to fight for my memories, but the assassin still gathered *some* information. I won't ever remember what it is."

"You mentioned some sort of Log," I prompt, now hungry for High-City information. Jude rubs a thumb over the back of my hand. A shiver breaks its way into my body and jolts me.

"A Testimony Log," he says. "People record their entire lives through video contact lenses so they can sift through it at their leisure and not worry about remembering. The problem is, every Testimony Log must be contained within a Testimony Bank. You can access your memories only by visiting the bank. It's much easier to break into someone's memory when it's recorded in a bank than when it's recorded in their head."

This new onslaught of information makes me wish for a bank of my own so I can sift through the details he's feeding me. "That's amazing."

Jude's eyes darken. "When I went missing, the government sifted through my brother's Testimony Log like kids in a sandbox, looking for clues of my whereabouts. That's how they discovered I crossed the Wall." As if realizing he had turned the conversation into a serious corner, he brightens. "So when do we leave?"

"Whenever you're better and when Black and Ash are ready."

Jude taps his right arm. "I'm better."

I smile. "Tally ho."

Four days later, Ash and Black approach me, but it's hardly the help I prayed for.

"Four ropes, three mounting devices, ten slats of dead-standing wood, and a rope ladder." Ash gestures to Black.

He sets the items on the ground and then addresses Jude and me. "We've never been to the Wall. This is all we can give. You must decide what you will do with it."

"Thank you." Jude kneels beside the pile.

I try not to gape. A pile of stuff and a wish for good luck? I thought they were coming with me.

Understanding of what lies ahead settles in my chest. It will be Jude and me. Maybe, at some point, just me. But Jude's little sermon from the healing hut stands out in my mind. This is another opportunity to offer up my weakness.

My confidence and hope are in You.

Ash holds out my Bible. "Thank you for reading to us."

I look at the cover, now bent and softened from use. As much as I want to take it with me, I don't have long to use it. "Keep it."

She gives a single nod, and they walk away.

I hope they read more of it.

"That was kind of them." Jude wraps up the coils of rope with his good hand so they fit in our packs.

"Yes, it was, though I'd hoped they would gather the supplies from the *Ivanhoe Independent* when it arrives."

"You find help and yet you're still ungrateful."

At the cool tone behind us, I turn to meet Alder's stare. "We are a community, Parvin. We don't desert each other. Black came straight to me when he and Ash offered to help you. I gave them my blessing and offered those slats of wood." He gestures to the pile Jude attempts to pick up with his one hand.

"I'm not asking anyone to desert you." I loop a coil of rope around my shoulder.

He lifts both eyebrows. "It doesn't have to come in words. Your actions—your *infiltration* into our community—stir things up."

I close my eyes against the words of retaliation fighting my tight lips for release. "We are leaving now. Thank you for hosting and caring for us."

Alder turns and walks away. Silence dominates the cold woods.

The next morning we're packed and loaded with gear, including a small pouch of white pain pills for Jude. My left wrist tingles in a sharp reminder of loss as I hug Willow good-bye. She's not tearful or somber. She just bounces on her toes, her ivory hair swinging side to side. "Elm and I will get the Ivanhoe supplies."

Jude taps her nose. "We can always count on you, can't we?"

"Yup."

"Thanks, Willow," I say.

"Welks."

I look around at the bare autumn dogwood trees and swallow a bewildering pang of sorrow. This village of albino strangers carries an odd welcome in its canopy of branches. I want to stay with hot broth and burning coals, watching winter arrive and depart until the white dogwood petals sprinkle the moss with summer.

The people are strange. Alder is harsh, confusing, and somewhat vindictive. But everyone is unified. How? How can they ask questions, force each other to atone, and follow personal dreams yet remain unified? What do they have that my village doesn't? Yet . . . an emptiness resides behind their pale blue and purple eyes.

I press my finger into the button on my sentra as we leave. If I get a chance, I'll give it to Reid or Mother so they can understand that I did, at one point, desire something more for Unity Village—for someone other than myself.

Jude and I enter the portion of forest burned most permanently in my memory. The glades of fallen logs and moss are now half brown, half green, showering dying leaves upon us with every strong gust of wind. We cross the river on the same log I used during my early travel. Jude's stamina withers after a few hours and I request rest often, for his sake.

My pack is heavy, laden with the ropes, mounts, and food from Willow and Ash. No cooked cattails this time, it's the wrong season. I'm disappointed. I want to try them cooked, if only to rid my memory of the raw ones we ate in the Dregs.

Three days later, we veer into a new stretch of forest. It looks the same, but our direction has changed.

"We need to stay above the cliff bottom," Jude says, "Neither of us can climb the cliff you've described with one hand and packs full of supplies. We'll have to circle around the canyon and walk parallel to the Wall until we reach the Opening."

I follow him with blind trust. He knows how to lead us there. "Do you think we'll get there with enough time?"

"We'll be fine, especially with Willow and Elm bringing the supplies later."

Days pass and the trees thicken. I grow more and more tense. "Are you sure you know the way?" I didn't travel this long when I first crossed, did I?

He remains calm. "Yes." But more days roll on and his yeses accompany a self-spoken whisper. "We should be there soon. Any day now."

One morning, we rise to grey clouds. The brisk weather seems appropriate as I glance at my watch. "Wow, it's September twenty-fifth. Today marks the fifth permanent zero on my Clock."

Jude shudders and meets my gaze with wide eyes. "September . . . twenty-fifth?"

"Yeah." I give a wobbly smile, but we both know what this means. I have nine days until my Good-bye.

I'm in the single digits.

Skelley Chase will be waiting at the Wall soon. So will Tawny. And Reid. And Mother. And Father. I can't seem to bring their faces to mind. They stand in shadows.

Is nine days long enough to build a form of survival for the Radicals and to save Reid?

It's not raining yet, but Jude is rigid as he rolls up his bed pelts. "September twenty-fifth," he says almost to himself. "I know this date."

My head snaps up. "You do?" Goosebumps lift each hair on my body like a beacon. "Why . . . do you . . . think you know it?"

"I don't know, I don't know," he says in a rush. "Maybe I don't."

I can't bring myself to ask if this is the day he zeroes out. He said himself he couldn't remember when. It could be after I cross. We're in the middle of nowhere in a forest. We're safe.

Jude favors his shoulder with each movement. Maybe the pain is agitating him. "Do you need to take a couple white pills?"

He considers this and takes out the small pouch before hoisting his pack onto his shoulders. "No. You should carry them, actually."

"Why? I don't need them." Even so, I consider sneaking a few for my sore muscles and occasional arm spasms.

"I'd prefer you hold on to them."

I shrug and tuck them into one of my many skirt pockets.

He leads the way without a moment for breakfast. Perhaps he wants to beat the rain. "Are we close to the Wall?"

"It should be within our sight soon." His pace is so quick it makes me dwell again on our goal: Reach the Wall and create some sort of survival option for the Radicals before I go through.

I imagine Jude's orphans, eighteen and alone, standing on the ledge and, instead of seeing death below them, they find a bridge leading to a small hut on the plateau with information and food. Hope.

Eighteen. That's my age. What would I have given for hope before this journey? *You gave it to me through the West, God. This is something I can give them.*

Jude weaves his numb fingers into mine. I look at his face. His brow is wrinkled. We must look funny to an outsider with our missing limbs. At least we can hold hands.

This time, I'm not awkward. I squeeze his hand. He lifts mine to his lips and kisses the back of it. My stomach twirls and I look at my feet.

As the day progresses Jude shares tips on tightrope walking and explains how to tie secure knots. The clouds leak their tears onto us, but Jude keeps trudging and talking.

"It shouldn't have taken this long, but I think I know the way now. I forgot a few directions. Probably the pirate chip, but I know the way now."

I clench my teeth against the question, *Do you* really *know the way?*

He sighs. "Parvin . . . forgive me. I'm sorry I pushed you when we were traveling . . . and yelled at you. I'm sorry I've forgotten important things. Solomon told me to look out for you, to protect you. I haven't done a good job."

I tug on his arm to make him stop and turn toward me. The rims of his eyes are red, but his eyes are dry. Wrinkles of strain and hopelessness stand out in his young skin.

"Stop that." I cup my hand on his cheek, breathing in the thrill of touch. "Do we need to rest? It's past noon and we still haven't eaten."

His lips are tight and his jaw fights small quivers. He nods.

I follow him to a small clearing of trees, watching the back of his head as if I can monitor his emotional state. His brokenness reminds me of when he was shot in the Dregs. His fear and tears were all raw. I was the strong one. Is he afraid of returning to the East? Is this remorse something more?

We sit in silence, eating the last of our dried meat and carrots. To give Jude some privacy to rest and stabilize, I send Skelley Chase my last journal entry.

9.28.2149 – 13:53

I'm on my way home. I had to come because Skelley Chase is threatening to kill Reid if I don't.

He'll probably cut out that sentence before publishing it, but I include it anyway.

I found out my brother is married. I want to meet his wife. She'll be waiting for me on the other side of the Wall. This journey has felt like another life. It's strange traveling through the scenery where it started. Thank you, everyone, who has traveled this with me. Hopefully . . . maybe . . . I'll see you on the other side.

I don't know what else to write. I don't want to share our plans to save Radicals, I can't mention Jude because of the shooter. I guess this is enough. I press the Send/Save button. Jude is already packing up the remains of our meal. I stand up. The stillness of resting invited the cold from the misting rain back into my bones, though I'm thankful we haven't reached a downpour. I consider putting on my Vitality suit before we continue to help manage the cold.

I pull it from my pack and, when I straighten, Jude stands in front of me, close enough to brush noses if I hiccup too strongly.

"Parvin . . ." His husky voice sends shivers running through me.

I force myself not to move forward or backward. I look into his face. He's breathing fast and sweat lines his forehead, or is it rain? His fingers startle me when they curl a stray strand of hair behind my ear.

This action increases my nervousness and I step back, breathless. "Yes?"

He seems to catch himself and withdraws from the intimacy. I bite my lip. "I . . . I'm glad I met you." His voice has lost the throaty tone and sounds embarrassed. "And . . . I want to give this to you." He holds out the whistle he carved.

I close my fingers around the smooth wood, running my thumb over the indented holes. It's such a gentle gift. Why is it for me? "Thank you," I whisper.

He gestures to my NAB. "I know you knew Solomon first but . . . I hope you've found my company pleasant, too."

My throat squeezes. "I have."

"Are you ready to continue?" His heart doesn't sound in it. He doesn't look ready to move at all. If anything, he looks worse than when we first sat down to rest. Maybe the rain is chilling his wound.

"Yes." What broke between us when I stepped back? Why did he come so near? Was he going to say something else? What spurred this closeness?

"Good, because you're going alone."

I straighten. "What? Why?"

He shuts his eyes tight. "Because I can't put you in danger. I'm dangerous. This is your pilgrimage and you have to finish it by yourself."

"No! You think you zero out today, don't you?" This explains his momentary tenderness. He was saying good-bye before deserting me. "Please don't leave me."

"I have to. It's not about zeroing out."

I reach for him. "I won't go without you."

He lifts his chin and looks away. "I'm set, Parvin. You need to do this for the Radicals, for the orphans. For Reid."

Fighting the downward swirl of despair, I hold up the Vitality suit and ask in a hollow voice, "Do you mind if I change? To keep me going through this weather?"

His tone turns sharp like a leader. "Be quick about it."

I swallow. "Could you turn your back, then?" I plan to pull the suit over my leggings and undershirt, but still feel exposed doing this in front of another person. Especially Jude.

Maybe, in putting on the suit, I can convince him that I have extra protection. Maybe, after it's on, I can persuade him to continue.

He turns around and I find my learned skill of dressing with one arm annoyingly impaired. He keeps his back to me, but his right hand clutches the hem of his coat.

He wants me to leave. My eyes smart. Does he think this is best?

"Okay," I murmur.

"Okay." Jude turns to face me.

"It's not okay," says a voice behind me.

I start and, before I can turn around, an arm wraps around my torso. Something sharp presses into the side of my neck. I jerk away from the point, but the captor follows my movement.

"Don't struggle," he says in a collected voice and the sharp weapon pierces my skin with a twinge. "There's now a needle in your neck. If you flinch, jerk, or pull away it will snap in half and you may even end up swallowing it."

Black dots fly across my vision. His arm is firm, pressing my ribcage together and stilting my breath. It's his voice that ices my nerves. I heard it on the ledge of the Dregs before he shot Jude with a pirate chip. I remember his smooth gaze on the Ivanhoe train platform.

No.

Jude stands frozen before me, staring over my shoulder. "Let her go. She was about to leave." His eyes flick to my neck.

"Hello, Hawke." The assassin wiggles the needle enough to keep me aware of its presence and to churn my stomach contents into poison.

My eyes snap wide open. "Hawke?" But the small movement bumps the needle and I whimper back into silence. Is Hawke here to help us? I look around the clearing, trying to spot his tall shadowed form, but the brief flare of hope quenches when Jude speaks.

"Hello." Jude jerks his head toward me. "Let her go."

"A valiant request, but we both know that won't happen. When my pirate chip took your memory of your Numbers, the leverage opportunity was too good to pass up." He holds an emotigraph in front of my face. "Plus, your girl gave me this."

It's a picture of Ivanhoe—the one I lost when riding the *Ivanhoe Independent.*

"Every time I click it, the first emotion has your name swimming through it—*Jude.* I knew wherever she'd be, you'd be. You've been together too long. She may know something. Give me what I want or I'll take it from *her.*"

I struggle to maintain focus on the conversation, even though my understanding is shaken by the usage of the name, Hawke. I scan Jude's face. He's not Hawke. They look completely different. They have different names, but the assassin speaks only to him.

"Is it what *you* want? Or what the Council wants?"

The assassin moves, possibly in a shrug. "Both. I want their money; they want your information. The pirate chip gathered a little of what I needed, but then its signal went dead. You fought hard, but not hard enough."

Information. "Jude, don't." I speak soft enough that the needle stays in place.

"Let me speak plainly, so that we all know how this is going to work." The assassin's warm breath battles the ice of raindrops on my ear.

He wiggles the needle again and a high-pitched squeal escapes my throat. My skin feels violated by its presence, but I'm afraid to jerk away. "This is a syringe with a toxic injection designed for situations like this. As you can see, it's quite full. The longer it takes you to give me the rest of your information, the more I insert into her neck, and the faster she'll die. For example . . ."

A pressure fills my neck, hitting my nerves like a branding iron.

"That"—says the assassin—"is one-tenth of the toxin. Over the course of two weeks, it will eat away her nervous system, shutting down the function of her brain, until she finally dies. Now, if I follow Miss Blackwater's X-book right, she should have nine days left to her supposed Clock. So far, she's not a dead woman, but"—another ounce of pressure hits the walls of my neck muscles—"she could be soon. Shall we find out if the Clock is really hers, Mr. Hawke?"

"Stop." Jude reaches out with his hand. "Please stop."

"Jude?" I croak. *Jude Hawke?* I can't ignore what I heard. I want to understand, but with a syringe in my neck, I ignore my curiosity. "You heard what he said. I have nine days. He can't kill me even if he wanted to."

Both Jude and the assassin are silent. Jude looks in my eyes—a tender look similar to the one he gave mere minutes ago when we were inches apart.

The assassin's left hand releases me for a moment and flicks something small at Jude's feet. Then his arm returns like a rubber band around my chest. "I'm waiting."

"No!" I shout and swallow a moan as the needle shoots another squirt into my neck. I imagine sickly liquid mixing with my blood, confusing my nerves, and swimming toward my brain.

"We're now at two-tenths, Hawke. That's another pirate chip at your feet. Uncap the needles and push them into the base of your skull. It will do the rest."

Jude looks down at the small green square—another invention of the High City. "*Just . . . a pirate chip?*"

"Jude! Think about the orphans and Radicals you're protecting."

He bends down. His hand quivers and it takes two tries to pick up the chip. His face is scrunched and pale.

"Stop, Jude." My voice is harsh. I'm angry. What is he doing? Is he worried I'll die? "Don't think about me."

"I always think about you." He looks up and the thick emotion in his eyes reminds me of the look Solomon Hawke gave when I was dragged out of the Containment Center. That's when I connect it.

They're brothers. I'm blind. They're *brothers.*

"If that chip isn't in your skull in five seconds, she gets a double dose."

"Why are there two needles on here?" Jude holds up the pirate chip. The assassin doesn't answer, but after a brief pause, Jude lets out a soft, "Ah." He smiles in a sad way. "So today is the day. Now I'll finally find out who has power over the Clocks."

"Clocks are power." The toxin the assassin pushes into my vein blurs my vision, or maybe it's my stomach churning. All I know is the next words out of my mouth come in a desperate wheeze. "I'm going to be sick."

Perhaps the assassin hears it in my voice or he sees this with his other victims, but the needle slides out of my skin as I collapse on the forest floor and vomit into the dead leaves. The hammer of a gun clicks above me and I don't need to look to know he has both Jude and me covered in case we try to bolt.

Upon the exertion of my last cough, a knee presses me into the ground, my face inches from my own sick. The needle enters my neck.

"Half of this is now in her body, Hawke. She's got four days. Do you want to lessen that?"

Four days, I think in a daze, trying to straighten my thought. *That's not enough.* My fingertips grow numb and tingle. Something is spinning.

"No I don't," I croak, but I can't remember what I'm arguing.

"Dose number five," the assassin shouts in growing anger.

"Hold off!" Jude yells. "You'll get your information." In an undertone, he says, ". . . and I'll get mine."

"No!" I screech against the movement of the needle. "No, Jude!" I twist to look up at him, but he avoids my eyes.

He uncaps the needles. I suddenly don't care if the syringe snaps inside my neck. I fight the assassin with my draining power, pushing with both arms. Stump and hand both sink in the wet dirt.

"Jude, don't!" My muscles collapse. "Your orphans will die! He can't kill me. It's a trick. Please. Don't give up *now!* Not after sacrificing your entire life to protect this—" My voice is cut off with a groan as another choking toxin dose causes my muscles to shriek.

"Shut up! She got another for that, Hawke."

"Please . . . *please* stop." Scuffle comes from where Jude is and the needle sinks deeper into my neck. Jude's movement halts and he groans. "The chip is in."

The assassin digs his knee into my spine, keeping me pressed into the earth like a trodden twig, and flops something onto the ground with his free hand. An electronic whirring reaches my ears. When the assassin speaks next it's with triumph in his voice. "Very good. A few more seconds."

The trickling string of hope inside me swirls into black despair. Jude gave up. His life work. The lives of his orphans. The lives of innocent Radicals. He's gone against his family. Against me.

He didn't listen.

"Parvin." His voice is a hollow breath. "I don't have faith in your Clock like you do. And I can't risk your life, even if it means giving up this information. Please . . . don't hate me. Remember to hope. Remember Who is stronger."

The assassin slips the syringe out of my neck. "Perfect. The sappy farewell has been given and the information is downloaded."

I remain, numb, on the ground.

"She has two days. And you have ten seconds, Hawke."

Jude runs toward us. For a fleeting instant, I flare with hope that he has a backup plan. He's about to tackle the assassin and crush the electrobook that just drank the secrets of his mind.

Instead, Jude rolls me over and brushes the leaves off my face. Before my eyes can focus, a tear drops on my forehead. He kisses my cheek below my eye as if he's desperate to gift me a kiss no matter where it lands. His lips leave my skin and he takes a quick breath to whisper, "Tally ho, Parvin-girl. I'll see you soon."

"Why?" Why did he give up?

His voice is soft by my ear. "Ask Solomon."

Two loud pops split the air. My eyes focus in time to see Jude blink once slowly, but when his eyelids lift he's a blank mannequin with the echoes of concern-wrinkles fading like forgotten time. Life is supplanted by breathless silence. And heartbeat is replaced by inert body weight slumping against my chest.

41

The assassin pulls Jude's dead weight off me, but hollow pressure remains on my chest. My throat convulses against the thickened toxin coating my veins. Footsteps crunch against the silence.

"Jude." I arch my back against the forest floor. His dropped tear slides down my temple and panicked energy propels me to a sitting position.

The assassin is gone. I guess now that he got what he wanted, he's returning to the Council. Instead of relief, alarm surrounds me at his absence.

Jude's body is folded against the ground like an ironed hem, his arms flopped to one side and his head lolling back.

My breathing jolts like a racehorse. I shake his good shoulder. "Jude?" I recall the blankness in his eyes and reckless screaming overpowers my sanity. "Jude?" I push him weakly. "Jude!" I crawl to see his wooden face. The chip in the base of his skull is covered in blood from the puncture points, but one sickly green word blinks on the tiny face.

Terminated

"Jude. *Jude!*"

It's the only word in my vocabulary and it grows like an orchestral crescendo until it's so loud in my ears it impales my muscles. I roll on my back in the rain, exhausted, ill, allowing the swollen drops to hit my face, my hand, my body, my hair. Then I sob, wrapping my fingers in his dirty black coat. I sob until dirt cakes my face, until my ribs and lungs beg for deliverance, until I allow myself to drown under God's eyes alone.

Darkness accentuates my defeat and I succumb to the misery like a pitcher of water poured into a soulless drain. Morning arrives and departs with crusted tears on my cheeks and in my hair. I stare dazed at the thick line of trees waving to me over the wind. My body exudes emotions, soaking the dirt with sentimental fertilizer. Maybe trees of abandonment and surrender will sprout around me. Black leaves. Black trunks. Void of oxygen and life.

"... Jude ..."

The sun rises and sets in a pattern I can't keep track of, stuttering between the swirling yellow aspen leaves. The rain stops, but knots of muscles twitch along my body. Spasms. They prick at my body like animal nips. I can't seem to focus, to think, to care.

Darkness blows in, once, twice, carrying a hollow feeling of hopelessness in the deepest crevice of my heart, leaving no room for fear of nocturnal noises or creatures crawling over my still, damp body. My thoughts rest in my head like an abandoned pool of water in a silent glade. I stare until I see nothing more through the darkness. My muscle jerks become a second hand. Soothing. I close my eyes once more.

Another sunset touches its colors on the white tree bark and I can no longer fight the snake squeezing my organs. I roll over and vomit. My muscles cry out at the sudden movement. Some sections are numb, others convulse in renewed spasms.

Toxin.

I'm sitting up. The world swirls, stirring my equilibrium with it. A body lies beside me. Jude. Jude's dead. Jude's gone.

I touch his hand.

He's ice. He's cold. Too cold. *I'm* cold. We need to warm up.

Fire.

In a dazed state, I stumble around the forest like a drunk on stilts. With one hand, it takes hours to pile enough wood beside us. As I stagger, pulling fresh branches from their trunks and dragging away dead ones, hallucinations meet me with swirling pockets of reality: Jude's tattooed arm burns in my unlit fire. His snake tries to bite me as I lay another stick on the pile. It's venomous. It will kill me.

I'm already dying. I'm already infected.

I shake so hard I drop my tiny supply of matches. They scatter among the leaves like escaped worms. I find one. Two. Strike.

Flame.

The wood is wet. My tears are wet. Why am I crying?

The match dies. "God! Fire!" I suck in shuddering breaths. "Fire. *Please!*"

My second match catches with the barest of movements and His miracle breath blows it to light. With the fire comes mental illumination. I straighten and swallow the tar of emotions.

"I'm on a pilgrimage." My voice is hoarse and broken.

Jude's cold body looks stiff. Heavy. Alone.

I knew he would die. But I hoped . . . I hoped he'd outlive me. The thought was selfish. I glance at my watch. Seven days left to suffer. One week. My finish line.

A deep shuddering breath stills my poisoned nerves. I wipe a trembling hand against my forehead and it comes away coated in sweat. My hair is stringy with leaves trapped in its tangles. I'm sick. I'm dying, but I'm dying slower than the assassin said. He gave me two days.

I have seven.

He can't defeat my Clock. My Vitality suit is fighting the weakness the toxin carries to my body. I know how long it will fight. But can *I* fight?

"Jude, can I fight?"

He doesn't answer. He's dead. I jerk from the reminder. He needs a burial. I can't bury him. I can't say Good-bye so thoroughly. The ground is too cold. The wolves will find him. I have no shovel.

I'll bury him in light. In ashes. In fire. The same way I want to be buried—not in the ground, not wasting earth.

Nighttime brings me back to my own fire after organizing branches around his body. They will smoke. The albinos will be angry, but they're far away. This isn't their forest. This is Jude's and my forest.

I light his fire at dawn and take an emotigraph. For me. For Hawke. *Hawke.* Does he know Jude is dead? I swallow hard. Why didn't I know? Their connection and friendship makes so much more sense.

As I click the sentra, I try to recall all the brave things Jude did, but all that sticks in my mind is his surrender to the assassin. His last act . . . of cowardice.

I lower the sentra. Why did Jude relinquish his information? Why did he go against his life convictions? Was it only because he feared for my life?

Ask Solomon . . .

His funeral pyre burns through the afternoon and I watch it until it turns to embers. The smoke blackens the air like clouds of sorrow.

I take his pack against the pounding in my muscles and add it to mine. I don't have long before the assassin's toxin will bow me to the ground to fade away. I can't accomplish much in a coma. I need to reach the Wall.

"Tally ho, Jude-man."

The clearing stays behind like a blot on my timeline. It's the moment when Jude gave in with a fruitless attempt to save me. Why didn't he listen?

Another day passes with as much progress as a slowing merry-go-round. I don't see the Wall and don't know how to get there, so I head toward the sunrise. My tongue sticks to my mouth, but water doesn't quench. Shadows seem to shift into people. At one point, I find myself asking one for guidance.

I collapse and force a swallow of dinner, but it resurfaces almost immediately. Who needs food anyway? I'm dying.

At noon the next day, both my arms are numb with the familiarity of amputation. I can't seem to remember why the albinos took my hand. I did something bad. It was an accident.

Jude. Jude Hawke. Hawke.

My NAB feels old in my hand. I haven't touched it in a while. There's been no need after I sent Skelley Chase my last entry. But does Solomon Hawke know his brother is dead?

I pull out Jude's NAB. It's small. I navigate through the many contact bubbles until I find one labeled "Solomon."

~Hawke, My numb lips work against the cold to speak to the NAB. *~Jude was . . . killed by the . . . assassin. He gave away his memory to . . . save my life. But I'm dying. I'm poisoned. I . . . can't think straight.*

As if to punctuate this last sentence, I stare at my message, trying to remember what I wanted to write.

~You are brothers?

I stare at my message and my throat squeezes out my air. I'm alone. I'm going to die alone.

PRESS ON TOWARD THE PRIZE.

God's written words float into my mind as consolation. *But I'm dying, God.*

TRUST ME.

Trust. It seems so simple, the act of finding calm in the midst of my Last Days. I knew these were coming. The question of my childhood is being answered at last: What will my Good-bye be like? Drowning? Accidental? Painless? Sickness?

Sickness. The shutdown of my nervous system.

I sink to my knees. How much can my will battle my body? I smile at God and pluck at my Vitality suit. "I'll bet"—I manage between shortened breaths—"You made sure"—I hold a fist at my sternum—"Wilbur gave me the Vitality suit . . . just for this . . ."

God prepared me for my death . . . and for my pilgrimage.

Skelley Chase's name bubble blinks when I reopen my own NAB. Out of instinct, I sniff for the scent of lemon when I tap his message.

~Parvin. The Wall Keeper has agreed to open the door at one o'clock each day for five minutes. He starts October first. Keep me updated on your progress. I expect you through early. Reid will be there, under my watch. -SC

This message came two days ago, hence his follow-up message:

~Parvin. Where are you? -SC

I lean against a sodden log and type a reply to spare my breath.

~Mr. Chase.

~I've been attacked. Jude and I were traveling to the Wall when an assassin found us, killed Jude, and inserted a toxin into my neck. I'm trying to find the Wall. I'm lost and sick and it's getting worse. I don't know if I'll find the entrance, but I'm trying. Don't touch Reid.

I don't mind using Jude's name now that he's dead. I want people to know he died. It seems important he doesn't fade into ignorance.

Fade.

I want to fade. The farther the sun sinks behind the trees the more I want to join it in its mystery bed. Where does the sun sleep? Is it warm? *God, can I join You there? Where You bring peace and constant light?*

You will.

I don't know if it's my hallucination or if His words enter more consistently into my mind now that I near my Good-bye. During the death of His children in the Bible, He always seemed nearer to them, like with Stephen the martyr. I want to see into Heaven.

Do you see me as Your child?

He doesn't answer this time, maybe because I already know the answer. Of course He does. He smiles like Father's crinkled face every time He looks at me. Even if I mess up and desert my companions for a ride to Ivanhoe, or lead Jude to his death by allowing him to come with me, or break albino laws to build a fire. Because He is the essence of shalom—the way things were intended to be.

"Parvin!"

I gasp so hard from surprise that I choke and hiccup through repeated deep breaths to keep my stomach still. When I open my eyes again, Willow kneels before me. Behind her stands a young albino boy with child muscles showing he's worked with the men since his first toddler step. His white hair spikes at different angles and varied lengths, giving him a fierce, but playful appearance. His most noticeable feature is his one eye, the other is patched with a stretch of brown animal skin.

Elm. Willow's grafting partner.

"Elm and I decided to follow you and Jude-man to help with the Radicals. We saw the smoke from a giant fire and tracked you."

"You burned a lot of green wood," Elm says in a voice forced a notch lower than what sounds natural.

"It's not your part of the forest. I . . ." I raise a hand to my head and try to form floating words into a sentence. *I needed to bury Jude. I wasn't thinking straight when I gathered the fire. What are you doing here? Please don't make me atone.*

A tiny hand feels my forehead. "Parvin, you sick?"

I nod. "Jude . . ."

"I know Jude-man's dead. Elm and I want to help you."

I give a tired laugh. "Thank you."

She pushes against my shoulders. I open my eyes, disoriented, and realize I'm now lying down. To my left, Elm takes out a bag of coals and prepares a small fire.

"Rest," Willow says in her light soothing tone. "Get better tonight and we'll leave tomorrow."

"I can't get better . . . I'm poisoned."

"Then we'll leave tomorrow anyway." A hum of disconcertion lines her words.

My sleep is delirious, combed with whispers between Elm and Willow. The morning dawns as the worst so far physically, but the most calming mentally. Overnight I seem to have accepted my Good-bye. I'm not alone. I'm not lost.

Elm takes the lead in the morning and adjusts my traveling direction so we head east. Willow walks with me, taking my hand to help me every few steps. They carry my packs on top of their own. Now that they're with me, I realize how slowly I've stumbled along the past two days. They adjust their pace for me, but still push me faster than my poisoned brain wants to accept.

"My legs," I cry at one point the next day, falling to the ground. "I can't feel them. Where are they?"

"They're here," Willow soothes, rubbing a hand up and down my calves. "Right here."

"Are they?" I must lie for a few hours because when we walk again it's dusk.

My mind plays a reel of pictures from my life to keep me company as we travel. I remember Reid giving me my cross ring a week after I told him I believed in God with my heart *and* my head. He said the hardest part about growing closer to God is remembering what He's done.

"Use this as a reminder . . ."

What has God done? I collapse when Elm says we're stopping for the night. Willow covers me with a fur. It smells dusty, but blocks the cold.

I think of small answered prayers—surviving the wolves, finding water, discovering Independents, reaching Ivanhoe, but the one that shines brightest overarches the other like a dome. *God, You answered my prayer for purpose.*

I found purpose in Him. With a meager year left, He filled my life to the brim with meaning. I discovered the meaning of shalom and how crucial it is to weave into my thinking. Jude taught me a new sense of freedom from the Clocks, though I don't fully grasp it yet. I experienced the loss of my hand, but saw God's provision through my weakness.

Weakness. It's okay to be weak.

I thought I knew what the Preacher meant when he asked what I'd want to do when on death's doorstep. I thought it'd be to save Radicals and reverse deaths. Now I know it's so much deeper. What I *really* want to do is share every ounce of passion in my heart for shalom, for God, for purpose, with every other person in the world. But that would have been a lifelong pursuit. My life wasn't long enough. My passion came too late, but I'm ready.

God will use someone else to accomplish what I should have.

"Come, Parvin."

Willow drags me up a crested hill midmorning the next day, beyond the aspens and pine trees until I'm crawling on my hands and knees up a plinth above the world. When we crest, Elm and Willow kneel beside me and point ahead.

The Wall.

It's so close, carrying a strange welcome. My family is on the other side. Mother is there. Father may cry. Reid will hold the two perfect hands of his stranger bride to introduce to me. And, if I make it across, then Reid will live. I'll save his life.

Solomon Hawke will be there. How is he feeling, knowing his brother is dead?

"We're close," Willow says. "We can be there by noon. A little more forest and then we climb that incline on the edge of the canyon."

I follow her pointing finger. So close. I look down at my hand clenched in the grass and cock my head to one side when I see my stump. It doesn't revolt me anymore. It's a scar from the West.

My blue watch reflects the sun into my eyes. I squint against the spinning in my vision until I make out the time on the bright face: *11:02 a.m.* and ticking. October sixth in the year twenty-one forty-nine.

I die tomorrow.

42

I stagger down the hill after Elm and Willow, tumbling part of the way and gathering crackled leaves on my clothing. We bid good-bye to the golden aspens and enter yesterday's forgotten world of red, orange, and purple. I never thought death could be beautiful, but now I witness the eighteenth autumn of my short life with new eyes.

The leaves peak with a rainbow of stunning color waiting to fall, and when they do fall, it's beautiful, like jeweled feathers dancing their descent. Once on the ground, they bring life through their deaths. I push through a supple tree branch, letting drops of dew rain on my face.

It was predestined I die in October. I wouldn't want to die in any other season. The world looks most alive to me now. Maybe I'll carry this same aura to those waiting at the Wall. Maybe my presence and my story will bring the same life these dying leaves bring to the ground.

Uphill steals my last energy. I disregard my pride and sink to all fours. Wet dirt soaks my knees. I crawl through the undergrowth. Elm and Willow walk beside me.

"Stand up so we can support you." Elm presses a hand on my shoulder.

They're too small to help. "Let me crawl."

Blood dries from scratches on my hand, but I don't feel them. The rocks denting my knees leave no pain. I'm swimming. Swimming through air toward the Wall. Sick. Ridden with pain.

Willow offers me water. I shake my head. I hurt too much to swallow.

"You must drink some," she says.

For her sake, I do. It tastes like acid. I choke and can't seem to draw enough breath. My sight blackens.

I'm floating. Flying. Angels carry me. I relax what few muscles still obey my mind and allow the will of God to take me. I wake in Elm's arms, a steady up and down motion rocking me like a ship's bow.

"The angels?" I breathe.

He looks down at me with a surprised jerk. "What angels?"

"They were carrying me to the Wall."

He gives a pained smile, creasing his animal skin patch. "No, *I* am carrying you."

My heart sinks. I want the angels to take me. "But you're a little boy."

He looks ahead and lengthens his strides. "I'm autumn fourteen—almost autumn fifteen—and attended dead-standing at autumn seven. My strength far surpasses the task of carrying a dying sapling like you."

His face stays serious, but I chuckle, which makes me want to vomit. "Dying sapling . . ." I chuckle again. Elm sets me down and I dry heave my stomach acid into a tree well.

I close my eyes. I can't remember where I'm going. I can't remember why.

Shalom.

Why?

SHALOM.

I open my eyes after what feels like a long, sickened slumber. Cold, damp, dirt cradles my aching body. Above me, the Wall arcs like a giant talon.

We're here.

The sun holds the clouds apart to shine on my icy body. I see its warmth, but don't feel it. In twenty-four hours, I'll be in eternal light and warmth.

Shalom.

A hammer breaks my thoughts and I turn my head toward the noise. Willow holds a metal mount against the ground beside the open canyon. Elm pounds it in. Deep.

Tears burn my eyes and throat. "The wolves will hear you . . . the wolves!" I roll on my side.

Willow comes to me. "We're above the wolves. Above the canyon by the ledge. See the Opening?"

I follow her pointed finger, following the stretch of Wall over the empty air. The wolves are far below us in their own graveyard of bones. We're safe. I don't have to climb.

"You're almost home," she says.

I shake my head, keeping my eyes closed. "It's not home anymore."

"We need to secure the mount so you can get to the door." Against my will, she pulls me into a sitting position. I fight her, but my muscles are as useless as a stamped horsefly.

"Parvin." Her voice is no longer soft or musical. "Wake up."

I open my eyes. Blinking several times, my vision brings the Opening back into focus. The metal door is thirty yards to my right, standing guard over the wavering canyon edge. Crumbled earth lines the base of the Wall, careening into nothingness.

"I flew off that," I whisper, but shake my head wondering why my words don't sound right.

"No more flying," Willow says firmly. "How do you open the door?"

I cock my head to one side and try to remember. "Skelley Chase?" I look at my watch. *12:46.*

A veil lifts from my eyes and I sit up straight, defying the gnawing anguish beneath my skin. "One o'clock." My voice is strong. Clear. I meet Willow's eyes. "It opens in fifteen minutes, but closes after five."

Elm resumes his hammering. Willow rejoins him and pulls from her bag a flat sturdy strap laden with strange metal clamps. Elm examines them, glances at a small crack in the Wall, and detaches three by their metal clips. He squeezes them into the crack, clips the rope to the metal rings, and gives it a few firm tugs. The other end of the rope, he winds under Willow's arms around her chest.

"What are those metal things?" My voice is losing its strength.

"Spring-loaded camming devices." Elm tugs on the knot under Willow's arms.

Willow looks back at me and brushes her long pale hair from her face. "They're anchors that fit in cracks to help you climb. We will use them as a rope station for a rope swing until we can get supplies from the train next week."

Elm gives her a nod and she loops the strap of camming devices over one shoulder, my two packs over the other, then places a tiny bare foot on the thin ledge.

I gasp. "Willow."

"Be silent!" Elm's bark reminds me of Black.

My blinks grow slower, but I can't take my eyes from Willow's small white body splayed along the edge of the Wall, standing on tiptoes as weak canyon rock crumbles into the misty bottom, feeling for cracks with her tiny fingers. Every time she finds one, she grips tight and takes another small shuffled step toward the suspended door, leaning against the Wall as if she and it are magnets. Each step takes her farther from solid ground—farther from us.

Elm watches with a wide eye and tight lips. He's not breathing.

Then she starts climbing. I don't know how—I see no holds. Inch by inch, she scales the Wall like a lizard weaving to and fro. At a crack, she inserts one of the camming devices and loops the rope through a clip. She scales back down, safer now with the anchor in the wall. She reaches the door, panting, but it's not open yet. My watch swims before my eyes. I hold it up until I make out the time.

"Three more minutes," I announce.

"Get ready to come, Parvin," Willow calls back to me.

Ready? How? "No, I will go through tomorrow. I need to help on this side."

Willow stares at me with fire eyes. "Parvin, you come *now*. Elm and I will make the station. You can't help. You're sick. Come save your brother."

I try to push myself to my feet, but my arms don't work. My brain doesn't seem to control my body anymore. Elm walks over and hoists me up. Once I'm standing, I realize he's almost as tall as I. Maybe I'm short. My knees are locked. He tugs me forward and they buckle.

"This isn't going to work!"

"Yes it is!" Willow's angry. At this moment, the door slides open and she falls inside the Wall. "It's open! I can see light far away. Hurry, Parvin!"

Elm tugs on my arms again, but his efforts seem half-hearted, like he's already giving up on me.

Don't give up! I can do this.

I push against the ground and his hold tightens. We stumble toward the cliff edge. Hammering comes from the entrance as Willow attaches her end of the rope somewhere inside the Opening. The rope is now an upside-down *V* along the Wall—one side here with Elm and the other side with Willow.

"Loop this around your hips like a swing," Elm instructs, shoving the rope at me.

Obey. Obey. Obey. I can't find reasons to protest, but my hands tremble too much. My mind swims too deep. What am I doing, again?

Elm takes the rope from me and winds it around my hips and waist three times. Its fibers cut into my spine. The pain is a welcome distraction from the ache of toxin. He ties a knot and now I'm relaxing in the rope. My legs shake. I can't stand much longer. *God?*

Elm gives me a small nudge. "Swing across."

As if on cue, my knees buckle and I fall into the open space above the wolves. I don't even have the energy to scream. Having no grip on the rope, I fall back into the air—all weight entrusted to the rope. Fingers grab my boot but lose the grip as I swoop back to Elm.

My side scrapes along the Wall, but I don't move. The rocking is soothing.

"Elm!" Willow calls from somewhere above me. The soft wind mutes her voice as I swing up, backward. Swing. Mother pushed me on a swing once. Only once.

Hands snag my loose clothing from behind and jolt me to a stop. "Sit up and hold the rope," Elm snaps.

I'm on solid ground again. I wind my fingers around the grains, commanding them to tighten. I think they do. I'm not sure.

My family is so close, I imagine their smells wafting through the Wall. Mother smells like oatmeal and cinnamon. Father is soap and saw-dust, the perfect mixture of fresh. Reid will smell like forest and travel. Or maybe he'll smell like Tawny. He's married now.

I have to do this for them. I want to see them.

What will Hawke smell like?

Willow screams at me. "Hurry!"

Elm pushes me. Hard.

I swing back across, this time gripping the rope with every last ounce of energy in my five remaining fingers. *God, keep me strong!*

I can collapse inside the Wall.

No, I must make it to the East.

Willow's arm stretches out to me from the door. I can't see my watch, but I'm certain my five minutes are almost up. The rope rubs my aching skin. I want to peel it off to relieve the pain. I reach for her. Torment steals my vision.

Warm fingers touch mine. My eyes snap open. At the height of my swing, Willow slices through the rope with a dagger—my dagger. I fly against the wall inside the Opening. I collapse on the ground, knocking my already pounding head against the inner stone.

"Quick." Willow urges me to my feet. The loose end of the rope flies in the sky.

The light flickers on the other side of the tunnel. The East. It steals my breath. "Can you smell them?"

"Who?" Willow sounds nervous.

"My family . . . Mother . . . Father . . . Reid . . ."

"Come *on*, Parvin!"

But with her words of urgency, both doors slice shut, forcing a demon of darkness around us. The darkness quenches the noise of wind and breathing.

Silence is welcomed. The twisted tortured animal of poison inside me rests long enough to hear Willow breathe, "Parvin?"

"I want to sleep."

"Are we trapped?" Her tiny voice quivers and her hand grips mine. She's childlike again, no longer a leader.

My ring bites into my pinky. "Only until tomorrow."

Tomorrow. Another twenty-four hours of wretchedness. *God, I think I'm ready to die.* My body pleads for it. My mind pounds the "shut-down" button. My Vitality suit only prolonged my suffering. It stretched two days of death into nine. I don't want to survive until tomorrow afternoon. I want to die. I want to *rest.*

"Willow, you and Elm *have* to save the Radicals."

Her fingers twitch. "We will, just like Jude-man saved me. We will do it. More Jude-mans will come through and we'll help them."

I can't breathe enough to say thank you, but shalom curls into my soul, bringing peace. *Is it true, Lord? Can I say Good-bye with peace?*

I pull out the tied wads of maps, trade tickets, and instructions I wrote up for the Radicals and place them in her lap. "Make sure they get these, too."

"I will."

I squeeze Willow's fingers until my muscles fade enough to match the darkness of the tunnel. I wake to an annoying *pop* from my NAB. Willow still holds my hand and Mother's skirt covers me. The rope is no longer bound around my torso.

Snug, I relish the warmth. "I need to wear this for Mother."

"I'll tie it around your waist," Willow whispers, pressing my NAB into my lap.

I release her hand to read the glowing messages while her tiny fingers fiddle in the dark with my skirt ties. The letters swim before my eyes, but I see two name bubbles. *Unknown* is back. Hawke. He's recontacted me on my NAB.

I don't know whose name bubble I press first, but messages unfurl.

~Parvin, what type of poison? Tell me details. I'll try to find an antidote. ~SC

~Are you alive? ~SC

~Parvin, you didn't come through the Wall today. Tomorrow you zero-out and we'll have twenty-five minutes after you get through. You're dooming Reid if you don't come. ~SC

"I'm in the Wall," I reply. "Send."

Hawke's message is long and I wish Willow could read it to me. The light hurts my eyes and my concentration stabs my body like a dagger when I try focusing.

~Dear Parvin,

~Are you sure Jude's dead? Yes, Jude and I are brothers, but . . . he can't be dead. It doesn't make sense. He would never give away his information. How did he die?

I blink and refocus. I've dropped the NAB onto my lap and the glow reveals Willow's face, scrunched in fearful sleep. Did I fall asleep? I pick up the NAB and continue.

~I'm worried for you. I don't know how to combat toxins. I've tried contacting the Nether Town physicians, but they deny knowing any cure or medicine that will help you. They won't come to the Wall for your reentrance because you may be a Radical. I feel so helpless. If you return, I will take you to the nearest hospital myself.

"I am in the Wall," I reply, as I did to Skelley Chase, but I take an emotigraph to send to Hawke. Maybe he will feel my desire to rest and won't try to save me. Who can fight the Clocks, anyway?

Willow wakes up. "We should go to the other door."

I shake my head, which makes it drum like an execution march. "I'm too tired."

"You've slept for hours," she whines, pulling against me. "*Please.* There are dead people in here. Bones." Her voice grows higher and frantic. "Let's go to the other side so when the door opens you can just go through."

I sigh. "Okay."

Willow leaves her pack and the pile of resources I gave her against the wall. I manage to crawl and close my mind to the mental image of bones rolling toward me. My movements are stiff and I put my weight on my elbows, sparing my throbbing stump.

Almost there. Almost tomorrow. Almost Good-bye.

When we reach the opposite door, I lie flat on my stomach, half my face pressed into the cold dirt. Shivers stampede my form, crushing my will to fight like wine-stompers. What is sleep and what is darkness? What is time when it's invisible?

My hand rests by my face.

Click. Click. Click. The tick of a blue watch lowers the drawbridge for Death.

Voices. Muffled. My whispered name. Silence.

Click. Click. Click. Where's my Clock? Where are my Numbers? How many zeroes do I have now?

"Parvin!" Willow shakes me.

"Hmm?"

Light illuminates my wrist. My watch. I squint. Willow holds the NAB above me like a candle. "What does the watch say?"

I've forgotten how to read. I've forgotten what these numbers and moving lines mean. Why does it matter? "Let me sleep."

"What does it say? What time is it?"

Time. The numbers and lines fall into place like a long forgotten memory. "Twelve fifty-eight."

Twelve fifty-eight. 12:58. One-two-five-eight. Fifty-eight minutes past noon. October seventh. Eight zeroes. My Clock is branded on my mind.

000.000.00.27.12

An awakening lightens my body. I claw the inner wall with my fingertips, fighting the flood of life memories as I pull myself to my feet. My toes scuffle against the loose rocks. My spine straightens like a soldier's and I lift my chin, not in defiance, but in determination.

I will welcome these last zeroes standing. I will allow my quickened heartbeat to count the seconds. I will remember what God has done.

I press my splayed hand against the cool door as if feeling for its heartbeat. Neither side is my home. My new home is above, waiting.

I'm ready to discover it.

43

000 . 000 . 00 . 25 . 59

The door slides open with the hiss of a snake. I squint against the sunlight of a thousand proclaiming angels. The space between my fingers closes and I raise my palm to shadow my eyes. With a single blink, my breath of imagined Heaven transforms into an earthly scene.

There they are: Mother, Father, Reid, and a pale twig of a girl wearing my old handmade clothes. They're paper cutouts of a forgotten life.

A line of regal Enforcers curves beside them, leaving an oval of space between me and a crowd of frozen cardboard strangers. The mystery faces are more numerous than the inhabitants of Unity Village and Nether Town put together. No one's breathing. No one looks real.

One Enforcer holds a softer posture, leaning forward on the balls of his feet as if ready to run toward me.

Solomon Hawke.

To my left, Skelley Chase leans against the Wall, one hand in his pocket and the other resting on a gun at his side. Imagined or real, I smell lemons. It's not the scent I crave.

I take a single step forward, toward my family, and crumble. My head hits grassy dirt like a mallet on a drum.

Get up, I grind at myself, but before I can make an attempt, I'm dry heaving so close to the dead grass my every gasp sucks in clouds of dust. The only sound reaching my ears through the deathly silence is my retching.

You can take me now, I think to God, wishing my audience consisted only of Mother. Instead, I'm showcased as the dying Radical. I don't need to be in a glass box clothed in spandex this time. It's real life. Everyone is watching. No one is moving. How long will I lie here, exhausted? How many people are disgusted?

Cameras and sentras click around me.

Three pairs of hands close on me, one lifting me, one smoothing hair from my face, and one poking something cold and tight into my left shoulder.

"Parvin." The second set of hands pulls me tight against a chest smelling of travel and something artificially masculine—cologne. It's familiar, yet strange.

The other two pairs of hands release me, the last of which removes the tight prick from my shoulder, leaving behind a foreign squirm in my skin. To my left, through the swirling black sickness, Skelley Chase holds out a sentra.

"Go away," I rasp, but I squeeze the button anyway and bury my face in Reid's coat. I sense someone standing near us—the first pair of hands, the strong ones.

Hawke?

I don't know how long Reid holds me. I can't comprehend what he's saying. I compute increased mutterings from the crowd and wonder if they came only to watch my Good-bye.

Parvin.

Who's calling?

Parvin.

I take a deep breath, submitting to the weariness pulling me toward the earth, but Reid holds me up, an arm's length away, with his firm working hands. He looks hard into my unfocused eyes.

"Parvin, you're home."

I glance up at the sky and shake my head, allowing the sun to draw out burning tears. *Not yet.*

"You need to leave. You're not safe. Skelley Chase . . ." Surely Reid knows all this. "I'm back, now go."

He shakes his head. "Didn't you read my journal?"

How can he still believe it's his Clock, when it's clear I have minutes of breath left? "Please. Let me go. Let me die. I'm okay with it."

He doesn't seem to hear me. "Do you know who this is?"

I look over his shoulder into Hawke's resolute, tattooed, light-skinned face. My mouth opens, but Hawke gives a faint shake of his head and raises his eyebrows toward a person on the other side of Reid.

I frown and follow his gaze.

Tawny.

Her hands grip Reid's bicep with fingerless gloves. The moment our eyes meet she looks at Reid, down at the ground, over my head, up at the Wall.

She's nervous . . . But as I take a deep breath for greeting, her doll face transforms into a harsh frown, focused past me. Then it morphs into openmouthed horror.

A scuffle of movement reaches my ears from behind. Reid's grip slackens and a familiar small voice shrieks, "Parvin!"

I spin on the dime of adrenaline. Death flees my mind when I see Willow kicking the air with her dirty bare feet, clenched in the arms of an Enforcer.

"Willow!" I stumble toward her.

Willow writhes so violently she manages to slide from the Enforcer's grasp, but he snags a handful of her skirt.

"Elm! *Elm!"* She screams toward the tunnel, digging her toes in the dirt, reaching for the Opening.

"Let her go." I tumble to the ground in my weakness. "Please! Let her go home."

Two more Enforcers run toward Willow and her captor. The sunlight from the West illuminates the pinprick arch at the end of the tunnel. The light is interrupted when a fourteen-year-old muscled silhouette, the size of a toy soldier, crawls into the tunnel, scrambles to his feet, and sprints toward us.

"Close the Opening!" an Enforcer calls to the Wall Keeper. "More are coming through! She's brought Independents with her!"

"No!" I gasp as the Wall Keeper sprints to his hut. "No! Hawke, help them!" The door zips shut, missing the tips of Willow's fingers.

"Elm!" She screams, long and hard. Moments later, faint pounding comes from the other side.

Almost all the Enforcers are now gathered around Willow. I dig my fingernails into the ground, paralyzed.

They want Willow.

They trapped Elm.

Guns are drawn, waved in the air. People start shouting. Mother and Father enter the swarm of Enforcers. Mother shields Willow from the forceful hands of the black hornets. Father shouts at the Enforcers, pointing at the Wall door and then holding up his hands for calm.

An Enforcer strikes him with the butt of a rifle. I scream as he slumps to the ground. I turn around for Hawke, for help. Behind me, Tawny is yanking Reid's arm, pulling him away from the chaos and back toward the crowd. He gives her a quick kiss, a crushing hug, and then sprints for Father—for the Enforcers raising their clubs over Father, Mother, and Willow.

Skelley Chase is looking at his pocket watch . . .

And suddenly I know what's coming.

Call it triplet intuition, but the feeling is more sickening than the toxin in my blood.

"Reid!"

A snap of explosion cuts every throat into silence. My nerves collapse.

Reid's halfway between the Enforcers and me when he folds to the earth like a dropped dishtowel. My lungs shrivel into raisins, choking out my gasp. All I can do is watch his body double like a closed matchbook, his limp form unable to stop gravity's hammer.

I gape at the body. Immobile. This . . . isn't right.

Skelley Chase slides his gun back into its holster.

Tawny screams like a strangled animal, her hands clutched over her mouth, and stumbles toward him. Her noise shakes me. I cower. Her wails increase and she tries to lift Reid's head into her lap.

I lurch toward him. He needs help up. He needs to be washed. I can't see his face. Reid's never fallen before.

My arms shake. My voice shakes. A tiny bubble pops from my mouth, releasing his name. "Reid."

I lift my trembling hand covered in his blood and my face tightens of its own will. "It's me. Your Brielle." I look him up and down and straighten his arm so it looks right. "You . . . You didn't say Good-bye."

Mother swoops beside me and wraps me tight in her arms, pressing my face into her shoulder. This movement, this action, breaks my brittle dam of control.

"Mother." I clutch her sleeve. "Mother, it was supposed to be *me!*"

She says nothing, just rocks back and forth, her chest heaving. Tawny continues to wail and examine Reid's wound as if it will disappear. I pull away from Mother and reach toward Reid again.

"My—his journal." I reach over my shoulder for my pack, but my hand falls limp. "I . . . I . . ." Sucking in a breath, I look into Mother's face through my blinding tears. "His b-blood g-got on your skirt." My fingers grip the worn cloth. "I didn't mean to." It seems important she know this.

"It's okay," she moans, rocking even harder.

Someone lifts me off the ground, out of the blood. Mother doesn't hold me back. Is it my turn now? Are these the arms of the angels?

"I'm taking her to the hospital," says a voice, laced with sorrow and fury, by my ear.

"No, Hawke." Someone speaks from close by. "She called your name for help. How does she know you? We'll take her and this white child back to Unity's Containment Center. Once there, you and I will . . . talk."

Hawke doesn't lower me. "She's nearly dead, sir." His voice breaks on the last word and he coughs.

"Just don't . . . bury me. Burn . . ."

"I put a Medibot in her," Skelley Chase shouts from somewhere distant. "No need—" His voice cuts off with a cry.

I twist in Hawke's arms to look. A slice in Skelley Chase's forehead releases a gush of blood. By the Wall, an Enforcer yanks Willow's sling from her hand.

Skelley Chase fishes the hurled rock from the ground, tosses it once in the air, catches it, and places his fedora on his bleeding head. He picks up his briefcase and walks away.

"Wait," I say, deadened. "Wait, he shot my brother."

He slips through the wide-eyed crowd. Why don't the Enforcers stop him?

"He went against his promise. I'm here. I came back to save Reid." I scream after him. *"Why?"*

What does Skelley Chase gain from this? I don't understand.

Hawke's arms squeeze me tight and I catch a new smell: Wind. Thatch. Blueberry ink.

I struggle against him. "Hawke, stop. He—"

"We can do nothing about it right now, Miss Parvin." He sniffs.

My muscles tense against my forced movements. "I'm sorry about Jude. I didn't know his Numbers." Our brothers are dead and it's my fault.

"His death was his choice." Hawke's words are barely audible.

"Ch-Choice? But . . . a pirate chip terminated him."

Hawk shakes his head. "Only because he let it."

I cough twice before finding my voice. "Wh-What do you mean?"

"Not here. Not with Skelley Chase nearby."

Skelley Chase. The name rakes nails over my heart and I curl against Hawke's chest, too exhausted to sift through the mysteries and sorrows surrounding me. "Chase went against his promise," I whimper. "My brother's *dead*."

Dead. Dead. Dead.

The word turns into a mocking heartbeat. Against my will, my mind becomes clearer, my memory turns sharper, and my breathing starts to regulate.

"You're not going to die." The way Hawke says it carries remorse, like he knows how terribly I *wanted* to die, like he wishes he could ease my pain.

But he's right. I look at the blood-smeared gift encircling my wrist, given to me by a betrayer and murderer. The watch is no longer blue, but still blinks the time.

13:32.

I'm seven minutes late for my Good-bye.

Now I know. The question that immobilized my childhood is answered. Who's going to die? Who's going to die?

Reid.

Reid is going to die.

Somehow, he knew it. He tried to warn me. He was able to prepare himself. Jude knew, too. He saved my life. They both seemed to see something in my future that I was blind to. Now, I've lost them both. I've been left behind.

Why?

I AM CALLING YOU.

Calling. I thought this death was the end of my calling, the climax and final act to save a life—Reid's life. But now I see God is beyond the Clocks. He's beyond my misplaced faith.

I AM CALLING YOU.

And I will answer. I must answer, for I am now an empty shell open to a new vision—a greater vision. Against my will, I came back to the East. God wouldn't let me survive my Numbers—He wouldn't force me to live past Jude and Reid—if He didn't have something even more tremendous in store for me.

Right?

Shalom is not yet here. Maybe I'll be the one to bring it.

I have Radicals to save. I have an albino girl to protect. I have an assassin to hunt down. And I have a bone to pick with the Council about Jude and a certain biographer.

I know secrets. And they need to be revealed.

Jude's Good-bye echoes through my mind. *"I'll see you soon."* Now Reid is saying it, too.

I'll see you soon, I send to them both, *just not as soon as I thought. First . . . I have a calling.*

My heartbeat grows stronger, sapping up the stolen beats from Reid's sleeping frame. Pounding.

Pounding.

Pounding a fresh new rhythm of invisible Numbers.

And for the first time in my life, I don't care that I don't know them. All I care about is that I will use them. For Reid. For Jude . . .

For Shalom.

Acknowledgments

So many people have been influential in my process of seeing A Time to Die in print. To walk the path toward the publication of a debut novel has been longer and more exciting than I ever could have imagined. Very little of it would have happened without the many instrumental people God deemed crucial to my writing process.

First and foremost, I attribute every ounce of joy, process, growth, and success to my Lord and Savior—the bringer of shalom. He interrupted my busy life with this story, one I'd never planned to write. Now it's changed my life. I love You, too.

Now on to the mortals. Thank you to:

My husband, the first person to really grasp my passion for writing. You push me to write no matter how dirty the house is, because you know I love it. Thank you for listening to my ramblings and for reading thirty different versions of my book.

Jeff Gerke, for seeing the story the way it was intended to be seen and for inviting me to be a marcher lord. Thank you, also, for inspiring me to be a better writer far before you ever considered me as an author. I will always admire your vision.

Steve Laube, for your continued patience as this newbie wades through the waters of publishing. You've put forth every effort to make my book stand out. Thank you for believing in it.

Kirk DouPonce at DogEared Designs for a phenomenal cover. Karen Ball, for pulling my manuscript up the last step between a hopeless ending and a hope-filled one. You forced me to ask "why" about everything I wrote. I'm so glad you did.

Melanie, for being my writing buddy for life. Our brainstorming capabilities when combined over chai in Barnes and Noble will take over the world someday. Count on it.

Mom (aka. "The Typo Queen") and Dad, for reading to me as a child and for accepting my love of writing despite putting me through grad school for a completely different profession.

Binsk, for having more feedback than I'd expected from my non-bookish brother. Beth, who led me down the path of imagination before I knew how to appreciate it ("A story is brewing . . . don't talk.")

My Brandes family, for supporting and encouraging me in more ways I'll ever be able to thank you for. I'm honored to be a Brandes. To Jason, for always asking, "How is the book going?" (That's more encouraging than you know.)

Cailyn, for letting me spout all manners of enthusiasm regarding writing that made very little sense. Both you and Brad helped me find new understanding in the word shalom. Life changing.

Brenda, for being the first person to ever read my fiction (you didn't know that, did you?) and for being a fellow imagineer. Jennifer Griffith, who took me to my first writer's conference and helped me survive the aftermath of realizing I knew nothing about writing. Megan David, the first person to read the full manuscript. Thank you for your feedback and your friendship. Maggie Foulk, for being a story-loving, word-weaving roommate.

Micah Chrisman—the first fellow author with home I was brave enough to meet and have coffee-writing sessions. Thank you for also pushing me to be bold about my writing. Seth Branahl, for challenging me to write a female protagonist (seriously, A Time to Die without Parvin? No way . . .)

Angie Brashear, my fellow critique partner, friend, supporter, and prayer warrior. Your encouragement has been priceless. Meagan, Ashley, Katie, Eleanore, Ben, Anna, and all my other beta readers.

The Inspiriters—my priceless critique group who supports me with friendship, encouragement, and constructive criticism. Angie, Clint, Nancy, Carol, and David...thank you.

My Biola Family: Julie, for late-night chats about characters; Melinda and Lauren, for constant enthusiasm; Jonathan, for endless imagination and passion for life; Andrew, for support and encouragement only a Biola family member can give; Jared, for inadvertently showing me how important meaning is behind my writing.

Lastly, but so important, thank you to every single reader who has picked up this book. You took a risk in dedicating hours of your time to reading my words. You know I don't take "time" lightly. Although not everyone will like Parvin's story, I pray for each of you and pray that the story leaves you better off than you were before you read it. May your time never be wasted.

Tally ho.

About the Author

Nadine Brandes learned to write her alphabet with a fountain pen. In Kindergarten. Cool, huh? Maybe that's what started her love for writing. She started journaling at age nine and thus began her habit of communicating via pen and paper more than spoken words. She never decided to become a writer. Her brain simply classified it as a necessity to life. Now she is a stay-at-home author, currently working on next book. *A Time to Die,* is her debut novel.

Visit her web site: www.NadineBrandes.com

 Facebook: NadineBrandesAuthor

 Twitter: @NadineBrandes